Praise for Swan Deception

"This is a spell-binding thriller that hooks the reader in the very beginning, building tension and suspense on every page."
— Long and Short of it Reviews

"Swan Deception is a gripping, suspenseful novel filled with secret pasts, secret identities, aliases, murder, betrayal, and deception. The writing style is unique and superb; the plot is intricate and jammed-packed with surprises, and the characters are complex and well developed. It's a must-read that will keep you turning the pages until the very end!"
— Ana E Ross, *New York Times* and *USA Today* Bestselling Author

"What a brilliantly written book! I cannot wait to read another title by this author. A definite must read for anyone who loves a well-written, carefully crafted thriller full of twists and turns!"
— VoraciousReaderofFiction

"The writing is absolutely phenomenal. That's the first thing that hit me when reading this book. The twists and turns just keep coming throughout the book and kept me on my toes with each passing chapter. Glede Browne Kabongo has made it to the top of my "to read" list whenever she has a new book!"
— Angie Martin, Award-Winning and Bestselling Author of *Conduit*

"The book scared the living crap out of me at first, then it ripped my heart out."
— Alea B.

"I'm an avid reader of Patterson, Baldacci, Clancy, Sheldon, Koontz ... well, this rated up there."
— Kathleen T.

"Truly diabolical psychological thriller. I have read many psychological thrillers, a great number of them much gorier and more sadistic than this, but few with a more twisted bottom-line. If at any point you think you have this one all figured out, you probably don't."
— LaDonna P.

Also by Gledé Browne Kabongo

Conspiracy of Silence

SWAN DECEPTION

GLEDÉ BROWNE KABONGO

Swan Deception

ISBN: 978-0692249727

Cover Art by Najla Qamber Design

Printed in the United States of America

First Published in America in 2014 by Gledé Browne Kabongo

Dedication

To my husband Donat whose idea was the catalyst for this book. Thank you for giving me the space to bring the story to life and encouraging me to stay true to the vision. For helping me face my fears head on, and for asking the tough questions, even when I didn't have all the answers.

PART I:

DECEPTION & HOAXES

Chapter 1

I catch a glimpse of the man who just walked into Pennybakers Café, and my fingers tighten around the steaming cup of green tea. The chatter of happy diners who look like they just stepped out of a Ralph Lauren advertisement surround me, yet this routine slice of suburbia does little to ease my panic. Trouble has come looking for me.

"What's wrong? You look like you just saw a ghost."

The verbal intrusion startles me. I knock over my cup, spilling the tea. I grab some napkins from the dispenser on the table and spring into action before my drink finds its way all over the gingham tablecloth and causes a huge mess. Or worse, burns the children.

I attempt a lame joke. "I guess that's my cue to lay off the caffeine."

"It's not the caffeine, Shelby. What's got you spooked?"

My husband, Jason, sits across from me at our booth near the window, eyeing me through ridiculously long lashes, the kind women envy on a man. The multicolored, tube-shaped lantern dangling over our table illuminates his GQ good looks, highlighting the potent masculinity he wears with a casual ease and sensuality that women find irresistible. Our daughter Abigail is texting a friend she saw less than two hours ago. Her thick, black tresses cover most of her pretty face and big, doe eyes—so like mine. I'm tempted to snatch the phone from her, but that would confirm Jason's suspicion that something is off. Miles, a mini version of his father and quite tall for his eleven years, is irritable, his peevish attitude grating on my frayed nerves. He'd rather be home playing *Clash of Clans*.

"It's nothing, just work. I missed another deadline to turn in my research to the journal. "

He reaches over and gently runs a finger down my cheek. "Then consider cutting back on your workload. You're overextended as it is."

I work in the competitive scientific field of bioinformatics, which is dominated by men. A tiny percentage of women of color are represented, and publishing my research is one of the ways I get ahead. However, work is the farthest thing from my mind tonight.

"I love what I do and see no reason to slow down. Besides, why does the woman always have to be the one to make career sacrifices?"

Abbie snaps to attention, sensing that an argument is about to occur. Miles makes obnoxious slurping sounds with his hot chocolate.

Jason arches an eyebrow in that way that says he's annoyed by my question. "You're not yourself tonight," he says finally.

I place my small hands over his enormous brown ones. "I'm sorry. I shouldn't have snapped at you. I'll get a full eight hours of sleep tonight. That should take care of my surliness."

"Are you sure that's all it is?" he asks, unconvinced.

I don't have the balls to make a show of pretending to be offended by his doubt. I murmur thanks when my cell phone vibrates, a welcome distraction. I return the phone to the side pocket of my bag when I see the incoming number. The caller is insistent, as the phone continues to vibrate.

"Aren't you going to get that?" Jason asks.

"It's Vivian. I'll call her later."

"Who knows what part of the world she's calling from? Pick up."

As if in agreement with Jason, the phone vibrates yet again. I have no choice. I must take the call.

"Hey, Vivian, what are you up to?"

"I need to see you. It's urgent."

"I'm at Pennybakers with Jason and the kids."

"Meet me out back."

The caller hangs up.

I keep the phone pressed to my ear in spite of the silence on the other end of the line.

"Can I talk to Aunt Vivian?" Abbie asks.

"Not right now, honey. I think your aunt just met a new man. She's anxious to give me the details. Knowing her, it's probably X-rated, so I must take this call in private."

I signal to Jason that I'll be right back. I wade through the noisy crowd to exit the café. It's late October and dark out with temperatures dropping by the hour. I adjust my scarf then tighten the belt of my Burberry coat as I arrive in the parking lot behind the bakery. I find the source of my panic leaning up against my car, the light from the lamppost illuminating him. He's sporting a fitted brown leather jacket with a double collar and jeans. His jet-black hair is an unruly mass but it can't conceal his sexy grin and vibrant blue eyes.

"Why are you here?" My eyes dart over the parking lot, looking for nosy neighbors or acquaintances who might spot me and report to my husband. "Jason could have seen you."

"It is a free country, yes?" he asks in accented English.

"You can't be here."

He pats the front bumper of the Mercedes S Class sedan. "I like the new toy. Your husband doesn't know you've been a very bad girl."

"Shh. Keep your voice down before someone hears you."

He winks at me in that sensual way that draws me to him, but I must remain cool and in control. "I'm sorry, Princess. I had to see you."

"Why? I said goodbye months ago. We agreed it was for the best."

"You agreed. I respected your wishes."

Alessandro Rossi is a Brazilian entrepreneur I met during my stint at one of his physical therapy centers. Very early in the year, I had a terrible crash with my motorcycle and ended up with multiple fractures to my limbs and a concussion. There were times I wasn't sure if I would ever walk again. His tenacity and patience gave me my life back.

I jam my hands in the pocket of my coat to ward off the chilly New England night. "You didn't risk coming here and calling my personal cell phone just for old times sake."

"I came to say goodbye, princess. I'm leaving. For good."

I stay silent for a beat, unsure of what to say. His pending departure has a finality to it that jolts me. Pokes at my spirit. Makes my heart ache.

"When did you decide?"

"My daughters deserve better. I don't want them growing up this way. It's very bad. I must leave now, while they still have a chance at a normal childhood."

"Did something happen recently?"

"Morgana was beaten for refusing to eat her dinner. I took offense. The police showed up."

"I'm so sorry Alessandro. How are the girls? Did the police make you leave?"

"Isabella changed her mind when they arrived. The girls are afraid to speak to their own mother. "

He didn't need to say the rest. He lived in fear of his wife, never knowing when some object aimed at him would come hurtling through the air, or when a kick or blow would materialize.

He's tired. New lines have formed around his eyes since I last saw him, a few months back when I ended the affair.

"What do you need me to do?"

"Help us leave. Undetected. In exchange, I'll sign over half ownership of the business to you. All of the centers are profitable. It will be a good investment."

"You don't ask for much," I say, mustering a half-grin. "No compensation necessary. You built that business from nothing and you should continue to be the sole owner. Even from a continent away."

"So you'll help us?" he asks, his eyes lighting up.

"Of course I will. You have to protect your children, no matter the cost. Always remember that."

I give him a quick hug then break free.

"Get a new burner phone. Don't change your routine in any way. Wait for my call."

Chapter 2

The sun is blinding, and I pull down the visor to shield my eyes from the glare. Traffic is fluid on Route 9 heading east, the gridlock of the morning commute forgotten. As I pass the plaza known as Shoppers World in Framingham, a suburb twenty miles west of Boston, a black SUV cuts in front of me. I slam on the brakes, frightened by the near miss. The driver behind me blares his horn. He missed rear-ending me by a split second. The smell of burned rubber attacks my nostrils. The aberrant driver maneuvers back to the left lane. The license plate says Colorado. I accelerate before the driver behind me honks again.

With Framingham behind me, I zip past Natick on my way to my destination. I check my rearview mirror. Fear rears its ugly head again. The SUV is on my tail and gaining speed. The earlier run-in was no accident.

I rev the V8 engine of my Mercedes. The nearest car is still several hundred yards in front of me, so I get as close as I can then switch to the left lane. My stalker does the same. I try to make out the driver but can't. The Wellesley police station is only minutes from where we are. I contemplate exiting to the side street that would lead me there. I doubt the driver will hang around once he realizes where

I'm headed. I switch to the right lane in anticipation of exiting. To my surprise, he speeds past me, disappearing around the bend in the road. I don't realize I'm holding my breath until I exhale. My heartbeat is louder than the sound of Miles wailing on his drum set.

My cell phone rings, dragging me out of the mist that is my fear of getting into another accident. The memory of my motorcycle crash and coming so close to death is ever present with me. I fumble for the phone on the passenger seat without taking my eyes off the road.

"Hello."

"Are you having fun yet?"

I don't recognize the male voice. Could it be the driver of the black SUV? What would he want with me?

"Who is this?"

"It doesn't matter, for now."

"Did you just try to run me off the road? If you did, who you are and what you want matter to me."

"Don't be so dramatic, Shelby. I was just having a little fun."

"So you admit you tried to kill me. Why?"

"Patience, my dear. The answers will come, although you're not very good at practicing restraint, are you?"

"I don't know what you're referring to."

I want to keep him on the line long enough, hoping he'll slip up and give me a clue to his identity and intentions. I'm sure he's using a burner phone so the call can't be traced.

"You disappoint me, Dr. Cooper. You've been so clever up until now. Surely, you must know what I'm after."

Fear ripples through me because I sense danger. He called me *Dr. Cooper*. He has my private cell phone number and knows what car I drive. His research is meticulous. It's clear I'm his target. But why?

"Obviously I don't. Stop wasting my time with your ridiculous game."

"We're just getting started. There's much to discuss: the rules of the game, punishment for disobedience, how and when you will pay for your sins."

"Go to hell."

Chapter 3

I exceed the speed limit at every turn on my way to my appointment, one I can't afford to miss. I must avoid the speed traps, though. Local cops love playing hide-and-seek with unsuspecting motorists. I replay the conversation with the stranger in the SUV in my head—the confidence in his voice, the specificity of his words, the glib warning.

My cell phone rings again and I feel for it on the passenger seat. I glance briefly at the number: unknown. He's not ready to give up. With trepidation, I continue the battle of wills.

"Yes," I say, rudely.

"Don't ever hang up on me again, dear." His voice is calm with a cold, concrete determination that leaves me suffocating under its weight. "Consider this your first and final warning."

"Or else what? I'm already tired of this game."

"You're not cooperating, Dr. Cooper." He speaks in soothing tones, like I am a toddler who just threw a temper tantrum and needs to calm down. "I want us to get acquainted. Why so hostile?"

"How about you get acquainted with my attorney and the police instead?"

"That would be a fatal mistake."

"Why is that?"

"You don't breathe a word to the police or your husband, Jason. If you do, both your children will end up in wooden boxes. I will not be kind in my methods."

My hands are trembling and I can barely hold on to the steering wheel. My heart beats at the speed of a runaway freight train. He has found my weak spot. My children. With great effort, I manage to sound normal.

"Hmm. I was wrong about you. You're not a man. You're a thug impersonating a real man. Do you get off on threatening women and children? Are you whacking off right now?"

He hangs up. I pull over to the side of the road and an oncoming Mack truck barely missed hitting my car. The driver honks his horn loudly as he drives past. I take deep, calming breaths and pull myself together, then call The Carlisle School to check on Miles. I also check on Abbie, and then leave Jason a voicemail, letting him know I'm thinking about him.

I feed the parking meter next to the tall snow gauge that indicates very little snow has fallen, although there will be plenty of blizzards to keep the gauge busy as the winter wears on. I absorb the quaint village feel of the area with its boutiques, restaurants, businesses, and parked cars lining the street. I've arrived at my destination, perhaps a little more tattered after my run-in with the psychopath in the black SUV.

I stand at the entrance of Citibank, a nervous energy overtaking me as I contemplate if I'm doing the right thing for the umpteenth time. Despite my earlier detour, I'm only a few minutes late for my appointment with Andrew Clarke. Andrew is built like a tank, his expensive dress shirt overburdened by his massive chest, a fact that is barely concealed by his baby blue silk tie and designer jacket. The full-time banker and volunteer firefighter came into my life five years ago. He has been my go-to guy for many financial matters, both simple and complex.

He ushers me into his posh office on the third floor, with dark red and gold oriental carpeting, a large oak desk with family photos and files, and a few paintings strategically placed on the wall. I decline his offer of Fiji water as he takes a seat behind the desk. I remove my gloves and undo the top two buttons of my coat. I occupy the seat across from him. I don't anticipate a long visit.

"Always good to see you, Shelby. How are the kids?"

"Abbie has a major crush on her friend, Ty. I think she's falling for him. Miles wants to play Peewee football. We'll see about that."

"They do grow up fast. Soon, Abbie will be heading to college. You're still pushing for her to go to Duke?"

"You bet. I have to save her from her father's influence, though. He keeps telling her she can go to any college she wants to and I agree—as long as it's my alma mater."

We both chuckle, but I'm anxious to get on with the reason for my visit.

"Do you have what I asked for?"

"Yes. The funds were taken from your individual account, not the joint ones as you requested. I'll take care of any paperwork without inconveniencing you. Do you still think it's a good idea to walk out of here with that much?"

"I don't have a choice."

"That's okay. My job is to make sure you have what you need when you need it."

I sense there is a "but" coming. The normally straightforward Andrew is hesitant, hedging his bets as to whether or not he should speak his mind.

"Shelby, you're more than just a client, I consider you a friend—"

"What's the problem?"

"I want to make sure you're not in trouble of any kind."

"A friend needs help. She's starting over, coming out of an abusive relationship." I have no idea why I'm explaining this to Andrew, yet I feel compelled to, as if I need him on my side.

"That's awful. I'm sorry to hear that."

His reaction spurs me on. "There are children involved. I want her to get as far away as possible and stay safe. What's the point of having money if you can't use it to help others, right?"

"Your friend is lucky to have you."

"She certainly thinks so."

I bid Andrew goodbye and walk out of Citibank with more cash than the average American makes in a year, all carefully hidden in what looks like a conventional ladies' tote bag. Alessandro and his daughters deserve to live in an environment free of violence. I had no one to save me. Perhaps I can help write a different story on the slate of their lives.

I open the front passenger door of the car and dump the bag inside. When I walk over to the driver's side, I notice a white piece of paper trapped beneath the windshield wiper. I snatch it and read the contents.

Have you forgotten what you've done? I haven't. Game on, Princess.

My eyes dart in every direction like a nervous thief. I expect the black SUV to come barreling down the street any minute. It takes great effort to hold on to the note as I unlock the driver side door. Fear pools in the pit of my stomach. I'm being followed. Everything that's precious to me hangs in the balance.

Chapter 4

Abbie Cooper's elegant fingers flew over the letters on her smart phone.

Need 2 c u. Urgent!

She sent the text message and made a hasty exit from the student lounge. She hurried down the main hallway of Saint. Matthews Academy, bumping into fellow students on their way to class. Abbie was a sophomore and a day student at the elite boarding school, founded in the 1800s. The school sat on a sprawling 250 acres of mostly brick and Tudor style buildings in her hometown of Castleview.

She arrived at Westford Chapel, eager to unburden the secret she'd been keeping from her parents. She didn't know what to make of the note. The Chapel was an intimate interfaith structure with rich architectural detailing and beautiful, stained glass windows that illuminated the chapel when sunlight seeped through, creating an atmosphere of serenity. Two angels on the back walls, one on either side of the organ pipe, reminded Abbie why this chapel was so special to her, a place she turned to for comfort when life threw her a curve ball.

She spotted him seated in the first row. Butterflies roiled in her stomach. She plopped down next to him, dropping her backpack at her feet.

"This had better be good, Cooper," he said. "I almost had a date with Kerri Wheeler before your text threw me off my game."

Abbie cut him a scornful look. "You have no game. As for Kerri, no comment."

"Thanks for supporting a brother," he said, grinning. "I thought we were friends."

"We are. If I don't give it to you straight, who will?"

He winked at her. "I love it when you boss me around. So, what's up?"

Ty Whistler Rambally adored Abbie. When they first met at a school function her freshman year, he was a nerdy kid with braces, a few quirks she found adorable, and a head of thick wavy hair he inherited from his Indo-Guyanese father.

However, things had changed. When he returned to school in September for the beginning of his senior year, Abbie noticed he was several inches taller. The braces were gone. He now sported a short tapered haircut. His hazel eyes exhibited a new shrewdness, as if the boy she had known vanished. And, he looked like he was working out beyond his regular routine as a member of the crew team. God help her, just being near him turned her insides into knots. But Abbie would rather rip her fingernails out one by one with a rusty old pair of pliers than confess her growing attraction to him.

Abbie reached for her backpack and removed an envelope from the side pocket. She handed it to Ty. He removed the thick cream-colored paper and read aloud.

Dear Abigail:

Sometimes, the ones we love deceive us. Don't be alarmed when the Universe attempts to correct this injustice. The storm is gathering speed. It will explode with a bang. Remain calm. All will be well.

Ty wrinkled his nose. "What does that mean?"

"I'm not sure. It sounds like a warning or something."

Ty handed the note back to Abbie, his expression solemn. "When did you get it?"

"It came in the mail yesterday."

"It did? Were there other notes before this one?" Worry crept into his voice.

"No. Why?"

"Cooper, someone sent you a weird note in the mail, someone who could be dangerous. They also know where you live."

"A lot of people know where I live. Every time my mom speaks at some conference, her bio ends the same way: 'Dr. Durant Cooper lives in Castleview, Massachusetts with her husband, Orphion Technologies CFO Jason Cooper, their two kids, and a lovable Golden Retriever.' It's not that hard to find our house."

"Okay. But we still have to find out who sent the note and why."

Abbie liked that he said we. *We* have to figure this out. They were a team. That thrilled her.

"The envelope might be a clue. It was mailed from Washington, DC. I don't know anyone who lives there, though."

Ty considered that for a moment. "Whoever mailed it might not live in DC. They could live in Maryland or Virginia. Many people who live in those states work in DC. Weren't you born in Maryland?"

"Bethesda. My mom was a postdoctoral fellow at the National Institutes of Health when I was born. We left the state when I was four. I don't see how there could be a connection after all this time."

"So, you think this has something to do with your mom?"

Abbie sighed. "It could. She's been acting kind of funny lately."

"Funny how?"

Abbie shrugged. "Like something's bothering her. Something big."

"Did you ask her what it was?"

"Not yet. She knocked over a hot cup of espresso when we were at Pennybakers the other night. Then she left the café to take a call from Aunt Vivian. That was weird."

"Why?"

"They're practically sisters. Why couldn't she just talk to her right there in front of us?"

"Maybe it was girl talk. You know how you women are."

Abbie play-punched him in the arm. "When did you become

an expert on women?"

"Wouldn't you like to know?"

The mischievous glint in his eyes told her he was joking, yet Abbie's analytical mind went into overdrive. Was there more meaning in that sentence than he meant to let on? What happened over the summer? Now, he was chasing after that conceited, hateful Kerri Wheeler. What did he see in her, anyway?

"Oh, puh-lease," Abbie said, rolling her eyes at him. "But you're right about my mom, though. She made some lame excuse about Aunt Vivian meeting a new man and the conversation being X-rated. I don't buy it."

"Why not?"

"She jumps every time her phone rings, like she's scared of whoever's calling. She also sends me like fifty text messages a day, just to check in. She does it to Miles, too."

"That's strange," Ty said. "The note is just creepy, though. Are you going to tell your parents about it?"

"Hell no. They'll put me on twenty-four hour lockdown and take away my phone, possibly my computer. I want to see if I get another note. If it gets bizarre, then I'll tell them. No point in getting them all freaked out right now."

Ty edged closer to her. "I know you, Cooper. There's something else you're holding back."

Abbie decided to go for it, to tell him everything. She knew he had her back.

"I got a couple of strange calls after the note arrived."

"You mean like a stalker?"

"I guess. Whenever I pick up, there's just silence, then the person hangs up."

His lips formed in a grim line. "It's probably the same person who sent the note. I don't think you should keep this from your parents. The guy could be a psycho and try to hurt you."

Before Abbie could cook up an appropriate response, the infectious beat of a Taylor Swift pop tune sprung from her cell phone.

"Hello."

Silence.

She looked at Ty.

"Who is it?" he mimed.

She signaled him to stop talking.

"Is anybody there? Say something."

"Hello, Abigail. Don't be afraid."

It was a man's voice. One she'd never heard before. It was oddly soothing. "Who is this?"

"Don't worry about that, angel. Did you get my note?"

"What do you want from me? Why are you stalking me? I'm telling my parents, asshole."

"You're smarter than that."

Abbie swallowed hard. She would be brave, in spite of the chill in her spine that told her this person meant harm. "You don't know anything about me. You don't know what I would or wouldn't do."

He chuckled. "I know more than you think, little one. So much more."

"What's your name? Why did you send that note?"

"We'll be in touch, Abigail. And, remember, it's our little secret or else."

"Or else what?"

He ended the call.

Ty eyed her intently. "Well, who was it?"

"It was *him*.

Abbie relayed the conversation to Ty.

"I don't like this. Did you mean it when you said you would tell your parents?"

She looked him dead in the eye. "No. I said that to scare him. He's up to something. I want to know what it is."

"He could be setting a trap."

"For what?"

"Who knows? Don't you think it's scary that this guy called your cell phone number and doesn't want your parents involved?"

She poked him in the ribs. "You're just a kid yet you worry like an old man."

"Damn it, Cooper, I'm not a kid. This is no the time for jokes, either."

He reached over and tucked a loose strand of hair behind her ears. "You know I care about you, right? I don't want anything bad to happen to you. I couldn't take it."

It made her feel all tingly inside to hear him say that. It meant that she was still special to him, that she was still his number-one girl, even if they were the only ones who knew it. "I'll be fine. No need to worry."

"Promise me that if this nut calls you again, you'll tell your parents. Let them handle him."

"I can't do that."

"Why not?"

"Because it could put them in danger. I had the feeling he wasn't kidding around when he used the phrase "or else".

Chapter 5

I've been staring at a 3D model of the same gene cluster on my flat screen computer for quite some time. My mission is to identify which genes in the cluster need to be shut off, effectively preventing an individual with a genetic predisposition to diabetes in this case, from ever developing the condition, if we can design a drug based on my findings. I'm determined to continue my daily routine, in spite of the paranoia that creeps up on me from time to time. I haven't heard from the stalker since he contacted me three days ago. I can't shake the feeling I'll hear from him soon.

Someone taps me on the shoulder. I spin around in the swivel chair with such force that I almost injure myself.

"You all right?" Emma Chan, my postdoctoral fellow looks concerned.

"I'm fine. What's going on?"

"Inez wants to see you. She says it's important. Something about a group of kids visiting the lab."

"Shoot. Thanks for telling me."

I bump into a few colleagues as I make my way through the narrow aisle of the lab, apologizing on the way out. My assistant, Inez Diaz, meets me at the door. "You've been looking forward to this for weeks. It's not like you to forget."

"Sorry. Time got away from me. Where are they?"

"Milan Conference Room. I have refreshments ready for after the tour."

"Thanks, Inez. You're a life saver."

Half a dozen high school girls are visiting as part of GeneMedicine's STEM (science, technology, engineering, math) program, implemented when I came on board. The STEM fields are crying out for more female representation. I do my part to further that agenda. Twice a year, I host students from various parts of the state, explaining what we do and what's possible for them in the STEM fields.

After the lab tour is over, we sit in a circle around the conference room table. It's time for Q&A, my favorite.

"What made you decide to become a scientist?" The question comes from Anita, a junior from Everett High School.

"I found that I liked science classes in high school, and college. I discovered there are many ways to use science to change the world."

"Did your parents encourage you? They must be proud."

My lips lock of their own accord. The innocent question from a Dorchester High School freshman shouldn't have caused me any distress. I was certain I had put those issues behind me. My emotional response to the question puzzles me.

I pin a smile on my face. "Parental support is important. If your parents aren't available, don't let that stop you. Stay focused. Hang out with people who have the same ambition you do. Take advantage of all opportunities. Never give up."

I'm pacing in my office after my near meltdown in the conference room. There's a knock on the door. I open it to see Inez standing there, concern etched on her features. "This just came for you by messenger," she says, holding up a manila envelope.

I take the envelope from her and head back to my desk.

"Can I get you anything?" she asks, still standing in the

doorway.

"What's on your mind, Inez?"

"Nothing. Just making sure you're alright."

"I'm fine."

After Inez leaves, I take a closer look at the envelope. There's no return address. My name is typewritten on an address label. Alarm bells ring in the back of my head. I reach for a letter opener on top of a stack of papers. I rip the envelope open. I pull out an eight by ten photograph of Abbie on her way to class. I gasp. My pulse races. The time stamp on the photo indicates it was taken yesterday, two days after the stalker first contacted me. I look closer to make sure my eyes aren't playing tricks on me. They're not.

Abbie favors the preppy chic look. In the photo, she's sporting a flouncy navy blue skirt that stops above the knees, a white, open-collar blouse, and gray, cardigan sweater. Her footwear is a pair of knee-high Prada boots I bought her last year for doing well on her report card. Whoever took the photo was able to get a full-length shot of her at close range, inside the school. Game on indeed.

I don't get an opportunity to digest this latest menace. My cell phone is ringing. I reach for it in the pocket of my lab coat. I know who it is.

"Hello."

"Now, do I have your attention?"

I don't have the stomach for this so I lace into him. "You're targeting my underage daughter because you can't handle me? You're a sicko. I hope you got your kicks with that photo because you will never go near Abbie again. I'm only telling you this once. Stay away from my daughter. Stay away from my family. I don't care who you paid off to get that photograph. Heads are going to roll at Saint. Matthews."

He cooks up a hearty, deep-throated laugh. He's truly amused, which pisses me off further.

"Your attitude stinks so I'll give you some time to cool that temper of yours. Don't get any silly ideas, like mouthing off to the administration at Saint. Matthews or the Carlisle School. You especially need to remember not to contact the police. You are aware of the consequences."

"I don't take orders from you. Crawl back into your hole and stay there."

"We'll be in touch, Shelby."

After he hangs up, I resume pacing. My children are exposed. He made his point. He could get to them at any time, any place. How can I protect them without Jason finding out there's a problem? Would the stalker carry out his threat? Or is he just a tough guy wanna be? As the thought occurs to me, I squash it because it isn't true. He's given me all the proof I need to know he's dangerous.

I pick up the photo again. I turn it over. There, handwritten in black ink, is Abbie's class schedule. Tears of frustration and fear sting my eyes. I have to get my head in the game. A determined swipe of the back of my hand gets rid of the tears. I need to think, strategize, and protect my family.

Chapter 6

Early afternoon snow flurries pelted *The Planner* as she exited her vehicle in the parking lot of the Sheraton Framingham Hotel. The blustery November wind whipped her blonde hair around her face, forcing her to take refuge in the hood of her winter coat.

She took the elevator up to her suite, a temporary living arrangement until her apartment was ready. The stage was set. Now, she would watch the dominos fall. Her little visit to Castleview earlier was the last piece to be put into place. The first time she visited the town, she thought she had stepped into a postcard, complete with rolling hills, wide-open spaces, and a European-style town center dotted with independent markets. The town boasted sprawling colonial and Chateau-style homes with backyards that could double as football fields.

She couldn't imagine residing in a place like that, though. She would slit her wrists within twenty-four hours.

She tossed her coat on the king-size bed next to the outfit selected before heading out on the excursion. She stripped down to her underwear, laughing aloud as the Duke University sweatshirt hit the floor. It was hilariously ironic to someone like *The Planner,* who had a limited sense of humor. She grabbed the cashmere sweater off the bed. It went on with ease. Skinny jeans coupled with Lanvin leather ankle boots completed her look.

Three quick raps on the door announced it was time to set the plan in motion. She assessed her visitor after opening the door—early fifties with slightly graying hair, dark eyes, and glasses. His multi-colored argyle sweater screamed college professor.

She sat across from him on a striped burgundy couch, and tucked her legs under her. She reached for her electronic cigarette.

"I trust everything went as planned?"

He removed his glasses. "Yes. Everything was done to your specifications, just as you scripted."

"Tell me more."

"She's a spitfire, as you Americans say. She called me an asshole."

A slow smile spread across her face. "Like mother, like daughter."

"She wasn't afraid. In fact, it was just the opposite."

"Oh, she'll be plenty scared. Just remember what I said. I need her alive, unharmed."

Her guest raked his hand through his hair and chewed on the frames of his glasses.

"Do you have something on your mind?"

"I thought you liked Abigail. I don't understand why you want her scared, especially since she's not the target."

The Planner was annoyed by his question. She took a puff of the cigarette and took her time letting out the smoke. The sweet scent of mint enveloped the space. "It will all make sense soon enough. Let's leave it at that for now. How did it go with the target?"

"She's guilty, just as you said. She won't go quietly."

"I'm aware of that. You don't come from where she has, achieved what she has, without knowing how to fight and claw your way out of the gutter. She'll be out of our way soon enough. Don't worry."

"What do mean clawing her way out of the gutter? When she came to work for GeneMedicine, her credentials were impeccable: Duke undergrad, doctorate from Johns Hopkins. Her research was already being published in top international research journals. From what I know of her personally, there was nothing about her that indicated she came from meager circumstances."

The Planner untucked her legs, planted them on the thick carpet, and leaned forward with great urgency. "Perhaps you haven't been paying attention, which really concerns me when I think about the importance of this project. Shelby Durant Cooper is not who she says she is. She's a fake, a phony, and a poser. She has done awful things. My family and I were her victims. I intend to see justice is served. My way. Now, are you ready for phase two?"

Her guest retreated in his seat like a startled rabbit. "Um…do you have a glass I could use to get some water from the bathroom faucet? My throat is parched."

"Not a problem. I can do better than that."

She walked over to the large desk drawer with the flat screen TV perched on top and removed a twenty-ounce bottle of spring water from the left drawer. Her guest guzzled it down like someone who just came in from the desert.

"Do I need to remind you of the stakes?" she asked. "You can have your life back, the life she stole from you. A position befitting someone of your talent, money, and prestige."

"She had no compassion. I begged her not to say anything, even after I promised to stop. Everyone makes mistakes. My pleas were ignored."

"And, for what? Because you tried to make some extra income, to give your family all this country has to offer to hardworking, driven people?"

"Exactly. That's all I was trying to do. I wasn't hurting anyone. Frankly, innovation is what this country is about, isn't it? What I did just spurred the innovation race. It was simply a matter of which company would win in the end."

"Absolutely," *The Planner* said, walking towards the window. "Think about your current circumstances. Slaving away as an instructor at some obscure college, barely getting by on what they pay. A wife who left, children who are ashamed of you. When you migrated from your home country to study at Harvard, is this the life you envisioned for your family?"

"Not at all."

"Good. Whenever you question whether or not you're doing the right thing, I want you to think about Shelby Cooper."

His eyes widened. "You do?"

"Think about all she took from you and all she has gained. Think about her speaking at conferences all over the world, the large consulting fees venture capital firms pay her for her advice. Think about the fact that she's training the next generation of scientists in her lab. I believe you did that once?

"She has a family, a husband, and kids to go home to every night. Where's your family? Oh, that's right. Gone. They abandoned you when your troubles began."

The Planner turned around, her eyes boring into the nervous man. "So, don't you dare question me or my methods. Think about what the success of this project could mean for you."

He shrank back in his seat.

"Just stick to the plan as we discussed. I can do wonderful things for you. I can also make your current life seem like a picnic on the grounds of Topkapi Palace. Don't ever cross me," she warned. "Not even by accident."

"You can count on me," he said, eager to please. "I won't let you down."

"Good."

Her guest stood up to leave. She escorted him to the door. His hand reached for the handle and then he turned around, as if he forgot something. "I don't suppose you're going to tell me your real name?"

She knew this moment would come and was prepared for it. She extended her hand to him. "Lansing. Mia Lansing."

Chapter 7

After her guest left, Mia yawned. She had slept very little in the past few days, staying up until dawn, sustaining herself with less food than a bird would need to function. She pulled out a photo from the purse on the bed and held it up to the light. "Why couldn't you see through her act? Don't you know she's evil? Now, look what you're making me do. It's the only way to make things right. You'll understand, won't you, darling?"

The sound of hands clapping startled Mia. "Who's there? What do you want?"

There was no one to be seen.

You really think you're going to get away with this?

The old woman was mocking her again. It was only a matter of time before she appeared.

Mia squeezed her head in anguish. "Shut up! Shut up! She's going to pay, old woman."

Mia hadn't heard from that visitor in a long time. She thought she had banished her, but here she was, trying to mess with her plans.

You were always a disaster waiting to happen. Nothing was ever enough. This will end badly for you. Heed my warning.

"You don't know what you're talking about. She'll get what's coming to her this time."

What will you gain?

Mia began to pace around the room, perspiration running down her back.

"You can't get to me, old woman. You're all talk, you're not even real."

So reckless and self-absorbed, as if the world owes you. If you think she won't catch you, think again."

"Liar," Mia screamed. "You're just trying to scare me. You can't stop me."

You've been warned.

"Who asked you, old woman? No one asked your opinion about shit. Stay away from me, you hear? Stay away from me."

There was no response. The only sound came from outside the room, in the distance. The sound of traffic on Route 9.

Chapter 8

I'm knee-deep in paperwork. There is not an inch of wood to be seen on my desk and the paper trail has made its way to the floor of my office as well. I asked Inez to push back my meetings for the day. I've narrowed down my choices to two private security firms. I'm leaning towards Bryant International.

I'm angry. I resent that I can't share this with Jason. I need him. However, I can't afford to take the risk that the psychopath won't carry out his threat if I breathe a word to anyone. Neither can I afford to do nothing. I glance at the file prepared for me by Greg Marr, co-founder of Bryant International. Their resume is impressive: they've created threat assessment systems for former Governors, the Supreme Court Police, and Defense Intelligence, and handled private security for some of the nation's most prominent families and Fortune 500 executives. Their employees have special ops and Secret Service training. These guys are the real thing. Exactly what I need to squash this bug.

My decision is made. "Greg, it's Shelby Cooper. Thanks for sending over the information. I like what I've read thus far. Can we do dinner tonight?"

I sense his hesitation, which tells me his schedule won't allow for it. I don't care. I need a security detail on the kids right away.

"Well, tonight's a little tough. How about lunch tomorrow?"

"No can do. I need to see you tonight. I'll keep it brief."

I meet Greg at a restaurant and bar down the street from the Federal Reserve Bank of Boston. It's crowded, noisy, and perfect for our discussions. We sit at the end of the bar. Greg is fit, with salt and pepper hair and a tan in the middle of November.

"I'm surprised you contacted us. I know the guys who handle executive security for your husband's company."

"I'm sorry I couldn't be more specific over the phone. That's why I needed to meet with you tonight. A few days ago, I received a phone call from a stranger who started stalking me, making threats. I dismissed him as a nut job." I dig inside my purse and retrieve the photograph. "Two days after the initial call, I received this," I say, handing it to him.

He examines the photo, his expression unreadable. "Your daughter?"

"Yes. He wrote her class schedule on the back."

"How is the security at her school?" he asked, turning over the picture.

"Everyone who enters school premises must sign in."

"So, he had someone on the inside take a snapshot."

"My thoughts exactly. He made it clear that if I complain to the administration—well, you can figure out the rest."

"You have no idea who he is or what he wants?"

"Not a clue. At first, I didn't take him seriously. His threats just seem outlandish and made no sense. The photo changes everything."

"An escalation of the threat. Our area of expertise."

"I have two children who both need protection, using all the training and expertise at your disposal, up to and including lethal force if necessary."

"Understood."

"They can't know your team exists."

"Got it."

"Furthermore, you work for me, not my husband, if you catch my drift."

"I do."

"You'll have the non-disclosure agreement for your signature in the morning. I'll make myself available to interview members of your staff you deem appropriate for this assignment. There will be more details provided then. How soon can your team be put in place?"

Chapter 9

It's date night at Casa Calypso, a hot new Spanish Caribbean restaurant in Boston. The intimate atmosphere and attentive staff is just what I need. No slaving over dinner for me tonight. For the first time in a week, I'm able to relax. My stalker has been silent since I hired a security detail for the kids.

"A penny for your thoughts," Jason says. He's elegant yet sexy as hell in an Iberian blue, cashmere sweater with a quarter zip, and charcoal gray, wool pants.

"That's all my thoughts are worth? So depressing. All that education for nothing."

He smiles broadly. "That's why I only offered a penny. If I had to pay market value for your thoughts, I'd be broke."

We both break out in giggles. A couple the next table over smiles in our direction. The waiter comes over and deposits dinner on the table: salted cod fritters for me, shrimp in coconut sauce for him. The aroma is undeniably mouth-watering. After the waiter leaves, Jason raises his glass in a toast. "To health, happiness, and longevity."

I clank my mango smoothie with his Pina Colada. I've barely put my glass down when my phone rings.

"Can you believe our kids? You'd think the whole world was

coming to an end just because we're not home for a few hours."

"Your fault. You spoil them rotten."

I know he's teasing yet it stings. I'm so desperate to be a different kind of mother than the one I had. Maybe I go overboard.

I pull out the phone from the side pocket of my purse. I freeze when I see the "unknown caller" label. It's not the kids. I have a split second to make a decision.

"Hello?"

"You're not in the game, Shelby. That worries me. I sent you a photo of Abigail, so what's your response? Do you need an incentive?"

I peek at Jason to see if he's curious about the call. He is.

"I'll take care of that tomorrow. No problem," I say.

"Oh, your husband is with you. Date night? How romantic. How many date nights have you had with Alessandro Rossi, hmm? Bad Shelby. I didn't think you were capable of such duplicity. What example are you setting for the lovely Abigail? Don't worry, dear, I know you ended the affair. I just wonder what Jason would do if he ever found out?"

"I must get back to my evening," I say. I hold the phone in a death grip so Jason won't notice my unsteady hand. "Thanks for calling."

"You're slow to act, Shelby, so you lose your chance. My turn. Can't wait to show you my next move. It's to die for. Goodnight, Mrs. Cooper."

I take my time returning the phone to its place in my bag, willing my riotous insides to calm down. However, Jason is impatient.

"Who was that?"

"What?"

"On the phone."

"Oh nothing, just one of my lab assistants."

I turn to face him. He looks at his watch then arches an eyebrow. "It's my fault, I asked him to call me. I needed the answer to something he was working on."

"It couldn't wait 'til morning?"

"I wanted to get a head start. The information was coming from one of our European labs."

He stares at me intently. "Why are you lying to me, wife?"

Whenever he calls me "wife," it's his way of distancing himself from me, so his emotions don't get in the way.

"I…why do you think I'm lying to you?"

"We've been together eighteen years. Now, what is it? You looked like you wanted to die just now. That call rattled you. And, don't tell me it's work."

I scratch my head with my index finger and look around the crowded restaurant, as if courage would miraculously see me across the room, come over, and hold my hand. I'm trapped between Jason's wrath if I tell him the children are in danger and I kept it from him, and the rage of a psychopath who was threatening to kill them, blowing my life to dust in the process. I just can't take the risk.

"I was disappointed, that's all. You know, I mentioned I was behind schedule turning in my latest research to the journal. I just suffered another setback. Nothing major."

"I think there's more on your mind than turning in a late manuscript."

I poke my fritters with the fork, unable to meet his gaze. "Whatever gave you that idea?"

"Perhaps you can explain to me why thousands of dollars is missing from our Bank of America account."

That got my attention. My fritters are no longer appetizing.

"You're going to deny that, too?"

"No. I just can't believe I forgot to mention it."

"Why is that?"

"It's one of the worst kept secrets in biotech right now. Word is Heron-Smith is about to get FDA approval for their new Gene Therapy-based drug."

"So, you wanted to make a purchase before the price per share skyrockets."

"Exactly. Nothing wrong with making a tidy sum when the price soars."

"Why didn't you just tell me after you made the withdrawal?"

"I don't know. I guess I've been so focused on getting this research published."

Jason gets up from his seat and comes around to my side of the table. He kneels beside me, reaching me at eye level. "I love you.

I hate to see you so stressed. Let's go away somewhere, just the two of us. My mother can stay with the kids. I want you all to myself, no interruption, for days on end."

"Sounds divine. Don't you have a long Asia trip coming up?"

"I can adjust my schedule accordingly. Charlie won't like it. Oh well, gotta keep the wife happy."

"What? Don't put this on me," I say, in mock offense. "It's your idea."

He leans in and demonstrates exactly what would be in store for me if I give in to his demand. For a moment, everything falls away, the stalker, my lies, even the patrons at the restaurant. I revel in the deep penetrating kiss and melt into him. When it's over, I take a minute to get my heartbeat and breathing under control. "Well, you make a compelling case. Your mastery of the facts can't be denied."

"Excellent."

"Let me get over this hump at work, then we can plan the trip."

"Oh, you're such a tease. Perhaps you need more convincing. Let's go home."

"We haven't even touched dinner," I say, laughing.

"Who cares about dinner? Let's go straight to dessert. I believe you have a wicked sweet tooth."

"Sure. Go ahead, make me feel guilty."

"My dessert has all of the pleasure and none of the guilt. I guarantee it."

Chapter 10

I made it home early today to snoop without the family around. My spirit is uneasy. In a matter of days, Alessandro and his daughters will be whisked out of the country on a private jet I've chartered for the occasion. Private pilots aren't required to file a flight plan, which comes in handy when one is fleeing the country.

Someone has been in the house. I feel it in my bones, the intrusion, the violation of our privacy while our backs were turned. I already ransacked the kitchen. I'm in the living room now, in front of the fireplace. There is a giant painting above it, our wedding day. Jason lifts my hand and brushes the back of it ever so lightly with his lips. I gaze up at him adoringly, my wide smile making promises of things to come.

An idea strikes me as I stare at the painting. I dash to the kitchen and grab the tallest chair I can find. I stand on the chair directly in front of the fireplace and gently lift the painting from its place on the wall. I place the painting up against the back of the chair, then jump down. I examine it for any listening devices or cameras. Nothing. I painstakingly replace it and straighten it out so it doesn't look crooked, messed with. When I jump down again from the chair, I almost knock over the glittering pair of crystal swans atop the fireplace. Jason had them commissioned. He presented them to me as an anniversary gift. He said he drew inspiration from the swans that live at the edge of the reservoir in our town because they reminded him of us, mates for life. If anything happened to them, he would never forgive me.

My next stop is our bedroom. I lie face down and close my eyes, hoping to calm my anxious nerves. My thoughts are still swirling, so I open my eyes and flip on my back. My phone is on the nightstand and beckons me. I pick it up. There's a new text message. I jump up from the bed as if a fire was just lit under me. The message reads:

What's right with this picture?

A family photo taken at Gillette Stadium during a New England Patriots football game follows it. My head is cut off from my body in the photo.

Rage rises up in me, sudden and thick. I want to hurt this person as much as he's hurting me. I delete the offensive photo and message. There's no need for the reminder that my every move is being watched and someone wants me decapitated. Perhaps the solution is simple. We could disappear and start a new life somewhere. However, I know the idea is silly. I'm not one to run from my problems. I face them head on, no matter the cost.

However, my adversary keeps upping the ante. He's right. What's my response? The .357 Magnum hidden in the walk-in closet? Jason bought me the gun for protection when he's away on business trips, not that anything ever happens in Castleview. He trained me how to use it and I've never had a reason to. Still, I have to consider the severity of the threat and whether my closet is the right place for the gun.

It occurs to me there's one place I haven't looked. I dive under the bed, hoping I'll hit the jackpot. Perhaps there's something hidden there.

"What are you doing?"

I'm startled, and I bump my head as I crawl out from under the bed. Abbie, hands on her hips with major attitude, looks like a school principal reprimanding a not-so-well-behaved student.

"I can't find my iPad and thought it might have ended up under the bed somehow."

"Under the bed, Mom?" Abbie can't hide the suspicion in her

voice. "What's really going on?"

"Nothing is going on, honey," I say casually. I stand to my full height and fluff her hair.

"Something is wrong and I'm worried. So is Dad. You've been acting weird lately. "

"Did your dad say something?"

"I know when you're not yourself, Mom. Like when you found out Dad cheated on you."

"What?" I ask innocently.

"I know what happened. I thought you and Dad were going to split. You guys had some pretty awful fights about Stephanie Hunt. Soon after, you crashed your motorcycle."

I can't lie to her and even if I did, she wouldn't believe me. I hug her tightly. She's growing up too fast. Or, it could be the way fifteen-year-olds are these days. I don't recall being that precocious at her age. But I had something Abbie doesn't: Nurse Ratched for a mother.

I sit on the bed and pat the spot next to me so she can join me. "Your dad and I love each other. We have issues like most married people. All you need to know is that you and your brother are the most important things in our lives. I don't want you to worry about grown-up problems. You're going to be an adult soon enough. Enjoy what's left of your childhood."

It sounded like a lecture, but I'm grateful the conversation took this turn. There is no way I can explain to my daughter that I'm scared shitless and some psychopath is threatening to do disgusting things to her if I don't cooperate in some evil plot he has yet to reveal to me.

"I'm not a kid, Mom," she points out. "In three years I'll be old enough to vote, go off to war, get married."

Married? Where did that come from? Oh lord, I hope she's not doing anything I don't want to think about her doing.

I drape my arms around her shoulders. "You came looking for me for a reason. What's going on with you and why all the questions about your father and I?"

She's deathly quiet. Knowing my daughter, she's running a risk benefit analysis in her head right now, contemplating if she should tell me her real reason for coming to my bedroom to find me. She scrambles off the bed and stands in front of the full-length mirror in the corner near the window.

"Do you think I'm pretty, Mom?"

I'm caught off guard by the question. Abbie is not one of those teenage girls obsessed with her looks. She's levelheaded and keeps the drama to a minimum.

"Of course, Abbie. Why would you ask me that?"

She turns away from the mirror and approaches the bed. "This is important, Mom. I need you to be honest with me and not feed me some line."

All right," I say hesitantly. "I don't think you're pretty."

She looks at me, horrified for a split second, and I make the time out gesture with my palms.

"I don't think you're pretty. I think you're gorgeous."

"Really, Mom? You're not just saying that?"

"No, Abbie, I'm not just saying that. Go see for yourself. Look in the mirror again. You have an inner glow that comes through to the outside. That's a sign of true beauty. No amount of cosmetics, plastic surgery, or any other artificial enhancement can compete with that. Why are you so concerned about your looks all of a sudden?"

She grabs a throw pillow near the headboard and stares at it aimlessly.

"What is it, Abbie? You can tell me. And, if you don't want me to tell Dad, I won't."

Her eyes go wide for a second or two then she blurts it out. "I want Ty to be my boyfriend."

I'm shocked. Still, I have to play this out and make sure I don't come off as the petrified parent I am.

"Well, you could do worse, believe me. What changed? You two have been the best of friends for a while."

"That was before. I mean, we're still good friends, but I…he's just different now. When I'm with him, my heart beats faster. I feel funny, like I'm catching a fever. Is that weird?"

"No, it isn't, sweetie." I hug her and let out a deep sigh. "I believe you're experiencing the pangs of first love with someone you already care for deeply."

She looks at me sheepishly, searching my face for some clue that tells her there's nothing wrong with her feeling this way. In theory, it's just fine. I also know what it's like to be her age and madly in love, at least what I thought was love, and no one could convince me otherwise. What I thought was love had life-altering consequences for me. I walk around fearful that one day, those consequences will come looking for me. On the other hand, I won't allow my past to ruin what could be a wonderful experience for my daughter, when she's ready.

"Does Ty feel the same way? Have you told him?"

Her response was swift. "Hell no! I mean no, ma'am. I'd rather die than tell him."

"Oh. I see. So, you're just going to suffer in silence?"

"No. He needs to put his cards on the table first. Then we'll see."

I burst out laughing, and soon we're both cracking up. I rumple her hair, so proud of her for controlling the situation. As the giggling subsides, I wipe a tear from my eyes and put on my serious face.

"I'm not going to lecture you, Abbie, but please take things slowly. Real intimacy is serious business and I don't want you to do anything you'll regret. You're a smart girl and I know you can think for yourself and not give in to peer pressure."

"I can think for myself, Mom. You and Dad have been teaching me to have an independent mind before I could walk or talk. I know you're scared. Don't be. I won't be doing anything I'm not ready for. Plus, there might be complications."

"What do you mean?"

"I think Ty likes someone else. Kerri Wheeler," Abbie said, disgust written all over her face.

"Did he tell you that?"

"No. They've been texting each other, though. He's trying to get a date with her."

Now I see what the problem is. Abbie has a rival for Ty's affection and she's worried about competing. "Is Kerri beautiful? Is that why you're concerned about your looks?"

Abbie pooh-poohed. "I suppose so. If looking like Beyoncé with big boobs and a serious head of hair is considered beautiful. My friends and I nicknamed her Rapunzel."

"Are you afraid if Ty gets involved with Kerri you two won't be as close as you are now? Because I don't think that will happen. There's only one incredible, spectacular, super smart, Abbie Cooper. Ty knows that and when the time is right, he'll recognize it."

"So, I'm just supposed to pretend I don't have feelings while he does God knows what with Kerri?"

"No, honey. You keep on being his best friend. You two have a special bond. The best relationships often begin with a strong friendship as its foundation. Let things unfold naturally."

I'm trying to do damage control before she may need it. If Ty is into this Kerri girl and Abbie shows her hand, she may get hurt and the rejection may be devastating to her self-esteem. That could spell the end of their friendship. Besides, if Ty wants to be with my daughter, he's going to have to earn that privilege.

"Thanks for being cool about this, Mom. I'm glad you didn't get all preachy cause that would really suck."

"I was a teenager once, Abbie, strange as it sounds."

"Am I going to be grossed out?"

"Hey, your parents are people, too. People who make mistakes."

Chapter 11

Yeah, it's me. My mom is definitely hiding something and she feels bad about it."

"How do you know?"

"I just talked to her."

Abbie lay on her bed with her feet up against the wall as she gave Ty the rundown on her conversation with her mother. Things were getting tense in the Cooper household. Her mother had major anxiety issues.

"Well, I could get her phone data from the Cloud. It won't be much help though. With her tech skills, she wouldn't leave anything incriminating on her phone or computer."

"Ugh. I hate this. At least that creep hasn't called me in a few days, so that's good news. I hate waiting for something to happen. There must be a way to find out who my mother was talking to that night at Pennybakers. I feel like my family is about to fall apart and everything depends on finding out."

"I got it!"

"Got what?"

"I can use SIM card data recovery software to retrieve any deleted data on your mom's phone."

"Knock it off with the nerd speak. Plain English, please."

"I need access to your mother's phone. With special software, I can retrieve any information that was deleted. If she didn't mess with her SIM card, I can get that number."

Abbie pulled her legs off the walls and bounced off the bed with excitement. "Ty, you're a freaking genius. I love you!"

Awkward silence descended on them.

"Oh, you don't think…what I mean is… oh hell, get over yourself, Ty. You know what I mean."

"I know."

Abbie breathed a silent sigh of relief. The last thing she needed was Ty finding out the truth about her feelings for him. She had to keep her emotions in check if they were going to work together on cracking this mystery. She couldn't afford any slip-ups.

"When can you come over?"

"How about tomorrow?"

"I need a couple of days to come up with a plan. A good excuse as to why I need to borrow her phone."

Chapter 12

The ringing cell phone broke his concentration. He snapped it up from its position next to the computer.

He gave a hurried hello. There was no answer.

"Who's there?"

Dead air. He looked at the incoming number and it said *unknown*.

Annoyed at the intrusion that was obviously a wrong number, Jason hit the end call button and returned to his task. He was going over revenue forecasts for the next two quarters and they had to be revised upwards, which pleased him.

He was chief financial officer at Orphion Technologies, a global powerhouse in the technology hardware and software space. A few years ago, things weren't looking so rosy. Back in 2008 when the global economy was falling apart, he had to get creative fast to stop the company from bleeding red ink. While most companies were shedding jobs faster than investors could dump mortgage-backed securities, Jason fought to minimize layoffs, streamlined operations, won the fight to freeze executive pay increases, and closed underperforming plants.

His unwavering leadership during that time is what now had

him on the fast track to becoming the next CEO when Charlie Sommers retired next year. That tidbit of information was the worst kept secret at Orphion, and every time he was interviewed in the financial press, the story always referred to rumors of his ascension to the CEO post, although he constantly denied it publicly. His dad would be proud. Erasmus Denton Cooper knew what it was like to climb the corporate ladder, often dismissed and second-guessed. He had to work twice as hard just to be considered part of the game. The fact that he made it to senior vice president at a major brokerage firm was a testament to the old man's iron will to succeed. Jason would complete the family legacy. Only one thing potentially stood in his way of becoming CEO. He had buried that part of his past long ago. It would be near impossible to dig up now. The cell phone interrupted him again and this time he let his annoyance be known.

"You're obviously calling the wrong number. Don't call this phone again and then hang up."

"Jason, it's Charlie Sommers."

"Charlie, I mistook you for a prank caller." Jason was surprised his boss was calling him so late at night. As far as he knew, there was no crisis looming.

"It's late so I'll keep this brief. I'm hearing things I don't like, Jason—personal things about you that could spell trouble when you take over as CEO. Set me straight and tell me the information I have is wrong. I need to know you're ready to take Orphion into the future with no flies on your back."

Jason got up from his desk and stretched his legs in an effort to calm his nerves and think what Charlie could possibly be talking about.

"Go ahead, Charlie. I have nothing to hide. What's on your mind?"

"I don't pay attention to rumors and gossip but when this one reached my ears, it piqued my interest. If there's anything going on between you and any of your subordinates, cut it out. Now! I'm not accusing you of anything. Just saying to be cautious and mindful of your position."

"I can say with unshakeable confidence that there are no such issues in my ranks. You've known me both personally and professionally for years. I wouldn't compromise the IPO by putting the company through a scandal."

Charlie exhaled a huge puff of air as if he'd been holding it since he dialed Jason's number. "Glad to hear it. Looking forward to the Hong Kong trip."

After Charlie hung up, Jason's emotions were on tenterhooks. Charlie's warning made no sense to him. Jason wasn't perfect and had strayed once before. Shelby struggled to forgive him, and over time, they worked through the betrayal. He would never be so stupid to head down that path again, especially with a subordinate. He could think of one person who had other ideas, however.

"This ends right now. Am I clear?"

"I have no idea what you're talking about."

"Don't play games with me, Chloe."

"Jason, I swear I have no clue what you're talking about. You seem stressed out, though. Maybe I can help you with that."

Jason sat in the plush leather chair behind the giant maple desk in his office at Orphion's corporate headquarters in Waltham, a city eleven miles northwest of downtown Boston.

His patience had just about run out as he sat across from Chloe Grace, his financial planning and analysis manager. She was in her mid-thirties, a smart capable woman who worked her way from an entry-level job in the finance department to now reporting directly to him.

He suffered a setback a few days ago with the regulatory filing for the company's IPO. He was in a bad mood because he was used to bending things to his will. He found out the hard way that the Securities and Exchange Commission and other agencies regulating corporate finance didn't really much care what he wanted. Chloe had caught him fuming.

Next thing he knew, she was kissing him. He was startled at first, then pushed back instantly, scolding her for her inappropriate behavior. She was furious, said she was being supportive by trying to relieve his stress. He suspected she had a little crush on him but nothing to be taken seriously as their interactions have always been friendly and professional.

"I've always treated you with the utmost respect. Now, I'm ordering you to knock it off. Spreading rumors of a nonexistent affair is unprofessional and detrimental to a company with plans to go public soon."

He watched a plethora of emotions play across her features. Her brown eyes blazed with defiance. She pushed a loose braid away from her face.

"Just how fucked up do you think I am, Jason? If I wanted to screw you over, I would call Shelby directly and tell her about us."

"There is no *us*. There's nothing to tell."

"She doesn't know that. If office gossip is to be believed, didn't she hack your computer and find out you were having an affair last year? It wouldn't be a stretch for her to think you were doing it again, now, is it?"

One word from her could bring all sorts of trouble he didn't need right now, mainly being accused of sexual harassment, an ugly label for a would-be CEO.

He stood up, slipped his hands in his pants pockets, and walked over to the large windows near the small conference table and group of sofas he used for management meetings. His office was spacious, a good thing since he liked to roam when he had a lot on his mind. He stared out the windows, a view of the parking lot and naked trees rising up to meet him.

He walked back to his desk and leaned up against the edge.

"I respect you as a friend and colleague. I'm disappointed you feel the need to make up stories. I think it's beneath you. Perhaps I've given you too much credit?"

She looked mortified, which he wasn't expecting. For a few beats, neither one of them spoke, Chloe perhaps too embarrassed and not sure what to say next, and Jason waiting her out.

"I didn't mean anything by it," she said, quietly fiddling with her notebook. "Sometimes, I speak without thinking. I meant no harm."

He relaxed his posture and that must have given her confidence.

"I do value our working relationship but I want there to be more between us. I know I'm supposed to feel ashamed for saying it aloud. I don't."

He knocked over a small potted plant on his desk and made no move to retrieve it. He stared at Chloe, his gaze intense, unwavering. "I'm married, Chloe. I'm also your boss. I don't need to spell it out for you."

"Marriages end all the time. Nothing lasts forever. That's why you have to say what's on your mind and grab whatever share of happiness you can, while you can."

"This conversation is inappropriate, and I don't think we should mention this topic again."

Chloe stood up and planted herself mere inches from him, her eyes giving the appearance of a tigress about to pounce on its prey. He could smell her perfume and could see the cleavage spilling out of her blue silk blouse. Her tone was soft yet determined.

"No. I want to talk about it. I'm not asking you to leave Shelby, although that may happen on its own. I grew up with an addict for a mother who was either too drunk or too high to notice I existed or had needs. So I've learned, the hard way, to ask for what I want and to go after it without asking permission because nobody was going to hand it to me."

She backed away from him with a self-satisfied smirk.

He didn't know she'd had a troubled childhood. He admired her confidence and competence on the job. However, he had charted a course for his life. He would trample anyone who got in his way.

"This can't happen, for reasons I've already explained. However, I can be a mentor to you, help you grow in your career, and get you where you want to go. Or," he said, straightening the family photo on his desk, "I can make it difficult for you to get a job waitressing, let alone anything in corporate finance."

She remained unfazed. "I like you a lot. You have multiple check marks in the plus column. You're a devoted family man, you're honest, and you care about the people who work for you. Not to mention, your considerable physical and financial assets. It's damn near impossible to find that combination in one guy. So, when that gift shows up, no matter how complicated the wrapping, I'm going to open it."

Usually when women made a play for him, they would act coy or try to manipulate him. He knew all the angles. He could tell a lot about a woman by the way she simply said hello to him. Chloe Grace had caught him off-guard.

He retreated to the leather chair behind his desk and turned his attention to his computer. He brought up his calendar. "If I were crazy enough to take you up on your offer, it would be a liability to me and the company. One we can't afford. I can't drag my family into a mess that could have been avoided."

"I don't hear you denying you want me. All I hear are the reasons you shouldn't."

"This conversation never took place. Good day, Chloe. Show yourself out."

After Chloe left, Jason placed a phone call. "Get me everything you can on Chloe Grace. I'm especially interested in her finances and under what circumstances she parted ways with past employers."

Chapter 13

I exit the parking lot of the Carlisle School, a less than ten-minute drive from home. I don't head back to the office as planned. I use the voice command system to call Jason. He picks up on the second ring.

"How did it go?"

"It's a clear case of revenge. George Adamson hit Miles and our son took the passive approach. It was merely a ruse, though."

"I'm guessing there was trouble."

"There was. Miles waited for his opportunity, which came on the field trip last week. He decked George and a fight broke out on the school bus."

"That's my boy."

"Jason, didn't we teach our kids that violence solves nothing?"

"Yes. But I don't want them to be anybody's punching bags, either."

"You're incorrigible. Anyway, both boys have agreed to keep their hands to themselves from now on and Miles and George are no longer friends."

"He stood up for himself. That counts for something."

"So, now that our son has one friend less, are you going to tell me what's going on?"

"I don't know what you mean."

"Something is bothering you. Something you don't want me to know."

"You're way off base. Prepping for an IPO is stressful."

"You never sweat the work stuff."

"We've never had an IPO before. Let it go. Everything is fine."

I enter the beige concrete building with bright red and white signage that reads National Engine and Bodyworks. I have a fondness for mechanics and cars because of my father. I force my brain to focus on the current task and not meander down some memory lane loaded with booby traps I can't afford to spring right now.

The smell of brand new tires and rubber is strong as I enter the customer center. A husky man with wide girth, a bald head, and glasses stands behind the black granite. His nametag says *Russell*. He tries to shore up a smile, but doesn't quite succeed. Maybe customer service isn't his calling. "Can I help you?"

"Yes. I need one of the mechanics to take a look under my car."

"Care to be a little more specific?"

"I will if you give me a chance." I let out an exaggerated sigh and shoot him a dirty look. "I want them to see if there's a GPS tracker on the car. If there is, I need it removed. Today."

"Anything else?" Mr. Friendly asks, eyes narrowed.

"No. If there's anything else, I'll be sure to let you know." I notice a couple of customers behind me witnessing our exchange and giving me looks as though I'm the one being difficult.

Mr. Friendly picks up the grey phone and dials an extension. I stare at the wall behind him. It's covered with the pricing menu, a giant map of all the states in which they have locations, and several certificates for outstanding service. Obviously, those certificates were awarded before Mr. Friendly came on board.

A much more agreeable employee comes through the glass doors connecting customer service to the mechanics' work area. After a brief exchange about the problem and the filing of some paperwork, I hand over the car keys and head to the waiting area. I scroll through my phone and check my email. It's the usual, a few bioinformatics newsletters I subscribe to, the latest sale at Nordstrom's and a plethora of other junk that clogs up my inbox.

I'm tapping away at the trash icon on my phone when the screen lights up. I hit the answer button. I take a deep breath and dive headlong into what I'm sure will be another confrontation. "I told you I would think about it."

"He wants to go. He's waiting on you. He's got no more business on this earth, except you."

"I'm sorry, Michael, I can't get away right now."

He knows I swore never to go back. Yet here he is, making demands, trying to force me to make a commitment I can never keep.

"I doubt he remembers me. Our business ended on a summer night over twenty-five years ago."

"No use holding on to something you can't change. Meanness won't make you feel better about it, either."

"What do you want from me? You want me to feel bad that he's dying? Tell him all is forgiven?"

"Let it go," he says, his voice impatient. "Don't punish him because of what she did. She's the one you're really mad at."

"He made his choice. I adjusted to that reality in ways you can't ever imagine."

"What about your children, your husband?"

"What about them?"

"When are you going to tell them your real name and who you really are? I'm tired of carrying your secret."

"Are you threatening me?"

"No. I'm just saying that fancy life you're living up north with your rich husband and spoiled kids…well…it could be over just like that. Life is funny that way."

"Go to hell, Michael."

"After you, darlin'."

I'm spitting mad. Before I hang up on my baby brother, I need some information.

"Has anyone contacted you, asking questions about me?"

"No. Why?"

"Are you sure? Nobody asking questions about the past they shouldn't be asking? No weird calls?"

"Nobody has said anything to me. I could ask—"

"Don't! Please don't say a word to her. I mean it."

"You can't change your past."

"I can sure as hell try."

"If you say so. Why you so concerned all of a sudden?"

"I'm not," I snap, then soften my tone. This can't be easy for him. I've done what I can. I can't go back as long as *she's* alive.

"I'm sorry. I just can't make it. Please try to understand."

I hang up on my brother, the only connection to a past I'd rather stay buried. The pain is as much a part of me as my limbs or my face or head. I've tried to do away with it, like a box of unwanted things you store in an attic. Yet, it's there. There's no escaping it. One day, it will destroy me. For now, I don't need the distraction. The present has enough demons trying to slay me.

Sometime later, Dominic the mechanic comes into the waiting area to hand over the keys to my car and inform me that he removed the GPS tracker.

"It was near invisible where they hid it under the rear bumper."

He places a small, round device the size of a quarter in the palm of my hands. I find it offensive and want to ditch it as soon as possible. Dominic must have sensed my mood.

"I guess your husband can't keep tabs on you now that you've busted him."

That casual statement strikes terror in my heart.

What if Jason knows what I did and is trying to teach me a lesson? Not possible. The man who took such great care of me after my motorcycle accident—who bathed and dressed me when I was incapable of doing the simplest task, wouldn't send a stalker after me. I'm ashamed for even thinking he could.

I thank Dominic and head to my car, elated that I was able to outwit my stalker, at least this time.

I'm on Route 9 heading west to my Westborough lab. I call my assistant to let her know I'm only minutes away. After I hang up, my phone rings. Michael can be so stubborn. He won't let this go and I'm getting tired of it. I come to a traffic stop at the intersection of Route 9 and Edge Hill Road in Framingham.

"Michael, I'm on my way to the lab and can't discuss this now. Please. Give me a break already."

I'm mistaken, though. It's not Michael on the line. Instead, I hear a child crying. My brain seizes. The sound is pitiful. Gut wrenching. I struggle to fill my lungs with air. "No. Please stop. Please stop it. I didn't mean to."

Somewhere, between my agony and the fog that blankets my brain, I hear horns blaring in the distance. The sounds get louder and louder. The adrenaline high starts to dissipate. The child stops crying. I hang up the phone then notice the traffic light is now green. I accelerate and pull into the parking lot of a McDonald's a quarter mile down the street.

I reach for the bottle of water next to me and drink it all. My heartbeat is slowly returning to normal. The guilt I can't share with anyone, not even Jason, about what happened that day so many years ago, can't be erased. My stalker must know this. He wants to remind me constantly so I have nowhere to run.

Chapter 14

His hair is longer, brushing his shoulders. The new beard gives him a scruffy appearance and the sparkle in his blue eyes is diminished. Alessandro is on edge but he knows this is the only way. It's *the day*. I've chosen a Wellness room for our final meeting. These rooms are used for all manner of things, from nursing mothers who pump during the day, to tired employees who need a nap or a shower after a bike ride along the trails nearby. We're unlikely to be disturbed.

He reaches for my hand and holds it in his for a few beats before I withdraw. "It's good to see you, Princess. I regret that it will be the last time."

"You have a new life ahead of you and your daughters will be safe. Think of it as the celebration of a new beginning."

"It doesn't feel like a celebration. I will never see you again."

"We make sacrifices for the ones we love. You understand that better than anyone."

"I worry about you. All the trouble you've gone through to help my daughters and I. It's at great personal risk to you. I don't take that lightly."

"I've covered my bases. We're good."

"And, Jason? It would be devastating to me if you had to pay the price for your generous assistance. And, my offer of half ownership of the centers still stands."

"You can run the centers from Brazil once things cool down. Besides, you left someone you trust in charge for now. As for Jason, we were discreet before until I broke things off. You can count on the same discretion with this situation."

My reassurances have the desired effect. He's calmer. I take the opportunity to turn the tables. "What about Isabella? Is she suspicious?"

"No. She's happy to have the girls out of her hair and me out of her sight."

"How do things stand between you two?"

I have no right to ask him such a personal question. That's between a man and his wife. Yet, I can't help but think about the fallout: what will happen once Isabella Rossi discovers her husband and children are gone? If my first and only run-in with her is any indication, she might think 'good riddance.'

"I tried to say goodbye. She told me to stop bothering her."

"I'm truly sorry. I never got a chance to apologize to you for sticking my nose where it didn't belong. I'm referring to the Whole Foods incident."

Back in October, I ran into Alessandro and his wife at Whole Foods. She was practically attacking him in the snack aisle. I hid around the corner so they couldn't see me. They caught me in the checkout line. Alessandro and I made eye contact. Mrs. Rossi looked at me like I was something she scraped off the bottom of her shoe. It didn't help that I looked like a fashion victim in jeans, sneakers, a sweatshirt, and a knit cap with a pom pom on top. It took little effort to feel ridiculous next to the stunning brunette, then I quickly realized she was a very ugly person in all the ways that mattered. When I arrived in the parking lot, I witnessed her punching and scratching Alessandro. I went over and threatened to call the police if she didn't stop. Not the best move on my part.

"No apology necessary. I only regret you witnessed my humiliation. "

I gently touch his shoulder. "You have nothing to be ashamed of. There's a difference between being unable to strike back and choosing not to. You stood up for your girls and your decision to leave everything you've built behind to protect them took guts. You're one of the bravest people I know."

"It means so much to me that you feel this way. Are you sorry, Princess? About us?"

"I'm sorry about all the lies we told to cover up the affair. I'm sorry we broke our marriage vows and compromised our families. I'm sorry we were both hurting and it was that pain that brought us together."

I was physically and emotionally devastated when Alessandro came into my life, having just found out that Jason was unfaithful. After my motorcycle crash, I required intense daily physical therapy sessions. Alessandro was patient and understanding. He wouldn't let me quit. One day, the emotional rollercoaster—nursing a shattered heart and the uncertainty about whether or not my marriage would survive, the psychological scars surrounding my recovery got too much and I had a meltdown. Alessandro wiped away my tears and told me everything was going to be okay, he would be with me every step of the way until I was one hundred percent me again. That was the first time he kissed me. I should have pushed him away but didn't. Along the way, I got to know him and the circumstances surrounding his own tortured life.

He cocks his head to one side. "Most people regret it only when they get caught, don't they?"

I smile at him, picking up the nuances of the question. I only said what I was sorry for. As for the things I'm not, I guess those shall remain unspoken.

I turn my attention to the back of the couch where I have a surprise waiting. I retrieve the gift bag. "Got these for the girls. Maybe it will keep them company on the long flight."

I present him with two dolls made in the likeness of his daughters. Gratitude is reflected in his eyes as he takes the dolls from me. "I don't know what to say. Thank you. My girls will cherish these dolls."

I stand up and so does he. Our time is up. "Are the girls excited about the trip to New York?"

"Yes. Anna wants to visit the statue of Liberty and Morgana wants to go to Dylan's Candy Bar."

"I took my kids there when they were younger. I'll never do

that again. They were the Roadrunner on steroids and I was Wile E. Coyote with my tongue hanging out, trying to keep up with them after the sugar high."

"I'll remember that when I'm chasing Morgana around the store."

The plan is to take his girls for a day trip to New York. No bags, just the clothes on their backs, cash in a nondescript overnight bag, and the best fake passports money could buy. Before the end of the day, a limousine would pick them up and take them to an airstrip, where a chartered private jet would be waiting for them. The pilot would drop them in Panama, where they would lay low for a few months, maybe Buenos Aires afterward to throw the authorities off the scent before they enter Brazil. The whole thing could take up to a year.

He goes solemn on me. "I can never repay your kindness."

"You couldn't use your own resources and make it easy to get caught. Be happy. That's how you can thank me. Let me go on with my life knowing you and the girls are thriving and happy. Who knows, I might even make it to Brazil some time in the future. I hear Rio has the best carnival in the world."

He grins and the sparkle returned to his eyes briefly. "That would be wonderful."

"I'll be praying for you and the children to have safe passage." He opens his arms and I go willingly. We hold each other tight, knowing it's the last time. I withdraw from his embrace. "Adeus, Alessandro."

"Eu amo você, Princess!"

Chapter 15

The sun is powerless against the frigid, mid-November temperature so I crank up the heat in the car. I adjust my rearview mirror, a nervous habit since my near car crash caused by my stalker. Thanksgiving is a couple of weeks away, and I'm glad we're heading to Connecticut to my mother-in-law's. I'm off the hook for hosting this year, although she still expects me to make leg of lamb, cheesecake, and coconut punch.

I glance in the rearview mirror again and don't like what I see. I'm on the Mass Turnpike heading west, and the Massachusetts State Police are trailing me. I recognize the navy blue and gray cruiser, different from local cops. My nerves are on edge. Is this the "next move" my stalker was talking about? Or, could it be something as simple as speeding without realizing it?

The siren wails, and I pull over in the breakdown lane just before exit eleven, near the Westborough Service Plaza. It's roughly three o'clock in the afternoon on a weekday so the traffic in both eastbound and westbound lanes is flowing at a steady pace.

I reach for the registration in the glove compartment; careful not to disturb the gun I now carry for protection. I have a license to carry it. I'd just rather not be questioned about it at all. The officer taps the glass of the driver side window. The power windows slide down with the push of a button.

"License and registration, please." He's roughly mid-forties, tall, blond, and stern looking. His nametag says *Hannon*.

I hand him what he asked for. "Was I speeding, Officer?"

"Is this your car?"

"Yes. What's wrong?"

"Wait here, ma'am."

He takes off for the cruiser just a few feet behind me. I tap my fingers on the steering wheel in a rhythmless tune. A couple of minutes go by. I explore all possible reasons for my detainment. I wasn't speeding. I have no broken taillights. The registration is current. The car is fully insured. He only wanted to know if the expensive German import was mine, as if I'd stolen it.

Then the truth slams into me like an NFL Linebacker. *Wait until you see what I have in store. It's to die for.* I replay the stalker's threats. What has he done now? For a brief moment, I consider just taking off. Then I remind myself to stop panicking. Police officers are trained to read body language.

I begin to hiccup and can now appreciate my habit of always making sure there is bottled water in the car. I don't feel good about this.

Chapter 16

I 'll make this brief. You're out of here."

Jason was all business as he dropped a green file folder on the desk and prepared to reprimand Chloe Grace. What his investigator found out about her was alarming. She had to go. Charlie agreed with him and backed Jason's decision. It would make things a lot easier. He had his assistant book the conference room on the second floor. The room was all glass, so anyone passing by could see who occupied the room. He wanted everything out in the open. In such a public space, Chloe couldn't try anything funny and then lie about it.

"What are you talking about, Jason?"

"I'm talking about the undisclosed settlement you received from your previous employer to 'not press charges.' It won't work this time."

"You invaded my privacy?" Chloe was furious and looked like she wanted to slap him. "How dare you?"

"I dare because there's a lot at stake, including my family and my good name. The last thing this company needs is to be embroiled in some artificially created scandal. I tried reasoning with you, to no avail."

"You think you can get rid of me that easily? I worked my ass off to get this job and to stay at the top of my game. My performance reviews speak for themselves. I'm an asset to this company. I'm not some fly you can swat."

"It's done. You'll be transferring to our London office, reporting to Jake Livingston. If you still want to work for Orphion, that is. You're always free to seek employment elsewhere."

"This is bullshit! You won't get away with this."

"I already have. Charlie is on board with this decision. You could have had a bright future under my guidance. You chose to throw it away."

Chloe began to toy with her phone. She shoved the phone in his face. "Take a look."

There was a photo of Jason with his arms around Chloe, both of them smiling for the camera. The second photo was of them kissing passionately outside a hotel. The third photo had Jason sitting in a chair, Chloe straddling him with her skirt hiked up to her waist.

He was going to be sick. She was willing to take this to obscene and absurd levels. Anyone looking at those photos would believe they were real. She wouldn't get away with it. He threw her phone across the desk. "That's disgusting and I don't take kindly to blackmail."

"You try to get rid of me and these go to all the top executives in this company, as well as Human Resources and the media. You can kiss the CEO chair goodbye before your tight derriere has a chance to make contact with it."

"You're out, Chloe!"

"I don't think so," she responded, self-assured. "So, let's stop this silly game right now. Since you were a bad boy and went behind my back to Charlie, you should be punished. I need access to your credit card. I have a wedding coming up in a couple of months and Chloe needs to look fabulous. My good friend Beth is marrying a rich hedge fund manager. How would it look if I showed up looking low-rent? I don't want to embarrass her, obviously."

"You're out of control and quickly losing touch with reality. You're playing a game you can't win. I have too much money, resources, and influence to let you get away with this."

Chloe was unflappable. "I also need the name of your jeweler.

I want ruby earrings set in platinum, like the ones Shelby wore to the Museum of Fine Arts gala last year."

"You need help. I'm sure you're aware that the company insurance covers mental health. You should call the employee help line as soon as possible so they can put you in touch with a professional." Jason closed the folder and got up from the table.

Chloe stood up too, and handed him her phone for the second time. Anyone looking in from the outside would think it was an employee and her boss working intently on company business. "Read that and tell me if it sounds like I'm joking."

Jason began to read the message and felt his rage growing by the minute. He wanted to shake Chloe until he rearranged the contents of her obviously deranged mind.

The email had his name as the sender in a blue hyperlink and Chloe's name in the "to" field. The subject line read: *Need to see you tonight.*

Chloe,

I can't stop thinking about you, about us. Meet me at the Westin tonight. I've booked a suite for us. I ache for you as I write this email. Can't wait to be inside you.

Eagerly yours,
Jason

If he gave in to her demands, it would never end. If he didn't, she could ruin him. He would handle this with brutal efficiency, beginning with a tech expert who could erase any digital trace of his so-called email messages to Chloe.

Chapter 17

I glance at the clock on the dashboard and can't believe it. Ten minutes have already gone by and the officer still hasn't returned. If his objective is to make me sweat, he just scored a home run. I can't keep the feeling of dread seeping into my bones at bay. I call Jason and begin to speak before he says hello.

"I got pulled over by the State Police and I don't know why. He's taking too long. I don't like this. Why can't he just give me the ticket and my flipping license back so I can go home?"

"Tell me from the beginning what happened. Stay calm and don't say or do anything to set him off. What did he say when he pulled you over?"

"He just asked if the car was mine and took off with the license and registration. You need to stay on the phone with me, okay."

"Of course, baby. Where did you get pulled over?"

"Westborough. Here he comes."

I wind the window down. "Ma'am, do you know you have a broken taillight?"

I'm stunned by the question and give him a blank stare. "No, I didn't. This car is only six months old and I haven't had any accidents or anything." I'm babbling now. I think I would have noticed a broken taillight when I drove off to work this morning.

"That's why I pulled you over. See that you get it fixed."

I breathe a sigh of relief as the officer hands me my license and registration. "Yes, Officer, of course I will."

I put the window up and place the registration in the glove compartment then slip my license in my wallet inside my purse. "All set, honey," I say to Jason. "It was just a broken taillight."

After I assure Jason that all is well, I hang up and my shoulders sag with relief. I close my eyes briefly. My phone rings again. Maybe Jason forgot to mention something. When I open my eyes and check the screen, the unknown caller label indicates it's *him*. I contemplate declining the call, then decide I'd rather have intel on his latest scheme.

My hostility is rising. "What is it now?"

"You're going to love this. I must warn you—if you end up before a judge and bail is granted, you must not post bond. At all."

"What the hell are you talking about?" I yell. "Why would I end up in front of a judge? I haven't committed a crime."

"You have, my dear. The police will have no choice but to take you in. Just remember what I said. No bail. I know everything there is to know about you, Shelby. Everything."

Rage takes over and it blows through me like a tsunami. "Listen, you piece of shit. I don't give a damn who you are or what you want. We're finished. I'm done playing your reindeer games. Now do me a favor and drop off a cliff."

Hot tears flow like lava. I'm shaking. My emotions won't be controlled. I feel everything at once: fear, hatred, anger, despair. A knock on the driver side window startles me. It's Officer Hannon again. I can't catch a break today even if they were falling from the sky like locusts. His face is as hard as a three-day old bagel. I slide the automatic windows down again.

"Ma'am, step out of the car, please."

"Why? What's going on?"

"Ma'am, it would be best for everyone if you did this voluntarily."

This is bad. If I stay in the car, he might drag me out by force—not that it would take much effort on his part. If I do as he says, I could be in a whole heap of trouble although I have no idea why. I take my cell phone and purse as I exit the car.

"Can you tell me what this is about?"

He doesn't answer. Instead, chaos ensues. No less than six squad cars with blaring sirens and flashing lights roll up behind his cruiser. Officers are exiting their cars, weapons drawn. My heart is hammering in my chest. What do they think I did?

Officer Hannon draws my attention to the trunk and that's when I notice the broken taillight, and the bloodstain on the bumper.

"Can you open the trunk, please, ma'am?"

"Huh?" The stress must be getting to me because now I sound like I have the IQ of a log. Officer Hannon stands next to me, feet wide apart, arms folded. The other officers form a semicircle.

"Are you refusing to open the trunk, ma'am?"

"No. I'm just confused."

"We have reason to believe this vehicle has been involved in a crime. Please open the trunk, ma'am."

"A crime? That's ridiculous. This car has been in an underground garage all day. I just came from work. I don't know where the blood came from. I'll show you there's nothing in the trunk except my gym bag and some bottled water."

Oh God, I hope that's still true. I don't know what nasty surprise that jerk has in store for me.

I hit the remote on the key chain and pop the trunk. I send up a silent prayer.

"See, there's nothing in there," I say.

Officer Hannon and his fellow officers tell a different story. I move closer to the trunk and peek inside to see what has them looking like they just lost a comrade. Then I see it. My legs feel like they're about to give way. I can't control my breathing and my chest is tightening. I don't want to have a heart attack at forty! Right there in the trunk of the car in the fetal position is Alessandro Rossi, with a gaping hole in the middle of his forehead.

Chapter 18

I gasp for air. Three more squad cars pull up. Officer Hannon is talking. I can't make out his words. I want to scream but my voice has deserted me and raw emotions take charge. Paralyzing fear. Shock. Disbelief. Devastation. He pins both my arms behind my back and snaps on cold metal bracelets that bind my wrists together. I'm escorted inside a police cruiser. I throw up all over the floor.

We arrive at the Weston Police Barracks. The long narrow white structure right off the Mass Turnpike looms before me like a disapproving parent about to dispense punishment. I'm ushered inside the main lobby with white walls, a bench, plaques on the wall, and an officer behind Plexiglas window swimming in an ocean of paperwork. I'm relieved of my wool coat after a female officer pats me down. I'm then taken into an interrogation room. The officers talk amongst themselves, and I'm left alone.

A rotten stench permeates the air. I look down and realize vomiting in a police cruiser was not one of my finer moments. The evidence made its way to my blouse. The room is impersonal, fluorescent lights embedded in the ceiling, walls bare and uninviting. I guess that's the point. I know they're watching me behind the glass window. The back of my eyelids burn, and I hunch over in my seat, holding my stomach. The past hour comes back to me in a montage. Flash: Mass Turnpike. Talking to Jason. Flash: police sirens and guns drawn. Flash: popping the trunk. I squeeze my eyes, and will the image to vacate my mind. It won't. Alessandro. Blood. My car. Dead. He's supposed to be in Panama with his daughters. How did the stalker get him to make a detour? Did I miss a clue? He threatened to kill my children if I didn't cooperate. Did he kill Alessandro as a warning to me? I don't have the mental capacity to figure this out so I give up for the moment.

The door swings opens and two detectives walk in: a strapping fifty-something, well over six feet, slightly balding with a graying moustache and world-weary eyes that say he's seen it all. I can see the bulge under his suit jacket, his gun in its holster. His partner is an attractive, fortyish brunette in a black pantsuit, and a permanent scowl.

The man speaks first. "Dr. Cooper, I'm Detective Eric Van Dorn and this is my partner, Detective Tess McCall."

I nod in their direction. Van Dorn asks if I need a drink before he takes the seat across from me while McCall stands against the wall, her eyes assessing. I rub my left wrist, the mark from the handcuffs evident and itchy. I have an idea how this is going to go and I will cooperate, up to a point.

Van Dorn clears his throat. "Dr. Cooper, we have a homicide on our hands and we're hoping you can give us some information that can help us understand what happened." He removes a small notebook and pen from his jacket pocket. McCall, arms folded, looks on. "We're not accusing you of anything, we just want to ask some questions."

Sure thing. And Alessandro is just a little bit dead.

"What do you want to know, Detective?"

"Do you know the victim and how he got in the trunk of your car?"

"Yes, I know him. He was my physical therapist, and no, I don't know how he got in the trunk of my the car."

"Where were you today between the hours of 11:00 am and 3:00 pm?"

"At work. I left at 2:00 pm."

"Where were you headed?"

"Home."

"What route did you take?"

"I left my office in Cambridge then got on the Mass Turnpike and took it all the way west until I was pulled over at the Westborough Service Plaza."

"Did you leave the office at all today, prior to heading home? Maybe to grab some lunch, run an errand?"

"No, I didn't leave the office at all. My assistant and several colleagues can vouch for me."

Van Dorn wrote something in his notebook. "What kind of work do you do?"

"I'm a research scientist, Director of Bioinformatics at GeneMedicine."

I couldn't tell if he was impressed or just pretending to be to establish a rapport. "Wow. Bioinformatics. Never heard of it. What do you do in your lab?"

"I build algorithms and use mathematical modeling, computer simulation, and a bunch of other technology-related tools to organize and interpret massive amounts of biological data. The idea is to extract information that could help lead to the cure to diseases like cancer and Alzheimer's."

"I see. Sounds complicated."

I don't respond and then it's McCall's turn to join the party. "Did anyone see you leave work?"

"I don't know."

"Where was your car parked?"

"Underground garage."

Van Dorn scribbled in his notebook again.

"Did you notice anything unusual about your car when you left work?" McCall asks.

"No. I was in a hurry to get home, so I just left."

Two sets of eyebrows arch with curiosity.

McCall continues. "Why were you in a hurry?"

"My son has a bake sale at school tomorrow and I'm supposed to make petit fours."

"Where does your son go to school?"

"The Carlisle School in our hometown."

Van Dorn took notes. He'll no doubt be checking out my

story.

"Do you own a gun, Dr. Cooper?" he asks.

That Visa Olympics commercial that ends with the phrase "moment over" comes to mind.

"I'd like to speak to my attorney now."

I hug my body to stop it from shaking. Alessandro is dead. The finality of it hits me with brute force. It wasn't supposed to go down like this. I'm afraid for his daughters now. I'm afraid for my family and what will happen to me. By the time my attorney walks into the interrogation room, my tears are pooling on the table.

Alan Rose pulls out the chair across from me. He places his gloves neatly on the table and removes his coat, then hangs it on the back of the chair. I watch him open his briefcase and remove a notepad and pen, and finally, take his glasses from the pocket of his suit jacket. His presence is commanding. He reminds me of the actor Gregory Peck in the film version of *To Kill a Mockingbird*.

"First things first," he says, taking charge. "What did you say to the detectives?"

"Not much." I give Alan the run-down on the brief interview. He hands me the silk handkerchief from his pocket to clean my face, and I'm grateful.

"From now on, you talk to no one. All questions and requests come through me. So far, they haven't charged you with anything, so I'm going to try to get you out of here on personal recognizance. But I have a few questions of my own."

"How bad is it?" I ask.

"Right now this case is a felony homicide. It carries a maximum sentence of life in prison, with the possibility of parole in fifteen."

I lean back in my chair and let my arms dangle at my side. I feel beads of sweat breaking out on my forehead, and I use Alan's handkerchief to dab them off. Shit just got real, as the kids say these days.

"I didn't do this."

"I don't care. However, I do care about your memory."

Alan Rose is a high-powered defense attorney who has never lost a case. I met Alan and his wife, Bree, on a few social occasions. Jason's company is a client of Lockerbee, Rose & Nash. I'm certain that relationship has a lot to do with the reason Alan got here so quickly.

"The only thing linking you to the crime is the discovery of the body in your car. There's no proof you put it there and no eyewitnesses. How do you know the victim?"

"He was my physical therapist." I explain my crash to Alan.

"Take your time," Alan says.

I can barely speak I'm hiccupping so much. It wasn't fair. Alessandro didn't deserve this. His girls deserve to have their father with them. My heart breaks for them. It breaks for Alessandro. My heart breaks for my family. I don't know what the stalker will cook up next to punish me. It's obvious I'm his target. He has demonstrated his willingness to sacrifice those close to me to achieve his objectives.

"Sorry. It's because of him I'm able to walk again."

"Were you friends outside of the patient-provider relationship?"

I can't admit that up until a few months ago, I was sleeping with him.

"Casually. We would run into each other at Whole Foods occasionally. Once in a while, he would enlist my help with some computer-related problems."

I squirm in my seat. The fluorescent lights must be giving off some extra heat. I dab sweat from my forehead again with Alan's handkerchief.

"When was the last time you saw him?"

This may not be the best time to bring up my role in the commission of multiple felonies including aiding and abetting in the kidnapping of minors.

"It's been some time. I don't see him often since I stopped going to physical therapy."

"Do you know his family?"

"He has two young daughters, Anna and Morgana. He would bring them by the center sometimes. I know of his wife, but I've never met her."

Running into her crazy ass that one time was enough for me.

"Can you think of anyone who would want him dead?"

"No. He was well liked by his employees and patients. He seemed like an all-around good guy."

"You speak as if you had some affection for him."

Did I say that?

"We got along. He helped me walk again."

"That's it?"

"What else is there?"

"You're holding back. Look, Shelby, I need all the facts. We can't be blindsided by some crucial piece of information you neglect to tell me. It could come back to haunt us later on."

Alan's eyes bore into mine. I struggle to maintain eye contact. My stomach is churning and I feel like throwing up again. I cover my mouth with my hand.

"What's wrong? Are you sick?"

I swallow hard then breathe in and out slowly. "No," I squeak. "I'm having a hard time with this. With…everything that just happened."

"That's understandable under the circumstances. Now is the time to nail down critical information, while it's still fresh in your mind. Okay?"

I nod.

"Let's talk about the timeline. I want to know everything you did today. The coroner will establish a time of death. We have to be certain investigators can't place you anywhere near the vicinity of the murder."

"I woke up at my usual time."

"What time would that be?"

"6:00 am. I went downstairs, worked out for a half hour, then showered and got ready for work."

"What time did you leave the house?"

"Around 7:00 am."

"Did you check the trunk of your car before you left home?"

"No. I had no reason to."

"Anything unusual about the car? Did it seem heavier somehow? Was there anything out of place?"

"No. I backed out of the garage like I always do."

"What route did you take to work?"

"I took Route 9 heading east, exited on Route 30 in Framingham, then got on the Mass Pike. Took Exit 18 toward Cambridge."

"Did you stop anywhere?"

"No."

"Where did you park your car when you got to work?"

"In the garage."

"Did you notice any strangers or suspicious individuals who might be looking at your car?"

"Not really."

"Do you own a gun?"

Fear grips me. I breathe mathematics for a living and see the equation; a clever adversary who's always one step ahead of me plus a dead ex-lover shot to death, and the fact that I own a gun equals viable suspect.

Many people own guns; it doesn't mean they go around putting bullets in other people's heads.

"I have one. Jason bought it for me for protection when he's away."

"What kind of gun is it?"

"A Smith & Wesson revolver. The .357 Magnum."

"Where is it?"

"In the glove compartment of my car."

Alan winces and drums on the table with his fingers. "The car that the police have now impounded, the car that the crime scene techs are processing as we speak?"

For a moment, I just stare at him. My earlier math equation tightens around my neck like a noose. If everything follows that logic, the gun would have been fired. My prints will be all over it.

"Give it to me straight, Alan. Just how screwed am I?"

"If I had to use an analogy," he said, loosening his tie, "I would say the Thanksgiving turkey is far from cooked. There are many unanswered questions, which make the State's case purely circumstantial if they were to charge you. It's going to be difficult to pinpoint exactly where he was killed, which means they can't place you at the scene. Your alibi is solid and that will be ironclad once we go over the security footage of the garage where your car was parked, and you have no motive. Is there anything else you neglected to mention?"

"Yes. There's a call you need to make before you leave the station tonight."

He eyes me with a healthy dose of curiosity. "To whom and for what reason?"

"Call Greg Marr at Bryant International." I rattle off the phone number I had memorized. "Tell him the flowers still need tending to. If there's ever a problem with the gardening, he should let you know right away and you'll contact me to solve the problem."

Alan looks at me like I need admittance to a mental ward. He clears his throat. "What exactly are you asking me to do? If I'm going to represent you and get you back to your family ASAP, I can't hesitate to use any and all tactics and resources at my disposal. That means there can be no secrets between us as far as this case is concerned. This message is code for what?"

"I swear it's nothing illegal, and has nothing to do with this case. Look up Bryant International for yourself. And, Alan," I say, not blinking, "this falls under attorney-client privilege. I don't care how much Jason is paying you to represent me or how much he badgers you."

After a long silence, Alan sighs. "I see."

"I don't need you to see, I need you to do it. It's a critical call."

My hands quiver of their own accord and I place them in my lap, awaiting Alan's response.

"Look, Shelby, if the District Attorney decides to pursue you as his number one suspect, you and I will be spending a lot of time together. If you don't trust me to provide a vigorous defense and act in your best interest, this case will be a very difficult climb."

"I understand what I'm up against."

"Do you? This meeting is a precursor to a toxic storm that could rage for months."

Chapter 19

Mia clapped her hands and danced to Rihanna's "Don't Stop the Music" around the small one-bedroom apartment, banging into furniture and occasionally bumping into the cream-colored walls. She paid no mind. The music was intoxicating and she just wanted to dance and dance. Victory was finally within her grasp, and nothing and no one would snatch it from her.

The music got louder and she was floating on a big puffy cloud made just for her. She felt alive, invincible. She didn't want it to end but there was still much work to do. She had to sharpen her tools for the tasks ahead. Her masterpiece would soon be complete, the picture so perfect, everyone would wonder why they thought it should have been any other way in the first place.

She plopped down on the chair in front of the computer and muted the sounds coming from the police scanner. Her little setup against the wall in the far corner of the living room was perfect. She didn't need much. This was only a temporary place of operation. Soon, she would move on to a much grander residence.

She dialed the number for WBCY-Channel 8. She had timed this perfectly so the story would make the six o'clock news. She was transferred to the newsroom and spoke to a man who picked up the call. She put on her most seductive yet professional voice.

"I've come by some information regarding a murder. The State Police have picked up a woman for questioning in connection with the discovery of a dead body in the trunk of her car on the Mass Pike. I think I may know the woman. Her name is Dr. Shelby Durant Cooper, the wife of Orphion Technologies CFO Jason Cooper. Such a tragedy, isn't it?"

Before the man could lob a question at her, she hung up. The call was untraceable. If she knew anything about the media, they would be checking out this information in a flash and WBCY would have scooped the other stations. Tonight, nobody in the Cooper household would rest easy.

Chapter 20

A bbie was just finishing her homework when she heard what sounded like a helicopter buzzing overhead. When the sound got increasingly louder, she knew she was right. She ran out of her bedroom and yelled for her father as she slid down the long, winding staircase.

"Dad? Dad? Do you hear that?"

She found her father leaning up against the kitchen counter. Sagging against the counter would be more accurate.

"Dad, what's going on? Why is there a helicopter hovering over our house?"

Before her father could respond, Miles appeared with Mahalia, the family Golden Retriever, in tow. The canine whimpered and wagged her tail anxiously. The house telephone rang and Abbie reached for the one near the refrigerator.

"Don't pick that up." Her dad's tone was biting, disturbed.

"Dad, what's going on? Where's Mom?" Abbie sensed something terrible had happened.

"Take a seat. You, too, Miles."

They did as he asked. Mahalia sat at her usual spot at Miles's feet, whimpering. The dog's anxiety wasn't lost on Abbie. Whatever their dad was about to tell them was bad.

Jason chose to stand. "Come on, what is it?" Miles asked impatiently.

"There was an incident this afternoon involving your mother."

"An incident?" Abbie asked.

"What kind of incident?" Miles said.

"The State Police took your mom in for questioning about a murder."

Abbie and Miles exchanged panicked glances. "Why does the police think Mom knows anything about a murder?" Abbie asked.

"Alessandro Rossi was found dead in the trunk of her car this afternoon."

Miles was speechless. He held Mahalia's collar in a death grip. Alarm rippled through Abbie. What if there was a connection between Mr. Rossi's death and her stalker, Mr. Anonymous? She tried to remember what he said in the note. Something about the storm gathering speed, and that it would explode with a bang.

Abbie was breathing like she'd just run the Boston Marathon. She couldn't make eye contact with her father.

"Abbie?" Jason asked.

She wrung her hands. "It's just awful. Do they know how he died?"

"He was shot in the head."

Abbie clutched her stomach. "Excuse me," she whispered, and then bolted from the kitchen.

She sprinted up the stairs and barely made it to the toilet in her bathroom before she emptied her stomach. She rinsed her mouth with Listerine and splashed cold water on her face. She leaned up against the sink and closed her eyes.

Her wooden legs took her to her room where she unplugged her smart phone from its charger and speed dialed Ty. He answered on the first ring.

"Mr. Rossi got shot to death and the police are holding my mother for questioning. What the stalker said in the note came true. Oh my God, I'm in so much trouble. My mom is in so much trouble. I don't know what to do."

"Slow down, Cooper. What are you talking about? Who got shot?"

"Mr. Rossi, my mom's former physical therapist. Are you deaf? He was shot in the head. He's dead, Ty. They found him in the back of my mom's car, and the cops are holding her. They think she did it."

"Holy fuck!"

Ty rarely swore. His reaction told Abbie everything she needed to know about what she and her family were about to face.

"Should I tell my dad about the note?"

"I don't know, Cooper. Shit just got real. Okay, let's think about it for a minute. I mean, we're just kids, we don't have answers."

"I know that, idiot."

"Don't say that. You called me, remember?"

"Sorry. I'm freaking out."

"Me, too. This stalker guy just took it to another level. You have to tell your dad and let the police deal with it."

"I can't, I'm too scared. You see what he did to Mr. Rossi. He'll come after the rest of us if I tell."

"Yeah, maybe you're right."

"I have to go. I'll call you back. I'm heading downstairs and see what else is going on."

After Abbie hung up on Ty, she headed back downstairs to find Miles in tears and her dad looking like the living dead.

"I had to go to the bathroom," she blurted out.

"I just got a call from Alan Rose, your mom's lawyer," Jason said. "She won't be coming home tonight, Abbie. They arrested her. She'll be arraigned in court tomorrow morning."

Ty's reaction was spot-on, Abbie thought as she backed away from her father, terror stabbing at every cell in her body. She sat down quickly before her legs gave way under her, and covered her face with her hands. If she told her dad about the note, the stalker could get mad and try to hurt them. He wasn't playing around. Abbie decided her dad couldn't find out. They just had to focus on proving her mom didn't do it. This was the worst day of her life.

Miles clung to their father. Abbie got up from the chair and held him tight. Their dad embraced them in his strong arms, and tears flowed with abandon.

"It's going to be okay," Jason soothed. "You know your mother is innocent. The police just made a mistake. Once it's all cleared up, she'll be home with us where she belongs. Alan is with her right now. She'll be home soon, I promise."

Jason's day had gone straight to the crapper when he confronted Chloe Grace about trying to sabotage him. Then Shelby called, and his world had been spinning off its axis ever since.

The vultures were circling. It was after 5:00 pm when he told the kids. It was now forty minutes later and the press had already gotten wind of it. The house phone and his cell phone hadn't stopped ringing.

They lived on a quiet country road, with a private cobblestone path that led to the house. He hoped the news media wouldn't trespass but he wouldn't hold his breath. They would be waiting to ambush him at some point. Jason refused to answer the house phone. His kids were terrified, and he had to protect them. He instructed them not to watch the evening news, not that he was about to follow his own advice. There were a lot of calls to make, starting with Alan Rose. His sister, Robin, in Atlanta, and his mother would be next. His mom would have to leave Connecticut tonight to stay with the kids so he could be there for Shelby at the arraignment and bring her home.

Jason headed to his study on the first floor of the house, the place he retreated to whenever he was in crisis.

He stood in the middle of the room and turned on the TV to channel 8. No surprise, the murder of Alessandro Rossi was the lead story. "A shocking murder in MetroWest leads our broadcast tonight," the blonde female anchor said. A picture of Alessandro Rossi, taken in his office, flashed on the screen.

"State Police confirmed that a suspect has been arrested in connection with the crime but they have not yet officially revealed the identity. However, WBCY News has information from an anonymous source that Dr. Shelby Cooper, a top researcher at Cambridge-based GeneMedicine, has been arrested in connection with the murder."

A photo of Shelby at last year's company picnic flashed on

screen.

"Dr. Cooper is one of the most vocal voices nationwide for programs designed to encourage girls to pursue careers in STEM— Science, Technology, Engineering and Math. She's the wife of Orphion CFO Jason Cooper, who has been interviewed several times on this station."

He'd heard enough.

Abbie didn't watch much TV and mostly used the set to watch DVDs or stream her favorite shows on Netflix. She wanted to catch a few minutes of the evening news to see what the story was about her mother, in spite of her dad's warning to the contrary. She decided against it when her dad told her to keep an eye on Miles until he was through making some calls.

"What are we going to do, Abbie?" Miles asked, his eyes brimming with fresh tears. "What if Mom doesn't come home tomorrow or the day after?"

"She will, Miles. It's just a mix-up. Remember the time you brought home Max Mitchell's backpack by mistake because the two of you had the same bag? And, you almost got in trouble the next day? They figured out what happened, right?"

Miles nodded.

"Well, it's like that with Mom. It's just a mistake. Once the police find out she didn't do anything wrong, she'll come home and they'll look for the real bad guy."

"What if they don't find him? Does that mean Mom will never come back to us?"

Abbie knelt before Miles who was seated on the mini-couch. "No matter what happens, she'll find her way back to us. It just means we all have to say extra prayers when we go to bed. Mom would like that, wouldn't she?"

That got a grin out of Miles. "Yes. She wouldn't have to yell at me for skipping."

"That's right. You would score major cool points from her."

Abbie hugged her little brother tight. She had to keep an extra eye on him. Their Mom spoiled him rotten and he would be lost without her. They all would.

Part II:

THE PRISONER

Chapter 21

I sit next to Alan Rose at the defendant's table in courtroom three of the Worcester Superior Court.

My clothes are disheveled, the same outfit I had on yesterday—charcoal gray wool slacks, a pink open front cardigan sweater and matching blouse, and high-heeled ankle boots. I haven't slept. My bones hurt. I need a shower. I look straight ahead, avoiding the glare of the cameras and the stares of the few reporters who were able to snag a seat for the arraignment. I glance back at Jason seated in the gallery, his face expressionless.

Alan runs me through the proceedings that are about to take place. Once the case number is called, I'll be brought before the judge. The charges against me will be read. The prosecutor will give the specifics of the case at which point I enter a plea of not guilty. I shiver as I recall my stalker's statement. *If bail is granted, tell them you can't afford it. You mustn't post bond.* Tears prickle at the back of my eyes. For the first time since I became an adult, I'm no longer in control of my own destiny. The young, vulnerable teenage girl I was, unloved and lost, has been superimposed on the accomplished, confident adult I'd worked hard to become. A murderous psychopath has issued a challenge and he dares me to respond. But, the instinct to protect my children at all costs, that maternal drive my own mother so sorely lacked, is a powerful force my tormentor doesn't understand.

Judge Susan A. Donnelly enters the courtroom, a middle-aged blonde with a short bob and blue-rimmed glasses. The bailiff calls the case number. We move to stand before the judge, and so does the District Attorney to our right.

My lungs feel like they've been set on fire, and the blaze is quickly spreading to the rest of my body. It doesn't matter what's said in the next three minutes.

I plead not guilty to Felony Homicide, Improper Disposal of a Body, and Improper Transplant of a Body.

District Attorney Frank Barrows, a slightly overweight man who looked like he was in desperate need of a haircut and a shave, made his case against bail.

"Your honor, the victim was found in Dr. Cooper's vehicle while she was driving said vehicle. She knew the victim personally. She owns a gun, the same caliber that shot Mr. Rossi. The Coopers are wealthy and Dr. Cooper has access to resources that would allow her to flee the state or the country and stay away indefinitely. Due to the heinous nature of the crime, the Commonwealth requests that she be held without bail, and her passport be confiscated."

The cameras all go off in a symphony of clicks and flashes. Then it's back to the hushed silence, the silence that dares my lawyer to trump the DA's argument.

"Your honor, there is no proof that my client murdered Mr. Rossi or dumped his body in her vehicle," Alan says, with the confidence of a man accustomed to winning. "There are no eyewitness accounts of the crime, and the police have yet to establish where Mr. Rossi was killed, therefore they can't place my client at the crime scene. Everything that means anything to her is here—her husband, her children, and her work. She's been a law-abiding citizen and is anxious to clear her good name and reputation, which has been severely damaged by this tragic circumstance. We ask that bail be granted and Dr. Cooper be given the opportunity to prove her innocence, and restore her good name."

"I've heard enough and have made my decision," the judge says. "Based on the circumstances of the case, I grant bail in the amount of one million dollars, and Dr. Cooper will be required to wear a GPS tracking bracelet."

The gavel comes down. Alan looks pleased with himself. He stuffs some papers into his briefcase. The DA looks disappointed. The determined jut of his chin indicates this is far from over. Jason cracks a smile. The reporters are ready to pounce. This is a critical victory in the fight to clear my name, yet I feel as though my heart has just been ripped out of my chest. My head is swimming as I stagger under the weight of the decision I must make. If I walk out of this courtroom a free woman, it could spell disaster for my children. I can't gamble with their lives by pretending my stalker's threats are empty. He has proven they're not, with ruthless precision.

I put on a brave face as Jason and Alan usher me out of the courtroom. I stop and turn to Jason. "You know I love you and the kids but I can't come home right now. Please don't post my bail. If you do, it will be the end of our family."

Chapter 22

J ason didn't know how he was going to tell his children their mother wouldn't be coming home. How could he explain it to them when he didn't understand it himself? He was still reeling from the bombshell Shelby dropped after the arraignment. Something perverse was happening and she was caught up in the thick of it.

"Shelby is one of the most level-headed people I know," his mother Naomi stated. "She wouldn't do something like this without sound reasoning. She wouldn't put you and the kids through that kind of hell. Something dark and disturbing is going on, Jason."

"I know that, Mother."

Jason sat at the kitchen table with his head bowed as his mother rubbed his shoulders. He was glad she came. Naomi Cooper could always be counted on for her calming presence, and wisdom. The retired advertising executive in her mid-sixties now ran a bed and breakfast in Woodstock, Connecticut. Wrinkles barely registered on her cinnamon complexion. Her tall, slender frame lent itself to the regal air with which she comported herself.

"I'll help you deliver the news to the kids. They need to be surrounded by all the love their little hearts can hold because this will tear them apart."

I arrive at the Pre-Trial Unit, a maximum-security jail at the Bayside Women's Prison in Framingham. I'm on the second floor of the Health Admissions Building. That's all I'm capable of knowing for sure. The rest is a fog moving in slow motion: linoleum floors, white walls, blue doors. A corrections officer behind a Plexiglas window is yelling instructions at me. I can't keep up and I'm not moving fast enough for him, so he yells louder.

The worst is yet to come. The female guard assigned to get me through processing looks like she feels sorry for me. Maybe I imagined it. In no time flat, it's back to business. Information regarding my case is recorded. My property is searched, a small leather handbag with just my wallet and some makeup items. I take off the earrings I wore to court. The female guard looks at my hand. "The rock comes off, too."

I hand over my wedding and engagement rings. My brain goes into survival mode and finds a way for me to deal: numbness. I'm sent behind a plastic shower curtain and told to strip. The female officer photographs my naked body. I'm asked to hold my arms up and open my mouth while the guard pokes around. She asks me to squat, spread my cheeks and cough. I'm weak with humiliation and don't have the strength to attempt to cover up my body with my hands. I have to shower but not before throwing up in the sink. Afterwards I receive my new belongings. I change into an orange jumpsuit. I'm issued a military style blanket, sneakers that are too big, a towel, soap, toothbrush, toothpaste, cheap bra and panties, and a comb.

I'm escorted to my cell, where I already have a roommate. I must look a fright to her.

"It ain't that bad. Just takes a few days to adjust, that's all."

She's a few inches taller than me with long brown wavy hair, large, brown, glazed eyes, and lashes for miles. She looks like she's in a perpetual state of misery. That's going to be me if I don't get out of here soon. I collapse on the bottom bunk with the thin cheap mattress. I didn't even ask her name or which bunk was hers.

Jason strained to keep his voice even, matter-of-fact, to hide the emotional mushroom cloud that erupted in the past several hours. "Mom will be away just a little bit longer. It's going to take some time to sort out the legal issues surrounding the case."

"What? How is that possible, Dad?" Abbie asked, despair plain on her face.

A fleeting glance passed between him and his mother, who had joined them at the kitchen table. The dog already knew. Mahalia's whimpers grew louder and more intense as she lay in a defeated heap at Miles's feet.

"Mahalia, cut it out!" Miles yells.

He was rewarded with more whimpering and sorrowful eyes from the beloved family pet. Mahalia got up from Miles's feet and began pacing from one end of the kitchen to the other, wagging her tail. She stopped in front of the large stainless steel refrigerator, and started pawing at a photo with her two front legs. It was a photo of Mahalia, Miles, and Shelby building sand castle on the beach last summer.

"Mom isn't coming back, is she?" Miles asked, his lips trembling.

"Come here, babies," his mother said. "Come sit with Grandma."

Miles and Abbie obeyed. Jason could barely stand it, the look of sheer devastation on his children's faces.

"She's just temporarily detained," Jason said.

"Detained where?" Abbie asked, incredulous. She wanted answers and Jason knew there was no bullshitting with her. His mother gave him an encouraging nod. "Mom got taken to jail today."

"What? She's innocent. How could they take her to jail?"

It was a defining moment for Jason. If he wasn't up front with his kids, they would find out some other way and he wanted to be the one to put context around what they would hear from various sources, both online and offline.

"Abbie, I don't know what went wrong. She pleaded not guilty and the next thing I knew, she'd been carted off to the women's prison. Bail was granted but she asked that I not post it."

"So, Mom did it? Is that what it means?"

"No, Miles, your mother is not a murderer. We all know that."

He looked from Miles to Abbie. It tore him apart to see their world crumble before them. He would swallow his own grief as best he could. Shelby and the kids needed him to make the family whole again.

"I know this looks bad, kids. Whatever your mother is afraid of is the key to bringing her home. Something scared her so bad that she thinks going to jail is the only answer. We have to find out the connection between Alessandro Rossi getting killed and why your mother was framed for it."

"This bites," Abbie said, unable to hide her anger. "I thought yesterday was the worst day of my life. Today just took first place. I should just die now and be done with it. I'm the daughter of a jailbird. You know that Mom's life is over, don't you? Even after she comes home. Her career is over. All the hard work she put into her research, gone. Her company is going to pretend she never worked for them. They're going to find every paper she ever published and start a bonfire or wipe their servers clean. Good thing we're well off, because Mom is never going to earn a living as a scientist again."

How could he argue with that? Her logic was sound. Even he had to worry about his job. The crisis communications team kicked into high gear and put out a press release: Jason Cooper is a valued member of the management team. The company stands by him while he and his family go through this horrible crisis. They can't comment on an ongoing investigation, blah, blah.

"I understand you're worried about your mom's reputation. I am, too. But, the first priority is getting her out of jail."

"What are you going to do?" Miles asked. "How are you going to get Mom back? Jail is horrible, isn't it? And only bad guys go to jail. Are they going to hurt Mom?"

His mother jumped in. He was grateful.

"No one is allowed to hurt your mother, sweet pea. They punish people who do that in jail. Your mom is safe."

"I got Mom the best lawyer and we'll hire our own investigator," Jason said. "If either one of you," he said, looking from

Abbie to Miles, "hears anything, or sees anything, or something doesn't make sense, please come to me. For the next couple of days, I'd like you guys to stay home from school. I've already spoken to your teachers and principal. Homework will be emailed. Please stay off the Internet, especially social media. We have a lot of work to do, and it will be worth it when Mom walks through the door with that big smile on her face."

Abbie had heard enough and excused herself. She slammed her bedroom door and plopped down on her bed, face down. She would have a few choice words for Mr. Stalker asshole next time he contacted her.

Abbie's friends had agreed to a Skype check-in from Anastasia's room. Anastasia Cruz was Columbian, and came from a soccer-obsessed family. Abbie liked her because she was honest, smart and fun.

Callie Furi was the innocent in their group, always last to get the sexual innuendos they liked to throw around. Abbie's mother said she reminded her of a young Elizabeth Taylor.

Frances Lin was most like Abbie in temperament and behavior, although she could be obnoxious at times. She was first generation Chinese-American, had a wicked sense of humor, and no diplomacy. Abbie was the only local girl in the group; the others lived in the dorms. Together, they had dubbed themselves the Rainbow Posse.

The three faces took up the entire computer screen.

"Dish," Frances ordered. "What's going on with your mom?"

"It's not good, ladies. They took her to jail today."

"What?" they asked in unison.

Abbie adjusted the computer on her lap. "She told my dad not to post her bail."

"It's a conspiracy," Anastasia blurted out in her thick Spanish accent. "Somebody is pressuring your mom. Probably the real killer."

"State the obvious, why don't you?" Frances said.

"Abbie, we're so sorry to hear this awful news. We're here for you."

It was just like Callie to be concerned about her feelings. "Thanks, Callie. I don't know what to do."

"What does your dad say?" Frances asked.

"He's in shock like we all are. He says he got the best lawyer for Mom and he'll hire his own private investigator, but I don't know if that'll be enough. If somebody went through all that trouble to set up my mom, he's not going to make it easy to get caught."

"They always make a mistake," Callie said. "On all the TV crime shows, the killer slips up just once, and that changes everything."

Frances chimed in. "She's right. It takes a lot of work to set somebody up. There's a clue out there that could turn everything around."

"Don't be sad, Abbie," Callie said. "You have to believe they'll catch the real bad guy. Believing is half the battle."

"Thank you, guys. I appreciate the support."

"Are you coming to school tomorrow? There were a couple of reporters snooping around yesterday. Ms. Winthrop kicked them off school property."

"I don't know. My dad wants to keep us home for a few days until the craziness dies down a little. There are still reporters hanging out on our street, trying to get the neighbors to say something that will make the evening news."

The girls talked for a while longer, about classes, the upcoming Platinum Ball, and how ridiculous the amount of homework was. After they signed off, Abbie called Ty. He was sympathetic and supportive. "Check your email."

"Why?"

"Just check. I'll hold."

Abbie logged in to her email account and saw a message from Ty. When she clicked on it, the image of a roaring tiger appeared with the caption: BECAUSE YOU'RE FIERCE!

She completely lost it. She went to the bathroom and locked herself in. She sat on the cold tiles, leaning up against the giant tub for support.

"Cooper, are you there?"

She couldn't answer because she was crying so hard. She was

convinced one of the blood vessels in her eyes would pop. Yet, sweet, wonderful, supportive Ty understood the state she was in and just stayed with her on the line, soothing her battered soul.

Chapter 23

The earsplitting sound of a voice over a PA system ricochets off the walls and shocks me into consciousness. I slowly open my eyes to find out what the ruckus is about. The air smells of piss and something rancid I can't identify. I sit up and take in my surroundings and it all comes flooding back to me. The nightmare is real. I am in a jail cell. The steel bars, ugly gray walls, toilet, and sink are real, too. The woman I met yesterday, my new roomie, is staring at me like a strange specimen under a microscope in a lab.

"You're one of them college girls, ain't you?"

My eyes are sore and tired from crying. If I'm going to survive in here, I have to make friends. Isn't that what all the prison movies show?

"What's your name?"

"Elsa."

"Why are you here?"

She's confused by the question.

"What are you in for?"

She looks up at the ceiling then back at me. "What you wanna know for?"

"Just making conversation."

"None of your business, then."

"Okay. What's with the noise?"

"That's our own personal, fancy alarm clock."

"Well, it's obnoxious."

"Better get used to it."

"Why? I'm innocent."

She laughs at me. Her teeth are yellow and rotting. If I had to guess, I'd say she was in for dealing crystal methamphetamine. Or, maybe I've watched too many episodes of *Breaking Bad*.

"Why is that funny? I am innocent. Do I look like I belong here? What do you think I did? On second thought, don't answer that."

"It will start to feel just like home soon enough. You'll see."

"You have kids?" I ask, anxious to change the subject.

"One."

"I have two. A husband. A dog. A nice house."

Wretchedness puts me in a chokehold. Just saying it aloud draws a sharp contrast to what my life was and what it is now. I am an inmate, a number in the system. I belong to the Commonwealth. From now until Alessandro's killer is found, I'll be told when to wake up, when to eat, when to go to sleep, when I can have visitors, when to go to the bathroom. My new home is smaller than the closet of my five-thousand-square-foot home on three acres of pristine land. All of a sudden, my head is spinning. Hunger. I haven't eaten since I was brought in yesterday. Blackness.

Chapter 24

Jason led Detectives Eric Van Dorn and Tess McCall to the living room. He had a raging headache that wouldn't quit and he hadn't slept in days. He was running on fumes and was in no shape for police questioning, but he wanted to get it over with and cross it off his growing to-do list. It was after 10:00 am the day after Shelby's arraignment, and the sun was seeping through the window, giving the space a bright, cheery feeling. The sun must not have gotten the memo about his current mood. Or, maybe it just didn't care.

Van Dorn's sharp gaze meandered around the space and Jason could see his mind running like a calculator. McCall was younger, and not the soft feminine type. She looked like she wanted to string someone up by their eyelids.

The detectives sat next to each other on the sofa and Jason took the armchair opposite them. McCall wasted no time. "How well did you know Mr. Rossi?"

"I didn't. He was my wife's physical therapist after she suffered major injuries from a motorcycle crash."

"When was that?" Van Dorn asked, producing a pen and small notebook from his jacket pocket.

"Earlier this year. Late winter."

97

"Can you be a little bit more specific?" McCall asked.

"I'll get back to you on exact dates. The insurance company would have the records of her treatment as well as the names of Mr. Rossi's staff at the center."

Jason stretched out his legs and relaxed his body. He was dressed in black head to toe. He felt it was appropriate, though his wardrobe choice had not been deliberate. It was his idea to have the detectives ask questions without his attorney present. He had nothing to hide. He wanted to be accessible to the investigation. He wasn't about to allow them to railroad him, either.

"When was the last time your wife had contact with the victim?" An unspoken agreement had apparently passed between the two detectives. Van Dorn would take the lead for now.

"As I mentioned, her therapy went on for most of the spring. Occasionally, she mentioned running into him at the store. Nothing worth thinking about."

"Did Mrs. Cooper exhibit any strange behavior, change her routine? Anything seem to be bothering her in the weeks leading up to the murder?"

There was a loaded question if ever there was one. That night at Pennybakers back in October, she was jumpy and left the café to take Vivian's call. He wouldn't mention it to the police, though.

"No. Nothing changed about her behavior or her routine."

McCall crossed her legs, her eyes two orbs of hot coals. Van Dorn stroked his chin and concentrated on something he had written down in his notebook. This must be their good-cop-bad-cop routine.

"Where were you between the hours of 11:00 am and 3:00 pm on the day of the murder?" McCall couldn't help herself.

"In my office. Several people can vouch for my whereabouts. I was also on the phone with my wife when she was taken in."

That nugget of information animated the investigators. Van Dorn pounced. "Is that so? Care to tell us what you talked about?"

"Shelby was afraid, distraught. The state police pulled her over and she didn't know why. She asked me to stay on the phone with her."

"We'll look into her phone records," McCall said.

"You do that," Jason sniped.

Van Dorn cleared his throat and shifted in his seat. "Your wife must have spent a lot of time with the victim because of her therapy. Would you say they were close?"

"I'm not sure what you're getting at, Detective. Are you close with your doctor or any other person who provides a service to you?"

Van Dorn grinned. "Touché. What I mean is, did your wife have a relationship with Mr. Rossi, outside of therapy?"

"Are you asking me if my wife was having an affair? That's outrageous and I resent the question."

"No need to get bent out of shape, Mr. Cooper. No one said anything about an affair. Sometimes when people spend a lot of time together, they get close. Sometimes it's sexual and sometimes it isn't. Just trying to cover all the angles here. Nobody's accusing your wife of anything."

"It sounded like you were."

McCall wasn't about to let it go. "You and your wife have any marital problems?"

"No."

"Didn't she file for divorce at the beginning of the year? Then withdrew the petition?"

"That was a lifetime ago. Every marriage has challenges. We worked things out."

"Did your wife have any enemies or anyone she may have angered or had a beef with?" Van Dorn chimed in.

"No. She was well liked."

"Any gambling problems, debt, financial issues?"

"None."

Van Dorn appraised the living room again. His eyes landed on the baby grand piano off in the corner near the window. He moved on to the expensive art lining the walls, pieces Vivian had recommended and managed to procure at auction. He looked up at the coffered ceilings, and the crystal chandelier, and finally, the fieldstone fireplace before he flipped another page in his notebook.

"I see. Did she have many friends?"

"The women in her motorcycle club. Her best friend Vivian lives in Chicago."

"We're going to need all their contact information and addresses," McCall said.

Van Dorn flipped through his notebook again. "You're currently the chief financial officer at Orphion Technologies?"

"That's correct."

"I hear the company is going public soon. Should I buy some stock?"

Jason looked at him, expressionless and silent.

Van Dorn cleared his throat again, mostly out of embarrassment, and McCall took the opportunity to jump in. "Your wife getting arrested for murder must have really put a damper on your ambition to become CEO."

"No, it hasn't," Jason responded, his voice flat. "Whether or not I become CEO is irrelevant right now. Next question please," Jason said, looking at his watch. "I have somewhere I need to be."

"We're trying to establish a motive here, Mr. Cooper. By all accounts, Alessandro Rossi was a good man and had no known enemies. It just seems odd he would be killed in such a violent manner. Aren't you at all concerned that his body was found in your wife's car?"

"Not at all. Whoever is setting up my wife obviously put it there. Do you honestly think a person of her size and height could put a dead body in the trunk of a car?"

"Maybe she had help," McCall offered.

Jason ignored her. "Detectives, I really must go. If you have additional questions, please call me. I'm even willing to come down to the station and save you the trip."

"Can we look around a bit?" McCall asked.

"Not without a warrant, you can't."

"Okay. We'll get one, then."

Jason knew that a warrant to search the house was already in the works and could be executed later in the day. For now, he'd had all he could take. Everyone stood up.

"If you think of anything, give me a call," Van Dorn said, handing Jason his business card. McCall didn't bother. Jason escorted them out of the house, knowing this was only round one.

Chapter 25

Later that day, a uniformed guard behind the desk of the Pre-Trial Unit of the Bayside Women's Correctional Facility took Jason's Driver's License and asked him to empty his pockets. He was subjected to a search. He had done his research on visitor policies for the prison.

The cell phone was left in the car. He adhered to the clothing rules as well, wearing a simple sweater, jeans, and sneakers. The prison was only minutes from downtown Framingham. The environment was appalling. He didn't want to think about how truly awful it was for Shelby.

After a pat down, he was ushered into the visitors' room, a sparsely furnished area with Plexiglas on one side, white plastic chairs, tables, and a soda and snack machine along the wall. There was only one other visitor waiting for an inmate. He pulled up a chair. His heart was beating twice its normal pace. His nerves were on the verge of shattering.

When Shelby appeared, it took all the energy he had not to fall apart. She'd only been in for twenty-four hours. She already looked gaunt. She wore a hideous orange jumpsuit that was too big for her. She looked so out of place. Her eyes, framed in dark circles, were now enormous pools on her small face.

She pulled up a chair. Three uniformed guards were placed strategically around the room.

"Not exactly couture, but it will have to do," she said, pointing to her prison-issued uniform.

He was glad she could joke about this because he couldn't. "I have a million questions. Has anyone threatened or mistreated you? What are you eating? What do you need? I'll get it for you, I don't care if Alan has to throw his weight around or ruffle some administrative feathers, whatever it is …" he trailed off to catch his breath.

"It's not pleasant in here. That's the point though. It's scary and depressing and I just want to come home."

Jason curled and uncurled his hand, desperately trying not to reach out and touch her. "How are the kids?" she asked. "What is this doing to them?"

"It's hard. Miles is confused. He doesn't understand why you're here when you didn't do anything wrong. He cries at bedtime. Abbie, well, you know our daughter. She's angry and scared. She's playing tough, mostly for my benefit, I think. She thinks it's her job to keep the family together until you get home."

"She told you that?"

"No. She didn't have to. She's been spending more time on the phone with Ty than she does her girlfriends."

Shelby smiled. For a fleeting moment, it seemed like they were having their usual end-of-day conversation at home, about the children, work, things that might be bothering them or something funny that happened that day. Then, the harsh arm of reality promptly slapped him silly.

"What's so funny?"

"Abbie and Ty. She's falling for him. Hard."

"When did this happen?"

"It's been building for a while. She would rather die than tell him."

It was Jason's turn to smile. He knew this day would come but he always thought Shelby would be there to help Abbie navigate the trials and tribulations of first love. "She could do worse. Ty is a good kid."

"I told her the same thing. Just focus on the kids, Jason. I don't want you worrying about me in here. Let Alan do his job, and that investigator you hired. You need to be strong until I can come home."

He had to ask the question that had been burning a hole in his brain since the arraignment. Two questions actually. "What happened in court, Shelby? Why did you tell Alan not to post bail? We can afford it, so why did you choose to be here instead of home where you belong?"

"It's better that I'm in here. As long as I am, and Alan is working to prove I didn't do it, everything will be fine."

Her response was stupefying. Jason rubbed his temples with both hands. "What are you talking about?" He leaned in closer. "Did somebody threaten you? Do you know who murdered Alessandro?"

"Let it go, Jason. Job one is keeping the kids safe and happy. That will help me survive this hell hole until they find the real killer."

"It's also my job as your husband to protect you. How can I do that if you won't tell me what's going on?"

He just had to press a little bit more. He could see from the mist gathering in her eyes that it wouldn't take much for her to crack.

He lowered his voice. "What is it, baby? Please tell me. If it's something you don't want Alan to know, it will be our little secret. We'll figure out another way to get you out of here."

There was hesitation in her voice. "Um…I may have stuck my nose in where it didn't belong and the person decided to get even."

"What are you talking about? Who is this person?"

Shelby sighed. Jason braced himself. "Alessandro was a victim of domestic abuse at the hands of his wife."

He shut his eyes tight. An intense coldness gripped his core.

"That's awful," he said, opening his eyes. "How did you find out?"

"He told me."

That revelation made Jason uneasy. He'd heard of Battered Man Syndrome, the male equivalent of Battered Woman Syndrome. Why would his wife know such intimate details about the life of a man she only saw for health reasons?

"I feel terrible about what happened to him, but confiding in you about his domestic problems was crossing the line of the patient-provider relationship."

"He needed somebody to talk to. I had therapy every single day until I recovered from the accident. We talked. That's a difficult burden to carry and he needed a listening ear. Nothing strange about that."

Her explanation was plausible. Something was missing, though.

"So he felt comfortable revealing his darkest secret to a married woman he barely knew? Why not one of his employees or a friend? Why did he pick you?"

She looked down at her hands, unable to meet his gaze. Her body language spoke volumes and he didn't like what it was saying. His anxiety radar just went into overdrive. The sweater he was wearing suddenly made his body itch. Trying to remove it may set off the armed guards. Not a good idea, after all.

"I don't know why he picked me. One day last month, I got proof of what he had been telling me all along."

Jason let out a puff of air after Shelby told him the story of Alessandro being beaten up by his wife in the parking lot of Whole Foods and how she tried to stop it. "You think she had him killed, then put the body in your car as payback?"

Shelby nodded.

He pondered that for a moment. A wife wanting to get rid of her husband does so and frames someone else for it, because that someone threatened to report her for domestic abuse. The theory had some teeth to it, although he couldn't shake the feeling he wasn't getting the full picture.

"That still doesn't explain why you refused bail. Why are you sabotaging your freedom, dragging the family through this nightmare? Why won't you come home, Shelby? What's keeping you here?"

"I love you, Jason. Kiss the children for me."

"Who called you at Pennybakers the other night?"

"Vivian. Like I told you before."

"I love you, too. But, I won't let this go. I *will* find out what's got you so scared."

After Jason leaves, I go back to the concrete box I now call home. If only he knew how desperately I want to come home, to hold my children, to sleep in my own bed in his strong, soothing embrace. To be free to do all the things I took for granted before coming here. I won't ask Jason to bring me pictures of the family to keep me going. That I must do on my own so I can spit in the face of the demon who is determined to break me. I reach under the thin mattress and remove the note I received today. Corrections officers can only read incoming mail if there's a "Mail Cover" placed on it. That's usually used to track organized crime or gang members. My stalker is meticulous in his research and knows how the system works. From now on, whenever I feel my spirit waning, I'll whip out the typewritten letter.

Dear Shelby,

Thank you for your cooperation. Abigail and Miles are such wonderful children. I know how devastated you would be if any harm came to them. The world is full of tragedy and we must do our best to protect our loved ones, especially innocent children. You understand this principle very well. Your continued cooperation will go a long way towards ensuring their safety and well-being. Any attempt on your part to undermine this process, well…PTO.

On the other side of the letter are two 3D hand drawings of coffins, labeled with my children's names.

Chapter 26

After Abbie said good night to her grandma and her brother, she went to find her dad. He wasn't in the master suite and she figured right when she found him in his study, on the couch, staring into space.

"Dad?"

She joined him on the leather sofa. He wouldn't look at her. She knew he was trying the tough guy act for her benefit and didn't want her to know he was probably crying like a girl over her mom. She liked this side of him. It showed her just how much he adored her mother and that made her feel secure. "Dad, it's going to be okay. Mom is strong. And stubborn."

The tension in his face eased. "When did you get to be so smart?"

"I've always been smart, Dad. It's in the genes."

He chuckled and kissed her forehead. "So, you don't think your old man is lame for sitting here, almost comatose?"

"No. Your wife is gone and you don't know when she's coming back. That's serious, Daddy."

Abbie hugged her father tight, like she never wanted to let him go. Maybe that was true. He was the only parent she had for now.

Her phone was charging on the nightstand and she decided to take one look before she climbed into bed, and immediately regretted the decision. There were a series of text messages from him.

Him: I know you're hurting. Consider me a friend.

Him: Your mother is a deceiver. That's why she's in jail. She won't tell the truth.

Him: Hope u understand. Ur smart.

Him: u there? I know how to find u.

The phone trembled in Abbie's hands. Of course, he knew where to find her. He knew her cell phone number, where she lived, and probably what she had for breakfast every morning. She hated being so terrified all the time, feeling helpless, like her life was being controlled by an evil, albeit invisible, puppet master. Her fingers started typing before fully formed thoughts escaped her brain.

Abbie: My mom's in jail. U officially scared the shit out of a defenseless kid who did nothing to u. Ur a big hero, a real bad ass. U win. NOT!!

Abbie climbed into bed, pulled the covers up under her chin and ignored the droplets hitting her pillow.

"Why are you so jumpy?" Mia asked. "Did you do something you weren't supposed to?"

"Of course not," the man said, adjusting his glasses. "I didn't see you coming and when you got into the passenger seat, it startled me. It's dark out and no one's around."

Mia had arranged for them to meet in the abandoned parking lot behind Henry's Steak House in Framingham.

"First, congratulations are in order. You're competent after all."

He beamed at the compliment.

"The hard part is over, the rest should be easy."

"The rest?"

"You didn't think this was it, did you? I didn't spend three years planning this just to walk away after the hard part was over. The next phase is just as important, if not more so. It's what I've been working toward all these years."

"I see."

"Do you? I'm finally about to have everything I want. Now that that imposter is out of the way, it's time to ramp it up with the rude teenager."

"Abigail?" The man was alarmed.

"What, do you have a thing for her? Touch her and I'll bash your head in."

"No, that's not it. I was just wondering if that's the best way to get the results you want. She's determined. Angry. Defiant. She won't be easily broken. "

"I'll deal with her petulance when the time is right. Keep up the pressure."

She's not stupid, you know.

It was that damn old woman again. "Why can't you just stay dead?"

"I beg your pardon?" The nervous man practically jumped out of his skin.

"Not you. It's the old woman who won't shut the hell up."

"What old woman?"

"Get out of the car."

"But, it's my car."

"Okay. You can stay. Do you have any questions? You know what needs to be done?"

"Yes, I'm clear."

"Good. And don't screw up. For your sake."

Chapter 27

H ow are you feeling today?"

"I'll be a lot better if you give me something so I can sleep."

"Perhaps we can review your sleep journal together."

"How is a sleep journal going to get me eight hours of sleep so I'm not up at God forsaken hours every night? You may as well tell me to count sheep," Mia snapped. "I don't pay your exorbitant rates so you can give me pointless exercises."

Dr. Singer did not react. He never did. Mia had started seeing the prominent Harvard psychiatrist at his home office in Sudbury several weeks ago. She had chosen him carefully, and it wasn't solely based on his credentials. She observed him at several lectures, and saw how he interacted with students. His persona and appearance sealed his fate: grandfatherly, with mostly white hair, kind eyes, and non-threatening. He would be the perfect expert witness when the time came. Mia had also discovered through painstaking research that Dr. Singer's daughter Rachel suffered from a mental disorder.

Her eyes, through their own will, glanced at the photo of Rachel Singer with her parents, younger sister, and brother on a boat on Cape Cod. They looked like the perfect American family. Everything in this home office was perfect: Persian rugs, large bookshelf, plants, photos and paintings, even the dog that sat at his feet sometimes. Mia hated that damn mutt. He was always staring and growling at her so she told Dr. Singer it made her uncomfortable and she hadn't had to deal with it since.

"Well, let's exhaust all possibilities before we go the medicine route. Are you willing to do that? I'm sure you're aware that medications don't always work the way we would like them to. If we can get you to fall asleep for several hours by using positive behaviors that don't require drugs, that will go a long way towards healing."

Mia couldn't believe what he was suggesting. Was she wrong about him?

"I've suffered enough. If I don't get some sleep soon, I may not be responsible for my actions."

Dr. Singer removed his glasses and leaned forward. "What are you getting at, Mia?"

Where was his concern a few moments ago?

"I need to sleep so I can function properly, so I don't have to listen to that freaking old woman shooting off at the mouth. I need to sleep so I can get out of bed in the morning like a normal person instead of wanting to jump into the Sudbury River and never come out."

Dr. Singer scribbled something in his notebook. Mia felt like snatching it from him. Her frustration was growing by the minute. She glanced at the letter opener on the desk drawer next to him. What she was asking was simple, but no, he had to make it complicated. Damn shrinks, they're all the same.

Mia took a deep breath. She needed to remain calm. She couldn't go off the rails. There was so much more to be done. Her masterpiece wasn't completed yet. Not by a long shot.

When he looked up from his writing, Mia saw concern in his eyes, like she was worse off than he originally thought. She had to offer reassurances. She didn't want him poking his nose where it didn't belong. That would spell trouble for them both.

"I'm sorry. I don't know why I got all bent out of shape. That's what I've been trying to tell you. Not sleeping makes me crabby. And, then I have thoughts I shouldn't have."

"What kind of thoughts, Mia?"

"Like Shelby Cooper deserves everything that's happening to

her and worse."

"You're not sympathetic at all? You believe she's guilty?"

"Hell, yes."

"How can you be so sure?" Dr. Singer looked at her urgently.

"I know her. I told you before what she did to my family."

"You only indicated that she lied about something. Would you expand on that point?"

"No."

He replaced his eyeglasses to his face. "Mia, I'm really concerned. The only way to get to a place of calm and peace is to work through the difficulties in your life. Based on our previous sessions, you spend a lot of energy focused on Shelby Cooper. That isn't healthy for your psyche."

"You know, for what I'm paying you, I'm not seeing results. I expect results when I pay for a service." Her voice kept rising. "I told you Shelby Cooper took something very valuable from me and she's a fraud. How do you expect me to have sympathy for someone like that? Furthermore, the only way I'm going to be at peace with what she did is when she's rotting in a prison cell forever and ever and ever. Got it?"

Dr. Singer held up his hands. "All right, no need to get upset. I hear you. Your feelings are valid. If Shelby Cooper hurt you, it's understandable that you would want her punished. But, that's something for the law to decide, her guilt or innocence in the death of Mr. Rossi."

"They're idiots?"

"Who?"

"The police."

"Why is that?"

"See how long it takes them to convict her."

"Have you tried yoga or meditation?"

Mia looked at him like he had horns. "What?"

"What is your experience with yoga and meditation?"

"Yoga isn't so bad. I used to do it almost every day."

"Why did you stop?"

"Too busy."

"It sounds like it could be a valuable routine to return to. I'll give you a handout and some online resources to get you started."

"You better pray this works."

"Does threatening people get you the results you want, Mia?"

She cocked her head to one side, considering his question. "Some people only respond to threats. If they did what they're supposed to, I wouldn't have to resort to threats."

"Perhaps we can work on a healthier perspective. The world doesn't work that way."

"It does for me."

Chapter 28

Jason slid into a corner booth at Pennybakers on Main Street. Al Green's "Let's Stay Together" played on the sound system and long lines formed at the front counter as patrons waited to place their lunch order. He was meeting with Tom Bilko, the investigator he hired to help with Shelby's case.

Tom was retired from the Worcester Police Force. He was now an in-demand private investigator who also had expertise in security. It helped that he had old friends inside quite a few Police Departments in the state. At six-foot-five, with biceps as big as a python and a goatee that said *don't mess with me if you value breathing*, Jason felt good about his choice.

"What are your contacts at the state police telling you?" he asked Tom.

"Not much. The DA has political ambition and taking down your wife looks good. The case still has holes they need to close, like where he was killed. There's no crime scene other than your wife's car, and no motive or opportunity has been established. Until they do, state police homicide has the case."

"I can add to that," Jason offered.

"Let's hear it."

Jason gave Tom a rundown of his conversation with Shelby less than twenty-four hours ago.

Tom didn't seem fazed at all by his account. Jason figured a battle worn veteran like Tom had seen and heard it all during his crime fighting years.

"Does her lawyer know?"

"I gave him the basics. He's happy to hand the cops another suspect, a popular strategy with defense lawyers."

"I'm sure that lead will be pursued, too."

"You know the detectives assigned to the case?"

"Van Dorn is a good guy. His real gift is looking beyond the evidence. His methods can be unorthodox but he gets results. McCall is smart and capable. I'm guessing you're not buying into it, otherwise you wouldn't have called me."

"Nothing against the police, they have a job to do and I respect that, but I also have a family to protect and a wife to get out of jail for the simple fact that she's innocent. I have to do this my way."

Tom nodded. "I get that."

"I'd like to hear your take on the case before we nail down a strategy," Jason said.

"Did your wife have a beef with anybody? Outside of what you just told me. Something only close friends and family would know about? The more leads and possible suspects we have, the harder it could be to prosecute Mrs. Cooper."

Jason thought for a minute. Nothing came to mind. "Why do you ask?"

"Your wife was targeted for a reason. People don't drop dead bodies in random cars. We're talking some seriously twisted hating going on. Full-on psychopath. Whoever did this knows your wife personally and something went down between them. I once worked a case back in Philadelphia before I joined the Worcester PD. This guy was seeing a shrink for the longest time. Fancied himself in love with her. Let's just say the shrink didn't feel the same and she thought that was the end of that when she had him see another shrink. He bided his time. A whole nine months went by. Then just like that, one night she was working late. He broke into her office, hacked her to pieces, and dumped her body in the city dumpster."

"I'm not aware of anyone who hates Shelby enough to go to these lengths. It's sick."

"That's my point. To you and me, something might be insignificant, not warranting a second thought. To somebody who's not right in the head to begin with, anything can be construed as a slight or rejection and they blow it out of proportion. The poor victim usually never sees it coming.

"Maybe in passing, without even thinking about it, your wife may have said something or done something to someone and it was no big deal to her. To the other person, that slight was allowed to fester unchecked. Then they see an opening and they take it."

Jason rubbed his tired eyes. What Tom was saying made no sense to him. Shelby had little family or friends to speak of. Her parents perished in a fire when she was a teenager, and she was taken in by Rita and Daniel March, Vivian's parents. Vivian was the closest thing to a sibling Shelby had. Her friends were comprised of the ladies in her motorcycle club and a couple of mentors in her field. What Tom was suggesting was far more sinister than Jason could wrap his head around. He was the one harboring a devastating secret that could destroy his family and derail his plans to take over as CEO of Orphion. If Shelby had a dark past, too, he didn't know how he would handle it.

"That's a lot of speculation that doesn't trigger anything of substance we can use," he told Tom.

"How much do you know about your wife's relationship with her physical therapist?"

"What are you getting at?" The cops asked him the same question back at the house. And, Shelby confessed Alessandro confided his domestic problems to her.

"I'm wondering why they picked him. Don't tell me the thought never occurred to you?"

Jason rubbed his neck. "I haven't had time to think through anything. Shelby was pretty banged up after the accident. Couldn't walk for weeks. Alessandro Rossi, I give him credit for the work he did with her. That was the nature of their relationship."

Jason unzipped his jacket, took it off and placed it on the seat next to him. He was getting thirsty. It was probably a good idea to order food and drink.

"Maybe it's nothing, maybe it's something," Tom continued. "You asked me to leave no stone unturned so I had to put it out there. What about her past?"

"I've been more focused on the present. We don't know who's behind this and what their motive is, so I have to assume my children could be targets. As for Shelby's past, we met when she was a senior at Duke University, and we've been together ever since. Whoever did this is obviously insane."

Tom pressed on. "What about old colleagues? I did some research and found several articles about a fellow scientist who was selling GeneMedicine's proprietary technology to a rival biotech firm for a nice profit. Shelby discovered his racket and put an end to it."

"Ah, yes. It happened a while ago and it never even crossed my mind. Koczak. He left GeneMedicine in disgrace and went back to the Middle East, never to be heard from again."

"Are you sure?"

"Not a hundred percent. As you said, revenge is a powerful motive. Look into Koczak's whereabouts. If you find him, I want to talk to him myself. I want armed security guards on the property, cameras, the works. I also need GPS trackers that can be slipped into the kids' backpacks or some inconspicuous place. I need to know where they are when they're not home."

Chapter 29

M y God, Jason, what the hell is going on? How could this be happening?"

"I don't know, Vivian. It doesn't make sense to any of us. And, what's worse, the media frenzy hasn't let up. This morning I barely made it down the street to drop the kids off to school. News vans and cameras everywhere."

Shelby's best friend Vivian March had arrived at the house an hour earlier. She was sporting dark skinny jeans and her stylish sweater looked two sizes too big for her. She was always a thin girl but he could see her collarbone jutting out. Her elegant fingers were losing their luster, now only skin and bones. She was falling apart like the rest of them.

They were seated in the family room off the kitchen.

"What are you doing to bring our girl home? I try not to think about her being in jail. It's sickening. She won't survive. It's like the universe went and lost its damn mind."

Vivian was right. That's why he couldn't rely solely on Alan, as capable as he was.

"I hired a private investigator, Tom Bilko, to look in places the cops wouldn't think to look since they're convinced Shelby is the killer. They searched the house, took her iPad, and her laptop."

"I had no idea that all of this went down. Why didn't you tell me sooner?"

"I couldn't tell you all this over the phone."

Vivian rubbed the back of her neck and Jason went to the kitchen, returning with a bottle of spring water he handed to her.

"Thanks. This feels like it's happening to someone else, not Shelby. Did they say why they think she did this? Sounds like they have a purely circumstantial case."

"Well, besides the body being discovered in her car, her gun was fired. The bullet that killed Alessandro Rossi came from her gun. It was in the glove compartment of her car."

"What are you saying, Jason?" Vivian asked, her lips trembling. "Are you saying that Shelby did this?"

"There's a simple explanation for her prints being on the gun, I was teaching her how to use it. It's her property. "

Vivian took a few sips of the water then placed the bottle on the large coffee table, strewn with copies of *O Magazine*, *Vogue* and *The Economist*. Jason noticed her eyes linger on the publications, and a maudlin air overtook her features. Perhaps the reflection of what her sister's life used to be, before it was ripped from her and replaced with steel bars, in a place where she was treated as barely human was too much for Vivian to take.

"How are the babies doing? This must be unbearable for them."

"Abbie is on an emotional rollercoaster."

"How do you mean?"

"The timing couldn't be worse. She's struggling with her feeling for Ty and her mother isn't here to help her."

"Ty, her best friend?"

"Yup. See how cruel the universe can be?"

"You said it. And Miles?"

"He doesn't understand. He's keeping his feelings inside. I don't know how successful I've been in getting him to open up."

"So, what's next?"

"Keep pressure on the investigators to pursue other suspects. Get Shelby out of Bayport."

After dinner, everyone gathered in the family room to watch TV and try to relax. It felt almost normal to Abbie. Having Grandma Naomi and Aunt Vivian with them gave her a small sense of peace she hadn't felt in a while. She loved Aunt Vivian. She was glamorous and cool. Not fake wannabe cool like some adults. God's honest cool. Her job was awesome too. She owned her own successful art consulting business and flew all over the world on behalf of her clients. She had even picked out a few pieces for her dad's office and the house.

She also hung out with fashion designers, movie stars, and a bunch of rich fogies who spend millions of dollars on art that looked like Miles painted it. Best of all, she didn't treat Abbie like a baby. She was always telling Abbie's mom that Abbie was a young lady who needed to know how the world really was. If Abbie had any awkward questions that she was embarrassed to ask her parents, she knew Aunt Vivian would keep it real.

"How long are you staying, Aunt Vivian?" Miles asked.

"Oh, baby, I can only stay a few days."

"Oh, man," a disappointed Miles, remarked.

"I'll be back as soon as I can," she reassured him. "You know your Aunt Viv loves you guys," she said, as she rubbed Miles's head.

Then Abbie noticed that Grandma Naomi gave Aunt Vivian a look. She couldn't be sure, but it looked like Grandma frowned at her. Abbie hoped she wasn't seeing things because that would just be weird.

"I'm glad you're all here," Vivian said. "I wanted to float an idea by you, Jason, since it affects the kids."

"Well, let's hear it," Jason said.

"I just thought it would be good if Jason had someone who could help out with the kids so he can focus on bringing Shelby home."

"You mean like a babysitter?" Abbie asked, chagrined.

"No, nothing like that. Since I can't be here every day and Mrs. Cooper is knee-deep in renovating the Bed and Breakfast and can only be here part of the time, I thought it might be helpful having someone who can keep the house running, make sure the kids have a home-cooked meal when they come home from school, maybe pick them up and drop the off to appointments, things like that."

There was a brief silence, which was broken by Grandma. "It's a good idea. Someone needs to keep an eye on the kids when you can't, Jason. I suppose you have someone in mind, Vivian?"

"I do. I was thinking about it on the flight to Boston. Her mother was a mentor to me when I was a Fellow at the Art Institute of Chicago."

"I'm listening," Jason said, leaning forward.

"Her name is Rayne Revington. She's in her twenties, has a bachelor's in education and has taught kindergarten. I think she's working on her master's, but she's taking some time off to earn some money to help pay for graduate school. She's good with kids, smart, polite and completely trustworthy. I thought I could help her out as a favor to her mother who has been so good to me."

"Well, kids, what do you think?" Jason asked, looking from Abbie to Miles.

Abbie thought about it for a second and although the idea of some strange girl living in their house was a concern, the pros outweighed the cons. Aunt Vivian really seemed to like her and she sounded like a nice person. It would be good to have another woman in the house until Mom came home.

"We'd have to check her out," Abbie said.

"Miles?" Jason asked.

Her brother shrugged.

"Okay, then, Vivian. How soon can we meet her?"

"She can be here in a few days, a week maybe. I hope you don't think I'm meddling. I just want to help as much as I can. I feel bad that I can't be here daily. I have a few deals in the works and they'll take up more of my time than I would like. Between Mrs. Cooper, Rayne, and myself, we'll have you covered."

"Thank you, Vivian," Jason said. "I'm sure Shelby will be pleased."

"I'd like to go visit her."

No one said anything.

"What's wrong? Did I say something I shouldn't?" Vivian looked puzzled.

Abbie reluctantly took charge. "Mom doesn't want anyone

visiting her except Dad and her lawyer."

"What do you mean? We're her family."

"She doesn't care. We begged Dad to take us, and Mom refused. She said she doesn't want anybody visiting her. Not even her friends from the motorcycle club."

Vivian stared at Jason, incredulous.

"Abbie's right. Shelby refuses all visits. She even tries to convince me that I should visit as little as possible."

"I don't understand," said Vivian. "Why wouldn't she want to be surrounded by her family, to give her strength, to keep her spirits up?"

"You know Shelby. She's stubborn, and once she makes up her mind, that's it."

"That makes me sad, Jason. It really does."

"I know."

"We'll have to change her mind then, won't we?"

Jason's mother found him in the living room, staring at the gigantic wedding photo above the fireplace.

"Honey, why don't you go to bed?" she said, as she rubbed his shoulders. "Tomorrow is another day and you'll feel better after you rest up."

"I will, Mom. Soon."

"You know, that was always my favorite picture of your wedding. The two of you look so happy. The only thing missing is a halo around your heads."

That got a smile out of him. It seemed like a long time since he'd had something to smile about. "It was the happiest day of my life. No exaggeration. I owe Vivian. If it wasn't for her, I never would have met Shelby."

"So you keep saying," his mother said skeptically. "But, fate has a way of bringing people together. What's meant to be will be, no matter what anybody does, or doesn't do."

"I'm just saying Shelby saved me, and she doesn't even know it."

"So, you never told her about the Mazas?"

"No."

"Are you ever going to tell her?"

He faced his mother head on. "What good would it do? We've been married fifteen years, together eighteen. With the exception of my indiscretion with Stephanie Hunt, we've been happy until this nightmare reared its head."

"The murder may have changed all that. You can't be sure who's watching you or who's waiting to take advantage of your vulnerability. You're this close," his mother said, connecting her index finger and thumb, "to taking over the helm of a multi-billion dollar company. Somebody could see it as perfect timing."

"I've considered that, Mom." Jason gestured for her to take a seat on the couch. "Every day closer to the CEO post, I think about it. But, Nicholas Maza and I are even. His father is dead. If he wanted to expose me, he would have done it years ago."

"What about Vivian?"

"What about her?"

"Come on, Jason. Crises have a way of bringing people together and not always in a good way. I don't like it, especially given your history."

Jason forced a smile. "You're overreacting. She's just looking out for us. Shelby is like a sister to her. She is her sister where it counts most."

"Shelby doesn't know the two of you share a past. You're vulnerable. I don't want you doing something stupid in your grief."

Jason shook his head. "Vivian and I happened a very long time ago. You know it was brief and casual. If she didn't encourage me in my pursuit of Shelby, I don't know if we would have ended up together."

"Just remember where your loyalties lie. Get rid of unnecessary distractions. Your father would tell you the same thing if he were here."

Chapter 30

S omething is terribly wrong. I know it the moment I arrive. I pull out the chair across from Alan Rose in the tiny, claustrophobic room set aside for attorney-client meetings. The furniture is minimum: a table and two chairs. The walls are white and bare.

"Help me keep you out of prison."

I take a deep breath as my heart beats wildly. "What happened?"

Alan removes a folder from his briefcase and hands me several sheets of paper. A quick scan indicates they're my cell phone records.

"What am I supposed to be looking for?"

"Turn to the incoming call on October 28 at 6:23 pm."

One peek at the number and I'm momentarily speechless. How could I have been so careless? How could he have been? We were always meticulous, no calls on private cell phone numbers, only the burn phone.

"I know it looks bad," I say, coughing. "It doesn't prove anything."

"Up until now the investigators have been unable to connect you to the victim in any meaningful way. This call strengthens the DA's circumstantial case. It establishes a personal relationship between you and the victim that continued after your physical therapy ended. You told me there was no contact with the victim except an occasional run in at the supermarket.

"And, this one really had me going," Alan said, his frustration growing by the second. "You withdrew a large amount of cash from Citibank and Bank of America within days of each other. Right before the murder."

He looks down at some notes in his folder. "A friend of yours needed help to start over, you told Andrew Clarke at Citibank?"

Part of me cringes when he refers to Alessandro as "the victim" as if he were some random John Doe found murdered. I know what he's getting at and what he wants from me. I quickly weigh the pros and cons of disclosing to my lawyer what I haven't told anyone else, including my husband. Attorney-client privilege makes the decision for me. Alan is right, I have to help him keep me out of prison.

I bite my lips. I can feel my heartbeat accelerating but I can do this. Now is not the time to be modest.

"I knew Alessandro outside of physical therapy."

His expression tells me he's waiting to hear something he doesn't know.

"I didn't say anything to you earlier because I thought it would make me look guilty. I'm not. He was a friend."

Alan doesn't say a word and gives off the air of a man who's incapable of being shocked.

"Jason and I were in a bad place. Our marriage was falling apart." I explain to Alan that I had discovered Jason was unfaithful and his betrayal indirectly led to my accident. I explain the intense Physical Therapy that followed.

He cleared his throat and straightened his tie.

"When I was released from the hospital, I spent two hours every day except the weekends with Alessandro. He wouldn't let me quit, no matter what I threw at him.

"One day, I just lost it, wanted to give up. He helped me fight. Said he'd keep working with me until I was healed. He kissed me. I kissed him back. Before I knew it, we were spending whatever time we could together, even outside of therapy. He told me about his wife and his home situation."

"The one Jason mentioned to me," Alan interjected.

"Yes. It was messy business."

"We'll get to that in a minute. Continue."

"When I started to recover and got back to my regular routine, whenever he was in the city, we would meet up at Hotel Marlowe in Cambridge. We communicated through burn phones to avoid detection. Eventually, I called it off. He understood my reasons."

"Until the day he slipped up and called your personal cell phone in late October."

Alan's voice brings me back to the present with a thud.

"That's correct."

"Why?"

"What do you mean?"

"Why deviate from the pattern? Why did he call you on your cell phone that day?"

I have backed myself into a corner. If I thought confessing to the affair was a way of proving I'm not a murderer, I am dead wrong. I have to go all the way or this whole thing could blow up.

"It was the only way he could get in touch with me. He called to say he was leaving the country and needed my help."

Alan winces. "Are you telling me someone foiled his escape plan by killing him?"

"Yes."

He removes his glasses and places them on the table. "This could be helpful. It depends on how we spin it. The preliminary autopsy results corroborate what you've said about the domestic abuse. Apart from the bullet that killed him, the coroner found multiple wounds on his body, some were older, some more recent."

I shuffle my feet under the table and fight back tears.

"He wanted to leave the country with his daughters, go home to Brazil, and never return to the States." I fill Alan in on the whole escape plan.

I am wrong for thinking that Alan is a man who doesn't shock easily. The look of incredulity on his face makes me want to disappear into his briefcase and never come out.

"So, you want to add multiple felonies to the charges against you?"

"What?"

"Involvement in the kidnapping of two minors." Alan runs his hand through his hair and returns his glasses to his face. "Okay. We have an abusive wife who may have wanted to get rid of her husband. It's possible she found out he was trying to leave her and take their kids. It's possible she found out about the affair. She could have hired someone to do the job and screw you over for screwing her husband, no pun intended. We have a motive and new suspect. That's good. You left a paper trail of illegal activity, bad."

"I'm not that stupid. We only used cash. There's no way to tie me to the passports or the private jet. I used a fake name. You'd be surprised what people are willing to overlook for the right price."

"There's still the issue of the gun, which the DA's case hinges on. The ballistics report confirmed the bullet that killed Alessandro Rossi came from your gun. In spite of that, we still have a strong case. There's a simple explanation for your prints on the gun and they still don't know where he was killed before the body was moved to your car. Your alibi is airtight and we have plenty of reasonable doubt to go around. But, I want a slam-dunk. Think harder."

"About what?"

"Enemies or frenemies. Who could have gained access to your car? Did anyone look at you the wrong way in church weeks ago? Anyone who didn't like the color dress you wore on picture day in the third grade? Think about things out of the ordinary. Did you park your car in the same spot every day? If someone was planning to frame you, they would know your routine."

I look away. My stomach curdles as if I've eaten dairy that was left out too long. If I tell Alan the truth, is it fair to keep it from Jason? Whether I like it or not, Alan is a neutral party as far as my sins are concerned. His only interest in those sins is if they will help him get the charges dropped.

"I don't think Isabella Rossi killed Alessandro. But, there is someone else who may have pulled the trigger."

Alan leans in. "Now would be a good time to tell me."

"Before all of this happened, someone was stalking me."

"Is that so?"

"I don't blame you for being skeptical."

Alan lets out a long sigh. "Why would you not tell me this from the beginning? Do you like being in this place?"

"Of course not. He said if I told anyone about the phone calls and notes, he would kill my children. Why wouldn't I believe that low-down, murderous, mother—"

I lean back in the chair. I cross my hands in front of my chest as Alan looks at me with a potent cocktail comprised of sympathy, apprehension and flat out confusion.

He shakes his head.

"What?" I ask.

"You. You're unbelievable. I'm beginning to wonder if you want me to represent you at all or whether you even want legal representation, period."

"That's ridiculous."

"Is it?"

"Say what's on your mind and stop aggravating me with stupid questions."

He spreads his hands out on the table, unable to hide his anger. "You've lied to me repeatedly since I've taken your case despite my efforts to gain your trust. You tell me what you want to when you want to. If you would prefer to be represented by another attorney, just say so. I refuse to put my reputation on the line for someone who doesn't respect me enough to give me what I need to mount a solid defense. I took this case as a favor to your husband. I shouldn't have to work this hard to get information that could possibly save you from a murder conviction. I suggest you get your priorities straight, lady."

"So, you just wanna quit?"

"Shelby, wake up! Wake up."

I slam both palms on the table and glare at him. "Now you listen. Until you have children of your own, you have no concept of what this is like for me." I bring him up to speed on the photo of Abbie taken inside her school, and the note with the caskets drawn on the back of it. "I can't tell Jason because he'll want to fix it," I continue. "The risk is too high. Don't judge the decisions I make to protect my children."

My body quivers with fear and anger. I remove my palms from the table and ease back into the chair. My tears burst through, like rain follows thunder and lightning. For the second time since we became a team, Alan hands me his silk handkerchief to wipe my face.

"What did this stalker want? What do you know about him?"

I inhale deeply then expel the air through my mouth. "Something about paying for my mistakes. I don't know who he is. He knows an awful lot about me, though."

"Do you have any proof, anything we can use at all?"

"No. I think he was using a burn phone. The calls would be on my phone records but you wouldn't be able to trace them."

I give Alan a detailed list of all the stalking incidents.

He scribbles some notes on his notepad. "Do you have any idea what he meant by *paying for your mistakes?*"

"Not a clue. He sounded unhinged to me and I thought he had the wrong person. When he started naming my children and other personal details, that's when I knew he was serious."

"Anything you remember about his voice, an accent, how often he would call?"

"I detected a faint foreign accent he was trying to disguise. He sounded well educated. He was angry at me, and he didn't just make phone calls."

"That's why you hired security for your children."

"Yes. What did Greg Marr say?"

"The flowers are being looked after, although Jason might hire his own gardener. You have to tell him the truth about why you're in here and about the affair. The homicide detectives will find out if they're any good, and they are. If physical evidence exists, it could be another shit storm for you and your family. Not to mention, the DA will latch onto it as motive. It will make our battle more challenging."

I couldn't hide the panic in my voice. "What evidence? What are you talking about?"

"Hotel security footage, for example. All that's needed is the two of you being seen together. Your stalker worries me for obvious reasons, but also because we don't know what cards he holds or when he will play them."

I bang my head on the table in frustration. I must have been high on stupid pills during that time. I thought we were being so careful. It never once occurred to me that security cameras could be everywhere. Pressure mounts in my chest. My head feels like a sandwich being flattened in a Panini machine.

"Okay, Alan. Do what you have to. I'll do the same."

Chapter 31

Her dad had issued a stern warning to stay off social media sites and he banned Abbie and Miles from watching the news, but Abbie was curious. She knew how mean kids could be. She just had to know what she was up against when she returned to school. She had woken up a half hour early to see what the latest buzz was without her dad finding out. He wouldn't check her computer. One of the benefits of being a good girl was that her parents trusted her.

It would only take a minute. No big deal. Her dad would never know. No harm done.

She took her laptop from its usual position atop her homework desk and sat with it on her bed, legs tucked in under her. She logged on to her personal Facebook page and scrolled through the usual crap: posts from school friends about upcoming concerts, where they spent the weekend, the Platinum Ball, and meaningless posts about stuff in their everyday lives. She seriously needed to de-friend some of these people.

The logo of one of the local news stations and the headline: STILL NO MOTIVE IN FRAMINGHAM MURDER caught her attention. Instead of clicking on the story, she clicked on "comments" and began reading.

Dave Barros
I hope they catch whoever did this.

Paul Kingsley
Maybe they already did, lol.

Dave Barros
Shut up Paul. I feel bad for Dr. Cooper. Like why would she kill someone when she had so much going for her?

Gayle Thomas
Stop acting like you know her. We don't have all the facts. Stupid!

Abbie was feeling lightheaded, as if she were reading these comments about someone else. People who didn't know her mother were judging her, making guesses about who they thought she was, and whether or not she committed this horrible crime. They were all idiots. Running their stupid mouths just because they could. She kept on reading.

Eric Marks
He was her Physical Therapist. You never know. Maybe things got physical, lol.

Abbie was disgusted and had enough. Nothing she couldn't handle. Something caught her attention again, Kerri Wheeler's profile picture. She and Ty were cheek to cheek.
Abbie's heart hammered in her chest. She felt betrayed. Ty didn't have the guts to tell her that he and Kerri were officially dating. She calmed herself down long enough to read the post. It made her sick. Made her want to throw up all over Kerri's stupid face.

Kerri Wheeler
I think it's tragic that a member of our school community is going through such a difficult time. Abbie is a great girl who deserves our sympathy. Ty and I are praying for her and her family.

Jason shivered as the icy water poured from the showerhead, pounding his body. Maybe the punishing stream would help quell the pain. His heart was chopped up into tiny pieces, and he couldn't put the pieces back together in the right order. It took one phone call to bring him to his knees, a single phone call to shatter his children's lives.

The cold shower wasn't helping so he shut off the faucet and wrapped himself in an oversized towel. As he exited the bathroom, he peered over her sink and noticed her mascara had fallen in. He left it the way it was and entered the master suite, landing on the edge of the king bed. The empty bed set off a fresh wave of anguish. She never slept in the dark. She always had a night light on. He never asked why, too afraid of an answer he might not be able to handle. There would be no nightlight in jail. Her reading glasses sat on the nightstand next to the bed, perched on top of her bible. A bioinformatics journal she subscribed to lay upside down and opened on the antique armchair.

He hadn't realized how precious a simple morning routine could be until it ceased days ago. All the shoes in her closet were designed to add at least three inches to her five-foot frame. She wore minimal makeup, just some pressed powder and mascara. Abbie complained that it wasn't fair that they wore the same size clothing, although Abbie was taller by a few inches so sharing jeans was out of the question. Shelby's drill sergeant routine to get the kids out of the house on the mornings she dropped them off to school was amusing. One of the kids always forgot their lunch on the kitchen counter.

Jason refused to believe that all he had left were memories. He would find out who was behind this. They would pay in the most painful way imaginable.

He picked up his ringing cell phone off the nightstand although he should have known better. These days, any phone call, even ones he didn't want to take, could be important.

"How are you, Jason? How are the kids holding up? You must all be going through hell."

It was Chloe Grace. Jason had put a stop to her blatant blackmail scheme the only way he knew how. By hiring someone to erase any digital footprint of her so-called evidence of a non-existent affair.

"Is there a problem at the office?"

She faltered for a moment. "No, I just wanted to—"

"Then we have nothing to talk about."

"Don't hang up!"

"What do you want?"

"I'm really sorry, Jason. It's just terrible what happened to Shelby. I'm here for you if you need anything. I mean it. If you need anything at all, just say the word."

"You really mean that?"

"I do."

"Then stop calling me. Unless it's business related, I don't want to hear from you."

"I know what I did was messed up, Jason. I'm sorry. I hope you'll give me a chance—"

"You were already given a chance, a very generous one. You still have a job. I shouldn't have had to get Charlie involved. It was an embarrassment and almost compromised my leadership credibility within the executive ranks. I won't soon forget that. As for your concern about my family, it's not needed."

Jason hung up on her. Chloe wanted to use his family tragedy to weasel her way into his life and he wouldn't stand for it.

He dragged his weary bones off the bed, got dressed, and headed downstairs to face his children. His guts were once again turned inside out when he entered the kitchen. There was a breakfast spread on the kitchen table: chocolate chip pancakes, scrambled eggs, sausage, and a jug of orange juice. Plates and glasses occupied each setting along with linen napkins and silverware. There was the faint smell of burned food in the air, mingled with the frightened stares and sadness on the children's faces. The refrigerator hummed. He heard the distant sound of a vehicle passing by the next street over. He was rooted to his spot, unable to form the appropriate words.

"I'm just helping out until Mom gets back," Abbie said, breaking the stillness. "Don't get used to it."

"She burned the sausage," Miles chimed in. "I think we should give them to Mahalia."

Abbie glared at her baby brother, daring him to criticize her cooking again.

Miles shrugged his shoulders. "I'm just saying."

Mahalia growled then put a paw over her face as if she were embarrassed over the burned sausage. She sat at her usual mealtime spot, the foot of the kitchen table, next to Miles, who overfed her by using her as his personal food disposal unit.

"Thank you, sweetheart. Everything looks great. I can't wait to dig in. Where's Grandma?"

"She said she had some calls to make so we can go ahead without her."

Jason took a seat and placed a couple of pancakes and eggs on his plate. He wasn't hungry, but he didn't want to disappoint Abbie. Her maturity and foresight never ceased to amaze him.

He knew what was expected of him. They wanted answers, an explanation, something to help them grasp why their world no longer made sense.

"When is Mom coming home?" Miles asked. "She's innocent, so she shouldn't be in jail. They can't put innocent people in jail, can they?"

How could he explain to his eleven-year-old son a complex legal system that wasn't always fair?

"It's up to us and the police to make sure everyone knows your mom is innocent. They're holding her until we find the person who killed Mr. Rossi. We have a great lawyer helping us. It just takes a little time, that's all."

"So much for innocent until proven guilty," Abbie said in disgust.

"Are you guys ready to return to school?" he asked, desperate for some level of normalcy in the kids' lives.

Chapter 32

Jason parked behind a blue Audi across the entrance to Saint. Matthews Academy. He barely missed hitting the rear bumper. Morning drop-off for non-boarding students was in full swing. Backpack-wearing teenagers bundled up in sweaters and scarves exited their parents' cars and sprinting toward the main brick building. The large football field, now frozen tundra of wide-open space, was to his right. He shut off the ignition and turned to his daughter in the front seat next to him.

"I will take care of everything. Don't listen to the malicious gossip of people who don't know our family."

Abbie stared straight ahead. He noticed the defiance in her eyes, her mother's eyes. He could only imagine what she would face in the coming days at school. Kids could be cruel. That's why he contacted the teachers and administrators both at Saint. Matthews and the Carlisle School to make sure his kids wouldn't be harassed. Abbie in particular would be all over him and accuse him of treating her like a baby if she found out. He didn't want them moping around the house, hiding out like they did something wrong for any extended period. Two days was enough.

"Sweetie, did you hear me?"

She turned her head slowly towards him. "Yes, Dad, I'm not deaf."

Was it too soon? Was he wrong to push them to go back to school right away? Did they resent him for it? This is what Shelby would want.

"Just making sure you'll be all right. Don't take what people say to heart."

"Stop treating me like some fragile little flower you need to handle with care, Dad. I know how the world works. I know people are going to talk and say nasty things about our family. I don't give a shit. They can all go drink raw sewage for all I care."

He wanted to reprimand her for her crass language but he understood her need to protect herself with her attitude. She would need that armor in the coming weeks. He was proud of her for not making it obvious to the outside world that she was devastated beyond comprehension on the inside.

"I love you, Abbie. More than I can ever express."

She actually rolled her eyes at him. Teenagers. "I know. Let's not get corny. All families go through crap. It's just our turn. Now, can I please get out of this car and get to class?"

"Sure thing, sweetheart. Have a good day and don't be shy about calling if anything happens or you just want to come home."

Abbie unstrapped her seat belt. "Dad, I really think you should go back to work."

"Tired of your old man already? Abbie, I'm so hurt," he said, clutching his chest in mock offense.

She rewarded him with that gorgeous smile that could melt the polar ice caps. "You're all right, Dad," she said grudgingly.

Abbie shuttled down the hallway of the main building on her way to her Principles of Economics class. Everyone was quiet whenever they passed her by. Student after student refused to make eye contact with her or those who did gave her pitying glances. Usually, the hallway was noisy with the chatter of multiple conversations or someone yelling to a friend from one end of the hall to another. It was all part of the daily routine. At that moment, there was nothing but the clicking of footwear on the hardwood floor.

It was torture. Like they had just attended her funeral. She wanted things to go back the way they were before her mother was accused of murder. Even the kids she joked around with in class wouldn't look at her. Ah well, they weren't her real friends, anyway. At least she had lunch to look forward to with the girls from the Rainbow Posse. Those were her real friends who would never turn their backs on her.

She felt someone tap her on the shoulder as she was about to round the corner. She spun around and came face-to-face with Kerri Wheeler. All the rage she felt earlier about the Facebook post resurfaced in an instant. Long seconds ticked by. Everyone walked around them to their classes.

Kerri's hair was in a French braid that went all the way down her back, giving a clear view of her blemish-free caramel face, and cat-like grey eyes.

"Hi, Abbie. Got a second?"

Abbie pinned a fake smile on her face. "I'm heading to class. Can we catch up later?"

"This won't take long."

Abbie looked at her watch and let out an exaggerated sigh. "What's up, Kerri?"

"We're here for you. If you ever want to talk or hang out to get away from it all, we're here."

"We?"

Kerri blushed. "I mean, I know that you and Ty are friends—"

"Best friends. He's my best friend."

Kerri shifted her weight from one leg to the other. "What I meant to say was it must be tough. With your mom being in jail and all."

"Are you going somewhere with this? Because I have to get to class."

"Since Ty and I are together now, his problems are my problems, and I just wanted to reach out—"

"Problem?" Abbie balled her fists at her side. Where did she get off calling Abbie's friendship with Ty a problem? They'd been

136

friends long before Kerri started batting her eyes at him and went after him like a Lioness stalking her prey. "You've been with Ty all of five minutes and all of a sudden you're an expert on our relationship?"

"I didn't mean to offend you, Abbie. I was just reaching out, one sister to another."

"I'm good. I have all the support I need. My mom will come home soon and our family will go back to normal. I would think you of all people would understand that. I mean, wasn't your dad accused of negligence in the worst environmental disaster in U.S. history?"

"That's not fair," Kerri said, shooting daggers.

"I didn't mean to offend you. I was just saying that your dad was cleared of any wrongdoing and my mom will be, too. See, we have stuff in common other than Ty."

Abbie stormed off to class.

Chapter 33

"This seat's taken."

"Says who? I always sit here."

"Not today. Not ever again," Frances said.

"Really? How about I shove this tray of food down your throat. Then can I sit?"

The three girls at the table burst out laughing and Abbie breathed a sigh of relief. She couldn't take it if her best friends turned on her because of her mother. It was lunchtime at Saint. Matthews and the dining hall buzzed with the usual lunch crowd, students meeting with their advisors and friends and classmates catching up. This dining hall was endowed with wooden floors, long rectangular wooden tables and chairs and walls lined with portraits of important alumni, and a series of mounted deer heads.

Abbie placed her lunch tray of lobster salad, a bread roll, and bottled water on the table and pulled out a seat.

Anastasia started the conversation. "What's new and how are you doing?"

"Fine," Abbie said, then took a bite of her salad. She knew her friends were anxious for fresh details of the ongoing investigation straight from a trusted source, and not from the media reports, rumors, and flat-out malicious gossip.

"My mom is hiding something and she's scared, but she won't say why."

Callie touched Abbie's forearm. "This is just awful, Abbie. Mrs. Cooper doesn't deserve this."

"Yeah," Frances chimed in. "It took a lot of planning to pull this off. It's the work of a pro. According to the news, Mr. Rossi was shot in the head, execution style."

Abbie could always count on Frances to get to the point quickly.

"I'm confused right now. It's not like my mom to be afraid of anyone. Going to jail when she could have been home is just plain whack."

"Yeah. It's weird that they picked Mr. Rossi, though," Frances said.

"What do you mean?" Abbie's antenna perked up.

"Think about it. There had to be something about Mr. Rossi and your mom that made him a target for the killer."

"You're not making any sense," Abbie said.

Frances leaned in closer. "There had to be a strong connection between Mr. Rossi and Dr. Cooper. The killer had to make it look convincing that Dr. Cooper was capable of killing Mr. Rossi. Otherwise, the frame wouldn't work. Something was happening between your mom and Mr. Rossi for the killer's plan to work."

Abbie reached for her bottled water, and in her haste, knocked over the tray. She picked it off the floor quickly. Frances drummed on the table. Callie looked at Abbie, worry in her eyes, and Anastasia chewed on a carrot stick from her lunch tray. Frances spoke first.

"What's going on, Abbie? Do you know why your mother was framed?"

"No. Why would you ask me such a stupid question, Frances?"

"It's not a stupid question. You just freaked out for no reason."

As much as she was tempted, Abbie couldn't tell her friends about her stalker. Only Ty was privy to that detail of her family troubles. "I didn't freak out. Stop exaggerating."

"You were too freaking out. You've been holding out on us.

You know something, don't you?"

Abbie's aggravation grew by the second. "Cut the crap, Frances. I knocked over the tray by accident."

"I don't believe you."

"Frances, stop it," Anastasia pleaded. "This is hard for Abbie, and you're not making it any better."

Frances had the decency to look embarrassed. "Sorry. I forgot to take my chill pills today."

Abbie didn't want to spend another second talking about her mother's legal woes. It was putting her in a sour mood.

"Have you guys seen Ty? I haven't been able to get in touch with him since yesterday."

"Did you two have a lover's quarrel?" Frances asked slyly. "Oh, sorry," she said, placing her hand over her heart. "You can't have a lover's quarrel if you're not lovers."

Abbie didn't want to appear anxious when it came to Ty. He hadn't returned any of her calls or text messages since yesterday afternoon and she was worried. Was he pulling away from her? Was her family drama too much for him or was he just too busy with his new girlfriend?

"Come off it, Abbie," Frances said, never passing up an opportunity to rag on her friend. "You and Ty haven't done the deed, so technically, you're not lovers. Maybe if you did, he wouldn't be with that skank, Kerri Wheeler." Frances screwed up her face in disgust.

Abbie knew Frances was just defending her. Her friends knew she had it bad for Ty. In their minds, he belonged to Abbie and anyone who dared upset that order of things made their shit list.

"I can't do that, Frances."

"So, you're just going to die a virgin?"

The other girls giggled under their breath. When Abbie and Frances got into it, it was best to stay out of it. "I'm just saying screwing around for the sake of it isn't my thing. Besides, my first time is going to be earth-shattering, mind-blowing, sizzling, can't-breathe wonderful."

"The first time always sucks. Or, so I hear. By the way, is that why you're all dressed up? Because you're meeting your lovah?"

Abbie blushed. Today she had chosen a pair of fitted khaki

jeans that hugged her burgeoning curves and accentuated her tiny waist. Off-white, V-neck sweater encrusted with pearls along the neckline and an animal print silk scarf set off her ensemble. On her wrist was a black onyx and gold charm bracelet.

"Ty and I are friends. My appearance has nothing to do with him. What's wrong with looking nice?"

"You always look beautiful," Callie interjected. "Frances, stop embarrassing her."

"Why should she be embarrassed about wanting to look good for her man?"

"Ty!" Anastasia burst out. "We didn't see you."

Abbie went still, her heart thumping against her ribcage. Anastasia and Frances were seated against the wall, while Callie and Abbie were on the opposite side, their backs to the diners across the aisle. Anyone could creep up on them and they wouldn't know it. Apparently, Ty had. Abbie hoped he didn't hear what Frances had said. She would be mortified and would probably jet out of the dining hall to go die of embarrassment in the student lounge.

Abbie turned slowly to see Ty grinning down at her. She couldn't help but smile back at him. At least now she knew he wasn't ignoring her and it looked like he came to find her. He was wearing a long-sleeved polo shirt, dark jeans, and a pair of lace-up Vans.

"Hi," she said, trying to sound cool and in control, and not like the blubbering mess, she really was.

"Hey, Cooper. Got a minute?"

"Sure. I'll meet you at the chapel."

After Ty left their table, Abbie turned around to two pairs of brown eyes and one pair of blue trained on her. "Awww," they said in unison.

"You guys make me sick. Frances, take care of my tray, will you?"

When she arrived at the chapel, Ty was waiting, as was their usual practice. He had his hands in his pockets and removed them when he saw her walking down the aisle. She stopped in front of him. No words were exchanged between them. Next thing she knew, he pulled her into his arms. She went willingly and allowed herself to bask in the peace and comfort of his embrace, like a perfect summer day where the breeze was gentle, and the sun made everything sparkle like new.

She didn't want the hug to end but of course, it did. He broke away first. Abbie placed the blame squarely on Kerri's shoulders.

"How are you holding up?" he asked.

They both sat on the bench in the first row, and faced each other. "If my mother goes down for this, my dad won't make it."

"What happened?"

"He moved out of their bedroom. He says it's too hard to sleep there without her next to him. He's overwhelmed."

"I thought he hired a private investigator."

"He did, but how is that supposed to help him deal with his wife being in jail? Besides, investigations move slowly, I'm finding out. I've been reading up online on what life is like in prison, and it's awful. Did I mention the police searched the house the other day? And, just to make sure my entire existence is one big suckfest, Mom doesn't want to see us."

"I wish I had a magic wand, Cooper. I would make it all go away, and nothing and no one could ever hurt you again." He palmed her face with both hands, his hazel eyes filled with compassion and something else. It was too fleeting for her to put a name to it. And just like their earlier embrace, he broke away first. They sat in silence, each lost in thought.

Abbie cleared her throat, breaking the stillness. Ty stood up, and paced the aisle, hands in his pockets.

"The killer wants to punish your mother. We just don't know why."

"How do you figure?"

"All the references to her past. If the guy who's stalking you and the killer are one and the same, they know each other."

She let his words sink in. They made sense. *Sometimes the ones we love deceive us,* the stalker had said in his note. After Ty swiped her mother's phone, the data from the SIM card revealed that the mysterious call she received while they were at Pennybakers came from Mr. Rossi. Abbie had been sitting on that potential grenade for a while, hedging back and forth as to whether or not she should tell her dad. It could be that her mom and Mr. Rossi were just friends, simple as that.

Ty stopped his pacing, and walked over to Abbie who was still sitting. "What a mess, huh?" he said.

"I'm scared." She didn't think about the words. They simply came from that place where vulnerability and honesty existed, close neighbors with raw emotions she tried hard to suppress.

"I know." He brushed away her tears with his thumb. "It will get better. You can't quit, Cooper. You have to stay strong for your mother. Besides, who's going to be my go-to girl if you crash?"

"Sorry," she said between sobs. God, she had to keep it together. She wiped away her remaining tears. Ty was right. She needed to be his go-to girl, the way it had always been.

"Everything okay with you?" she asked him.

"Fine. I'm worried about you."

"You got all your applications in?"

He resumed pacing. "I don't want to talk about it," he said, staring off into the distance.

Abbie joined him in the aisle. She shook his shoulders. "What is it? You have to tell me. Why are you freaking out?"

"I'm not. I'm just a little stressed, that's all."

"About Yale?" She forced him to look at her. "You'll get in for sure. No one has better grades than you."

"It's not enough. Everyone in our graduating class has good grades, takes a ton of AP classes, volunteers, and plays sports."

Abbie knew the pressure seniors were under to get into top-tier colleges and universities, especially the Ivy League. Ty was planning to apply to all eight. Yale was his first choice so he applied for early decision and planned to send the remaining applications by regular deadline in February. Abbie knew in a couple of years she'd be sitting in that same seat. Her parents had high expectations.

"I get it, but you're putting way too much pressure on yourself. No matter what, you're going to get into a great school."

"Who wants to get into their safety school and not their first choice?"

"Ty, your safety schools are some of the top universities in the world. You'll do just fine. Is there something else going on? What is it?"

"Stop making a big deal about it. Everything is fine."

That sentence again. Everything was not fine. Abbie knew when he had reached his limit and pushing him would just lead to a fight. She pulled out her smart phone and realized she'd be almost late for class. Christmas was three weeks away. She would have to pray harder than she ever had in her life for a miracle, a Christmas miracle that would have her mom walking through the door and decorating the Christmas tree, baking her amazing gingerbread cookies, and making homemade eggnog.

"What are you doing for winter break?" she asked.

"Heading home to Westchester for Christmas. After that, the Bahamas for a week, and then I'm not sure after that."

Ty's mother Jenny was originally from the Bahamas. The Ramballys visited Jenny's family home once a year, during the winter. For the first time since Abbie fell for Ty, she wouldn't be seeing him for a while. Between missing Ty and her mother being in jail, this would be the crappiest Christmas ever.

"Tell me the truth. Did your parents tell you to stay away from me because of all the news coverage?"

"Cooper, I'm here talking to you right now. No one is going to keep me away from you."

"It's okay if they did. If it were me, I wouldn't want the press finding out that my kid was friends with the daughter of an accused murderer. I can't pretend it doesn't hurt because I think your parents are cool. But, I understand if they did."

Ty tinkered with one of the charms on her bracelet. "Stop it. My parents haven't said anything like that to me. They asked how you were doing. They know how I feel about you so they wouldn't tell me to stay away from you. Even if they did, I wouldn't listen."

"What do you mean, how you feel about me?"

"Come on, Cooper. You're my best friend, we tell each other everything."

The stinging in the back of her eyes would only lead to her embarrassment, so Abbie faked a yawn and told Ty she had to head to class.

PART III:

WHO IS MIA LANSING?

Chapter 34

Anton Devereaux pulled up the hood on his winter jacket and stuck his hands in his pocket as he exited the underground trolley service known as the green line in Copley Square. The square situated in Boston's Back Bay neighborhood was known for stunning architecture. It brought back memories of his first visit to Trinity Church, a stone's throw away from the John Hancock Tower. The La Marge murals, stained glass windows, and the wide-open interior made him think that just maybe, a little slice of heaven existed down here on earth.

He strode hurriedly against the December chill, dodging traffic and the blaring horns of taxis as he made quick work of the walk to the Fairmont Copley Plaza Hotel on Saint. James Avenue. He hadn't seen his childhood friend, Martin Wells, in many years but they had kept in contact by phone and email. Martin had made it big in Houston real estate and was in Boston on business.

Devereaux cut in between two cabs lined up at the curb and nodded to the doorman and a couple of bellmen helping guests with their luggage. He strode under the bright red canopy bearing the gold insignia of the Fairmont Hotel chain and between two large, golden statues of lions on either side.

The lobby was filled with guests, opulent French antiques, and marble floors covered by lush, patterned Persian rugs. He was to meet Martin for lunch at the OAK Long Bar and Kitchen, the hotel's American brasserie-style restaurant. He spotted Martin seated at a cluster of cream-colored armchairs with red cushions and tables in the middle.

Martin looked every bit the former athlete and ladies' man he'd been in their days at the University of Texas Austin. The suit was obviously tailored to his bulky five-foot-ten frame, which confirmed that Martin had stuck to his rigorous workout routine over the years.

After exchanging greetings, the men sat down. "Thanks for agreeing to meet me," Anton said.

"It's good to see you, man. I can't believe it's been ten years. The last place I would have expected you to end up, a Yankee town. Ain't that something? Thought you would have stayed down south and become some legal eagle, pulling down the big bucks, racking up the conquests, living the life." Martin gave him that look that said, *What the hell happened?*

"God had other plans," Anton said.

A waitress came by to take their order and neither man had even glanced at the menu.

"What's good here?" Martin asked with a slight southern drawl. Texas born and raised, Martin would never lose that drawl, no matter where he went, no matter what kind of lifestyle his wealth afforded him.

"I take it you gentlemen are from out of town," the waitress said. "In that case the New England Clam Chowder is first rate. How about a flatbread appetizer to start?"

The men ordered drinks together with their food. Martin had a flight to catch. The waitress disappeared to fill their orders and Martin gave Anton a questioning look.

"Lay it on me, man. What kind of trouble you got going these days?"

Anton skirted the question. "You know I got the call from the Lord so I'm a pastor now."

Martin let out a hearty laugh. "I still can't get over that one, man. You. A pastor. God is one funny dude."

Anton smiled. He didn't blame Martin for the skepticism. He was a hellion in their college days where self-indulgence, be it women, alcohol, drugs or anything in between was the order of the day. He still didn't know how he found the time to study and graduate with good enough grades to get into a top-tier law school. "No one was more surprised than me. I didn't let go of my old life that easy, though. Everything changed after I lost my parents a year apart. I figured God was trying to tell me something and I had better start listening."

"So, you cleaned up your act, went on the straight and narrow and now you're saving souls."

"Maybe my soul is the one that needs saving."

"What's that now?" Martin leaned forward and the waitress suddenly appeared, balancing a tray in one arm. The conversation ceased as she busied herself placing the food and drink in front of them. When she left, Anton looked at Martin intensely.

"You heard the story about the woman who's accused of murdering her physical therapist?"

"Yeah, it's been all over the news. A damn shame if you ask me. A woman that fine and that accomplished accused of offing some dude. Why are you bringing that up, man?"

"She's a dead ringer for someone from my past. Someone I *have* to find."

Martin shook his head, confused but curious.

"What are you saying, Anton? What are you mixed up in?"

Anton was silent for a beat. He needed Martin's help and had to be careful with his words.

He cleared his throat. "The summer before freshman year of college, my girlfriend told me she was pregnant. I told her I wanted no part of it and sent her off to deal with it alone."

Saying it aloud for the first time in twenty-five years brought an unfamiliar feeling of calm, as if his mind and soul had been in chaos until that moment.

"For real, no joking?"

"No joking."

"Break it down for me."

Anton couldn't meet Martin's eyes and neither could he control his shaking knees under the table. No one had ever questioned him before, forced him to own up to what he did. Now after all this time, there was no place left to hide.

"I accused her of sleeping around even though I knew it wasn't true. My parents didn't care for her. They thought she wasn't good enough. Then I insisted that she didn't tell anyone I was the father."

"Wow," Martin said. Was that disappointment swirling around his eyes? Anton couldn't tell for sure.

"So what happened to the baby?" Martin asked.

"I don't know."

"You never looked for them?"

The innocent question grated on his nerves. Martin was judging him. He knew what he did was despicable, but he was young and ambitious and not a very nice person at the time. He wasn't that person anymore. That had to count for something.

"No. That's why I have to find her."

"Yeah, man, you gotta do right by her and the kid."

"I especially need to find the kid."

"Why is that?"

He didn't mean to place such an emphasis on the kid even though that was the main reason he wanted to find Mia. Finding his child could change the course of his life.

"I want to make amends. I'm not expecting anything, just to let the kid know that I'm alive and to ask him or her to forgive me, too."

"So, what do you need me to do? Have someone dig into this Mia's past or what?"

Anton had asked himself a million times what he would say and do if he ever found Mia. How would she react to seeing him after all these years, knowing he probably derailed the plans she had for her life? Over time, the questions got more complicated and when the news story broke about the Framingham murder and a picture of Shelby Cooper flashed on the screen, the fabric of his life got another wrinkle he couldn't afford. He was in a race against time to find Mia and the kid they conceived.

"A private investigator. Start in Kenner. Mia Lansing's parents might still live there, although they may not be much help."

"You sure you wanna go down that road? No matter what,

lives will be turned upside down, man. This Mia girl could be married with a family of her own. What if she never told her spouse? And, what about the kid? If she gave it up for adoption, which is most likely since you said she was fifteen, you snooping around could affect the kid's adoptive family and disrupt their lives, too. Plus, who's to say they want anything to do with you? What if the adoptive folks never told the kid he/she was adopted? There are many scenarios to play out, friend. Think about it before you open this particular Pandora's box."

"It's the right thing to do. My run-in the other day was a sign from God."

"What run-in?"

Anton had been attending a workshop at the Fairmont and was heading home. As he reached for the door handle to exit the hotel, he felt someone bump into him. He turned around, and then froze. As if his recent thoughts of her had conjured her up in the flesh, he was staring into the almond-shaped, sable brown eyes of Mia Lansing.

Time stood still as they sized each other up, like two prized fighters before the big match. Anton took in the creamy chocolate smoothness of her skin. She was more mature now, although her face still had a girlish quality about it. She was several inches taller than the Mia he remembered, but she was wearing high heels. He was never so happy in his life to inspect a woman's attire. She had on a bluish grey, belted dress coat—cashmere, if he had to guess. Her jewelry probably cost more than his car. All of this meant one thing. That Mia Lansing was doing just fine.

She mumbled an apology and said she would use another exit. She was walking back to the lobby and he couldn't let her get away.

"Please. You don't have to take another exit on my account. How about I hold the door open for you?"

"That's not necessary." Her tone was brusque, dismissive. She was in a hurry to get away from him. He wouldn't let her. "It's no trouble at all, Mia," he said to her retreating form.

Her spine stiffened. She turned around and he closed the space between them.

"What did you call me?"

"Mia. You're Mia Lansing. You grew up in Kenner, Louisiana.

I'm Anton Devereaux. You don't remember me?"

"I'm sorry, sir, you're mistaken. I grew up in North Carolina."

She was about to leave when he grabbed her arm. They were in the middle of the lobby, forcing guests to walk around them. He didn't care. He had waited twenty-five years for this moment. She pulled away from him. "Sir, get a hold of yourself."

"I'm sorry. It's just that you remind me so much of someone I knew growing up. You look exactly like her. You sound like her. It's important that I find her."

"Look, I hope you find your friend but I can't help you. They say everyone has a double. I'm Shelby Cooper, not this Mia person you're looking for. Now, if you'll excuse me, I really must go."

He felt like an ass and it was futile to pursue her further. He'd accosted a total stranger and given her the third degree, all because he wanted to clear his conscience.

Martin stared at him, his mouth gaping open. "Are you saying this chick looks exactly like your ex-girlfriend, to the point where you called her by name?"

"It was so real, Martin. The woman I saw *was* Mia, no doubt."

"Then who is this Shelby Cooper woman, the one in the news?"

"I don't have the answer, but I intend to find out."

"I'll get one of my people to work the Mia angle. I hope this doesn't blow up in your face, man."

Chapter 35

They'd been communicating through instant message using Tor, a program that allows anonymous communication and prevents tracking. Was it dangerous? Sure. But Abbie needed to draw him out by pretending to be some naïve teenager who was no threat to him.

Him: How are you today, Abigail?

Abbie: Sad. Depressed.

Him: Don't be. Sometimes even the ones we love must pay for their mistakes.

Abbie: I don't understand. What did my mother do that she deserves to be taken from her family?

He didn't respond immediately. The seconds ticked by. Did she scare him off? Pushed too hard?

Him: Sometimes, we don't know our loved ones as well as we think we do. Your mother has done bad things, even destroyed lives.

Abbie: What are you talking about?

Him: Goodbye, Abigail.

Abbie: No, don't go! I'm sorry. I didn't mean to upset you.

He was gone, his screen name grayed out.

Abbie pounded her fist on the desk in frustration, and almost fell off the chair when she heard two quick knocks on her bedroom door. If it was Miles, she was going to wring his little neck. She loved her little brother to death but he had the worst timing, always.

She let out a sigh loud enough to be heard two streets over as she shut down the computer. "What is it, Miles?" she yelled, without opening the door.

"It's Dad. I have a surprise for you."

"Give me a minute, Dad."

She groaned inwardly. Her dad acted like she and Miles were made out of eggshells. He was always asking them if they were okay, how they felt, if they wanted to talk. He always got the same answer. When he wasn't satisfied, he would start mumbling about them seeing their school psychologists or he would threaten to take them to a private shrink for adolescents.

She walked over to her solid oak antique dresser and pulled open the first drawer. She found a scrunchie from her pile of hair accessories and pulled her hair into a hurried ponytail off her face. She opened her bedroom door ever so slightly.

"Dad, I'm fine. You don't need to worry about me. I'm not going to do anything stupid."

"I know, sweetie. I thought this would cheer you up."

"I'm really not in the mood—"

Her eyes widened. Out from behind her father stepped the boy she had spent so many of her waking hours thinking about.

"Ty, what are doing here?"

Her heart was doing more back flips than a cheerleader at the national championships. She ripped the scrunchie from her head and let her hair fall past her shoulders.

"I asked your dad if I could come over and help you with AP Biology since I aced it last year, and he said yes."

"I'll leave you kids alone to catch up on your *biology*," Jason interjected. "Ty, remember what we talked about?"

"Yes, sir, I won't forget."

"Good." Then her dad disappeared.

Abbie felt her toes curl. She couldn't believe Ty was entering her bedroom. He'd come over a few times before, but they were usually confined to the living room under the watchful eye of whichever parent was around at the time. Her dad must be worse off than she thought to allow them to be alone in her room.

"Are we going to just stand in the hallway?" Ty asked. "What's up with you, Cooper? You act like you've never seen me before."

"Oh, sorry. Come in," she said, opening the door wider. "I'm just surprised, that's all."

"It smells nice in here," he said, jamming his hands in his pocket as he strolled in. "What is that scent?"

"Jasmine oil. I heat it up a couple of times a week."

She watched him take in the details of her room. She was a neat freak. When she turned fifteen, she told her mom she wasn't a kid anymore and didn't want a room that looked like she was five years old with a princess fixation so her dad repainted the room in a dark ivory color. She got a new bed and carpeting that matched the wall and for contrast, she had a burgundy rug at the foot of the bed, and matching curtains. The ivory overstuffed armchair and mini couch had burgundy throw pillows for a pop of color. Her dresser was painted ivory with gold floral accents.

Black and white family photos hugged the walls. There were three photos in particular she treasured: her inspiration, Doctor Keith Black, one of the leading neurosurgeons in the country and head of the Department of Neurosurgery at Cedars-Sinai Medical Center in Los Angeles. She wanted to follow his example and even exceed his accomplishments. The second was of ballerina Misty Copeland, and the third of Lewis Hamilton, the first black race car driver to win Formula One. Her dad's company was a sponsor at that event last year and she was thrilled to meet the British hottie.

"I was always curious what your room would look like," Ty said. "It's pretty cool. Not too girly, yet elegant."

Butterflies fluttered in her stomach and heat rushed to her cheeks. Her room. It seemed such an intimate thought for him to have. Or maybe she was grasping at straws, making a big deal out of a casual comment.

"Thanks," Abbie said as she gestured for Ty to take a seat on the mini couch. "What did my dad mean when he asked if you remembered what you two talked about?"

"Oh, that. He said I needed to keep my hands to myself or he would cut them off. I told him I would never do anything to mess up our friendship. I respect you way too much."

Abbie was willing to bet her allowance that he had no problem getting his hands all over Kerri Wheeler.

She forced a smile. "I'm glad you respect me so much. We wouldn't be friends if you didn't. Does that mean you don't feel the same way about Kerri? Rumor has it that the two of you were all over each other at General Assembly the other day." She sounded like a jealous idiot, but she didn't care.

Ty stared at his shoes for a beat then let out a puff of air. "I don't understand what you're asking me, Cooper," he said looking at her. "What does Kerri have to do with you and me?"

"Nothing. I just thought as your best friend, you would tell me that you had a girlfriend instead of me finding out on Facebook."

"What are you talking about?" He seemed genuinely bewildered.

"So, she's not your girlfriend?"

She could see the tension rising in him. He went quiet, his lips pursed in a firm line, his jaw set.

"Look, I like Kerri. We hang out. We kissed a couple of times, nothing to make a big deal about."

Anger and sadness tugged at Abbie. She was angry because he kept insisting Kerri wasn't a big deal in his life when the evidence said otherwise. Sadness welled up inside her because he would never see her as anything other than his best friend. It hurt. The kind of hurt that made her want to march up to Kerri and scratch her eyes out with Sandpaper. She would have to settle for friend status, an awesome consolation prize if she could just erase her feelings for Ty.

"I'm sorry," she said, squeezing his hand. "You didn't come here to get the third degree. I don't want you to get hurt."

"I like that you care so much about me. That's why you're going to be a talented surgeon one day, and a great mom, too."

Why did he say that she was going to be a good mom? There's no way he could know. Sometimes in class, she fantasized about the two of them. She would write her married name in her notebook: Dr. Abbie Cooper Rambally. They would have three kids—two boys, Blake and Lucas, and one girl, Alexis. Abbie quickly dismissed the fantasy and focused on the present.

"You going soft on me, Ty? What's that crack about me being a good mom? I don't even know if I want kids."

"You do. And, you'll have them."

"What about you? Do you see kids in your future?"

"For sure. I want a big family. Being an only child isn't all it's cracked up to be."

"I feel sorry for your wife, having to pop out all those babies so you can have a sports team."

He grinned at her and her heart almost stopped. "She'll be fine. She'll love having babies."

"Dude, it's the twenty-first century, and that was way sexist."

He leaned in closer to her, his face mere inches away. She could feel the heat of his breath on her face. Her body was doing that weird thing again. She was overwhelmed, not knowing if she should just go with the flow or what. For the first time, she noticed there were little green flecks in his eyes. She always thought his eyes were all brown. Why did she never notice that before?

"No, it isn't. Not if we're on the same page. Do you know anyone who would be on the same page with me when it comes to family?"

"Maybe," she said, her voice hoarse. "I might know someone." Abbie was sure he was going to kiss her. Her senses were going off like firecrackers on the Fourth of July.

Ty ran his index finger across her lips, ever so gently. She shivered.

"Abbie, Grandma's back." Miles was on the other side of the bedroom door. Loud, obnoxious banging followed.

Ty retreated to his corner of the couch and the spell was broken. Miles marched in, his face beaming with excitement.

"Haven't you ever heard of knocking?" Abbie shrieked, tossing a throw pillow at him.

"I did knock," Miles responded. "Were you guys kissing?"

"No," they said guiltily, at the same time, and got off the couch.

"Yes, you were," Mile said with a mischievous glint in his eyes. "I'm telling Dad."

Abbie was aggravated. The last thing she needed was her little brother telling their dad something that wasn't true, especially since their dad promised to cut Ty's hands off if he didn't keep them to himself. "You do that and I'll tell him you've been sneaking your Nintendo DS in your backpack when you know Mom told you a million times not to take it to school."

"Miles isn't going to say anything, are you, Miles?"

Ty was right behind Abbie.

Miles knew he was beat. "I guess not."

"Tell Grandma I'll be right down," Abbie said to Miles's hunched frame.

After Miles left, Abbie turned to Ty, who now sat on the edge of her bed, twirling around one of her stuffed animals.

"I guess we won't have time to go over AP Biology," Abbie said, playfully punching him in the arm. "That was a great excuse to come over."

"It wasn't an excuse. I really thought you could use my help. I know you're doing well in the class, still I figured I could share my studying techniques with you."

"Studying. Is that what we were doing?"

"I can't help it when I'm around you sometimes. I have to remind myself you're my best friend, and I shouldn't do anything inappropriate."

"We have to go. If I keep Grandma waiting, she'll come find me and have something to say about it."

Ty stretched. "What's she like?"

"You'll see."

Chapter 36

Grandma Naomi Cooper was preparing dinner in the kitchen, perfect makeup, black high boots, a fitted sweater and a leather skirt with a hemline that Abbie was sure her dad had a problem with. Abbie helped her with dinner: grilled pork chops with green beans and tomato in a chimichurri sauce. Grandma added sweet potato fries as a side dish. She said they could use some comfort food since she doubted their father cooked anything since their mother left.

After everyone was seated at the dinner table ready to dig in, Grandma was Grandma, saying exactly what was on her mind.

"Stop mourning my daughter–in-law, she's not dead. She's in a tough situation right now but have faith that she'll come back to us soon. Where is that big old tree she puts up every Christmas? Where are the toy soldiers? Jason, do you think your wife wants you and the kids sitting around acting like people with no hope?"

"No, Mother. I suppose not."

After Grandma Cooper was satisfied with that answer, she turned her attention to her next victim: Ty.

"Young man, you must be pretty special if my granddaughter asked you to stay for dinner. What do your folks do? Where are they from? Do they have a good relationship? That will determine the kind of man you'll become. You have any siblings?"

A mortified Abbie came to Ty's defense. "Grandma, stop it. He's just having dinner with us, that's all."

Her dad chuckled, and Miles licked his fork with one hand and stuffed Mahalia's mouth with a piece of pork with the other.

"It's okay, Abbie. Your grandma just wants to make sure you're hanging out with people who share your values."

"Handsome and smart. I like him," Grandma said to no one in particular.

Ty continued. "My family lives in Westchester County. My mother is originally from the Bahamas and my dad from Guyana. I'm an only child. Both my parents are surgeons at Columbia Presbyterian Hospital in New York City."

"I see. So you're not a day student like Abbie then."

"No, ma'am. I live in the dorms."

The clanking of silverware provided a backdrop for the continued interrogation.

"Miles, how is school?"

"Good."

"And?"

"And that's it, Grandma."

"Are you keeping up your grades? Are kids being mean to you about what's going on with your mother?"

"Everything is okay. Mr. Atkins made a big deal about it in class so everyone knows they're supposed to be nice to me."

She moved on to Abbie. "What about you? Anything to add to your brother's 'okay?'"

Abbie didn't get a chance to respond. A way too excited Miles interjected, "The Platinum Ball is coming up soon. I heard Abbie talking to her friends about it."

Grandma's eyes brightened. "Oh really? I hope you're going," she said, turning to Abbie.

"I don't think so."

Abbie noticed her dad shifted interest from the pork on his fork to his mother.

"Nonsense. You're a beautiful, intelligent, special girl and any young man in his right mind would be lucky to take you."

Abbie tried hard not to look at Ty, who was extra quiet.

"It's no big deal, Grandma. It's not like it's the most important thing in my life right now."

"Sweetheart, your grandmother is right. You shouldn't allow what's going on with your mother to stop you from enjoying high school. She would be the first person to tell you that."

Trust her dad to act like she was some fragile flower whose petals would fall off if he didn't say and do all the right things.

"Even if I wanted to go, I couldn't. The ball is for juniors and seniors only and you'd have to be asked by one of them to go. I don't think they would ask a sophomore."

Grandma scoffed. "That doesn't matter."

"Ty is a senior," Miles piped up, his mischievous grin not lost on anyone at the table.

Awkward silence followed. Abbie didn't dare look Ty in the eye. He suddenly found his green beans interesting scientific specimens. Unfortunately, Miles took the silence to mean that he should proceed with his particular brand of eleven-year-old wisdom.

"Ty and Abbie, sitting in a tree, k-i-s-s-i-n-g."

Abbie lunged at him from across the table. "I'm going to rip your head off and then feed it to the dog. You know she'll eat anything."

Mahalia placed her paws over her face, chagrined. Miles wasn't fazed by the threat hanging in the air. "Everyone knows you're in love with Ty and you write his name in your notebook all the time. There's no reason to be embarrassed, Abbie. Ty will be a great boyfriend. He can play video games with me when he comes over."

Miles looked pleased with himself.

Her father and Grandma offered up sympathetic glances. She could see it in their eyes. "Sorry your brother just embarrassed you in front of the boy you're in love with. You'll live. We promise."

Did they not understand that her brother just dropped a nuclear bomb on her life? She had no choice but to leave the table. She offered no apologies, she just upped and left, a stream of silent tears the only witness to her inner turmoil and complete humiliation.

Chapter 37

Mia was more miserable than ever and getting more depressed by the minute. She was paying him to take care of these problems and instead they kept getting worse. She had to be alert and focused at all times and didn't need whatever "this" was getting in the way. His usual cup of tea sat on the coffee table. She didn't say anything, just sat in the armchair across from him. For a moment, neither one of them spoke. Dr. Singer's hand shook when he lifted the cup of tea to his lips. He was careful when he laid the cup down on the coffee table.

"What do you want to talk about today?"

She didn't respond, instead she stared out the basement window that gave a view of the frozen ground above them. It was a cold, sunny morning. The sun's rays came through the windows, as if it knew this session needed some brightening.

"Why do you think the old woman keeps appearing and talking to you?"

"Because she hates me," Mia responded, without looking at him.

"Are you sure?"

"Yes."

"Are there periods of time she appears more often than others?"

"When I'm busy, going about my day. She likes to make me feel stupid and inadequate."

"Hmm." Dr. Singer scribbled some notes again. "Does she ask you to do anything?"

"What do you mean? Like telling me to jump?"

"What I was getting at—"

"I know exactly what you were getting at," Mia said. Her voice was low and menacing as she turned to look at him.

Something vibrated. Dr. Singer reached into his pants pocket and looked at the screen of his cell phone. "Could you excuse me for a moment, Mia? This might be an emergency."

The notebook he was just scribbling in sat on the desk, calling to her. She watched him disappear then made a beeline for the desk when it was safe. Mia snatched up the notebook and thumbed through it from the beginning. Nothing much, her name, age, why she came to see him in the first place. Boring. She kept turning the pages. She had trained herself to be an expert speed-reader and anticipated she'd be able to get through the entire thing before Dr. Singer came back. Then she hit the jackpot. Or maybe not. She could feel anger swelling inside her.

Patient exhibits random episodes of rage and hostility. Could lead to destructive behavior. Feelings of entitlement are prevalent. Has difficulty showing remorse or guilt.

Highly intelligent, but uses charm and manipulation to get her way.

Unhealthy obsession with Shelby Cooper. Unable to process perceived wrongs in a healthy manner.

Antisocial Personality Disorder?

Mia wanted to rip the notebook to shreds. Her eyes fell on the letter opener, bright and shiny on the desk. She forced herself to remain calm and kept flipping through the pages of the notebook. More psychobabble.

Patient's lack of sleep affects her ability to function.
Don't think sleep aid will help. There are missing pieces to her story.

Mood swings, thoughts of suicide, made more perplexing by my belief patient...

Mia heard a noise and turned around, startled. She was caught red handed. Dr. Singer was pissed.

"Could I have my property, please?" he asked, hand extended.

She handed him the notebook without a word.

"Why were you going through my private notes? There are boundaries surrounding the doctor patient relationship."

"I thought you cared about me as a patient. I guess not."

"I do care. I want you to get better. "

"So, what's all that nonsense in the notebook?"

"Please, have a seat."

Mia obeyed and Dr. Singer took his usual spot. "Sometimes psychiatry can be like hunting for treasure. You look at all the symptoms and clues, and combine them with your expertise to see if you can pinpoint a diagnosis. Only then can a course of treatment be prescribed."

"I don't think I should see you anymore."

He arched an eyebrow. "You're perfectly within your rights as the patient to decide which professional should assist with your care and treatment."

"I'll think about it."

Mia didn't wait for a response. She left Dr. Singer sitting in his chair, looking somber.

She banged her hands repeatedly on the steering wheel of her car parked in his driveway. She couldn't trust him anymore. It wasn't supposed to be this complicated. Dr. Singer seemed relieved when she said she didn't want to see him anymore. Mia hated that.

Chapter 38

Rayne Revington arrived on an icy December morning. She was everything Vivian had said, Jason observed—sweet, caring and kind. Her meeting with the kids went better than he anticipated. The kids were usually guarded, and given what they'd been through over the past weeks, he was surprised at how quickly they took to Rayne and her to them. Rayne was a pretty girl with big brown eyes and a bohemian edge.

"So, tell me, Rayne, do you think you would be comfortable running this house?"

"Well, Mr. Cooper—"

"Please, call me Jason."

"Okay," she said, wringing her hands then placing them in her lap. "The house is enormous. Intimidating. Everything in it is so expensive," she said, her eyes running across the expansive granite countertop, top-of-the-line stainless steel appliances, and gleaming hardwood floors. "But, Mrs. Cooper did a great job of making it homey."

"You don't have to worry about the heavy lifting. We have a cleaning service that comes in twice a week to do that. Shelby took care of the cooking, laundry, and light housekeeping. The service is still in place. Besides, I want your primary focus to be the kids. Dropping and picking them up from school, taking them to appointments, that sort of thing."

"I can cook, too."

"That's fine if you want to take that on. Vivian is family and she had great things to say about you so I trust her judgment."

"Thank you. She explained the situation to me and I want you to know I will do all I can to help until Dr. Cooper comes home. And, you can count on my discretion. Abbie and Miles are great kids so we can make this work. To answer your question, yes, I can handle it."

The stalker had contacted Abbie again and she was in no mood to tiptoe around him. He was texting her this time. She sat at the edge of her bed. She was desperate to get him to slip up. She would archive the text messages, even if the origin couldn't be traced. They might come in useful. With Rayne in the house now, she had to be extra careful.

Abbie: What do u want?

Him: Ur angry.

Abbie: Ur going 2 kill us all now?

Him: Don't be silly.

Abbie: u murdered a man to set up my mother. Monster!!!

Him: Don't forget whom ur talking to.

Abbie: Not afraid. Loser!!!

Him: Shelby isn't who she says she is.

Abbie: u keep saying that but it's all bull.

Him: She didn't love u enough to tell the truth.

Abbie: What truth? Ur the liar.

Abbie: My mom's already in jail.

Abbie: Should just tell my dad about u.

Him: That would be a tragic mistake.

Abbie: Already made a mistake trusting u. It ends now.

Him: Ur mother's real name isn't Shelby Durant.

Abbie: *???*

Him: She hasn't been honest.

Abbie: About what?

Him: Ask her for her birth name. Ask what really happened to her family.

Him: TTYL

Why would he say that about her mother? He was a killer and would say anything to keep her from telling her father, Abbie surmised. Why come up with a lame story about her mom's name, though? He sounded so convincing.

A knock on the door broke through her troubled thoughts. "Come in," she snapped. It was Rayne. She stood at the door, shy and cautious.

"Sorry to bother you, Abbie. I was wondering if you needed a snack before dinner. I made some sandwiches."

"I don't bite. You can come in."

"Thank you."

Abbie assessed Rayne. She was polite to the point of being annoying. Pretty but was one of those girls who didn't know it and didn't care much. Just one look at her hair, all puffy and wild, told the story. She didn't wear makeup, which Abbie supposed was all right. Her mother always told her too much makeup all the time ages the skin.

Abbie chuckled. "Seriously Rayne, you need to learn to relax. Stop walking around here like the boogeyman is going to jump out and grab you. We're pretty laid back in this family."

"Sorry," she said, smiling nervously.

"And, stop apologizing for everything."

"I'm just not used to this. It's a little overwhelming."

"Used to what?"

"This is the fanciest house I've ever been in. I'm afraid to touch anything."

"It's just a house. We're like everyone else. You being here is a big clue."

Rayne sat beside Abbie on the bed. "Because of your mother's situation, you mean."

"You can say it out loud. My mother is in jail. It doesn't matter if she's innocent. That's what our family is dealing with."

"You're so brave and matter-of-fact about it. You're really mature for your age."

"My dad says I'm an old soul."

"Your dad, he's intense. So…"

"Hot?"

Abbie had embarrassed Rayne, who opened and closed her mouth, mortified. "Well, I was going to say—"

"Don't worry about it. Even my friends at school drool over him. It's harmless. He comes across a little scary sometimes, but he's a good guy with a good heart."

"I can see that."

It was nice having a younger woman in the house to talk to, even if it was temporary. "Do you have a boyfriend?"

She was startled by the question. "I was seeing someone, mostly just talking on the phone and going on a few dates. Nothing serious."

"So, how does he feel about you being all the way in New England?"

"He understands. I'm happy that Vivian brought this opportunity my way. I can save up some money to pay for grad school."

"What do you want to be when you grow up?"

"Social work. So many kids are neglected and need help."

"So, you want to change the world, one kid at a time?"

"Something like that. A lot of kids aren't wanted by their parents."

"Really?" Something in Rayne's tone told Abbie there was a story there. "Do you have experience with that? Aunt Vivian said you came from a nice family."

"I do. But, I'm adopted."

"Oh. Do you know who your biological parents are?"

"No."

"You want to find them, don't you?"

"Yes. I want to ask my mother why she didn't want me. She can tell me about my father."

"Wouldn't that make your adoptive parents feel funny? I mean they raised you and love you and all that."

"They'll always be my parents no matter what. But part of me is still missing because I don't know where I came from."

"Is that why you want to be a social worker, because you're adopted?"

"That's part of it. It's also because too many kids end up in foster care, either because their parents abandoned them or were abusive. I want to help. You wouldn't understand."

"Why wouldn't I?" Abbie asked. Her temper flared. "Just because it's not my experience doesn't mean I can't sympathize."

"I didn't mean to imply that because you're—"

"Yes, you did. You were being a reverse snob. By the way, I don't feel guilty about having a comfortable life. My parents work hard to provide my brother and me with financial security and access to numerous resources. It means one day, we can give back."

The discussion was getting too intense, and Abbie may have come off a bit harsh. "Sorry, Rayne. I didn't mean to go postal just now."

"It's ok," she said with a wry smile. "You're right. Sometimes I come on too strong. How about that sandwich I promised you when I came up?"

"No, thanks. I'll just wait till dinner."

Chapter 39

W hat are you doing here?"

"You didn't think I would stay away, did you?

"Jason didn't tell you about my bad attitude?"

"He did. I'm stubborn, too."

Vivian disregarded my request for no visitors with the exception of Jason and my lawyer. Now, she sits across from me in the visitor's room. I barely know what day it is, but by her clothes, I know that it's still winter. Despite her bravado, she's stunned to see me in this condition. Hearing someone is in jail and seeing the effects with your own eyes are two different things. Vivian's way of dealing with it is to talk to me as if we were sipping a glass of merlot on the patio at home.

"I think we should take that trip to Dubai we always talked about, just the two of us. One of my clients lives there and would treat us like royalty."

"Yeah? An exotic vacation sounds good right now. Not like the vacation in here. Can you believe they don't even have a pool? There's no room service, and don't get me started on the accommodations. The thread count on the sheets is in the single digits. No ocean view from the room and no spa. How do they expect people to live under these horrible conditions? It's just awful, I tell you. I'm writing a strongly worded letter to the management when I leave."

Perhaps I took our little game too far because Vivian is drenched in tears. She wipes them away with the elbows of her sweater, an odd move for her. Vivian is meticulous about her clothes, chiefly because they cost a fortune and are mostly imported from Europe. "I don't want you to be sad," I say. "Just keep an eye on Jason and the kids. I hear you recommended someone to come help him. Thank you for that."

"I wish I could do more. I just want you to come home so we can resume our lives and forget that you were ever in this godforsaken place," she said looking around. "You don't belong in here, Shelby."

"How is Jason? I mean really?"

"Barely holding on."

"I figured that was the case despite his protests to the contrary."

Vivian's eyes land on my hands. "Where is your wedding ring?"

"They took it."

"That's just plain wrong."

"I'm in jail, Vivian, at a maximum-security prison facility for people accused of or convicted of horrible crimes. I have no rights here. No one in here cares that I'm innocent."

Conflicting emotions play out on her face. I don't think she really gets it. For a woman like Vivian, this is an unthinkable, unbearable situation. If we were to switch places, she would be on suicide watch from day one. She grew up a pampered, spoiled girl with a father who overindulged her and a mother who couldn't control her. Hardship and difficulty are two words she can't spell, let alone comprehend.

"I can't take this, Shel. I can't see you like this," she announces, her breathing uneven as she tries to control her emotions. "Can't the police find the real culprit? What's taking so long? And, I don't understand why you told the court you couldn't afford to post the bail. It makes you look guilty and I want to know why you did it."

I want her focused on keeping Jason sane and making sure my kids are okay. I love her to death, and we have an unbreakable bond, but I cannot tell her the truth. Over the years, we've kept each other's secrets and I've come to realize that some secrets should stay buried. It's time to end the visit.

"Don't worry about me. As long as my babies are okay, I'll make it. Help keep Jason together. And, yes, I will go to Dubai with you when I get out of here."

She smiles for the first time since she entered the visitor's room. "I'll hold you to that. You're paying for the trip. It's your punishment for getting yourself arrested. Just saying."

I stand up to let her know the visit is over. "Please don't come back here. I mean it. I'll see you in Dubai."

"You're scared. Why?"

"What do you mean?"

"I know you. There's something you're not telling me."

"You know everything you need to. Stop worrying so much."

The next day, I expect a visit from the prison chaplain. I need guidance, and an end to the nightmares. I see Alessandro in all of them. He's not at peace. It's always the same. He's at the edge of a cliff. It's dark. Angry waves crash below us. I don't know where we are. "You lied, princess," he says to me, then dives off the cliff. I wake up screaming. My cellmate is usually dead to the world around this time. I don't know what lie he's referring to. I offered to help him and instead he wound up dead. That would be enough to piss off any ghost. But, he's not just any ghost. I cared deeply for him. I feel overwhelming guilt about his death. He was targeted because of me, and that I will live with for the rest of my days.

When I enter the visitors' room, I can't believe my eyes. The chaplain has pulled a disappearing act and in his place is someone I thought I'd never see again. He's wearing thin, clear glasses, black slacks, a black jacket with a dark purple shirt, and a white collar, the type worn by religious clerics. The universe has a sick sense of humor.

He removes his glasses when I sit down. He's nervous and unfocused.

"What are you doing here, Anton?" I ask, my tone measured, controlled. Why pretend anymore? We both know we ran into each other at the Fairmont Hotel lobby weeks ago.

He rushes headlong into a series of random questions. "You have no idea how happy I was to see you at the Fairmont…I never knew what happened…I asked around and no one in your neighborhood or your friends from school knew where you were or if you were doing okay. I'm so sorry, Mia. When I saw the news story, I knew they had it all wrong. You would never do anything so heinous. I know I'm the last person you want to see…I just had to come."

He removes a handkerchief from his pocket and dabs the sweat pouring from his forehead.

"That color looks good on you. The shirt, I mean. Then again, you could put on a potato sack and make it look good. Are you still in possession of that particular gift? And, what's with the collar, anyway?"

He looks at me as if I'm not right in the head. I've never seen Anton at a loss for words. He's forty-three now, and I can see the years were kind to him. He put on at least fifteen pounds, which isn't that bad considering he was a bony eighteen-year old when I knew him. For years, I hated him. I blamed him for using me and then discarding me at the first sign of trouble. When I got older, that logic didn't make sense anymore. How could I blame him when the woman who gave birth to me threw me out like garbage the first opportunity she got?

"Mia—"

"Shelby. My name is Shelby. Mia Lansing is dead."

Chapter 40

When he saw the news story of her arrest, he was stunned. Why would the police believe she was capable of murdering a man and stuffing him in the trunk of her car? She was barely five feet tall and probably weighed a hundred pounds soaking wet. He was having difficulty seeing her as anyone other than Mia. Something about the new name she had adopted, Shelby, seemed familiar to him—some factoid that escaped him for now.

"I'm sorry, Shelby. It will take me some time to get used to your new name. Why did you choose that name?"

"You came all the way to this jail to find out why I changed my name to Shelby?"

"I thought that might break the ice."

He could see the gears turning in her head. She gently tapped her fingers on the table. "Okay. Even exchange. I'll tell you why I changed my name to Shelby and you tell me why you're here. The real reason."

She wasn't going to make this easy for him. Shelby Cooper was no fool. She had an edge to her, a somewhat jaded, *everyone is full of it and don't even think about messing with me* kind of edge. He had to gain her trust, tread carefully. If there was a way they could help each other, he had to find it and convince her he was in her corner.

"Sounds fair."

"My daddy's favorite car in the world—"

"Was the 1964 Shelby Cobra Roadster," he said. "You're surprised I remember that, aren't you?"

"I am. Why?"

"I remember everything you ever said to me. The things that were important to you, anyway. I remember you and your daddy were close. That he owned a mechanic shop and he taught you about cars and motorcycles. That the two of you would go through his stack of *Popular Mechanics* magazines. That his dream car was the Shelby Roadster. It was your way of holding on to him? The name, I mean."

"What do want, Anton? Why are you here? No bullshit this time."

"I've thought about you a lot over the past twenty-five years. I wondered if you were okay and what happened to the baby. Then I ran into you at the hotel and you looked wonderful, and I was relieved. I came because I know you didn't do what you're being accused of. I thought, after everything that went down between us, I owed you. The least I can do is visit, pray for you. I know you were raised in a Christian home and it's important to you."

"How would you know what's important to me, Anton? We knew each other when I was fifteen years old. Now, I'm forty. As far as I'm concerned, we're strangers."

She was still angry with him. She didn't trust him. He had a monumental task ahead of him, getting her to see him as a man who wanted to help her and not the boy who almost ruined her life.

"I don't know what's important to Shelby Cooper, you're right about that. However, we're not strangers. I did care for you. I just couldn't let my parents know how I felt. They would have pressured me to stop seeing you. When you told me you were pregnant, I panicked. I wish I could take it back, all of it. A few days after you told me, I went by your house to apologize and make things right. Your mother said you didn't live there anymore and I should never come back. I'm truly sorry for the pain I caused you, Shelby."

She looked at him with those big doe eyes he remembered so well. They were giant pools of wariness. "Thanks for the apology.

But, that's not the only reason you're visiting."

"I'm pastor of the First United Methodist Church in Framingham. I needed to find you and ask for your forgiveness. When I met your family in church last Sunday, I knew that was a sign from the Lord."

"What happened to Pastor Bridges?"

"He moved on to a larger congregation in Oklahoma."

"How did you end up here? I never pegged you for someone who would like living up north."

"People change."

She leaned away from him and folded her arms. "I know why you're here and what you want."

"You do?"

"Yes. The question you've been dying to ask me before you got here. The question you've turned over in your head a million times over the years. You want to know what happened after I left your house that day."

"If it's not too much trouble, yes."

"Okay. I'll tell you."

Chapter 41

Kenner, Louisiana 1988

I was hiding in my bedroom before she got home from work, jamming to Whitney Houston on my Walkman when my little brother Michael knocked on the door. He was eleven going on twenty. Michael and I hung out in my room a lot. She wouldn't hit me if he were in my room.

Michael and Daddy were the only two people in the world who loved me, and maybe Anton, but I don't think so. Not after what he said. The jerk! Maybe she'd stop hitting me once I told her the news. Anything would be better than being hit with pots and pans, shoes, the belt, or the switch. Listening to music was my escape. I could pretend I didn't live in this house, on this street where all the houses looked the same and everyone went to the same church on Sunday, and were always gossiping.

Michael walked over to my dresser and picked up the latest issue of *Teen Beat* Magazine, then sat on the edge of my bed and thumbed through it. Kirk Cameron from the TV Show *Growing Pains* was on the cover. I untucked my legs from my sitting position and told him to move over. "Can you keep a secret, Michael?"

"Sure. What is it?" He continued to thumb through the

magazine.

"I'm going to have a baby."

His head popped up and his eyes went big. "You're lying. No way."

"Yes. I'm serious."

He frowned and put away the magazine. "How do you know for sure? Your stomach doesn't even look big."

"I just know, okay, I—"

"Mia, open up." It was Daddy knocking at the door.

"Shhh," I told my brother. "Don't say anything."

Daddy walked in with a brown paper bag and a big grin on his face. His clothes were dirty and greasy from working at the garage. Daddy was the best mechanic in town and owned his own shop. I scooted off the bed and grabbed the paper bag from him. I was happy when I opened it and found the best bread pudding in Louisiana from the bakery across town. All the kids went there after school because they had the best beignet, bread pudding, and petit fours.

Michael and I started eating away like two greedy little pigs. We didn't even offer Daddy any. He just stood there, laughing at us.

"So, what are you kids up to?" Daddy asked.

"Mia's going to have a baby," Michael blurted out.

Silence enveloped the room. The bread pudding didn't taste so great anymore. I stopped eating and slowly looked up at Daddy's face. Michael ran out of the room, slamming the door behind him. I was going to kill him.

Daddy walked over slowly and stops just in front of me. He knelt down so he could be at eye level with me. I've never seen him look so serious, and sad.

"Is it true Mia? Are you pregnant?"

I couldn't look at him. It hurt too much. I disappointed him. I looked out my bedroom window and noticed the sun was setting. The last rays of daylight burst through my window, like it was casting light on my secret, which was no longer a secret. Now, everyone would know that I'm not pure anymore and I brought shame to my family. I would probably be kicked out of school. I started crying and couldn't stop.

"I'm sorry, Daddy. I didn't mean to get in trouble. Anton said it was going to be okay and it wouldn't hurt but he lied. He said he loved me and wouldn't let anything bad happen to me. When I told him this afternoon, he didn't want anything to do with me. He acted like he didn't even care. I was so stupid. I believed everything he told me. It was just that one time, I don't understand…and…"

I felt Daddy's arms wrap around me and I held on tight. His shirt was drenched in my tears. "Anton Devereaux did this to you?"

His voice sounded strange, like it didn't belong to him. I let go of him and still couldn't look at him in the eye. "It was my fault, too. I let him."

"Why, Mia?"

"Because I loved him, and he said he loved me, too, and he would wait for me even after he went off to college."

"This is bad. I'm going to have a word with his parents. He has to take responsibility for this."

I tugged at his arm. "No. You can't. Don't you say one word to him."

"What did you say to me?"

"You can't do that Daddy. Anton said he didn't want his family name dragged through the mud. You know how the Deverauxs are. They're all hoity-toity and they could make real trouble for us."

"I'm not afraid of Thornhill Devereaux and his clan. His son got my daughter pregnant, and they're going to hear about it. They're going to have to deal with it, too."

Fresh tears streamed down my face. I was in a full-blown hysteria. I felt Daddy's rough hands wiping away my tears. "Go wash up before your mother sees you."

I opened the door and ran smack into my mother. I slowly backed away from her, and bumped into Daddy, who since stood up. My legs felt like overcooked spaghetti. I looked at Daddy and he didn't look so good, either. Mama's face was the same way it always was whenever she saw me—all wrinkled like one of the California Raisins, except she never smiled. She was wearing her nurse's uniform, the white dress with white stockings and white shoes. Her nametag was still pinned to her dress. Betty Lansing, RN, Stafford Memorial Hospital.

Some people in the neighborhood claimed that Mama was

pretty. I never saw it. All I saw was how mean she was. I'm glad I didn't look like her. I took after Daddy who was always kind and special.

"What's going on? What did you do now?"

Daddy and I didn't say anything.

"Girl, don't try my patience. I asked you a question."

I felt frozen in time. My brain wasn't working well. I didn't know what to say.

Daddy spoke first. "Betty, we need to talk. It's important, but I don't think we should do it tonight."

Mama came all the way into the room. "No, we're gonna talk about it right here, right now. What trouble did Mia get into?"

Mama stood close to me and turned my face towards her. "I'm not going to ask you again. What did you do?"

I started bawling all over again. My heart was beating erratically and I felt sick. I held my stomach so I wouldn't throw up. "I'm…going…I'm…pregnant."

Mama looked at Daddy, and then back at me.

"Anton Devereaux did this," Daddy said.

Mama was quiet, which was strange, because she was always yelling and carrying on about something or the other. I didn't see her raise her hand. I almost fell down when she slapped me hard across the face. It hurt. Good thing Daddy caught me before I hit the floor.

"Betty, stop it."

Mama acted like Daddy didn't even speak. "So, now you're the town tramp who got knocked up? You just couldn't keep your legs closed after all the talking I did. All the warnings I gave you. I always knew you were no good from the day you were born."

"I'm not a tramp, Mama," I whispered. "I don't sleep around."

I didn't know why but it was important for me to tell her I wasn't slutty. She never thought anything good about me. It didn't matter that I got all As in school.

Maybe I shouldn't have said anything because she got angry. Her eyes were bugging out of her face, and she pushed me down on the bed. Then she started hitting me in the face and stomach.

"Stop it! Daddy, make her stop."

Daddy pulled her off me and I rolled to a corner of the bed and curled up with my back to her so she wouldn't hit me. Her breathing was heavy.

"I want this no good filth out of my house."

"Stop it. You don't mean that," Daddy said.

Mama put her hand on her hips and let out a big sigh. "Okay."

Daddy and I looked at her like she'd lost her mind. She was never this agreeable.

"Richard, I need to speak with my daughter. Alone."

Daddy's eyes darted all over the room. Then they landed on me.

"Are you sure I can't stick around?" he asked, Mama.

Mama just cut her eyes at him. When he wouldn't leave, she shoved him out the door. "Don't make me place that phone call, Richard."

Daddy looked at me with sad puppy eyes. He did what Mama said and left the room. I looked up at Mama, and she was almost smiling. She started looking around the room. I sat up straight on the bed and followed her movements with my eyes. She went into the closet and started looking through my clothes. I've never seen her do that before. She pulled out a wooden hanger, got close enough to the bed and whacked me across the face.

I screamed in agony and grabbed my face. It felt like someone poured boiling hot water on me. She hit me again in the stomach. I fell to the ground and yelled at her. "Stop it! Stop it!"

She stopped for a second and I ran for the door. She was too quick for me. She pushed me back, and I stumbled. I take refuge in the bed again. "You think you can defy me? I will kill you."

Mama looked like a wild animal out of control. I snatched a pillow and placed it around my stomach. She tried to wrestle the pillow from me. I was getting tired but if I let go, she would kill me.

"Let go of the pillow."

"No." I left the bed and backed into the corner near the window. If I went for the closet, she would drag me out. It was better to be standing because at least I could fight her.

"Mia Caroline Lansing, get over here," she said. Her tone was like dirt being shoveled down my throat.

I touched my cheek, the place where she hit me with the hanger. It felt like a hundred bees stung me, and I started to cry again. I knew she would come get me from the corner, and grab me by my hair. That's why I cut it whenever it grew past my shoulders. I had to keep the short version in a bun so she wouldn't notice the blunt edges.

I was sick of her. I wasn't going to be scared anymore because it just made Mama feel important but made me feel lower than dirt. I decided I was going to survive, just to get even with her. I would grow up. I would be happy. I would go to college and study something important. I would have a family and I wouldn't be mean to my kids. I would love them and comfort them when they were sad or scared. I would marry a man who was strong, and not afraid of anyone or anything, a man who was really brave, but kind and would protect our children. Not like Daddy, who ran away like a coward.

"I'm not leaving this corner. You're not going to hit me anymore."

"Shut up! Who asked you to speak?"

"Nobody. I'm tired."

"You're tired? You haven't seen tired yet." She dragged me from the spot near the window and hit me again. I wrestled the hanger from her. She punched me with her fists. I pushed her hard and she fell to the ground. I didn't feel at all sorry. She grabbed me by the ankles and I lost my balance, falling hard on the wooden floor, next to her. I cushioned the fall with my hands. Mama jumped on top of me and we started wrestling each other like WWF contenders in WrestleMania.

"I hate you!" I yelled. "You're not my mother, you're a monster."

She appeared dazed by my outburst. Her body stiffened, then she rolled off me. I got up from the floor and so did she. We were both breathing heavily but she recovered first.

. "What did you say to me? You looking to have all your teeth knocked out?"

"No, ma'am. Just done with you hurting me. Done with you making me feel ashamed to be part of this family. Done with you hurting me every day of my life.

"What did I do to you that was so bad? Why can't you love me because I'm your daughter?"

She was at a loss for words. She just stared at me like she

couldn't comprehend what I was asking.

"This won't work," she said, calmly. "You think because you let Anton Devereaux feel you up and got you knocked up that you're grown? You think you can disrespect me?"

"No. I was just telling you how I felt."

"You should know by now that your feelings don't mean diddly-squat to me. I want you gone. Tonight."

I knew Mama hated me, but I didn't think she meant it. Maybe if I asked nicely she would change her mind.

"Where would I go? What if something bad happened to me?"

"I don't care. Now I can be finally rid of you."

I didn't want to cry. I didn't want to seem weak in front of her. Still, I was so sad and scared and my tears knew that too, so they just kept falling, soaking my favorite hot pink t-shirt. "That's not true. I've never been in trouble before this."

She put her hands on her hips and bit her bottom lip, the way she did when she made up her mind about an issue. "What kind of example would I be setting for Michael if I allowed his slutty sister to remain in this house? You ignored all the morals I tried to instill in you. I can still save Michael. Pack your clothes and get out of here. You have five minutes."

I dragged my luggage through the hallway to the kitchen. Mama wouldn't let me through the front door in case the neighbors saw me. Daddy leaned up against the kitchen counter. Michael clung to him. I've never seen Daddy cry. He squeezed a small envelope into my hands and whispered that I should hide it. He told me he didn't want me to go Mama wouldn't listen to reason. He said I should forgive her. Never! Michael sobbed and begged me not to leave. To survive outside that house, I had to forget they existed.

Chapter 42

Anton swallows hard and lowers his gaze. "Dear Lord. I had no idea it was that bad. How did you get—"

"I made it to New Orleans with some of the guilt money Daddy gave me before I left. When the money ran out, I lived in abandoned buildings, ate out of dumpsters and tried not to gag on my own filth. When I started showing, I ended up at a homeless shelter for runaway teens. Ironic, because in spite of my crazy mother, I didn't want to leave home."

He tugs at his collar. "I'm sorry...so s-sorry."

I don't want his pity. I survived him, and my mother's cruelty. I'll survive this nightmare, too.

I touch his forearm briefly, and our eyes lock. "I don't know what happened to the baby. I know his whereabouts is the only thing that matters to you."

He whips his handkerchief out of his shirt pocket and turns away from me. He dabs the corners of his eyes. When he looks at me again, something fleeting passes between us. A silent recognition of the pain we've both carried for over two decades.

"You gave him up for adoption?" he asks, his voice shaky. "What did you name him?"

What I did was cruel. If I live to be a hundred, the shame will never leave me. When he was placed in my arms at the hospital, I glanced at him for a few seconds. Then my decision was made. I couldn't, wouldn't allow myself to bond with him. I never named him. I didn't ask how much he weighed at birth or whether he was healthy or had any complications. All I knew was that if I was going to make it in the world, I had to leave him behind. So, I did. I left him in the hospital alone and unloved. Just like his mother.

"I didn't give him a name, Anton. I didn't know how I was going to raise him. In my teenage mind, leaving him at the hospital was the best solution. They would have to take care of him, and find him a family. I couldn't stay in a shelter with a baby. On the streets with me, his chances—"

I stop to catch my breath, and rein in my pain. I won't lose it in front of Anton, of all people.

"He was better off without me," I finish.

"You just left him?" Anton is incredulous.

I nod. I can see the veins in his neck pulsating.

"So, you have no idea where he might have ended up?"

"None, whatsoever."

"Did you ever feel anything for him, wonder where he was after you had gone on with your life?"

Does he think the title *Pastor* makes him morally superior? Bullshit!

"I didn't have the luxury of giving in to my feelings, Anton. As despicable as it was, leaving him was the most loving thing I could have done. Having him live on the streets, an uncertain and dangerous life, with a kid mother who couldn't provide for him would have been worse. Leaving him was the only shot at a life I could give him. Why can't you understand that?"

"You turned out okay."

"By a miracle. When I walked out of that hospital in New Orleans, I went back to the shelter. I knew I couldn't stay there much longer. I told them the baby was stillborn. While I was there, a woman named Rita March walked in. She was a donor and volunteer. For some reason, she took a liking to me. That chance encounter changed my life.

"Rita became my foster mother and within a few months, she

and her family moved to North Carolina, taking me with them. Rita and her husband Daniel raised me, along with their daughter, Vivian. When it was time for college, I got into Duke on a partial scholarship, and Rita footed the rest of the bill. After Duke, I went off to graduate school at Johns Hopkins. The rest, you probably know."

"Wow," he said shaking his head. "That's an incredible story."

"I can't help you. I don't know if he made it or not. You're chasing a ghost."

"Let's bow our heads in prayer and ask for forgiveness for our sins."

After Anton leaves, I go back to my cell and weep. I weep for the little boy I was too weak and scared to love. I weep for the family I lost because of one mistake. I weep because I will never know what became of him. I weep because I was too much of a coward to try and find him. I started the process, but gave up, convincing myself he would hate me and want no part of me, that I had no right to disrupt his life after what I did to him, that I didn't deserve him after I deserted him as a helpless newborn. It was better to leave well enough alone. I hold on to that rationalization as if my life depends on it. One thing is clear, however: Anton Devereaux is a liar. Father-son bonding is the farthest thing from his mind. He has a far more sinister reason for wanting to find our son.

Chapter 43

He walked up the stairs of their Ashland home, knowing Jade would pounce on him the moment he walked in. There were still patches of ice that hadn't quite melted on the stairs and he had to be careful he didn't slip and fall. He'd thought about what he would say on the drive home. He knew his wife wouldn't be pleased, but he just couldn't go through with it. Not after the dramatic story he heard from Shelby. It would have been cruel to barrage her with the questions he really wanted to ask.

"Did you get the information we need?" Jade asked, when he entered the kitchen. He removed his coat, and slung it over a chair. He gazed at her with an expression he hoped conveyed that he needed a minute to breathe.

She pulled out a chair hurriedly, the scraping sound on the tile adding to the pressure he felt. The kettle whistled on the stove, a good thing. He could use some hot tea.

His wife eyed him with apprehension, then slowly got up from the table and removed the kettle from the stove. She poured hot water into two mugs.

Anton met Jade when he was a senior at the University of Texas Austin. She was a theater and dance major who wanted to be a Broadway actress. A year behind him, Jade earned her way through college as a stripper. Years later, she had still maintained a dancer's body. She was a Texas gal with southern traditions and a pull-no-punches New York attitude. She had been by his side from the moment they met, and knew him better than anyone ever had or ever would. She never judged him for his past and he never judged her.

She placed a mug in front of him and he allowed the steam to caress his face. He then took a long, slow sip.

"It's harder than I thought it would be."

"What do you mean? What did she say?"

"She doesn't know anything."

"How can a mother not know where her child is?" Jade asked. She pushed away her mug.

Anton didn't understand it himself. How could he explain it to his wife without painting Shelby as a heartless, selfish woman, even though that's exactly what he thought initially?

"She didn't raise him. She left him in the hospital."

Jade placed her hand over her mouth, her eyes wide with shock. When she dropped her hand, Anton observed the tightness in her jaw. "She abandoned her child? What kind of woman does that?"

"She wasn't a woman back then, she was a frightened teenage girl that I deserted. She did the best she could under the circumstances."

"Don't give me that, Anton. Teenagers have babies all the time, they don't leave them in hospitals and walk away."

"She had nobody. Like I told you, her mother threw her out into the streets after she found out she was carrying my child."

"She's going to have to do better than that. Now is her chance to set things right."

"I can't force her to give me something she doesn't have, Jade. I understand our dire circumstances, but we can't pin all our hopes on her."

She shifted her chair so she could be closer to him. "Do you, Anton? Do you understand our dire circumstances? Ever since you told me about your past with this woman, I have been patient and understanding. I can't afford to be patient anymore, and neither can you. Get Shelby or Mia or whatever name she's going by these days to tell you as much as she can about when she gave birth, where, and anything else that can help us. We need to find that kid. Time is running out."

"Don't you think I know that? Badgering me isn't going to freeze time. Badgering Shelby could send her running in the other direction, especially since I never told her the real reason I'm looking for our child. She's in a maximum-security jail cell fighting for her freedom right now. I have to consider that. Also, don't forget Martin has offered his resources to help us."

They were in a pissing match and Anton was caught between loyalty to his current family and the loyalty he never showed Shelby. He didn't know which one would win out in the end. He did know that somebody was going to lose.

"We should keep our voices down," Jade said finally. "Was the baby a boy or girl?"

"Boy."

"And, his name?"

"I…I don't know. She never gave him a name."

Jade clamped down on the mug and with trembling hands, brought it to her lips. When she put it down with a bang, spilling a few drops, she said, "There has to be a birth certificate. Even if it's Baby Doe written on it."

His wife's aggressive interrogation, understandable in the face of an uncertain future, was doing something to him. Unnamed emotions threatened to erupt and rip him apart. Is this how Mia felt before she morphed into Shelby?

"I didn't ask her about the birth certificate."

"Lord help me, Anton," Jade said, rolling her eyes. "What did you and this woman talk about then? Old times? Did she hypnotize you? Did you forget your mission?"

"No, I didn't. I had to show some compassion. It hasn't been an easy road for her. She's not to blame for our current circumstances. She made the best of the hand she was dealt. I ruined her life, until God interceded. We can't lose sight of that."

"Your compassion is admirable and that's one of the things I love about you. I just hope your compassion for this woman doesn't cost our daughter her life."

PART IV:

THE HUNTED

Chapter 44

The crackling sounds coming from the fireplace in his study wrapped Jason in a blanket of calm he hadn't allowed himself to feel since this dreadful mess began. He sat on the sofa, facing his modular entertainment system that also contained his bookshelf—mostly history, biographies, and business and motivational books penned by the likes of Jack Welch and Malcolm Gladwell. He was trying to make sense of the investigation thus far.

Tom couldn't find any record of Mehmet Koczak re-entering the United States, so that lead was a dead-end. The police were slow to investigate Isabella Rossi as a possible suspect. Why would they when Shelby made a far more interesting target, one who looked guilty based on their so-called evidence?

His pocket vibrated and he pulled out his phone. He didn't recognize the number and stared at the screen. His finger hovered over the "ignore" button. He took the call, anyway.

"Cooper."

"Bro. It's been a long time."

Jason's body temperature dropped several degrees. His hands felt numb and he almost lost his grip on the phone. The voice was unmistakable. One he'd hoped never to hear from again.

"This is a surprise," Jason said to the caller.

"Is it though?"

"Yes. Frankly, I never expected to hear from you again. It's been over two decades."

"Who's counting?" he asked, dismissively. "I could never forget my old buddy. Never."

"So, we're buddies now? No recriminations about the past?"

"Water under the Rio Grande, amigo. And, a colossal waste of time."

Jason was puzzled and he knew it spelled trouble. It was no coincidence that Nicholas Maza was calling him after all this time. He was after something. Jason suspected that this call was the least of whatever problems were about to surface.

Nicholas Maza had taken over from his father as the leader of what was now one of the largest drug distribution enterprises in the country. There was a brief moment in time when Jason's path crossed with the Mazas, and it almost got him killed.

Austin, TX 1988

He threw his backpack over his broad shoulders and made use of his long limbs, sprinting up the steps of the Perry-Castanela Library. He had goofed off the past couple of weeks with partying and recreation. Now it was time to refocus on his studies. Jason Cooper was a twenty-year-old junior and finance major at the University of Texas, Austin. Turned out he had a knack for the field and breezed through his courses. His career plans were right on track. He already had an internship at a major energy company under his belt, and a couple of Wall Street firms were eyeing him. What he really wanted was to start his own company.

He found a good spot in the library and settled down for what would be a marathon study session. He had barely cracked the textbook open when someone plopped down in the seat next to him. He grinned at Jason through a maze of thick black hair and amused brown eyes.

"Hey, man, what gives? Can't you see I'm studying?"

"This won't take long, bro."

"I'm not your bro. What do you want?"

Nicholas Maza was a dickhead and too cocky for Jason's taste. They were in the same major, so he saw a lot more of Nicholas than he would like, mostly because Nicholas always needed Jason to explain the lectures to him. Too bad charm wasn't a major because Nicholas would be in the Ph.D. program by now.

"Word is you're a kickass finance dude. Got all the professors talking about you."

"So?"

Nicholas edged closer to him and whispered, "So, I know someone who could use your skills."

"What are you talking about?"

Nicholas pulled a piece of paper from his pocket and handed it to Jason. "Call me later. He would pay you serious dough for your advice. This finance shit comes easy to you. Why not fatten your wallet by doing what you're good at?" Nicholas stood up. "Gotta jet. Call me, bro. I'll be waiting."

Nicholas had piqued Jason's interest. Two days later, Jason was in Nicholas's car heading two hours outside of the city to a gated mansion. A week after that, Jason was on the payroll of Sebastien Maza, advising him on how to hide money, launder it, and funnel it into legitimate businesses.

Nicholas hadn't been joking about fattening his wallet. The drug trade Jason learned was extremely lucrative, and once he earned the trust of those in charge, he had it made. He didn't question why he was doing it or what the consequences would be. It wasn't that he was hard up for cash per se. His parents earned a good living and he and his sister Robin had a great childhood.

But, consequences did follow. One night during the spring semester, Jason, Nicholas, and Daniel, another Maza employee, were sitting at a table at the Last Call Nightclub. They were just a few guys hanging out, enjoying the club vibe. Daniel excused himself from the group with no explanation. In Daniel's absence, two tough-looking dudes approached the table. Both had tattoos on their necks. The shorter of the two was wearing an eye patch. Both donned expensive-looking suits.

"Y'all friends with Daniel?" the taller one asked. Jason and Nicholas looked at each other.

Nicholas responded. "Who wants to know?"

The one with the patch took a seat across from them. "Daniel owes us money. Since he left, I figure you two need to pay up."

Talk about random run-ins, Jason thought. This was absurd. The best approach was to reason with these thugs. "Look, man, we don't have any beef with you. Whatever Daniel is into has nothing to do with us. We're just two college kids hanging out, taking a break from school."

Nicholas nodded in agreement.

"College kids, huh?" the taller one asked. "Where you go to college?"

Jason figured the university had a large campus and as long as he didn't give his name, he would be safe. "UT Austin."

"Both of you?"

"Yes."

Jason noticed the usually charming, cocky Nicholas sat perfectly still, and was doing his best not to look the thugs in the eye.

The one with the patch placed a gun on the table. Jason's heart was beating faster than a Thoroughbred Race Horse at the Kentucky Derby. These guys were no joke.

"Well," said the one with the patch, "I'm Rico, and this here," he said, gesturing to his friend, "is Felix. Since you two pimply faced losers were nice enough to answer our questions, we'll give you a little bit of time."

"Time for what?" Jason asked.

"Time to come up with our money."

"Huh?" Jason was stumped.

Felix spoke up. "What Rico is saying is, you two ain't leaving here until we get our money." For emphasis, Rico placed his hand over the gun.

Jason and Nicholas exchanged desperate glances. "We don't know you and we don't owe you any money."

"Don't matter," Felix said. "Daniel skipped out of here so now his debt is your debt."

Jason guzzled down his drink.

Rico stood, and picked up the gun up from the table. "I'll let you fellas think about how you're gonna get us our money. We'll be back in twenty minutes."

"What are we going to do?" Nicholas asked after their newfound friends left.

"I don't know, man. Your father's connections got us into this club, no questions asked."

"My dad doesn't know I'm here," Nicholas explained. "He'll kick my ass if he finds out."

"Are you kidding me?" Jason was pissed. "You have to do something. We can't just sit here waiting for them to come back and shoot us."

"I don't know who these guys are any more than you do," Nicholas said. "Looks like Daniel had a side racket going. He's dead, man. My dad won't like this."

Jason could see Rico and Felix at the far corner of the club in conversation with another man, and nodding in their direction. Fear clawed at him. "Let's hit the dance floor," he said to Nicholas.

"What?"

"Let's hit the dance floor, ask some girls to dance. I need to think."

"Nah. I'm okay. You go."

Jason left Nicholas at their table and secured a dance partner in no time. The DJ was spinning a remix of Jody Watley's "Some Kind of Lover." His dance partner was a little chatty, which didn't bode well for his ability to think and come up with a solution, but he had to if he wanted to get out of that club alive. Two thoughts occurred to him. He could ask the bartender to call them a cab and make an escape when Rico and Felix weren't watching, or he could try reasoning with them again.

Jason thanked his dance partner when the song ended and headed back to the table. To his chagrin, the two extortionists were there, talking to a terrified Nicholas.

"You're back," Felix said. "We were just asking your buddy for our money."

"We need more time," Jason said, sliding into his seat. "We're just college kids." Jason reached for his wallet, and Rico reached for his gun.

"I'm just getting my wallet," Jason said.

"Hurry up, then," an impatient Rico barked.

Jason handed his UT Austin student ID to Rico, and asked Nicolas to do the same.

Another idea occurred to Jason. It might help him—not so much Nicholas—but he was sweating, scared, and desperate to get back to campus and forget this evening ever happened. He handed Rico his Connecticut driver's license, too. Rico took the two pieces of identification and scrutinized at them.

"I'm just here for school, man," Jason said. "Connecticut is home. We're not friends with Daniel. He just came over and sat with us. Isn't that right, Nicholas?"

"Yeah, that's right."

Rico was stroking his chin again. He returned the IDs. "We'll be back." He and Felix left.

"We gotta get out of here now," Jason said.

"How? They'll see us."

"I'll ask the bartender to call us a cab. Let's separate and use the crowd to our advantage. They'll be expecting to see the two of us together. See you outside in twenty minutes."

Jason pushed through the crowd of club-goers. The cigarette smoke in the air burned his lungs, but he figured it was a small price to pay to stay alive. So far, he hadn't seen either of the two tough guys. He breathed a sigh of relief when he made it to the bar. It was a busy night so it was difficult getting the bartender's attention. He finally did and, like he predicted, the cab would be there in twenty minutes. He had to find a spot and wait out the time.

Nineteen minutes passed by and he spotted Nicholas heading towards the door. He joined him. Then out of nowhere, Felix and Rico appeared. "Going somewhere?" Rico asked.

"We just want to get some fresh air," Jason said. "It's smoky in here and I have asthma."

"How about I shoot you to send a message to Daniel?" Rico said to Nicholas.

A petrified Nicholas begged. "Please, man, I got no beef with you. My dad would be grateful if you would just let us go."

Jason elbowed Nicholas. That was a dumb idea, using his father. If these guys were from a rival drug ring, both of them could be killed on the spot.

"Don't listen to him," Jason said. "He's scared shitless and doesn't know what he's saying. Look, man, we're just two kids trying to make something of ourselves. We just had the bad luck to run into Daniel here. I hope you find him and can get your money back, but this isn't our fight."

"I still want to shoot him," Rico said.

They were some trigger-happy assholes, Jason thought.

Felix leaned in closer, staring Nicholas up and down. "Say, ain't you Sebastien Maza's kid?"

Nicholas didn't answer.

"I asked you a question, boy."

"Yes."

Rico smiled. "The boss is going to love this. Y'all are coming with us."

Jason panicked. He may have been naïve to get mixed up with Nicholas and his family, but he knew with certainty that if they left the club tonight, they would both be killed. He had to think on his feet.

"Wouldn't it be better if his father owed your boss?" he asked Rico.

"What you talking about, college boy?"

Jason took a long breath. "I'm saying if you let us go, your boss has leverage over Mr. Maza. He's going to have to play ball with your boss. You know, out of respect for letting us go."

Jason didn't know what he was saying and had no idea who Felix and Rico's boss was. He could be starting a drug war for all he knew, but that was their problem, not his.

Both men considered the offer. "Get the hell out of here," Rico said. "And, if I see either one of you wimps around here again, I won't be so understanding."

They didn't need to be told twice. Thankfully, the cab was still waiting and they told the driver to step on it. After that, Jason wrote a letter to Sebastien Maza and asked Nicholas to deliver it. He was done. For weeks afterwards, he lived in fear that Maza would send someone after him. You don't just quit a crime lord. Nicholas must have told his father that Jason saved his life, because Jason's fears were unfounded. As for Nicholas, they agreed to never speak about that night to anyone under any circumstances.

Chapter 45

W hat do you want, Nicholas?"

"Always the businessman, huh, bro? I see it served you well. Soon, you'll be *the* man, running things, taking a big company like Orphion public. You did it, man. Felicitaciones. I mean that."

"Gracias. You've kept tabs on me. But, we're square, you and I. Nothing else between us."

"You have a lot going on, the wife being in jail and all. That must be torture. I feel for you, bro."

Jason's patience was disappearing by the second. Nicholas had always been that way, doling out the fake charm and concern in spades. He should save that for his minions, it was wasted on Jason.

"You're right. I do have a lot going on, so get on with it. Why are you calling me?"

"Need your help."

"What for?"

"An investment."

"You have people on your payroll for that."

"Only you are CFO of Orphion Technologies. I would be a fool if I didn't get in on the IPO action."

"Are you serious?"

"As a slug to the chest."

Jason had entertained the idea that his past with the Mazas could come back to haunt him. However, too many years had gone by. He had been at Orphion for almost a decade. He could see now that the predatory tactics that had made Nicholas successful when he took over his father's business were still intact. Jason was vulnerable. His wife's legal troubles and ascension to the CEO role was a twofer for someone like Nicholas. It became clear to Jason that either one of those situations could cost him more than he was willing to pay.

"I can't help you, Nicholas."

"Nonsense, bro. Still so modest after all you've accomplished. I'm just an old friend asking a favor. You tell me the price per share before Orphion goes public on the New York Stock Exchange, and I'll be sure to make a substantial purchase. You can hook me up, can't you?"

"What you're asking me to do is illegal. I don't need the SEC breathing down my neck."

"There you go again, underestimating yourself. You didn't seem to care how you were making your money back in the day, did you, bro? I'm sure the Orphion Board of Directors might be interested to know how you were able to start the software company that made you a millionaire. If I recall, my father's generous salary afforded you the start-up capital you needed, didn't it?"

Jason berated himself for picking up the call. He resisted the urge to burst out laughing. He wouldn't come apart at the seams with this latest threat, compliments of Nicholas. Acquiring shareholder status as a front for money laundering is exactly the type of thing Nicholas would do. Jason was just surprised that Nicholas decided to contact him at all.

"We've all made mistakes, Nicholas. All we can do is try to make up for them. I know I have. *Everyone* is vulnerable, susceptible to life's whims. You never know when you may get knocked off your ass."

"I'll be seeing you, bro."

Jason threw his phone against the entertainment system with such force that it ricocheted off the unit and barely missed him. It landed on the floor behind the couch. It was a childish act but he needed to release the tension. He stood up. It was hot, so he removed his sweater, tossed it on the couch, then unbuttoned his dress shirt and rolled up the sleeves. His head turned sharply when he heard a knock at the door and the knob turning shortly afterwards without an invitation to enter. It must be one of the kids. Before he could call out, Vivian entered the study.

"I thought I would check in on you. Do you need anything?" She locked the door behind her and approached the sofa. Her eyes rested on his exposed chest and lingered, all the way down to his waist and his crotch. Something flared in her eyes and burned brightly. Then like a shooting star, disappeared as quickly as it appeared. Jason buttoned up his shirt.

"I'm fine, Vivian. What about you?"

She took a seat on the sofa. "I went to see Shelby. I had to ambush her. It's not good, Jason."

He paced with his hands in his pocket. "I know."

"She deflected all my questions, kept telling me to look out for you and the kids and that would make her happy. She won't last in there."

Vivian shook her head, confused. "And, I don't understand why she passed on bail. She's scared, Jason. Something other than a possible murder conviction hanging over her head has her twisted up in knots. You have to find out what it is and bring her home."

Jason turned to face Vivian. "I'm trying. And, I know she's hiding something, something that could crack this case wide open."

"She said that?"

"No. She's my wife. She didn't need to tell me that."

"She needs you. The kids need you. You're stressed out and losing weight."

"I'm good." He gave her a faint smile.

"I need you, too, Jason. I need my friend to be himself again. I hate what this is doing to you. Not to mention, what it's doing to your career. I know you've thought about that."

"I have. As much as I want to, I can't control what happens next. Everyone has been supportive, the board of directors too but I don't know how long their patience will last."

"What does Shelby say?"

"I can't burden her with that right now. Although I know what she would say. 'Give them hell if they try to mess with you.'"

"Will you? If they try to mess with you?"

"I don't have the energy to speculate right now."

Vivian signaled him to join her on the sofa. "What is it, Jason? You can talk to me and it goes no further than this study. We used to be able to talk, share our problems. I promised Shelby I'd look out for you."

"I'm not sure what you mean. Don't I have enough on my plate already?"

"You're way past too much on your plate. The damn plate is overflowing and threatening to crash."

He was amused. Vivian was always a straight shooter, ever since they met at a party at the University of North Carolina, Chapel Hill, her alma mater, back in the early nineties. She was a bit of a wild child back then and he appreciated her candor and free-spirited attitude about life. One drunken night, he told her about his past with Nicholas Maza and his father. They ended up having sex and would hook up whenever they could, which wasn't too often. They were non-committal, content to have a good time simply because they liked each other as people, no strings attached. Then Vivian introduced him to Shelby one weekend when he was in North Carolina, and he was smitten.

Vivian had made fun of him then. "You like her, don't you? Maybe if you're nice to me I might convince her to give you a chance. She's a bit of a nerd, though. And seriously uptight."

"You would put in a good word for me?"

"Sure, why not. It's not like she's seeing anyone. Besides, you're not really my type. We were just having fun. Both you and Shelby are the getting married and settling down type. I like my freedom and I'm too selfish to be anybody's mother."

After that, he and Shelby got close. And that's when Jason and Vivian made the pact: Shelby would never know they had a sexual history.

"Nicholas Maza called me just before you walked in."

"What?" The shock on her face was thick enough to be scraped off with a knife.

"What did he want after all these years?"

"He wants to purchase shares in Orphion. Another money laundering scheme."

"Shit. Why couldn't he just stay out of sight and out of mind? Does he think you're going to break the law for him?"

"Nicholas thinks everyone's here to do his bidding. It's part of his charm."

"I hope you told him where to park it."

"I did, but with Nicholas, you never know."

Vivian sighed loudly. She was about to cry.

"We'll get through this," he said, clasping her hand in his. "No tears. Shelby will have none of it."

"Sorry, I can't help it. When will this end?"

He wondered the same thing. For now, the answers were elusive.

Chapter 46

I reach for the phone in slow motion. The beating of my heart feels like angry waves pounding an unsuspecting shoreline. It's him. He's been calling intermittently, pretending to be my lawyer, Alan Rose, I'm sure.

"Hello, Princess."

I detest that moniker coming from his lips. It makes a mockery of what Alessandro felt for me. It reminds me I had a hand in his death. "What do you want?"

"That is no way to speak to a friend, now, is it?"

Silence.

"Have I upset you?"

I want him to get tired of this game and leave me alone. I know he calls to taunt me, to get inside my head, to make me feel desperate and powerless.

"No. You haven't upset me."

"You miss him. Alessandro."

"You know nothing about what I think or how I feel."

"I know more than you think."

"Then you should know how this ends."

"You lose," he says with bravado. "The way it should be."

"That's where you're wrong. This game is just getting started. You think you're so clever. You're not. You're an errand boy taking orders from someone much smarter. The true brains behind this operation will get rid of you when you're no longer useful. Tick, tock, friend."

His erratic breathing comes down the line. I imagine his nostrils flared, eyes blazing with hatred.

"You forget who you're talking to. You forget I can eliminate your family in a heartbeat. I'm the one in control, not you. Not anyone else."

He was yelling now, unsure of himself, a crack in the armor.

"Give your boss a message for me. I accept the challenge. Game on."

As I schlep back to my cell, two things occur to me: this unraveling of my life has been meticulously planned for some time, and I've heard that voice before.

I must get away from him. I run down the long corridor on the fifth floor of GeneMedicine's Cambridge office. He's hot on my heels and he tugs at my coat. I manage to escape and keep running. I push hard against the door that leads to the stairs. I must make it to the ground floor, to the garage. The back stairs are dimly lit, and I must be careful not to trip. I run as fast as my legs can take me. He's just a breath away from catching me. I hold on to the metal banister as I take step after step. The stairs are never ending, the ground floor so far away. The clacking of my heels on the concrete steps spurs me on, though I can hear his footsteps, gaining on me, louder, heavier, closer.

I keep running. I'm getting tired and my lungs begin to burn. I gasp for air and feel my legs about to buckle but fear pushes me to my limit. Just a few more steps. Just when I'm about to collapse, the door that leads to the garage appears and I grab on to it like a thirsty man who finds water in the desert. I turn the silver metal handle and dash into the parking garage. But I can't find my car. There are rows and rows of red cars and mine is nowhere to be seen. I dart between the rows of cars in the hope of finding mine. I no longer hear my pursuer and I sag with relief as I lean up against one of the cars. I close my eyes and take a second to collect my bearings, perhaps catch a second wind that will give me the energy to escape unharmed. When I open my eyes, I scream. Alessandro is standing directly in front of me.

"Why are you running from me, Princess?"

I'm incapable of speech. His hair is long and unkempt. His usually vibrant blue eyes are pale and bulging from their sockets.

My body is chilled to the bone. I try to get out the words in between terrified breaths. "I thought…I'm not…What are you doing here?"

"I came to see you. What are you doing about it?" He was angry, accusing.

"I don't know. He said he would kill my kids if I didn't do what he wanted, if I didn't go to jail."

"Put your scientist brain on hold. This is not logical. It doesn't make sense. Who hates you? Who secretly envies you? Don't have this all be in vain, Princess."

"I'm sorry, Alessandro. I'm so sorry." I begin to sob. I crumple to the ground. And when I finally look up again to ask him to forgive me, he's gone.

I wake up from the nightmare, terrified. My hands are clammy and shaking. I must find his killer and free us both.

Chapter 47

My cellmate went off to the prison library, and I'm grateful to be alone. I sit on the lower bunk and remove the card from inside the envelope.

It's a blue holiday card with gold lettering and snowflakes on the front. Inside shouts out *Season's Greetings* and there are multiple notes and signatures all over. It's from my staff at work. In that moment, I clutch this piece of my former life and shut my eyes tight. It's an unexpected surprise and gives me much needed courage to renew my vow to catch the son of a bitch who's doing this to me. There are people outside of my family who believe in my innocence.

I read each note and signature, some multiple times. "Next year will be better," Chris Snowden, my research assistant says.

"I know this holiday sucks. We expect you at next year's office Christmas party." Greg Larson, a Bioinformatics Specialist.

"Still the best boss ever, Merry Christmas." My administrative Assistant Inez Diaz.

"You promised to take me to the conference. Will hold you to it." My postdoctoral fellow, Emma Chan. I read her note two more times. I did promise to take her to a Genomics and Bioinformatics

Conference in Salzburg, Austria. Emma is bright and will one day run her own research team.

I scan the contents of the card one more time. As I'm about to close it, I have a flash of memory. The Fairmont Hotel back in October. I was attending a Bioinformatics conference with Emma.

"I need to talk to you about something," Emma said.

"Oh. We can discuss it at lunch."

"That's okay. I'd rather talk to you without a crowd."

"Is everything okay?"

"Yes."

My antenna was on high alert. What could Emma possibly have to tell me that she needed my undivided attention? We got along great but she was guarded about her personal life.

"Ok. What is it?"

She nodded towards seating near the reception area and I followed. After we sat down, I waited for her to speak.

"I ran into someone at a networking event a couple of weeks ago and they were asking about you. I didn't make a big deal about it at the time. He knew so much about you so I thought you were friends. Then I Googled him."

"Who?"

"Dr. Mehmet Koczak."

I was startled by the revelation. As far as I knew, Koczak had gone back to the Middle East. "What did he want?"

"He asked if you were still at GeneMedicine and talked about how much he admired your work."

"I suspect he's trying to make a comeback and rebuild his reputation. I'm sure you got all the gory details about what happened from your Google search?"

"I did. Was he really selling proprietary data for a fee?"

"Unfortunately, yes. Strange that he would lead you to believe we were friends, though."

"I take it you weren't?"

"No. He wasn't a fan when I joined GeneMedicine, and I didn't have the stomach for his particular brand of sexism. We were constantly at each other's throats."

"So you don't hate him?"

"Hate? No. I wish him well and hope he doesn't do anything that dumb again. I don't waste emotions worrying about it."

"Well, I just wanted you to know."

The answer was right there all along, the accent, the formal speech, personal details about me. Mehmet Koczak has been planning to destroy me all along as payback for ruining his life.

"I checked out Mehmet Koczak like you asked. You're not going to like this."

Jason was meeting with Tom Bilko in his study. The kids were at school and Vivian had returned to Chicago to handle some business. Rayne was out shopping, so the men had the house to themselves.

"What did you find out?"

Tom handed Jason what appeared to be a dossier. He took a few minutes to read through quickly.

"This can't be right."

"I'm afraid it is," Tom said, as he peeked over Jason's shoulder. "Koczak re-entered the U.S. from Turkey under a different name by way of Canada. That's why we couldn't find out anything when we first started digging. We assumed he would come back to the States using the name we knew him by. He came back two years ago. Got a job as an instructor at a community college and lives in Cambridge."

"He could be the guy? Are you telling me this nightmare could be over soon?"

Jason was elated. Finally, the break that could restore Shelby's freedom and her good name.

"I spoke to Emma Chan," Tom said. He left Jason's side, opting for the couch instead. "Koczak gave her his new alias, but she recognized his face. She confirmed her conversation with Shelby. I think the guy was putting his revenge scheme in place and was using Emma to get information. Good thing she was smart enough to mention it."

"We need proof," Jason said.

"Working on it."

"Everything smooth with the kids this week?"

"Yes. My guys have nothing unusual to report. Fingers and toes crossed that Koczak is our guy so Mrs. Cooper can come home to you and the kids."

"That would be wonderful, Tom. Anything else?"

"You might be interested to know that your wife's assistant made a call to Alessandro Rossi the day he was killed."

Chapter 48

H er humiliation was too much and she just couldn't face him. After Miles just about ruined her entire high school existence by blurting out her secret feelings for Ty during that doomed dinner, Abbie avoided him like a popular senior avoided being seen with an uncool freshman. Apparently, he was embarrassed, too, because he didn't text her like he usually did. He wasn't in the dining hall having lunch, and she hadn't seen him in a few days.

"Should we tell her?" Anastasia asked as they sat in their usual lunchtime spot in the dining hall.

"Tell me what?" Abbie had tuned out her friends, content to pick at her food and drown in an ever-expanding pool of jealousy and misery.

The girls looked at each other. A decision was made silently between them. It was going to be Frances who would deliver whatever news they wanted to tell Abbie.

"Look, Abbie, it sucks what your brother did. Maybe it's for the best."

"Really? How is that? What twisted logic do you have to explain the fact that my life is over? I may as well show up to school wearing a ginormous paper bag over my head."

"You don't have to. I know you're hurting right now but the best way to get over Ty is to start dating someone who actually is in love with you and not afraid to show it."

"Frances is right," Callie said. "It's time to move on, Abbie. And, I think what we have to say will help you do that."

Didn't they understand? Nothing and no one was going to help her move on. She would love Ty forever and she had to accept that he would never feel the same way about her. She was sure the flashing neon "Loser" sign on her forehead was growing by the minute.

"I'm not interested in moving on to anyone else. This is exactly why I didn't want him to know how I felt. It would get in the way of our friendship. Oh my God, I miss my mom so much. She would know what to do."

The sobs escaped her, a small whimper at first and then a full-blown, body-racking ugly cry, right there, on the spot. Abbie put her head down on the table, not caring if her hair ended up in her food.

She felt someone stroking her arm and another her hair. She guessed her girls were rallying.

"It's okay, Abbie. It won't hurt like this forever."

It was Callie, the nurturer.

"I'm going to punch Ty in the face the next time I see him," Frances promised. "He asked Kerri Wheeler to the Platinum Ball. We are so over him."

If Frances was trying to make her feel better, it had the opposite effect. Fresh waves of pain and misery washed over Abbie in enough quantities to drown an elephant. She couldn't recall a time in her life she was so sad, not even when Grandpa Erasmus died. Curious stares from fellow students were sent their way.

"What are you all looking at?" Frances yelled.

"You had to tell her that now?" Anastasia asked Frances.

"It's better to rip the Band-Aid off than have her die a slow, painful death before our eyes," Frances countered. "This way she can start planning her revenge, and I know just where to start."

Abbie lifted her head and was sure she looked as hideous as she felt. Callie handed her a napkin. She proceeded to wipe her tear-stained face then blow her nose, which, by the looks she was getting from her friends, was gross.

"Eww. We need to get you to the ladies' room. Your eyes are redder than a hot chili pepper," Frances said.

Before the girls could head for the bathroom, someone approached their table.

"Are you all right, Abigail?"

It was Mr. Newman, one of the guidance counselors. Most of the girls at Saint Matthews thought he was the hottest guy in the main office and were always drooling over him. It also helped that he was probably one hundred years younger than the other teachers and administrators. He was polite and considerate, a little nerdy, but good with students whom he preferred call him Lee. Abbie never did. She raked her fingers through her hair and hoped it didn't look too messy.

"I'm fine, Mr. Newman. Thanks for asking."

"Good. Can you come by and see me in my office soon?"

"Sure."

The Rainbow Posse made it to the ladies' room and got to work putting Abbie back together again.

"So embarrassing. Now everyone is going to know I lost it at lunch."

"You're going through a lot, Abbie," Anastasia said. "It's okay to lose it."

Callie dug in her purse for a hairbrush while Abbie splashed cold water on her face. After she dried off with some paper towels, Frances handed her some lip gloss and took the opportunity to dispense beauty advice.

"This is why you need to wear makeup. You could walk out of here flawless, as if nothing happened. A little powder for your face would do wonders. This natural look is okay but soon, you'll need to glam up. You don't want guys thinking you're a little girl, do you?"

"What are you talking about?" Abbie asked, agitated.

Callie piped in. "I can brush your hair if you want me to."

"Thanks, I can do it myself." Abbie took the brush from her friend.

214

"Frances, what are you talking about?" Abbie asked, brushing her hair.

"Don't freak out," Frances said, backing away from Abbie. "I'm just saying that maybe Ty thinks you're too young or something. He and Kerri are both seniors, you're a sophomore, two grades behind."

"Frances, that's insensitive," Callie said.

Frances inched her way back to face Abbie. "I hate to see you like this. Ty's graduating in the spring. You can't follow him to college. Once he's there, he's going to be dealing with college girls. College girls who are willing to give it up."

Abbie hadn't thought about that. As much as she hated Frances for bringing it up, she made a point Abbie had never considered. Maybe Ty still saw her as a little girl. She just thought, naively, that their close bond would blossom into something, and he would see how good they were for each other. Okay, so she had never given him any indication that she was interested in him that way. She wasn't the kind of girl to openly flirt with a guy or flaunt her body to get his attention, so she couldn't expect Ty to be a mind reader.

"Oh my gosh, do you think Kerri is giving him the goods?" Abbie asked.

"Hell to the yes," Callie said.

Frances, Anastasia, and Abbie looked at her like she was suffering from a brain abnormality. "That's it. I'm going to find that urban dictionary and I'm burning it," Abbie promised.

"Come on. Everyone says it these days," she said defensively to Abbie, who went back to her favorite subject.

"When he was at my house, he claimed they were just friends and it was nothing serious. He also said they kissed."

"Look, why are we wasting energy talking about Ty? He's old news as far as I'm concerned," Frances said scornfully. "We have more important issues at hand."

"Like what?" Abbie asked. She finished up with her hair and handed Callie the brush back.

"Like the fact that my sources tell me Ajani Oni wants to ask you to the Platinum Ball."

All the girls except Abbie screamed in unison.

"Ooh, he's cute and a senior," Anastasia said. "That will show Ty."

"And, he's been crushing on you all year," Callie confirmed.

Abbie wasn't sure how she felt about that. It would be nice to show Ty that he wasn't the only hot guy around, and she could go to the dance on the arm of a senior. But the whole thing reeked of desperation to her. Besides, Ajani was a good guy and she didn't want to use him.

"Ajani is all of those things, but I don't want Ty thinking I'm just doing it to get back at him. If Ajani asks and I accept, it's because I want to go with him."

"It's settled then," Frances declared, reapplying her lip gloss.

"I haven't been asked yet."

"Minor details. We have to start deciding what kind of dress you're going to wear. We can come to your house and start going through the fashion magazines to get ideas. Then we should hit the Natick Collection and the Copley Mall. "

"Hire a stylist for your hair and makeup," Callie said.

"Hold on," Abbie said, putting up her hands. "We don't know anything for sure. We don't even know if Frances heard correctly. She did get the information secondhand. Until Ajani asks me himself, there's nothing to discuss."

A tiny little part of her was coming alive about the idea of going to the dance with a smart, hot guy who was totally into her. She just hoped it wouldn't backfire.

Chapter 49

I was surprised to get your call."

"Why is that?"

"Things ended on a sour note last session. You didn't want me as your psychiatrist anymore."

"I changed my mind."

"Oh?"

Mia figured she should have another session with Dr. Singer. What would be the point of starting all over again with another shrink? It was a waste and all the work she put into researching Singer would be for nothing. She had to find a way to keep it cool whenever they were in session. The weather today wasn't helping her mood. Rain. Wet snow. A watery mess, and she almost had an accident on Route 85 on her way here.

"It's obvious I need help. I can recognize when that's the case."

Singer crossed his legs. They both sat in their usual spot. "I'm proud of you for coming to that conclusion. It's not always an easy thing to ask for help."

"Yeah…well…what choice do I have?"

"Have you checked out some of the methods we discussed

last session?"

"I started up with yoga again. It helps to calm me down but sleep is still an issue, and the old woman..." her voice trailed off.

"She still appears?"

"Yes. It's getting to be a real drag. I'm sick of hearing what a saint Shelby Cooper is. If the old woman would just get the hell out of my head and stay out, I think this sleep thing could work out."

Singer contemplated her statement for a moment. "Can you pinpoint exactly when the old woman started appearing and what was happening in your life at that time?"

Mia looked straight ahead. She wasn't about to divulge that. It was none of his business, anyway.

"Just before I started seeing you."

"Did it get worse when the Cooper case hit the media?"

"What are you asking me, Dr. Singer?"

"I'm trying to pinpoint your triggers. We've spent a lot of time in your sessions talking about Shelby Cooper."

Mia could feel her blood boiling, her hatred of Shelby Cooper threatening to spill out in big gobs. "She's a liar, a deceptive woman who got where she is by manipulating people into believing she's something she's not. She has brought a lot of pain to innocent people. She's a heartless witch. Does it surprise you that somebody like that is capable of murder? Maybe the guy found out her secrets and threatened to tell. She offed him to silence him."

"The police don't yet have a motive. How did you come by this theory?"

"It just makes sense," Mia said, her confidence growing by the minute.

"Do you know something about this case?"

She sat up straight. "Why would you ask me that?"

"It's just a question. I want to make sure you're not compromising your treatment by getting too caught up in this case."

"Thanks for the concern, but I'm fine."

"Do you have any hobbies?"

Watching Shelby Cooper rot in a jail cell was Mia's new favorite hobby but she wasn't about to divulge that to Singer. And leaking evidence to the cops? She liked that even better.

Don't need a hobby."

Mia was only half listening the rest of the session. The highlight for her was the fact that Dr. Singer finally decided to write her a prescription sleep aid. When it was over, she couldn't wait to get out of there.

She was about to pull out of the driveway when she realized she forgot the prescription. She got out of the car and went down the steps that led to Dr. Singer's basement office. She opened the door. Dr. Singer didn't hear her. His back was to her. Her plan was just to quietly pick up the prescription off the desk, wave it to him so he understood why she came back, and quietly exit. As she got closer, she heard him clearly. He was in the middle of a conversation that made her fume. He was about to feel her wrath.

"Yes, Mia Lansing. What do you think of the notes I sent over? Aha. Yep. I came to the same conclusion. She could be dangerous. Absolutely. What about the Cooper case? Professional ethics definitely come into play. No doubt in my mind she knows something about it. I realized that this afternoon. The authorities will have to get involved. Yep. Well, thanks for the consult, Aaron."

Singer turned around, stunned to discover her presence. With lightning speed, Mia picked up the letter opener on top of the desk drawer and stabbed Dr. Singer deep in the neck. Blood spouted and he dropped to his knees, his eyes wide with shock. She grabbed the prescription and was about to run but she had to make sure he couldn't go running off at the mouth. She felt for a pulse after he hit the floor. Nothing. She knocked over a few objects, ransacked the place as much as she could, then got the hell out of there before trouble came looking for her.

Chapter 50

A robbery gone wrong was what the news reports were saying. Good. It meant no one would become suspicious. She was safe. The woman who called herself Mia had stayed up all night. Her only sustenance was a bag of potato chips and water. She didn't feel in the least bit guilty about Dr. Singer. He was about to rat her out to the cops. He'd left her no choice.

She needed to accelerate her timetable. Everything had gone according to plan so far but Singer was a complication she didn't anticipate. Was she slipping? Losing her edge? That nervous idiot she hired to help her carry out her plan said Abbie wasn't afraid of him. Her mother being in jail made her brazen. Mia would have to up the ante herself. Make the little brat want to wet her pants.

She pulled up a chair to her makeshift workstation in the living room and went through her tools. It was time to ratchet up the pain on Shelby Cooper. This time, being behind bars would look like a dream come true. The new girl they hired offered endless possibilities as well. She was a perfect backup plan if the Coopers didn't cooperate. Rayne Revington would be the collateral damage that would let them know they were dealing with a pro.

You're getting desperate now, aren't you? Desperate people make mistakes. That's how they're caught.

"Shut up, old woman. Leave me alone!" Mia pounded her head with her fists, shaking her head in rapid motion from left to right.

You can't get rid of me that easy.

The old woman took a seat on the sofa. Her hair was pulled back in a bun and she was wearing white. Always wearing white.

"Don't make me shoot you."

Go ahead. You'll be wasting your time. How long do you think you can keep this up?

"Mind you own business. I'm warning you. Stay out of my business."

How could you? How could you do this to her?

"She's a selfish witch. A liar who destroys everything she touches. She's gotten away with too much for too long. "

You don't know what you're talking about. You never did.

"Well, now, she's paying for her crimes, isn't she? She's going to rot in that jail cell."

You're such a stupid girl.

"Shut up! Shut up. I'm not stupid. I know exactly what I'm doing," Mia yelled.

However, the old woman had disappeared.

Chapter 51

Thank you for coming in, Abigail. I'm glad you did."

"You can call me Abbie. Everyone else does. What's this about, Mr. Newman?"

They were sitting in Lee Newman's small office off the central hallway of the main school building. The pale yellow walls gave the space a cheery feeling. There were papers in a neat stack on the left side of the desk and a personal printer. The computer sat on another small desk off to his left and behind him was a large file cabinet. A bunch of diplomas and awards lined the walls, as well as a Saint. Matthews flag, a calendar, and a bulletin board with several photos of recent Saint. Matthews's alumni.

Mr. Newman was a neat freak like her, Abbie observed. Everything was in its rightful place. He sat behind the desk, looking all concerned like the world was ending. He was intense like that. He definitely needed to lighten up. He was probably in his late twenties or early thirties, Abbie guessed. Today he was wearing a dark sweater with a dress shirt and tie underneath.

"I wanted to make sure you're okay and that other students aren't giving you a hard time. You can talk to me and it will go no further than this office. You have people who care about you among the administration and staff."

"Thanks, Mr. Newman. You don't need to worry about me, though. My mother will come home soon. I know it."

"That's a great attitude to have."

"There's no other attitude to have. She will come home," Abbie insisted.

She could feel her lips trembling but she refused to break down in front of Mr. Newman like she did at lunch the other day. What was wrong with her? If Ty hadn't tossed their friendship away, maybe she wouldn't be such a mess. She could focus all her energies on helping her dad stay strong. Instead, she felt like crying the minute anyone mentioned Ty or her mother. She had to put a stop to this. Her parents raised her to face life head-on. Her mom would be so disappointed in her, crying over a stupid boy.

"It's all right, Abbie. You can cry if you want to, it's perfectly okay."

"I'm not a crybaby, Mr. Newman. I'm just dealing with something else. It's stupid, really, but I'll handle it."

"Something other than your mother's situation?"

"Yes."

"Care to talk about it? I'm a good listener."

"That's okay, I'm good."

He leaned forward. "Abbie, you're only fifteen. You're not supposed to have all the answers. You're not supposed to understand all that you're feeling or why certain things happen. It's okay to be angry because you feel helpless, like you don't understand why things are unfolding the way they are."

That's exactly how she felt. Nothing made sense anymore. Her life was spinning out of control, and she didn't know how to put everything back in order. Maybe Mr. Newman did understand.

"Coopers don't whine about their problems," she informed him. "They wrestle with each problem until it's solved. Kind of like a math equation."

He smiled. And when he did, he didn't seem that much older than she was. She didn't notice before that he had dimples, the kind that made her want to poke her fingers in them to see how deep they would go. He should smile more often. His brown eyes were big and bright, like stars that light up the night sky.

"What's so funny?"

"You're brave, Abbie, and I respect that. Remember, all of us on staff are committed to keeping you on track. If anything changes, I want to know about it."

"Why? There are over four hundred kids at this school. Why so much attention on little old me?"

She was being a brat, but she didn't want anyone treating her like a charity case.

"I would do the same for anyone in your situation. I also think that you're an exemplary student and a wonderful young lady. Your teachers all say great things about you."

"I'm doing just fine. I have to. Otherwise my dad will tell my mom and they'll make a big deal about it. The last thing I need is them getting all over me about my grades."

"You're lucky to have parents who care so much. It's a gift, Abbie."

Mr. Newman sounded like he had frogs in his throat when he made that statement.

"I'm sure you had awesome parents, too. Look how well you turned out."

"Listen, I'm glad we got a chance to talk and now I feel better knowing that you're doing ok. Don't hesitate to call me or come by any time," he said, handing her one of his business cards.

Chapter 52

Jason pulled into the parking lot at Shoppers World in Framingham. It was pouring rain and the large puddles of melting snow from the previous storm just added to the slushy mess. He popped his umbrella after he exited the car and rushed into Starbucks for the meeting he hoped would provide him with additional facts to back up Shelby's innocence.

He settled into a seat and waited. It was a Wednesday afternoon and a few patrons were sprinkled throughout the café, many of them taking advantage of the free Wi-Fi. Inez Diaz would arrive any minute. He'd met Shelby's Administrative Assistant on a couple of occasions during GeneMedicine's holiday party or company picnic, he couldn't remember which.

Inez appeared looking like a drowned rat, which did nothing to quell her beauty. Her dark hair was plastered to her scalp, and her beige coat had patches of rain splattered all over. Jason rose and offered to take her coat.

"Thanks for coming. Can I get you a latte or a scone, anything?"

"No, Mr. Cooper, I don't need anything, but I was surprised to get your call. After the police searched Dr. Cooper's office and interviewed everybody, I didn't think there'd be anything left to ask."

"There's always something, Inez. How are they treating you at GeneMedicine? Anybody giving you a hard time?"

"Is that your way of asking if I still have my job?"

Jason smiled. "You got me."

"Don't worry about me, Mr. Cooper. I'll be fine. I still have my job. I support a couple of the more senior researchers, like I did for Dr. Cooper. It's not the same as working for her, though. She was more than a boss. I consider her my friend."

"And, she you. I'm glad you're doing okay. If anything changes, if you need anything at all, please pick up the phone. Promise me you will."

"I promise."

"Now, do you mind telling me why you called Alessandro Rossi just before he was murdered?"

She retreated into her seat as if she'd just been slapped, her face puzzled. "I don't know what you're talking about."

He didn't mean to come off accusatory but his wife's freedom hung in the balance.

"I have it from a trusted source that a call was placed from your office to Alessandro Rossi on the very day he was killed."

Inez stared at Jason like he'd suddenly sprouted horns. "Then your source is wrong. I'm sorry, Mr. Cooper, but I never heard of Alessandro Rossi until the news broke that he was killed and Dr. Cooper was accused of doing it."

Jason berated himself inwardly for grasping at straws. He had to try. Then a thought occurred to him. "What if someone wanted him to think you were calling on Shelby's behalf?"

"Why would they do that?"

"Because they were setting him up to be killed."

Inez looked like she could freeze to death. "How about I get you a hot drink?" Jason offered.

"Yes, please."

Jason returned to the table with medium sized mocha lattes for them both. She grabbed hers with trembling hands and tried to take a sip.

"I don't understand how someone could make it look like I made that call," Inez said.

"Your office number could have been cloned so Alessandro Rossi would pick up."

"But, Dr. Cooper only saw him for Physical Therapy, and that's been over for many months now. Wait a minute," Inez said, tapping her latte container. "I almost forgot. He was at GeneMedicine recently."

This news jolted Jason. "When was this?" he asked as casually as he could.

"A couple of days before the murder. I was heading out to grab some lunch and I saw Dr. Cooper with a man who looked like Mr. Rossi. They were leaving a meeting."

"Are you sure?"

"Yes. I didn't think anything of it at the time. I thought it was a business meeting she forgot to mention. It wasn't on her calendar. He seemed depressed. He looked up at me briefly. I remember his deep blue eyes. His hair was on the long side. When the news broke, I checked the visitor's log. I wanted to see if it was the same guy but when I checked the log, the name I found was a Sam Weston."

"An alias."

"Why would she put an alias instead of his real name?"

Jason didn't answer. It occurred to him that Shelby was more involved in Alessandro Rossi's life than she let on.

He thanked Inez for her time and reiterated his offer of help anytime she needed it. His wife had a lot of explaining to do.

PART V:

DEAD GIRL WALKING

Chapter 53

A visit to the student lounge was just what Abbie needed. An in-between-classes hub of relaxation and socialization, the lounge was a blend of leather sofas, multi-colored armchairs, bright open space and large bay windows.

Abbie was deep in conversation with Ajani Oni, who sat across from her, when the ringtone for her text messages went off. He had officially asked her to be his date for the Platinum Ball, showing up at her house and asking her father's permission. Way old-fashioned, but her dad appreciated the gesture.

"Excuse me, Ajani. I need to check my phone. It could be my dad or Aunt Vivian."

"Sure. Go right ahead." Ajani's keen eyes were trained on her as she took the phone from her bag and read the message.

Ty: *I'm sorry.*

A burning sensation formed in the back of her throat. She stared at the words as if they would tell her how to respond. When they didn't, she returned the phone to her bag.

"Bad news?" Ajani asked.

"Not exactly."

"I'm not stupid, Abigail. I'm guessing it was Ty who texted

you."

Her guilty countenance was all the confirmation he needed. She didn't want Ajani to think she was one of those girls who got off on having guys fight over her.

"You're right. It was Ty. How did you know?"

"The two of you are close. I don't want to get in the middle of it if there's something going on. If you're not sure about going to the ball with me, I'll understand."

"You don't need to understand anything. I'm happy that you asked me and I look forward to it. "

"Are you sure?"

"Yes."

He was satisfied with her answer. "In that case, I can't wait to brag to my friends that I will have the most gorgeous girl at Saint. Matthews as my date to the ball. And, my mom will be so pleased."

"What? You told your mother about me?"

"Of course. I told her about you from the moment I first saw you."

"Oh."

Ajani walked over and planted a kiss on her cheek. "I'll see you later."

He walked out of the lounge and nodded in acknowledgement of Ty, who just walked in.

Ty waved to a few classmates. Abbie went back to the couch and pretended to be engrossed in her German textbook.

A bemused Ty took the seat next to her. "So, that's why you didn't reply to my text message. You were too busy sucking face with Ajani."

Abbie didn't answer. She grabbed a hot pink highlighter from her bag, pulled off the cap, which she kept in her mouth, and began highlighting random paragraphs for which she already knew the English translation. She was afraid her voice would betray her tumultuous feelings if she spoke. Unfortunately, Ty was built to torture her because he looked even hotter than the last time she saw him. He was dressed in a black fitted turtleneck sweater, a gray puffer vest and a scarf. His muscles bulged through the stretch material of the sweater.

"I'm not going anywhere, Cooper," he announced. "You have

to talk to me."

Silence.

Ty reached over and removed the highlighter cap from her mouth. She didn't protest.

She shrugged her shoulders in resignation and in a voice she barely recognized as her own, she asked, "What do you want me to say, Tyler?"

"Tyler?" he asked, frowning, as if the use of his full name was offensive to him. "So that's how it is?"

"I'm really good at taking hints," Abbie said.

"What is that supposed to mean?"

How dare he sit there and pretend he didn't know what he'd done? After Miles dropped the bombshell, he went off the grid for days, not so much as a text or phone call to see if she was still alive. First, he denied and serious interest in Kerri which turned out to be a lie, and then he just abandoned her at that dinner, didn't come to her defense or play it off as a joke or anything.

"You lied. You wrecked our friendship."

His eyes flashed with anger. "You're flipping out, Cooper. How did I wreck our friendship?"

Abbie lowered her voice to a whisper. "Don't make me out to be the one who's losing it. It's insulting."

"I didn't mean it like that. Something is obviously bothering you. Tell me what I did and I'll fix it. I've been trying to, but you wouldn't answer any of my texts."

"You sent me *a* text a few minutes ago saying you were sorry and then you just showed up here."

"Um…I sent you like twenty text messages after that dinner at your house. You couldn't be bothered to answer even one. That was seriously messed up, Cooper, just plain rude. I expected better from you."

It was her turn to be indignant. "I didn't get any text messages from you. Maybe you got me confused with Kerri."

"That was bitchy," he snapped. "You're not behaving like yourself. And, as long as I live, I could never get you confused with any other girl."

Abbie rolled her eyes at him. Why would he claim he sent her text messages, when she hadn't received any of them? What did he hope to gain by lying, especially since lying to her wasn't one of the things he did? It didn't make any sense.

Then it dawned on her, a swift kick to the head. During one of her temper tantrums and "I hate Ty" diatribes, she'd blocked him from her phone so she couldn't receive messages from him and she forgot to reverse the block. So, it was her own stupid fault that she didn't get his messages and, of course, she had to go thinking the worst, even had her girlfriends dogging him out, too. She screwed up. But, she wasn't about to fess up.

"It's obvious that I didn't get your messages. I don't know what happened. Maybe my phone is screwy. I shouldn't have jumped to conclusions. So, why don't you just tell me what you said in those messages?"

"I will. But, not here."

They met at their usual place, the chapel. Abbie stood with arms folded, pacing up and down the aisle.

"Well?"

Ty floundered, searching for the right words. Abbie figured her pacing was getting on his nerves and making him more nervous than he appeared.

"Look, Cooper, I admit it was a little weird when your brother said what he said. You didn't deny it but I could tell you were so upset that you wanted to get out of there and never speak to me again."

"Forget what my brother said. Forget everything about that night. It was just my kid brother trying to act grown up. He thinks you're cool and we should date. That's all."

She felt like a total Judas for throwing her little brother under the bus. She couldn't tell Ty the truth, though. Not now. Maybe never.

"What about the notebook?" he asked.

"What notebook?"

"Miles said you would write my name in your notebook. What's that about?"

"Oh…no big deal. Sometimes I write my to-do list in my notebook instead of my phone. I must have written your name to remind me to ask you something."

That scared her, how the lie just rolled off her tongue with ease.

"And, that's it?"

"Yeah."

He came to stand directly in front of her. His eyes were mesmerizing, like a swirling current that was trying to pull her under. "I'm not clueless, you know."

"What do you mean?"

"Cooper, I've never met a girl like you before. You really get me. I like that we can sit together and say nothing at all and it will be just fine. You don't need to be running your mouth all the time. I like that you always look fantastic yet you're not obsessed with clothes and makeup, or trying to be sexy. I like that you're not full of drama or desperate for attention."

"Where are you going with this?" She knew she wouldn't like the answer.

"I'm saying I don't want you to change. You're my safe place. I hope you feel the same way about me. I don't want to screw things up between us."

Abbie wished the ground would open up and swallow her. If she was holding out any hope that they would end up together, that he would be her first kiss, her first time, he just took a machete to her dreams. It hurt to breathe. The pain was like a giant rock pressing down on her lungs. Up until this point in her life, everything had gone her way. She didn't know what it was like to want something and not have it. Now, how was she supposed to go on being his friend while she was dying inside?

"Sure thing, Ty," she said, her voice wobbling. "I don't want things to get complicated, either. But, next time you feel like flirting with me, don't."

"What do you mean?"

She turned around. "You were flirting with me when we were in my room. Before we went downstairs to dinner and my brother opened his mouth. You almost kissed me. And what was that crack about finding a wife who would give you lots of babies?"

"Oh," he said guiltily.

"That's all you can say?" She looked at him with disgust. She didn't wait for an answer. She picked up her bag and left the chapel.

Chapter 54

7:00 a.m. Christmas morning

There was not a sound to be heard in the Cooper household. The eeriness was paralyzing. Abbie contemplated whether she should even get out of bed. She clutched the spare pillow and placed it over her head. The only bright spot this holiday season had been her present from Ty. After their big blow-up in the chapel, she wasn't expecting anything, not even a goodbye before he took off for Christmas break. But, he surprised her. They met at the chapel again and he said he couldn't leave for the break without seeing her. Then he pulled out a gift from his backpack and made her swear not to open it until after he had left school and gone home to Westchester.

She hadn't gotten him anything. Before she knew it, it was almost Christmas and she hadn't given any thought to his gift. He insisted she didn't have to. She would rectify the situation as soon as she could.

On Christmas Eve, she locked her bedroom door and pulled the glittering red box with the satin ribbon from her desk drawer and sat on her bed. When she opened the box, she was greeted with the most gorgeous, blinged-out friendship bracelet she had ever seen. It was made of thick embroidery thread tightly woven together in a parade of exotic colors: hot pinks, aqua blue and green, fire engine red, vibrant purple and orange, topped off with shimmering crystals at the edges. She was blown away. The note at the bottom of the box read:

> *To my go-to girl, my best friend.*
> *Merry Christmas*
> *Ty*

Abbie was the last one to arrive downstairs. She took one look at all the faces in the living room: Grandma Naomi, her dad, Miles, Aunt Vivian, and Mahalia. Her dad had insisted Rayne go home to be with her family in Minnesota for the holidays. All Abbie wanted to do was to run back upstairs and pull the covers over her head.

"Who died?" she asked, rudely.

"Is that the way to greet your family on Christmas morning?" her dad asked, his voice thick with disapproval.

Abbie ignored him, grabbed a seat, and folded her arms, waiting to see how this depressing farce of a Christmas morning would unfold. Her dad looked pissed off, Miles was sulking and on the verge of tears, Aunt Vivian was stone-faced, and Grandma Naomi looked like she wanted to give everyone a good kick in the rear. Even Mahalia just sat there whimpering. The toy soldiers in the corner next to the tree even got in on the action, looking depressed. No one made a move towards the tree to unwrap presents. Then, they all looked to Jason for the appropriate Christmas etiquette. Hallmark didn't have a card for the occasion of Christmas in a household where the matriarch was in jail for murder.

Grandma spoke first. "I'm going to put on some music, the way my daughter-in-law would, then I'm going to get breakfast started. I know she wouldn't want us standing around like a bunch of fools with no common sense. Jason, don't forget to call your sister."

"Why don't you kids start opening your presents?" her dad asked.

Mahalia stood up on all fours and started wagging her tail excitedly. "I think that's a good idea," Aunt Vivian piped in.

Neither Abbie nor Miles made any move towards the tree. The slow opening notes of "Christmas Eve/Sarajevo" by the Trans-Siberian Orchestra drifted from the sound system.

"Face it, Dad, this family has been falling apart since the day Mom got carted off to jail," Abbie said. "Not even Christmas can fix that."

"I know, sweetheart. But Mom insists that we should carry on as usual. It helps her cope."

"We're in mourning in this house," Abbie continued, as if her dad hadn't spoken. She needed to get this out. "Even the dog is freaked out. Without Mom, we're just a bunch of zombies walking around. It's even worse for her. Locked up like an animal in some filthy jail cell, away from her family. She doesn't have anyone to tell her good morning, or ask how her day was, no one to tease her about being so tiny that she can't reach anything in the house without help. We can't stalk her in the kitchen when she's cooking because we can't wait to dig in. Miles and I don't get to pretend to be grossed out when the two of you are all over each other. It sucks. It sucks big time. Merry freakin' Christmas to us all." Abbie marched off to her bedroom, slammed the door with all the strength she could muster, and didn't care what anyone thought of her behavior.

Abbie entered the dining room, took one look at everyone and burst out laughing. The place looked almost as good as when her mom decorated for the holidays. There was a large bouquet of poinsettias in the middle of the table. Tall, lit candles offered a warm glow, giving the room a festive feel. And the food, what a spread. Grandma did well. What made Abbie laugh was that all the women had dressed up. The dress code for Christmas dinner was formal. That's the way the Lady of the House wanted it. Abbie hoped her mom would smile when she told her the tradition was alive and well.

Aunt Vivian wore a sophisticated red lace cocktail number with see-through long sleeves and Grandma wore a red pants suit, with a black beaded top. Abbie wore a short velvet dress with satin ribbon tied at the waist.

"I see everyone got the dress code memo."

"We're about to call your mom before we sit down to dinner and you know she's going to ask," Vivian said.

They all agreed.

"This is a surprise," Jason informed them. "Alan got special permission from the jail authorities. Shelby will be thrilled to hear all of you."

When her father got her Mom on the line, he immediately put the phone on speaker and had everyone gather around.

"Guess what?"

"What is it?" Her voice was strained.

"We have everybody here.

"Merry Christmas, Mom," the kids yelled. "We miss you so much. We can't wait for you to come home."

Dead silence invaded the space.

"Mom, are you there?" Abbie asked.

"Jason, take the phone off speaker," her mom said.

Abbie could tell that her dad was being reprimanded. He had that look. Knowing her mom, it was because she didn't want them remembering this Christmas, the one where she was in jail. Her dad did his best to look normal, but he was dying inside.

After a while, Jason held the phone in his hands, and stared at the screen.

"Why did Mom hang up?" Abbie asked.

"She had to go," was the only answer he could give.

Miles burst out crying and the doom and gloom atmosphere of earlier in the day returned. Miles ran out of the room with Abbie on his heels.

Her little brother was quick. He managed to reach the door to his room and shut it in her face before she could get in.

"Miles, open the door."

"No."

"I'm not kidding. Open the door now!"

"Go away. I'm never coming out of this room so you might as well just leave."

Abbie sighed heavily. "Fine, I'm going to get Dad and he can break down the door."

There was a brief silence, then soft footsteps. Miles opened the door.

Abbie kicked a soccer ball that nearly tripped her. "Mom will be glad to see your room is the same as it was when she left."

Miles's room was in a perpetual state of messiness. Various Percy Jackson books were strewn all over the floor. Some putrid odor was coming from the foot of his bed, probably his socks. Shoes, books, old homework assignments, a tablet computer, dirty dishes, old food, and dirty laundry were all competing for floor space. Abbie was sure the comforter on his bed was a different color when it first went on.

"It's disgusting in here. How do you live like this? Why didn't you take all these clothes to the laundry room? Can you even breathe the air in here? Aren't you afraid it's going to kill you?"

"I'm already dead."

Abbie was shocked by his response. Her brother was the comedian in the family, a smart aleck who was always getting in trouble for saying things he shouldn't. Miles was the happiest kid Abbie knew and although they were going through a crisis, this response was extreme for him.

She took him by the hand and sat him on the bed. She pulled up a chair and sat in front of him.

"You don't mean that."

He stared up at the ceiling.

"What is it? You can tell me."

"Mom's not coming back, is she?"

"Of course she is. Why would you say that?"

"She doesn't want to talk to us. She's getting us used to her not being around."

Abbie could see the logic in his line of thinking. Their mom had refused all attempts at visitation from them and she hadn't spoken to them once since she'd been in jail. The only communication from her was a brief letter telling them how much she loved them and they needed to behave for their dad. What if Miles was right? No way. Their mom was a fighter. She wouldn't give up on them.

"Mom is coming back to us. Count on it, do you hear me?"

Her brother stared off into space.

"Miles, I'm talking to you."

He didn't move a muscle.

Abbie shook his shoulders. "Stop it. Say something."

He wouldn't move. His face was frozen. "Oh no. Oh God, no."

Abbie ran to the door and screamed at the top her lungs in the hallway.

"Dad, you have to come fast. It's Miles."

When she returned to his room, her brother was flat on his back in a full-on seizure. She slipped her hand under his head and tilted him on his side. The convulsions were intense and his eyes fell back to the back of his head. A terrified Abbie could only hold onto him as tight as she could and pray. "Please, God, let him be okay. Please let him be all right."

Jason burst through the door and took over from Abbie. Miles still convulsed, frothing at the mouth now. "Call nine-one-one," Jason yelled at Abbie.

She disappeared from the room in search of her phone. Grandma Naomi dropped to her knees and started praying.

"I'll get our coats," Vivian said. "I can call his doctor so he can coordinate his care. I'll get the info from Abbie."

"Good idea. The ambulance will probably head to MetroWest Medical Center first."

Abbie came into the room again. "The ambulance is on its way."

Vivian left the room with Abbie. "Get me Miles's neurologist's information, I can call before the ambulance gets here."

"It's on the corkboard in the kitchen. I'll get it."

Three minutes and six seconds. That's how long his son had been seizing. Jason never got used to it. This was a surprise. Miles was diagnosed with Febrile Seizures as a baby. The neurologists said he would outgrow the condition brought on by sudden high fever. He finally did, when he was six. The medication had worked well and controlled the episodes, which were far and few between, yet devastating every time. Jason and Shelby thought they were gone for good. This episode blindsided him. Miles wasn't running a fever.

When the convulsions stopped, Miles was wiped out and fell asleep. Jason picked up his son and carried him downstairs. He contemplated whether to drive to the hospital, but he rationalized that the EMTs were better equipped to deal with the drive in case anything else popped up.

The flashing lights in the driveway signaled the arrival of the ambulance. He handed Miles over to the EMT who had a stretcher ready. Jason told Vivian to follow with everyone else in his car. He would go with Miles in the ambulance.

Chapter 55

Jason's impatience was threatening to swallow him whole. He needed answers only his wife could provide. When he delivered the news regarding Miles's seizure, Shelby was inconsolable. It wasn't the time to press her for the details of her clandestine meeting with Alessandro Rossi. Miles was better now, though his recent seizure was inexplicable. None of the tests revealed any brain abnormalities.

His eyes drifted around the room. As many times as he'd visited Shelby, he could never get used to the drab walls with peeling paint, the grimy floor and the rancid smell of despair. He pushed the morbid thoughts from his mind. The conversations of inmates and their visitors became background noise when Shelby was brought in escorted by a guard. His chest tightened. Once she was seated, he resisted the urge to allow his concern for her well being to take over the conversation.

"Were you ever going to tell me?"

"I don't know," she said, blinking rapidly. "I thought about what I could lose if I confessed."

"That's all you have to say? Even after he was killed, you continued to keep it a secret?"

"I thought if it got out, the authorities would nail me. I had to consider us, our children, what it would do to them if it went public."

"That's not good enough, Shelby."

Jason lifted his palms off the table and eased back in the chair. He needed to slow down. He was coming off harsh and judgmental. The goal was to get at the truth, not bring out her defensive streak.

"I was ashamed, Jason," she said, unable to meet his gaze. "When I ended things, I convinced myself there was no reason to put my family through emotional distress over an event that was in the past, and would never occur again."

"When you ended things?" he asked confused. "What exactly do you mean, Shelby?"

She bit her bottom lip and wouldn't make eye contact. "I thought…I thought that's why you came. To confront me about the affair with Alessandro."

Jason bit down hard on the inside of his mouth. He could taste his own blood. An affair. Right in front of him and he missed it. He was annoyed when the detectives asked him about the nature of Shelby's relationship with Alessandro. Dismissive when Tom Bilko brought it up. Naïve when Inez mentioned the visit. He was not a naïve man and his senses were usually razor sharp. The pain and betrayal were too much to take so he got angry.

"I've never thought of you as a lying tramp," he said, through gritted teeth. "I screwed up once in fifteen years of marriage. I thought you forgave me. When did you decide to get even?"

"It was never about revenge, Jason."

"Then what was it about? Break it down for me like I'm five years old."

She took a series of quick breaths. Her eyes pooled with tears. He wanted to comfort her and punish her at the same time.

"At first, I was angry about Stephanie. Then I was spending a lot of time with Alessandro. My emotions were all over the place. I was a mess."

"How long did it go on?"

"A few months."

"So, all the while I was begging you to forgive me, to give us another chance, you were sleeping with him?" Jason placed his hands in his lap, under the table, away from her line of vision. He didn't want to frighten her. His fists were primed, ready to punch a dead man for sleeping with his wife.

"No. When I started getting better…well, he was troubled. He was wounded physically and psychologically. I was, too. It's not an excuse. It's just that…as my husband, you deserve an explanation."

"Do you comprehend the torment I've been living through since you got arraigned, and then brought to this jail? Do you understand that our children are destroyed all because you couldn't keep your legs closed?"

"That's not fair. I couldn't predict that some psycho would kill a man in cold blood for no good reason."

"This is about you deceiving me for months. Am I supposed to tell the prosecutor there's no way you could have killed him because you were screwing him?"

She flinched, as if his words caused her physical pain. "Stop it, Jason."

"Why should I? You just gave the District Attorney his motive, gift wrapped on a silver platter. He'll argue that you killed Alessandro to stop him from revealing the affair."

"I'm so sorry, Jason."

He needed to get out of there, to think, to regroup. Staying a minute longer would only prolong his agony.

"I have to go."

Her tiny hand reached out and touched his forearm but, she quickly pulled it back. "Please don't. I have something important to tell you."

"It will have to wait. I've heard enough confessions for one day."

"Mehmet Koczak didn't just kill Alessandro to get even with me. He was stalking me for weeks leading up to the murder."

Jason rubbed the back of his neck. "Why should I believe anything you say to me concerning this case and the reason you're in here?"

"Because this could change everything."

"I'm listening."

"Koczak sent me a note with two coffins on the back labeled with our kids names. He said if I posted bail after the arraignment, he would kill them. I had no reason to doubt him. He somehow managed to call me after I ended up here. When I suggested that he was working for the real brains behind the plot to frame me, he got angry. I think Koczak is only an underling. This isn't over."

Nausea clogged his throat and rendered him speechless. He had failed her. He had failed his children. He didn't push hard enough. He knew a piece of the puzzle was missing, that her refusal to allow him to post bail was no ordinary thing. She was confined to a cage and he didn't want to add to the hell she was already living by digging for information she wasn't willing to give. His justification didn't matter. They were small and insignificant in the wake of her revelation.

. "That's why you're in jail? Because you were trying to protect our children?"

"I made the only choice available to me at the time."

How was he supposed to deal with the paradox? The woman who betrayed her vows to him, and deceived him for months was sitting in a jail cell for a crime she didn't commit because she wanted to protect her family.

"Jason, say something," she pleaded.

"I don't know what to say. I'm trying to grasp this, Shelby, and it's not easy."

"I'm tired of the lies too. I thought I was protecting our marriage by keeping the affair a secret. You would have walked away had I told you earlier. I made a terrible mistake. When the stalking began, everything turned upside down and my singular focus was making sure the kids were safe."

The revelations kept coming after that, how she helped Alessandro plan his exit from the U.S. and provided the resources to help him do so, the GPS tracker on her car, hiring a security detail for the kids, the picture with her head cut off, the calls, the notes.

The realization that she sacrificed her freedom for their children broke him wide open. It was his job to protect his family, and even though Shelby kept the truth from him, the sting of failure still spread throughout his body like a virus. His tongue grew heavy and words deserted him. He reached across the table and covered her small hands with his. He squeezed. He looked across at the guards and was rewarded with granite hard stares. No touching was allowed. The guards didn't make a thing of it, though. He was glad they didn't.

Chapter 56

S omething is wrong with Mr. Cooper," Abbie heard Rayne say to Aunt Vivian. She was about to enter the kitchen to grab a snack when she saw the two of them, heads huddled and looking intense. She stepped backed and hoped Miles didn't come running in and ruin her spying.

"Well, his wife is in jail. It's a lot to take."

"I mean besides that," Rayne said. "Yesterday when he came home, he looked distraught, like someone had just given him bad news. He's in a lot of pain. I wish there was something we could do to help him."

"I'll handle it. Thanks for letting me know."

Abbie pretended she just arrived downstairs and entered the kitchen. "What are you guys up to?"

Aunt Vivian didn't give Rayne a chance to respond. "Rayne was allowing me to express my gratitude, that's all. Say, isn't the Platinum Ball around the corner?"

Abbie was disappointed that Aunt Vivian just lied to her. She hoped that whatever bad news her dad had received, didn't involve her mother.

"Yes, it is. I'm counting the days."

"But?" Aunt Vivian asked.

She knew Abbie so well. "Ty is taking Kerri Wheeler. I have to face them as a couple for the first time at the ball." Abbie scrunched up her face as if she'd never heard anything so vile in her life, despite the fact that she'd had a few weeks to get used to the idea.

"Boo. Boo," Aunt Vivian said, making the thumbs down sign. It made Abbie laugh.

"Who's Kerri Wheeler?" Rayne asked.

"Abbie's nemesis. Ty is an idiot and should have asked you to the ball. He doesn't know what a gem you are, so we're going to show him."

"What do you mean?"

"I was going to wait until you settled on a style for your dress to tell you this. A designer friend of mine has agreed to sketch three dresses for you to choose from."

"Are you kidding?" Abbie was delighted at the news.

"Don't you want to know who the designer is?"

"Yes, yes. Please, tell me."

Aunt Vivian tapped her fingers on the table for a drum roll effect. "David Masutani."

Abbie shrieked with delight. She gave Vivian a big squeeze. "Oh my goodness. I can't believe it. Thank you. Thank you so much. How did you do that? Oh my gosh, my friends are going to die with envy."

"You're a special girl. You deserve a special dress for your first big date."

After another big hug, Abbie scuttled off to brag to her girlfriends.

He was on his second glass of scotch, hiding out in his study. One of his favorite TV shows failed to hold his interest, so he gave up. Jason had learned the hard way that dealing with this family crisis was akin to fighting for oxygen with every breath. There was renewed urgency to finding Mehmet Koczak so this ordeal would be over.

He threw back the remaining scotch in the glass and was about to pour himself another when someone knocked on the door.

"Who is it?"

"It's Vivian," her muffled voice came through.

He ushered her in and she took a seat. "What's going on, Jason?"

"What do you mean?"

"Don't try to play me. You reek of alcohol and you look like hell. Something has got you upset and I don't mean the fact that Shelby is in jail, although that in itself is enough to make us all go off the deep end."

He didn't think about it. It just came out. "Shelby had an affair with Alessandro Rossi."

Vivian's jaw dropped. Then she shook her head in denial. "Where are you getting this from?"

"You didn't know?"

"You ask me that as if it really happened."

"It did. She confessed. They used to meet at Hotel Marlowe in Cambridge."

Vivian's hand crossed her chest. "I had no idea. Shelby never said a word to me and you know we tell each other everything."

"She must have really cared for this guy, huh? She kept it a secret, even from you."

He was in urgent need of a second glass of scotch, so he poured one and downed it in one long gulp.

"Jason, please sit," she said, patting a spot on the sofa next to her.

He obeyed. Vivian placed his hand on her lap and covered it with hers.

"Look at me," she commanded. "I love you and Shelby. I'm truly sorry you're going through this. Don't do anything rash. You're going to bring her home and the two of you are going to fight for your marriage."

"We were doing fine, Vivian. At least that's what I thought. I'm not perfect but…if she wasn't happy, why didn't she tell me?"

"Only Shelby can answer that. I do know you're the love of her life. She would be devastated if she lost you."

"It doesn't make any damn sense. It was the way she did it."

"What do you mean?"

"So calculating and deliberate. There were no signs at all. No indication she was tempted."

"You feel robbed of the chance to convince her it was a bad idea?"

"She says it wasn't revenge. Maybe it's my fault."

"It doesn't work that way, usually."

"I know."

Vivian touched his cheek with the palm of her hand. "It's going to be okay. The pain will ease up."

"I can't focus on my marriage right now. We have to find the killer first. Do you know she was being stalked by this psychopath before the murder?"

Vivian furrowed her brows. "What?"

"He was harassing her before he put a bullet in Alessandro Rossi and framed her for it. He was calling her, sending notes, threatened to kill Miles and Abbie if she didn't do what he said."

Vivian looked horrified. "Oh my God, Jason. That's sick. Poor Shelby."

"The good news is we may be closing in on him."

"The killer?"

"Yes. Mehmet Koczak might be behind this. Can you believe it?"

Vivian repeated the name, trying to make a connection. "The guy Shelby busted for selling out GeneMedicine?"

"That's the one."

Jason let it sink in for a moment. Vivian was near tears but decided against it with the swipe of her hand. She sat up straight on the sofa. "How did you find out?"

Jason recounted the story Shelby told him and Tom Bilko's evidence regarding Koczak's re-entry into the U.S.

Vivian stroked Jason's arm. He knew he wasn't imagining that or the unmistakable look in her eyes. He wasn't that drunk. "It's a lot to take in," he said, removing his arm from her reach. "I can't spring Shelby from Jail just yet. I need proof when I go to the DA. It's the only way to save my wife."

Jason vacated the sofa and took a few steps to his desk. He

chose to lean up against it instead. Vivian followed, and placed her hands on both his shoulders. "You're in a lot of pain, Jason. I wish there was something I could do to ease it, even if it's temporary. I would do anything for you. I hope you know that."

"I'm going to check on the kids."

Chapter 57

Y ou won't be in here much longer."

"I didn't know fortune teller was part of your resume," I counter.

"You're losing faith?"

"Can you blame me?"

Anton Devereaux is visiting me again. With him, there's always something else, just beneath the surface waiting to reach out and shake me. That's the way I remember him. He's taking this visiting business seriously. This is his third visit. He's determined to keep my spirits up so I don't disappear into some rat hole with no exit.

Is this about his guilty conscience? Did he see an opportunity to score some points with God for almost destroying my life, and he grabbed it with both hands, and that scheming mind of his? It's Tuesday afternoon visiting hours. My cellmate and some of the other ladies went to arts and crafts. Anton saved me from boredom. It's getting increasingly difficult not to pass the hours and the days away in an emotionless stupor. Emotions are dangerous in a place like this.

"God's ways are not our ways. Sometimes, He uses difficult circumstances to reveal important things to us, things we can't see ordinarily," Anton says.

"Can you tell Him to hurry up and show me? My eyes are open and ready to see. Like I see you, Anton. You have unfinished business with me."

He removes his glasses and places them in his jacket pocket. "Don't hate me for what I'm about to ask."

"I don't hate. Except for the psychopath who framed me, and my mother but I got over that."

"My daughter's dying. Finding our son may be the only way to save her."

I stare at Anton for a long time, afraid to speak. I don't know which emotion I should let loose: compassion, anger or sarcasm? Which one deserves to run amuck? Or, do they each get a turn?

"That's why you've been coming to see me, to pump me for information to save your daughter? The only reason you want to find our son?" I make no effort to hide the loathing in my voice.

"Shelby, it's more complicated than that." He bows his head and clasps his hands together.

"Not from where I sit. You haven't changed at all. You're still the same self-serving bastard I remember. You sat here and tried to make me feel guilty about abandoning our baby. But you only pretended to care because you need him for parts?"

His head remains bowed. "Answer me, damn it!"

He slowly raises his head. When he looks at me, his face is a stubborn mask. "I came here with good intentions. I feel remorse for abandoning you when you needed me. I want to make amends to both you and our boy. Ask your forgiveness. But I'm also the desperate father of a thirteen-year old girl."

With that single sentence, my rage subsides. I can't punish his daughter for his mistakes. I can't deliberately withhold vital information that could save her life. Irony wins. I'm offering my compassion to his daughter, compassion I didn't have for my own child.

"Is it cancer?"

"Acute Lymphoblastic Leukemia."

"It's aggressive and fast growing. Where is she being treated?"

"Dana-Farber."

"She's getting the best care."

"Nothing's working so far."

"Blood transfusion?"

"Just buys us some time."

"Spinal chemotherapy and cranial radiation?"

"Jade doesn't want to. We're running out of options. Family came forward to be tested. No one was a match. Not even Jade and I."

"Nothing but the marrow of a sibling will do, huh?"

He stays silent. As a parent, I sympathize. I don't know how to reconcile my anger at him with the fact that he could lose a child to a horrible disease.

"I know some of the best researchers in childhood cancers at Johns Hopkins and The National Cancer Institute. They run cutting-edge clinical trials and design some of the best alternative treatments for cancer patients."

He gives me a blank stare. I understand. Time is running out. Trials take too long and there is the FDA drug approval process to consider.

I employ a different tactic. "If you find him, how are you going to explain the fact that you abandoned both him and his mother before he was even born? How are you going to convince a grown man to part with a piece of his body to save a random stranger, a stranger who happens to be his sibling, the only child his father cares about?"

He winces. Maybe I've gone too far. We can't change the facts, no matter how ugly they may be.

"I'll let God lead the way," he says finally, after failing to produce answers on his own.

"Do you have any idea where to start?"

"Need your help. Basic details like birth date, and hospital."

"April 15, 1989. Ladner Medical Center in New Orleans. I take it your wife is on board with this?"

"Yes. He was a Baby Doe, so that specific detail might jar the memory of the nurses on duty that night. I'm sure they're retired by now, but…"

The way he said *Baby Doe* wounds me all over again. "We both failed him, Anton. That collar around your neck doesn't absolve you."

I don't want to read his reaction, so I stare at an empty spot on the table.

"I started to look for him," I say. I refocus my attention on Anton.

His eyes light up. "You did?"

"Of course. I'm not heartless, in spite of what you think."

"You said you didn't know where he was or what happened to him."

"Because it's true. I stopped looking. He didn't deserve to have the woman who abandoned him disrupt his life."

"An old college buddy agreed to provide me with resources for the search. If I find our son, how will you feel?"

"I don't have a crystal ball."

He nods. "Does Jason know?"

"No. Once we had Abbie and Miles, too much time had passed and it seemed like a bad idea to bring it up."

I've helped him all I can. What happens next isn't up to me. "I'll pray for your family."

Visiting hours are about over. I ask him to keep me apprised of his progress. After he leaves, I go back to my cell and stare at the ceiling. Now that I've given Anton my blessing, what am I going to tell my husband who has no clue that I have a grown son out in the world somewhere?

Chapter 58

J ason stood at the bedroom door and knocked twice. There was no response. It was a spur of the moment idea, inviting Vivian to dinner, just the two of them. It would give him an opportunity to have a serious, uninterrupted conversation with her about the other night. He didn't want to ruin their friendship over a potential misunderstanding so, it was best to be clear about the boundaries between them.

He knocked three more times and was met with silence. He pushed open the door and stepped into the bedroom Vivian occupied when she came to visit. He wasn't sure why he decided to enter. Some invisible force beckoned him. It was a spacious room, and Vivian had decorated it with some of her favorite artwork, and photos. She added a bookshelf and a rocking chair with an ottoman.

Nothing seemed out of the ordinary. Then he heard a distinct sound, a classical piece he recognized but couldn't name right away. He followed the sound, which was coming from the bed, which was empty except for a few decorative pillows. The ringing persisted. It sounded like it was coming from the pillows. Strange. He lifted up an ivory throw pillow and found nothing. The sound was getting louder. He then removed the pillows one by one until he found a cell phone. He picked it up and hit the answer button. A panicked male voice came through.

"I've been trying to reach you all day. We have to talk. It's urgent. Meet me in the abandoned parking lot behind Henry's Steak House at 10:00 pm tonight. Please. It's of the utmost importance."

The caller hung up. Jason stared at the phone, his mind racing. Dinner plans were now off the table. He deleted the call from the incoming log and returned the phone to its spot under the throw pillows. He reached for the door and looked both ways before exiting the room and closing the door behind him.

Jason pulled into the abandoned parking lot. If he had to guess, he would say the caller was Mehmet Koczak. But why would he call Vivian? That question had Jason in knots since the call came in. Was he threatening her, too? Was she afraid of him? Did he mean to cause her harm and that was the reason for this meeting? It was five minutes before the appointed time. He parked in the far corner of the parking lot, away from the lamppost and shut off his headlights. Seconds ticked by. He was beginning to sweat and shut off the heat. It was a clear, brutally cold January night and Jason had made sure he was bundled up. He anticipated having to exit the car.

At exactly 10:00 pm, a dark SUV entered the parking lot. The driver killed the headlights as soon as the vehicle came to a stop. Jason flashed his headlights. Nothing. He flashed them again and waited. The door of the SUV swung open. This was it. Anticipation bubbled through him but he had to remember to be cautious as well.

The figure got closer. A man wearing a heavy coat, scarf and knit cap. The man cupped his hands and blew into them in an attempt to keep his hands warm against the brutal cold. Timing was crucial. Jason needed him close enough to catch him if the man decided to run. Then he figure came into full view. It was Koczak!

Chapter 59

Jason clutched the door handle. When Koczak approached the window, he opened the door with force, slamming it into his knees. The killer crumpled to the ground. Jason exited the car with lightning speed, shut the door, and knelt down beside him.

"Don't move," he commanded.

Koczak writhed in pain. His glasses fell from his face and landed noiselessly on the cold asphalt. Jason ripped off his knit cap.

"Who are you?" he asked, on a whisper.

"Jason Cooper. Shelby Cooper's husband."

Koczak attempted to get up under Jason's watchful eye. "Don't try to run."

With great effort, Koczak managed to stand, and Jason took the opportunity to pat him down. "What are you doing here? And don't lie to me."

"This was a mistake."

"No, it wasn't. You tell me what I want to know."

Jason grabbed him by his coat collar. Koczak held up his hands in defeat. "Please don't hit me again. Please, I beg of you."

"Then talk, you murdering psycho," Jason said, then, released him. "What urgent business do you have with Vivian March, and why did you ask her to meet you here?"

"I'm freezing," Koczak complained. "I'd like to sit in my car. As soon as I find my glasses, he said, looking down to the ground.

"You can sit in *my* car," Jason said. "Try anything funny, and you'll be eating out of a tube for a while. Understood?"

Koczak shook his head miserably. He bent down and picked up his glasses. He placed them over his nose, and opened the front passenger door of Jason's car. Jason got in on the driver side.

"Talk."

"Could you put the heat on, please?"

Jason glared at him, then obliged.

"Thank you."

Jason had run into Mehmet Koczak a couple of times when he visited Shelby at GeneMedicine and never liked him. Shelby's stories about how Koczak belittled her work because of her gender and her race made Jason's blood boil.

"You have a minute to tell me everything or else.

"I don't know anyone named Vivian," he insisted. "I called Mia Lansing. Perhaps I dialed incorrectly in my haste. It was a simple error."

Jason was baffled. Who the heck was Mia Lansing, and why would the call come in on Vivian's phone? An idea occurred to him. He reached into his coat pocket and pulled out his phone. He scrolled through some photos and settled on one.

He placed the phone in front of Koczak's face. "This is Vivian. She's the one you called."

Koczak looked confused. "She's black."

Jason wanted to punch him in the face. He resisted the urge. "Your powers of observation are astonishing."

"What I meant to say is that Mia Lansing is white. Blonde hair, green eyes, with freckles on her face and chest."

Jason was incredulous and was just as confused as Koczak was a few seconds ago. This didn't make any sense. Did Koczak really call Vivian by mistake? That didn't explain why her phone was hidden amongst a bunch of pillows. He would deal with the Vivian/Mia puzzle later. He had been waiting for this break. Finally.

"Okay. What's your connection to this Mia Lansing and what does she have to do with my wife being in jail for something she didn't do?"

Koczak stared straight ahead, looking like a deer in the headlights. "This is your only chance to set things right. Start from the beginning."

Koczak turned to him. "Please, I have a wife and children. If anything happens to me, they'll be in dire straits."

"I have a wife and kids, too. They *are* in dire straits because you decided to take their mother from them."

Jason remembered Shelby telling him that Koczak was just carrying out orders, that someone else was behind this. He had gotten angry when she pointed it out.

Koczak rocked back and forth, hugging his body. Jason was getting impatient.

"Start from the beginning. And don't leave anything out."

"I didn't want to do it but she insisted."

"Who?"

"Mia. She said Shelby had to pay for what she did, that she destroyed Mia's family with lies."

"Go on."

"She offered me the opportunity to get my career back on track if I would help her."

"Help her how?"

Koczak swallowed hard. "Get rid of Shelby. Said she wanted her to suffer. So she asked me to start stalking her, gave me information I could use."

"Where was she getting this information from?"

"I don't know. She said she knew everything there was to know about her. At first, I thought I wasn't causing any harm. I could make a few calls, scare Shelby, and that would be the end of it. I would collect my reward and never cross paths with Mia again."

"That wasn't the end, was it?" Jason couldn't keep the bitterness out of his voice.

"No." Koczak scratched his head. "Then when she introduced Phase Two, I realized I was in too deep."

"Phase Two was to kill Alessandro."

"Yes. She made it clear I would be punished severely and my family executed if I didn't go along with her plan. So, she stole Shelby's car from the parking garage at GeneMedicine, and drove to a park a few miles away, where I was waiting. She shot him at point blank range. He begged for his life. She wouldn't listen. She's not human. I tried to stop her," Koczak whimpered. "She did it anyway. Afterwards, with a gun to my head, I placed the body in the trunk of the car and she drove back to GeneMedicine."

Jason shivered. His head was spinning. What kind of person would do something so heinous? What caused this person to hate Shelby so much? Was the answer in Shelby's past as Tom Bilko suggested?

Jason spent another hour in the car with Koczak, extracting details about the set-up. Just when he thought he had heard every horrifying detail, Koczak shocked him yet again by producing an image that made his blood run cold.

Chapter 60

Abbie's bedroom had become Platinum Ball central. Clothes, shoes, accessories, makeup, hairbrushes, curling irons, blow dryers, and styling gel were all over the place, but for once, she didn't mind the mess. Tonight, she wouldn't allow the neat freak in her to spoil the moment. She wore a short silk robe with a floral pattern as Aunt Vivian put the final changes on her makeup. Rayne had fashioned her hair into an elegant pinwheel bun. She wore her hair loose so often that she had forgotten what her face looked like without hair covering it.

"There you go. Your skin is already flawless, so I kept the makeup to a minimum. Just a little mascara, smoky eyes for dramatic effect, and some loose powder on the face," Aunt Vivian said.

"Don't forget your lipstick," Rayne added.

"I've never worn lipstick before."

"Maybe a shiny lip gloss with a little sparkle might do the trick instead of lipstick," Aunt Vivian said.

"That's a good idea," Rayne said. "You don't need much."

"Thank you guys for everything. I'm so happy. I just wish Mom could be here. This is a big deal to her and I feel so sad that she can't see it."

"Oh Abbie, your mom will see you. I'm sure your dad has the video camera all ready and we'll take lots of pictures. You can tell your mother all about it when she comes home. She would be so proud."

"Rayne is right. We're doing our best to stand in for Shelby. We better do a fine job or else we'll have to answer to her." Aunt Vivian gave a sad little smile.

"Let's get to the main event, shall we? The dress," Rayne said.

Abbie didn't want to think about her mom anymore. It was just too sad. She knew in her heart her mother was with her and wanted her to have a wonderful evening, one that she could cherish forever and that's exactly what she would do.

Her dad's jaw dropped when he entered the bedroom and saw her. He just stood there, taking it all in for a full minute.

"You're wearing heels and makeup."

"Too much?"

Her dad pinched his nose and took in a sharp breath. Aunt Vivian told Rayne they should head downstairs because Ajani would be arriving any second.

"So, what do you think, Dad?"

"You're going to be the most exquisite girl at the ball, no question about it."

Abbie took his hands and walked him over to the mirror. "You really think so? You're not just saying that because it's in the Dad Manual somewhere?"

"Not at all. I call it as I see it. But, if Ajani tries anything, he's going to wish he hadn't."

"Dad, stop it. Ajani is a total gentleman."

"Maybe so. He may forget his manners after he sees you. I'm going to make sure he doesn't."

"I wish Mom were here."

"I know, sweetheart. So do I. But, she'll be with you tonight."

"She will?"

He reached in his pocket and removed a small velvet box. He opened it and handed it to Abbie. "I think she would want you to wear these."

Abbie was near tears when she opened the box and saw her mom's diamond cluster earrings—four marquis cut stones with the largest one, pear-shaped, in the middle of each earring. Ten diamonds in all. She removed the earrings from the box with trembling hands. Her dad helped her put them on. He hugged her tight afterwards.

"Dad, you all right?" she asked, concerned.

"Of course, sweetheart. Stop worrying about your old man."

Ajani was speechless after Abbie descended the elegant staircase and came to stand in front of him. He still couldn't speak as he attempted to pin a corsage on her dress and failed miserably. Rayne must have felt sorry for him because she stepped in and completed the task. Abbie figured having everybody gathered in the foyer to check him out was intimidating, especially her dad.

She thought Ajani looked dashing in his tuxedo. He opted for a purple satin tie with the black tux instead of the customary bow tie. Her dad was off to the side looking somber. Aunt Vivian helped Abbie into her matching cape, and Rayne handed her a silver clutch purse that contained her makeup, phone, and cash. After warm wishes to have a good time, Abbie was off for an evening she would never forget.

Chapter 61

Abbie and her date stepped into a Winter Wonderland at the Buckley Country Club in Chestnut Hill. Juniors and seniors were still arriving and the music was in high gear. A few die-hard dancers were already showing off their skills on the dance floor. It was clear that everyone had gone to great lengths to look nothing less than spectacular tonight. The competition among the girls for Best Dressed would be fierce.

The ceiling of the ballroom had turned into a starry night, comprised of hundreds of stars. Snowflakes circled the hardwood floors and white trees were strategically placed around the room. The centerpieces were large bouquets of white roses with lit candles that cast a warm glow over the diamond-pin-tuck taffeta tablecloths.

Abbie and Ajani had arrived fifteen minutes after the dance officially started. She shouldn't have been surprised that Ty and Kerri were seated at their table. Four couples per table. The other two were Michelle Dowling and her date Pete Cora, Ty's teammate on the crew team, and Aaron Bailey, and his girlfriend, Lea. Abbie felt the tug of insecurity, fleeting as it was. They were all seniors and she a lowly sophomore. Ajani did all the right things. He pulled out her chair, and made sure she wasn't cold or uncomfortable before sitting down beside her.

Kerri was shooting daggers at her and Ty seemed to have swallowed his tongue.

"That's some dress," Kerri said, trying to hide her inner bitchiness and failing.

"Yes, it is. It's a David Masutani original, made just for me."

"Shut up!" Michelle said. "Are you serious?"

Abbie had found an in with the senior girls. Michelle and Lea leaned toward her and wanted to know how she got such a famous, in-demand fashion designer to make her a one-of-a-kind dress. Ty kept staring at her as if he was seeing her for the first time in his life. Kerri pouted.

"Hey, Abbie, where have you been?" Aaron asked.

"What do you mean? You see me almost every day."

"No. I mean *where have you been?*" he said, arching his eyebrows with a mischievous grin. "I didn't know you were a total hottie. Ty, did you know?"

Lea slapped him upside the head. "You jerk, leave Abbie alone."

Kerri was glaring at Ty, daring him to say a word.

"Hey, that's my date you're talking about. Show some respect, Aaron." Ajani, her knight in shining armor, came to her defense.

"I didn't mean anything by it. I'm just stating the obvious. This is new information that until tonight had remained under wraps. Am I right, Pete?"

"Hey, man, don't drag me into your drama. I'm just here for the food."

Aaron dismissed Pete with a wave of the hand. "Chicken."

"Can we talk?" Jason stood outside Vivian's room.

"Sure, come in. Have a seat," she said, gesturing to the bed.

He hadn't planned what he was going to say. "I prefer to stand."

"You're scaring me, Jason. What's going on? Bad news about Shelby?"

"Why would you think that?"

"The look on your face. It's tragic."

"This whole thing has been a tragedy. Too many casualties."

"What do you mean?" She searched his face for a clue.

"Was Mehmet Koczak threatening you?"

"I...I...why would you ask me that?"

"It's important, Vivian. I'm not going to get mad at you, but I need you to be truthful. Did Koczak threaten to do you harm if you didn't keep your mouth shut about what he had planned for Shelby?"

Vivian sat down in the rocking chair. She looked frail and petrified. Jason knelt in front of her and lifted her chin so he could look her directly in the eyes. "Were you afraid for your life and kept quiet about what Koczak was doing? Were you threatened by Mia Lansing?"

Vivian almost fell out of the chair.

Chapter 62

Abbie and Ajani were in the middle of the packed dance floor getting their groove on to "Gangnam Style."

"I'm really glad you came with me tonight," he said.

"I'm glad you asked me. Why did you?"

"Maybe I had my eyes on you for a while. Maybe I was afraid to make a move because you're fifteen. The ball was the perfect opportunity to ask you out and I took it."

"That's a lot of maybes."

"You're not accessible."

"What do you mean?"

"Don't tell me you haven't noticed the "don't mess with me" sign you carry around with you?"

She chuckled. "I do? I thought my ways were transparent."

"No. If you were, I would have asked you a long time ago."

"Ask me what?"

He whispered in her ears. "Will you go out on a proper date with me?"

The request was unexpected. "Aren't we on a real date?"

"You know what I mean. I'd like to hang out with you, get to know the real Abbie Cooper."

"Oh," she said, nervousness getting the best of her. "I thought you were afraid of my dad."

"Terrified. But, that makes me want to go out with you even more. You're no ordinary girl."

Abbie was flattered. "Thanks, Ajani. You didn't have to say that, though."

"I said it because it's true. So will you?"

"Will I what?"

"Go out with me, silly," he said, grinning.

"Sorry," Abbie said, slapping her forehead. "I have to ask my dad. I think he'll say yes. Your timing is perfect. He'll do anything to get my mind off our family problems."

Abbie suddenly felt shy and excused herself to the ladies' room, where she sat on one of the brightly colored futons in the small makeup room. The backlit mirrors cast a soft glow over her face. She was dabbing her mouth with lip gloss when Kerri Wheeler took the futon next to her. Abbie continued with her task. Kerri started rambling.

"It must be hard for you. Knowing Ty will disappear from your life in a few short months. I mean, we're graduating in the spring, and he'll be heading off to Yale this fall, broadening his horizon, living new experiences."

Abbie knew what Kerri was trying to imply, that Ty would soon be a college boy and wouldn't have time for a young high school girl. Abbie didn't care. It was the reference to Yale that sparked her interest.

"Ty got into Yale?"

"Oh, I'm sorry, I thought he told you."

Abbie knew Kerri wasn't sorry at all and was pleased to know something about Ty Abbie didn't.

"It must have slipped his mind," she reasoned. "There's a lot going on senior year. I'm glad. He was stressed out because it was his number one choice."

Her reaction obviously wasn't the one Kerri was looking for, so she stormed off, leaving a trail of expensive perfume in her wake.

Abbie exited the ladies' room and felt someone grab her from behind. She was about to scream when a hand came over her mouth.

"Shhh, it's just me," Ty whispered in her ear. He dropped his hand from her mouth.

Abbie turned around to face him and hit him with her purse. "You scared the heck out of me."

He gave her the big old Ty grin that made her heart go pitter patter. "Sorry, Cooper. It was the only way I could get you alone. Can we go somewhere private?"

"Why?"

"I just want to talk to you without everyone spreading gossip about us."

"Ajani is expecting me."

"Don't worry about it. I told him you'd probably be a while in the ladies' room."

Abbie and Ty bobbed and weaved through the crowd of kids who had overflowed into the foyer. Ty spotted two empty chaise chairs off in a corner and they sat, their classmates obstructing a view of them.

"What is it?"

"I'm glad you're here. You've been through so much in the past couple of months, you deserve to have some fun."

His eyes told her the whole story, the way he lingered on her chest, then her mouth, with just a slight edge of nervousness to him, because he was seeing her in a different light. He'd chosen to wear a dark suit, white dress shirt, and a blue pocket square that matched Kerri's dress. Her mouth went dry. Abbie mentally admonished herself. She didn't want to embarrass herself in front of him by openly ogling him or saying something stupid.

"You've been through a lot, too. College applications, the stress of waiting to hear if you got in, and helping me deal with my family crisis."

"It's no problem."

"Congratulations on getting into Yale. Kerri told me."

Ty went quiet, as if that bit of news upset him.

"Ty, what's wrong?"

He turned away from her. Abbie was getting really concerned

now. She shook his arm. "What's wrong? You can tell me."

"It's nothing."

"It's something."

"It will only upset you."

"Now you have to tell me."

"I'm embarrassed, Cooper. I messed up."

"How?"

Ty looked at the kids milling around to make sure no one could hear what he was about to say.

"I did something bad and Kerri found out about it."

Abbie leaned in closer to him. "What did you do? You know you can tell me anything. Whatever it is, we'll deal."

"The stress was getting to me and I could have handled it better. Taking all AP classes and keeping up my grades to get into my top choices for college, pulling all-nighters constantly, it all got too much, so I when I heard about this guy who graduated a couple of years ago… well, he gave me some stuff to help me stay up all night to study. It was just a few pills and I only took them for a month or so, then I stopped."

Abbie was shocked. "You took drugs to help you keep up with classes?"

"Adderall."

"Holy shit, Ty, that stuff is really bad. You could get addicted."

"I know. It can cause heart problems and anxiety, too. That's why I stopped. You're disappointed in me, aren't you?"

He looked genuinely ashamed, as if he were waiting for her to tell him it would be okay.

"Why didn't you tell me you were thinking about it? I would have tried to stop you. I thought only college kids took that stuff. How did you find out about the dealer, anyway?"

Ty looked guilty. "Kerri told me about him. She didn't tell me to use. She just said she heard about the guy who was selling Adderall."

"Wow. So, that's the kind of girl you want to date?"

"It's not like that, Cooper," he said, straightening his tie. "Kerri swore she wouldn't tell anyone. She's a senior, too, and understands the pressure. She has it worse than me. You know her mother is a Dean at the University of Virginia, and all her brothers went Ivy League. If she didn't get into a good school, her parents were going to freak and cut her off."

The picture came into view. Kerri used Ty's secret against him by pretending they were in it together. That made him an easy target for Kerri to get her claws into. Abbie was disgusted with them both, Ty for being weak and Kerri for taking advantage of him.

"I'm glad you told me."

He looked relieved. "Really? I thought you would be steaming mad. You know that temper of yours."

"I'm disappointed. I get it, though. Don't ever do anything that stupid again."

"Scout's honor. I saw you getting all cozy with Ajani earlier. So, is he like your boyfriend now?"

"You jealous?" she asked brazenly.

"Hell yeah. What I mean is I don't want you to get your heart broken. Ajani is going back to London after graduation."

"Just like you're heading to Yale. I can take care of myself."

"I know you can. I'll still miss seeing you. A lot."

"It's only Connecticut. You act like you're moving to the moon."

He searched her face for a moment, then stood up and stuck his hands in his pants pockets. She stood up too. "You look incredible tonight, Abigail," he said. "You take my breath away."

Abbie felt warm all over. That heat she always felt near him was spreading from her head to her toes. It was making her giddy. He had called her by her full name. He never did. The way he complimented her, something had changed in his tone. "Thank you, Ty."

He removed his hands from his pocket and edged closer. The look on his face was intense, hungry. Abbie's heart began to beat like a wild thing in her chest. His hand snaked around her waist and he pulled her closer into his body. It felt natural to be in his arms like this, as if she'd been waiting all her life for him to do that.

She could feel his muscles under his jacket and inhaled his scent, a combination of his cologne that smelled of citrus, lavender, and ginger, and that sexy smell that was all Ty.

He lowered his head, aiming for her mouth. There was no misreading his intent. She couldn't believe it was finally happening.

His lips were soft and perfect as they caressed hers. For a few seconds, he lingered, but Abbie did what felt natural to her. She opened up. The kiss deepened. It wasn't rushed. He took his time exploring every inch of her mouth and she greedily responded. She wrapped her arms around his neck and pressed her body further into him, so not even the air could separate them. She wanted the kiss to go on for an eternity.

When he pulled away from her, they were both breathing as if they'd just run the one hundred meter dash. She spoke first. "Where did you learn to kiss like that?"

He winked at her in that way that made her insides turn to mush. Then he walked away.

Abbie brought her fingers to her lips. She could still taste him. A wide smile spread across her face and her heart soared. Her first kiss. The way she had fantasized about it. She couldn't wait to tell the girls how amazing it was. How she would remember it for the rest of her life.

The evening was far from over for Abbie, even though it was approaching 10:00 pm. The ball would start winding down in an hour or so before the midnight hard stop. She was hopping mad and on the hunt for Kerri Wheeler. She had a few things to say to her and Abbie wasn't about to hold back. She spotted Kerri with a group of people that included her ex, Kyle Davidson, in a corner near the main entrance of the ballroom. She walked up to them and poked Kerri in the arm. "We need to talk."

A pissed-off Kerri eyed Abbie up and down with a look that said, *how dare you interrupt me?*

"What do you want, Abbie?" All conversation ceased and everyone in their little clique was watching the drama they thought was about to unfold in front of them. Abbie was the intruder here.

"I just told you. We need to talk. Now."

Abbie didn't wait for a response. She headed for the little alcove she and Ty occupied earlier. She knew Kerri would follow.

Kerri showed up, her floor-length, beaded mermaid dress

sparkling under the lights. "I don't appreciate you interrupting me."

"Who cares what you appreciate?" Abbie said, as she sat down and gestured for Kerri to do the same. "I thought you cared about Ty."

"What?" Kerri shook her head in confusion.

"You introduced Ty to a drug dealer? You put his health and his future in jeopardy."

"I did no such thing. I just happened to mention what I heard the other kids saying."

"You're such a liar. You told him on purpose, knowing he might try it. You manipulated him by pretending to understand what he was going through. Once he started taking that crap, you had him. As long as he was with you, you would keep his secret."

"What do you know about what Ty was going through, little Abbie? You think you're so special. You think Ty only has eyes for you and would wait for you forever. You can't handle the fact that he's with someone his age who truly understands him."

"You can't be this stupid. If this gets out, Ty could be in big trouble. Then again, that's what you wanted, isn't it? Something to hold over his head."

"You're a selfish little brat who wants Ty to spend every waking hour he's not in classes focused on you. I'm the one who was there for him when he felt like his world was falling apart because he got one bad grade on an exam and panicked that it would hurt his chances of getting into Yale. I'm the one who was there for him when he struggled with getting out from under the thumbs of his strict parents because they have his entire life mapped out according to their plan. You know his mother is demanding and sometimes he has a hard time dealing with her. So, don't you dare question my feelings for Ty."

Abbie wanted to scream, mostly because she was confused. She had no idea Ty was going through such difficulty. Why didn't he confide in her? Isn't that what best friends are for? Was she so obsessed with her own problems that she let her best friend down and wasn't there for him when he needed her? Her heart was breaking for him, but she couldn't let Kerri see that.

"Nice speech and all. It doesn't change anything. You knew he was taking something that was bad for him, something that could have gotten him expelled if the Headmaster ever found out. That was selfish, because you wanted him all to yourself."

"You're the one who's selfish," Kerri said, pointing at her. "You dump all your problems on him and don't think about how it affects him. Thank God graduation is around the corner."

"You think graduation is going to kill our friendship? Think again."

"We'll just see about that, won't we?"

"I guess we will. I'll be there for him when you get bored and move on to the next guy, you know, like you got bored with Kyle, and the one before him and the one before that…"

Abbie pinned a devious smile on her lips and exited the alcove, leaving Kerri fuming and stamping her feet.

Chapter 63

I need the truth, Vivian. Koczak is going down for his part in framing Shelby while the cops pursue the mastermind, this Mia Lansing. Shelby will be home any day now."

"Can I trust you? I mean, really trust you?"

"Have I ever betrayed you?"

"No, you haven't," she admitted.

"So, tell me what's going on so we can all put this mess behind us and move on with our lives."

"You're right, Jason," Vivian said, abandoning the rocking chair in favor of pacing the carpet. "Koczak contacted me. Threatened to kill me if I got in the way of what he was planning for Shelby."

Jason swore. "So you just allowed her to suffer and watch the kids do the same? Not a hint to me? I thought we trusted each other, Vivian. I could have done something to try to stop it from escalating. Before Shelby got arrested."

"He didn't just stop there, Jason," she said, swiping a tear. "He said he would kill you and the kids, too. I thought it was a joke. Until he sent me this."

Vivian reached for a purse on an armchair and rifled through it. She removed a photo and handed it to Jason. Shelby described this very photo to him when she confessed she was stalked. He remembered the day that picture was taken at Gillette Stadium.

Jason was angry and confused all at once. "Kozcak said he doesn't know you. He didn't recognize you when I showed him your photo."

"The man is a killer. Do you think he's going to tell you the truth? Look, I'm not proud of what I did, Jason. I didn't say anything because I thought I would lose all of you. Ever since my parents died, you and Shelby and the kids are the only family I have left. I never thought it would go this far. I never in a million years believed that."

Vivian broke down into a full-blown hysteria, curling up in the corner near the door. In all the years he'd known her, Jason had never seen Vivian fall apart. Ever.

He continued to stand, pacing a hole in the plush, white carpet.

"I know you're disappointed in me," she said through short breaths. "I thought if I did what he said, everything would be all right. When Shelby was arrested, I figured she would be out in no time because she was innocent. That didn't happen. He kept getting crazier and crazier. By then, I thought at least you and the kids would be okay as long as I played along and we could find some way to outsmart him and bring Shelby home. I never intended this to happen, Jason. You have to believe me."

Vivian looked at him, eyes pleading for understanding. He didn't mean to raise his voice, it just came out that way. "I'm angry and disappointed, Vivian. Shelby could have been killed. The kids could have been harmed. You witnessed what this was doing to them, to all of us, yet you remained silent. How could you do this? How could you visit Shelby in jail and see the condition she's in, and say nothing? You say you were scared but you could have given me a hint, a clue, something to let me know you were in trouble."

Vivian wiped her tears and looked up at him with new grit and determination. "I did what I had to do. I was honest with you about why I did it. If you can't deal with the truth, I'll leave your house right now. I can't stay here if you're going to be passing judgment on me."

Chapter 64

Jason wanted to check in with Tom Bilko before he retired for the night. The past forty-eight hours had been draining. The only highlight was telling Shelby the good news about Koczak. He peeled off his shirt and tossed it on the chair and stripped down to his underwear. His phone buzzed and he picked it off the bed. It was Tom.

"Tom, I was about to call you."

"It's not good, Jason."

"What's wrong?"

"Mehmet Koczak is dead."

A stunned Jason plopped down on the edge of the bed. He felt like screaming. The realization of what this could mean for Shelby's release came crashing down on him, choking him beyond all reason. "What happened?"

"Not sure. State Police went by to interview him earlier this evening and when they got to his apartment, he was already dead."

"How?"

"Bullet to the head. Same as Alessandro Rossi."

Jason didn't say anything. He was incapable of forming a coherent thought.

"Jason, you there? Sorry, man. I thought we had this one in the bag. At least we know he was involved. His conversation with you is more information than we had before, so at the very least, now that he's gone, Shelby can get out on bail until they catch this Mia Lansing chick."

"We'll talk in the morning," Jason said.

A drink sounded like a good idea. He pulled out a black and gold silk robe Shelby had bought him from the closet and threw it on, not bothering to tie the belt. Everyone was asleep at this hour. He reached for the bedroom door handle, turned it, and then stumbled backwards in surprise.

"I didn't mean to startle you. I just didn't feel good about the way we left things," Vivian said.

"I'm heading to the study."

Vivian sat on the sofa in the study nursing a drink while Jason stood at the mini bar throwing them back, one after the other. He needed to be numb and it wasn't happening fast enough. Vivian got off the sofa and relieved him of his last drink.

"That's enough. This isn't you. We have to fight to get our girl back and it's hard. So what? You can't fall apart on her. Not on my watch."

"You're right. I'm still worried. Even when we post bail and bring her home, it doesn't mean she's in the clear. If investigators don't find concrete evidence of Koczak's involvement, and they can't find this Mia person, where does that leave Shelby?"

"I don't have an answer. But, just for tonight, can we pretend that it doesn't hurt so much?"

Vivian brazenly ran her fingers over his exposed chest. He shivered yet made no move to stop her. "Stop thinking, Jason. You need someone to hold you, to make you forget for a little while. I want to be that person for you."

Chapter 65

A lan arranged a call so my brother Michael could talk to me.
"Just don't make any sense. This is bad. How could you be in jail?"

"Somebody set me up. They think this is funny."

"Ain't nothing funny about my big sister hanging out with criminals in a jail cell. Mama's just down here acting like it's no big deal, like she expected this."

"I don't want to hear about that woman, and I told you she's not my mother."

"Daddy has a month or less left to live. I know you're in a tough spot, but I wanted you to know."

I stay silent, emotions rippling through me. I'm trapped and helpless. I haven't seen my father in over two decades and it looks like I won't get a chance to say goodbye. I begin to breathe hard, all the anger I've held onto for years threatening to sweep me away in a twister of regret and sadness.

"He wrote you a letter. He asked me to give it to you, said I would know when. I think this here time is the right time."

The letter finally arrived, courtesy of Alan Rose. The ladies from Cell Block D28 and E30 are outside, the one hour per day we see the sky. I sit on a small bench close to the barbed wire fence. I pick up the letter and put it down again. I do this at least four times before I gather the courage to read it.

Dear Mia,

You must think it's strange hearing from your daddy after all these years. If you're reading this letter, it means I'm either dead or close to it. If you're reading this letter, I know you made it. Thank God. Baby girl, I messed up bad. I was supposed to protect you but I was too scared. Too scared the truth would come out if I went against your mother and stopped her from hurting you.

I'm sorry I was weak and you had to pay for it. I can't undo what I did— letting you walk out of the house at fifteen, alone, pregnant, scared, and confused. Every day for weeks I tried to find you, to bring you home, to tell you it was a mistake. Every day, I went home empty-handed. Your daddy ceased to exist the day you walked out the door. Every night, I dreamt you would walk through the door, and your smiling face would make me so happy. I would have your bread pudding from LaFayette Bakery waiting for you. I was willing to take whatever your mama was going to throw at me. I came to that point too late. Maybe it was God's way of taking you away from a mama who was as mean as Satan and a daddy who betrayed you because he couldn't stand up for you.

You see, a long time ago when you were little, I did something terrible. Your mama knows what I did. Ever since that day, your daddy has been a prisoner to the secret and your mama the warden. I don't want you to blame her cause I messed up. I always taught you and your brother to respect your mama, and never talk bad about her but I think you're grown enough to hear the truth now.

When you were about two years old, before your brother Michael was born, I had a secret lady friend. I know it wasn't right and I'm not going to tell you all the reasons I did it. I just did. This lady also had a husband who wasn't very nice to her. We met when she came to my garage to fix her car because she heard I was the only shop in town that could fix her particular vehicle. Anyway, we got to chatting and before you know it, she would come by the shop almost every day.

One night, her husband showed up unexpectedly. He was mad as a swarm of bees when he found us, fit to be tied. He came after me and we got to tussling. He went for my throat. In self-defense, I pushed him away from me. He fell and hit his head on a dresser. The blow killed him instantly. My lady friend told me she would say he was drunk and fell and I was never there. Since nobody knew about us, it was easy enough to cover up. But my conscience wouldn't let it lie. I had to tell your mother. And ever since, your daddy had to do what she said.

I'm so ashamed, baby girl. I wish I was the kind of daddy you deserved. One who was strong, and would protect his little girl no matter what her mama said or did. I'm sorry I couldn't be the daddy you needed. If you're married, I hope you chose wisely, so my grandbabies can have a better daddy than you did.

I ask your forgiveness, baby girl. That's the only thing that matters to me now.

I love you.

Your Daddy

My heart melts into a puddle, like snow on a sunny day after a major storm. I can't imagine the guilt he must have lived with all these years, the fear of being found out by someone other than my mother. What terrifies me now is that I will never see him alive again. A large part of who I am will be gone, for good.

PART VI:

MOTHER, COME HOME

Chapter 66

W e've suffered a setback."
    I was expecting Alan to tell me that my bail has been posted and I can get out of here. Koczak was dead and he confessed to Jason that he was the stalker even if no one was able to find the mastermind behind the plot to frame me.

"What are you talking about? They can't keep me here, not with the main suspect running loose and her accomplice confessing."

"The DA is taking the case to a grand jury. Next week."

"That's bullshit, Alan!" I screech. "They can't do that. They should be looking for that psycho bitch who's running around using my birth name. Why aren't they?" I demanded.

"The police got an anonymous tip that you were having an affair with Alessandro Rossi and that was your motive for killing him, to stop him from exposing the affair to your powerful husband, who would take your children from you."

"That's not even remotely true. Jason would never take my kids from me."

"It gets worse."

I'm thinking about how I can be admitted for a mental health evaluation and treatment, tell them I'm suicidal. They'll pump me full of drugs. Once in a drug-induced haze, I won't feel a damn thing.

"Shelby, are you listening?"

"Sure."

"There's a recording."

"What recording?"

"A phone call between you and Alessandro. You threaten to have him taken care of if he tells your husband about the affair. The two of you were discussing what I assume is the incident with his wife you told me about. It makes you look guilty. The DA's office has the tape. They're about to go public with this evidence as the break in the case they've been waiting for."

I can barely breathe. Is this how it ends?

"It doesn't look good, does it?"

"It's disappointing, but far from over. There is one thing that really worries me, though."

"What else could possibly go wrong?" I gripe.

"Investigators claim they have in their possession, videotape of you leaving the parking garage at GeneMedcine and returning, all within the timeframe of the murder. The coroner says he was killed between 11:00 am and 3:00 pm on November 14. Either all your colleagues were lying when they backed up your alibi or you have a twin running around town committing murder."

"I swear on my children's lives, I did not leave the garage that day until it was time to go home. Maybe this psycho found someone who looked like me to drive the car and return it, but it wasn't me. You have all the documentation that proves I was in the office between those hours."

"I know. The tape hasn't been authenticated and I can argue that they were doctored. I'll also challenge the chain of custody on all the prosecution's evidence: the tapes, the recorded phone calls, etcetera. The burden of proof is on the prosecution, not us. I want you to focus on that.

"There are also photographs that were sent directly to the DA's office, anonymously, of course. My guys couldn't find any evidence of the affair because the killer had it all along."

"What are you talking about?"

"Photographs of you and Alessandro Rossi at Hotel Marlowe. Kissing."

I bow my head. Panic stabs me like a hundred sharp needles. My family's suffering was about to increase ten-fold. My husband would be publicly humiliated. Whether or not Alan suppressed the photos, someone would find a way to leak them.

"I fully expect to win this case, Shelby. The voice recording hasn't been authenticated, either. The person hasn't identified him/herself or explained how they got the audio recording of a private cell phone conversation. That casts doubt about the credibility of this witness. I can get that tossed out easily. Jason can corroborate your testimony about the stalking. I'm not worried yet. Concerned, yes, but not worried. A grand jury will see this for the shaky circumstantial case it is. We will win."

I only heard half of what was said. I was planning my funeral. What dress should I request? A dark color? Something pastel? Maybe a nice Chanel suit. May as well go out in style. I'll ask Anton to help me pick the right scriptures. Wouldn't it be funny if he performed the funeral service? At the thought, I laugh hysterically. Alan's eyes bug out of his head. He's worried. I laugh louder and can't stop.

Chapter 67

P lease, Mr. Newman. I don't have anyone else I can ask."
Abbie was desperate. She needed to see her mother. Her dad
wouldn't take her and Aunt Vivian said no way, Shelby would have
her head on a platter if she did. Abbie wanted to lift her mom's
spirits, let her know she was loved as fiercely now as she was before
she went to jail. The media was so mean. They were all hoping a
grand jury would give the DA the go ahead to make her mother stand
trial for murder. Her mom must be dying inside, Abbie reasoned.
She needed to see her, to help her fight.

Mr. Newman was the last resort. He was working on a report
when Abbie entered his office and luckily, he was nice enough not
to kick her out.

"You're asking me to go against the wishes of both your
parents, not to mention if the Headmaster finds out, I could be
fired."

Why does he have to be so logical all the time, so straight-
laced? "You gotta live a little, Mr. Newman. Life isn't a straight line.
You think all the people who changed the world played by the rules?
They didn't: Martin Luther King, Jr., Gandhi, Nelson Mandela,
Shakespeare, Sir Isaac Newton, Confucius, Ben Franklin...I could

do this all day."

"Okay, okay," he said, holding up his hand and grinning. "I get it. Can I ask you a question?"

"You can ask me anything."

"Why are you so determined to see your mother after both she and your dad made it clear they didn't want you or your brother in the jail environment?"

Abbie cleared her throat. "You don't understand. I don't know what it's like not to have my mom around all the time. I feel lost without her, like there's a huge hole in my heart and only seeing her can fill it."

His body stiffened. The pen he was holding looked like it could snap at any minute. "I do understand what you're going through Abbie. Better than you think."

"Really? You were separated from your mom, too?"

"I never knew my mother. That's all I'm going to say. I only mention it to let you know you have the listening ear of someone who gets it."

It made Abbie sad to hear that about Mr. Newman. She imagined he was a great kid. "So, you'll help me?"

"I'll think about it. We would have to do this on a day I'm out of the office."

"Just name the date and time and I'll be there. I even looked up the visiting rules on line."

"I'm not making any promises. And you do know that parental consent is needed?"

"Already thought of that. Saw it on the prison website. The consent form has to be presented when we go in. All I need is my dad's signature."

"How do you intend to get it?"

"I'll download the forms from the prison website. After that, the less you know, the better. I can't explain how I work my voodoo."

He shook his head. "There's nothing I can do to talk you out of it, is there?"

"Nope. And don't worry, I won't tell anyone."

"Not even the Rainbow Posse?" He smiled that adorable dimpled smile.

"You know about that?"

"I pay attention."

"Well, can't risk this getting out for the reasons you mentioned. So no, not even my girlfriends."

A week later, Abbie met up with Ty in the chapel to discuss details of the great escape from Saint. Matthews to Bayport Women's Correctional Institution— a fifteen-minute drive from Castleview. "Two hours will be plenty of time for us to get there and back. I'll call my dad on the way and let him know I'm going with you to the art supply store so the security guys won't get suspicious."

"You sure you want to do this? Your parents could get really mad at you and ground you forever."

"I wouldn't do it if there was another way. They've left me no choice."

"You've never disobeyed them before. Not on anything major."

"I've never had to. It's like I told Mr. Newman, sometimes you have to break the rules to get things done, and it's not like I'm doing anything bad. I just want to see my mother. Don't you think I deserve that?"

"You deserve everything your heart desires, Cooper. Everything."

"Thanks, Ty. I appreciate you saying that."

They would take a cab to downtown Framingham, where she would enter Creative Juice art supply store from the front entrance on Concord Street and exit in the back on Howard Street. Mr. Newman would be waiting for her and drive to the women's prison. The cab would return with Ty after 30 minutes with Sarah Giles, a classmate who was the same height and build as Abbie. They didn't look much alike but that was okay. The idea was to make it look like Abbie and Ty went to the store and left together with their purchases.

"Sure you can handle it? Seeing your mom like that, I mean?"

"I can't think about that. I'm not the first kid visiting a parent in jail, as horrible as it sounds."

"What about Mr. Newman? He could get in serious trouble. Your dad could go postal on him."

" I'll handle it my dad."

"He must really care about you to go out on a limb like that."

"It's weird."

"How?"

"He was always nice to me, but ever since Mom's been in jail, he's been going above and beyond."

"Really?"

"Yeah. He said he never knew his mother so he understands why I need to do this."

"Wow. That's deep. That explains it. I always thought he was way too uptight."

"Me too. He's been cool lately, though. Now I feel I can talk to him about anything."

"Hey, tell Mr. Newman the position of your confidante is already taken."

Abbie chuckled. "Jealous much?"

"Maybe. I don't want any other guy moving in on my number one girl, even if it's good old Mr. Newman."

Chapter 68

A re you okay?" Mr. Newman asked. "We don't have to do this now."

"I'm...I'm good." Abbie could barely speak. Her eyes darted all around the visitor's room of the women's prison. An older lady dabbed her tears with a handkerchief as she sat across from a much younger woman—her daughter Abbie guessed. Guards in dark uniforms were peppered throughout the room. The few inmates who had visitors were outfitted in hideous orange jump suits with serial numbers, just like on TV. It's as if they were branded cattle, not people. It occurred to her that her mom was one of the branded cattle.

Mr. Newman squeezed her hands. "It's going to be okay. You don't want your mother to see you like this, though. She'll worry."

"It's harder than I thought, being in this creepy place."

They were waiting for her mother to arrive in the visitor's room. Abbie sat upright in the cheap plastic chair and struggled to get in the right frame of mind, the one that would tell her mother she was doing great.

When she looked across the room and saw her mother walking towards them, her gait tentative, Abbie clutched her stomach. She tripped over her feet when she tried to stand and would have hit the floor were it not for Mr. Newman's quick reflexes.

Her eyes fastened on her mother who now stood in front of her, a weak smile pasted on her face. "Abbie, sweetheart, what are you doing here?"

"Mom," she cried, through trembling lips. "I had to see…see…for myself how you were doing. We miss you."

"I miss you too," her mother said, and then hugged her briefly.

"I'll leave you two alone," Mr. Newman interjected.

"Thank you for looking out for Abbie, Mr. Newman," her mom said. "I'll never forget your kindness to my daughter."

He nodded, and then made himself scarce, opting for an empty chair out of earshot.

Her mother sat and Abbie did the same. "Things have been tough lately but it will work out," her mom said. "I'll be home soon. For now, continue to look out for your brother, and obey your father. Can you do that for me?"

Abbie shook her head. Sure Mom, I can do that."

"How is Miles coping?"

"He hangs out in his room too much so I have to check on him often. Dad is threatening to take us to a child psychologist."

"Your dad is worried about the both of you."

"Nothing's wrong with us. We don't need a shrink; we just want our mother home."

"Hang on a little bit longer. We'll be a family again, the way things were before."

"You promise, Mom?"

Abbie clung to every bit of hope, every word, every reassurance, like a lifeline.

"Yes. I'm too stubborn to be in here much longer."

Abbie knew her mother was putting on a brave face for her benefit. She couldn't handle the visit or being locked up. The slumped shoulders, sunken cheeks and barely there smile all pointed to one inescapable fact: her mother's spirit had taken a severe beating. She wouldn't last much longer if the police didn't catch Alessandro Rossi's killer soon.

"It shouldn't have happened," Abbie said, her voice choked with tears. "Why can't the police see that they have the wrong person? You should be home, getting on Miles' case about homework and the state of his room, telling me to keep my nose out of grown people's business. Arguing with Dad, the same dumb argument about the greatest album of all time, *Thriller* or *Purple Rain*."

"I'm winning that squabble time. Your dad won't give up because he's a sore loser."

Abbie smiled, despite the turmoil churning inside her. "I'll think of a new topic the two of you can fight about, then."

"This is no place for you Abbie," her mother said, ending the brief teasing. "You shouldn't have come. Promise me you won't do it again."

"Only if you make me a promise in return." Abbie folded her arms and wouldn't take her eyes off her mom's face.

Her mom leaned back in the chair, and then looked away briefly. When she faced Abbie again, there were tears in her eyes. "What is it?"

"I want to hear you say you're coming home soon. This month. Not months from now or a year from now. This month of February."

"Abbie, sweetie, the legal system—"

"Say it. "I'm coming home this month."

"I'm coming home this month."

"Now repeat that one hundred times when you go back to your cell and it will happen."

"I admire your confidence."

"It's not about confidence, Mom. It's about what has to happen."

Chapter 69

Jason sat at the kitchen table, his head bowed. The media frenzy had descended on the Coopers again. This time, even the tabloids got in on the action. A photo of Shelby kissing Alessandro Rossi was splashed all over the newspapers, news websites, and social media. MOTIVE EXPOSED IN FRAMINGHAM SLAYING, the main headlines screamed. It was falling apart all over again, only worse. For the first time in his adult life, Jason was at a loss. Their lives were heading for the edge of a cliff and he didn't know if he could pull them back in time or if they were all going over together.

Vivian returned to Chicago. She promised to be back soon. The crisis trap his mother warned him about ensnared them both. After they slept together that night in his study, they dusted off their old verbal agreement. Shelby must never know. They both understood the stakes. Next week, the grand jury would convene to determine if there was enough evidence to proceed with trying Shelby for murder. Alan was confident the grand jury would rule in their favor.

The doorbell rang and Abbie scrambled to get it. When she opened the door, a man she didn't recognize stood there, a disarming smile on his face.

"May I help you, sir?"

"Yes you can, little lady. Is your daddy home?"

The man had a pleasant voice, a drawl of some sort. He seemed sweet, harmless.

"Who are you?"

Abbie could tell the man was freezing by the way he kept hunching over and she felt bad. She couldn't allow a total stranger into their home, though. She had to get her dad out here and sort this out.

"I'm Michael. You must be Abbie. I came to see your daddy. It's important."

"How do you know my name?" She now had her guard up.

The man just gave her an even wider grin.

"Wait here," she told him.

Abbie went into the kitchen, where she found Jason with his head stuck in the refrigerator. "Dad, there's some guy at the door looking for you. He says it's important."

"Who is it?" Jason asked, as he closed the refrigerator door with one leg and dumped his arm full of smoked Gouda cheese, lettuce, and tomatoes on the counter.

"I don't know. He said his name is Michael."

"I hope it's not another reporter here to badger me. I'm sick of them."

"I don't think he's a reporter. He doesn't seem to be from around here."

Chapter 70

"Who are you?" Jason asked the stranger standing at his front door.

"I'm Michael Lansing."

Jason stared at the man. *Lansing*. According to Koczak, Mia Lansing was white. This guy was black. Was this just a strange coincidence? "I don't know anyone by that name. Are you sure you have the right house?"

"Yes, sir. I'm Michael Lansing, Mia's brother. She's in a heap of trouble. That's why I'm here."

"Who sent you to torment us? Start talking or I'll have you arrested for trespassing."

"The man wasn't intimidated, not even a little bit. Then he snapped his fingers. "I'm here for Shelby, your wife. She's my sister."

Jason took two uneven steps backward, as if assaulted by a physical force. Whatever this stranger was after, he had Jason's undivided attention. He was invited in.

Jason asked Rayne and the kids to disappear for a while. It was Saturday, temperatures in the thirties. Rain showers were expected throughout the day. They had planned on staying indoors, watching movies and relaxing while he plotted his next move. Now an unexpected visitor sat in his living room, primed to be the narrator of what Jason was sure would be an outlandish tale.

"Start from the beginning, Michael," Jason said. "How do you know my wife?"

Michael looked annoyed, like Jason was a simpleton to whom he had to keep explaining the same thing repeatedly.

"She's my sister," he insisted. "I read about the murder and that she was arrested and sent to jail until the trial. I didn't have a way to get in touch with you. I remembered your address, though. Sorry for showing up like this. Mia left me no choice."

"My wife doesn't have a brother."

"She does, sir. Your wife, the woman you know as Shelby Durant, is my sister, Mia Lansing."

This had to be a joke. Jason couldn't entertain the idea that what this man was saying could be true. Two women named Mia Lansing, one white, one black, both with a connection to him? There were no such coincidences.

"What proof do you have that my wife is your sister?"

Michael fingered the gold chain with the crucifix he wore around his neck. "I don't know where to start. Mama used to say Mia was too hard headed for her own good, that it would get her in trouble one day. Maybe Mama was right. Look where Mia is now."

Jason recalled that whenever he had brought up Shelby's childhood, she always changed the subject. There were no pictures of her as a little girl around. She told him the story of her parents' tragic death in a fire and he took the story at face value. He believed she had every right to be reluctant to discuss such a painful part of her history. So, it made sense she only talked about her brief stint in a home for teens or how Vivian's mother, Rita March, saved her.

"Go on."

When Michael dug up Shelby's/Mia's backstory, Jason couldn't breathe. How could he believe this man? How could he not? He was married to two different women. The one he thought he knew, and the one who could pretend her family didn't exist.

"Three years went by and no news," Michael continued. He hadn't noticed Jason's distress, he was so caught up in his family's past. "Then one day, by the grace of Almighty God, a month after Mia would have turned eighteen, a call came in to the house. Mama answered and a woman named Shelby Durant asked to speak to me. Mama didn't even recognize her own daughter's voice. When I got on the phone, she told me to act normal, that it was Mia, and she had legally changed her name. She had been living in North Carolina with a nice family and was doing ok. That was the happiest day of my life. My sister was alive."

Jason shivered, although the thermostat was set at seventy-two degrees. His wool sweater and slacks couldn't protect him from the unusual chill ripping through his body. "You said she was pregnant. Did she give birth? What happened to the child?"

"Mia wouldn't say. My guess is she gave it up for adoption."

Jason swallowed hard in rapid succession. "Are both your parents still alive?"

"Mama is alright. Our Daddy doesn't have long. He's waiting on Mia so he can go home to be with the Lord."

PART VII:

THE MOLE

Chapter 71

Jason snapped his third pencil in a row. In one angry swoop, he cleared his desk of all objects—files, folders, photos, loose documents, and anything that wasn't nailed down scattered. Nicholas Maza was on the line again, like a pit bull that wouldn't let go of his leg.

"I've been patient, bro. Don't make me call Charlie Sommers. All I'm asking for is an opportunity to buy shares like any savvy investor. Is that so bad?"

"Buy the stock on the open market like everyone else."

Nicholas chuckled. "Why so hostile? We used to be buddies, we hung out, got to know each other."

"I'm not the person you remember, Nicholas. I was a kid during our brief acquaintance. I'm a man now, a man who doesn't respond to threats. Go pick on someone who's afraid of you."

The added pressure Nicholas was doling out had Jason feeling like he was swimming upstream against a strong current. The only way to deal with someone like Nicholas Maza was to take away the thing he wanted most. Jason's mind was made up.

"What?" Jason barked into the phone.

"Sorry to bother you, Mr. Cooper. There's someone here to see you. She insists. Her business card says Chloe Grace. She says she works for you."

Jason pounded his fist on the desk. The call was from Derek, one of the armed guards Tom Bilko had hired.

"What does she want?"

"She says she couldn't discuss it over the phone."

Jason wasn't going to run from Chloe Grace like a coward. He would deal with her and toss her out in three minutes, five tops.

"I'll be right there."

Jason stuck his hands in his pants pocket, and glowered at Chloe, who was seated in the living room. He observed that her dress was a little too tight, the heels a little too high, and her lips a little too red.

"Start talking," he commanded.

"They want you out, Jason. I came to warn you."

"Who's *they*?"

"The board. Your wife's legal problem is a liability they can't afford."

"Who informed you of this?"

"I hear things. I have friends. Charlie won't tell you this to your face. He'll come up with some carefully prepared speech that won't make him look like he's stabbing you in the back. The endgame is the same, Jason. The intense media scrutiny is making the board queasy. You're out."

Chloe Grace may have many faults, but she wouldn't lie about something this serious. Disappointment soared through him. The dream was dying a very public death. When Shelby got charged, Charlie told him the company would stand by him, give him as much time as he needed to be with his family, and Charlie was true to his word. Jason also understood the immense pressure that came with running a company the size of Orphion. There were thousands of employees to consider, vendors and suppliers, regulators, partners, the Board of Directors, as well as the press, both business and traditional. The damage they could do was not to be taken lightly. He thought Chloe Grace's blackmail was the biggest threat to his succeeding Charlie as CEO. The truth was much closer to home.

"Have you discussed this with anyone?"

"Nobody. I came straight to you once I confirmed some things. I didn't want to get caught up in rumor and innuendo."

"Why come to me?"

"Why not? I think you deserve to know. I respect you, Jason."

"Not so long ago, you were willing to ruin my reputation with lies and blackmail. What changed, Chloe?"

She got serious. "Whatever you think of me, I'm loyal. And you'll do great, whatever you decide to do after all this blows over."

It became clear. Self-preservation. A way to expand her options in case things don't work out at Orphion. There was always an angle with Chloe. He grinned.

"What's funny?"

"You. You know how to work all the angles. I don't know if I'm impressed or repulsed."

"You should resign."

"I beg your pardon."

"Leave on your own terms. That way, they can't run you out of town. Write the ending to your story, Jason. Don't let someone else do it for you."

She made sense. If the Board was planning to oust him from the company, he would need to beat them to it and create his own narrative. First, he had to find out if what Chloe said was true. Her smarts were never in doubt. Trusting her was something he couldn't afford to do. For all he knew, someone from the Board could have sent her to spy on him, get information they could use against him.

"Thank you for coming all the way out here, Chloe. I'll see you out now."

"What are you going to do?"

Chapter 72

Jason sits across from me in the visitors' room. His jaw is set in that stubborn, decisive way of his. His eyes reveal that the decision was made under duress.

"What is it?"

"I'm resigning from Orphion. The media scrutiny, the IPO, I'm not going to sit around waiting to be tossed out on my ass."

Humiliation, guilt and shame grab hold of me. I've cost him his dream, stripped him bare in two devastating blows to his ego: my affair with Alessandro and now this. For a moment, I can't meet his gaze. There is an uncomfortable silence between us. I take refuge in the murmuring of conversations around us from family and friends visiting other inmates.

"When will you officially resign?"

"It's already done. Only the formality of the announcement is left."

"What will the announcement say?"

"I've decided to relinquish my role as CFO in order to help my family through a difficult time. You can figure out the rest."

"Do the kids know, yet?"

"I haven't told them."

At least that's something. He told me first, and I hold on to that as if it's gold.

"They need you."

"Resigning frees me up completely to focus all my energies on getting you out of here. After that, I don't know what's in store for us."

"What do you mean?"

His eyes bore into mine. "Come on, Shelby. Do you honestly think we can go back to the way things were?"

I don't have an answer because I haven't allowed myself to think that far ahead. Just getting through life day by day, hour by hour is a struggle.

"I know it won't be easy, too much has happened, but we can figure out how to put it back together again when I get out."

"I don't know if we can."

"We have to try."

He looks away briefly. When he focuses on me again, what I see on his face scares me.

"Maybe we should cut our losses, once you're free. I don't know what the right thing is, Shelby. Will we ever look at each other the same way again?"

What he really means is he doesn't trust me anymore. "I love you. That has never changed and it never will."

"Your brother came by the house, Shelby. Or, should I say Mia?"

I lean back in the chair. I should have known Michael would show up eventually. I couldn't spend time dwelling on that while my world was imploding.

"What do you have to say for yourself?"

"Mia Lansing died a long time ago, Jason. She was a girl nobody wanted. When I met you, I was Shelby, the girl I wanted to be."

"So, you just lied about your past? Your family?"

"I had to leave them behind. It was the only way I could survive."

"What happened to the baby? Your brother said your mother threw you out for getting pregnant."

My shame, my scarlet letter. I tell Jason the same story I told

Anton. When I'm through, he gapes at me in disbelief.

"Why didn't you tell me all this when we met? I wouldn't have judged you. Why rob the kids of the opportunity to know their uncle and grandfather? "

"I had already lied to you about my childhood. It seemed simpler to keep the lie going."

"So, you have a son out there who has no idea who he is. That's not right, Shelby."

"I know it isn't."

I tell him that Anton is the father of my son, and he has mounted a search for him.

Jason is stunned to find out that the new pastor of our church is the father of my first-born. He struggles with the emotions on the heels of these revelations. His jaw tightens. His eyes are almost bloodshot with stress and grief.

"I don't have any words left."

"That's the last of my secrets. I'm fresh out now."

. In spite of this, he still manages to put my interests first.

"So, if you're the real Mia Lansing, who is this other chick running around, causing mayhem?"

"I don't know, Jason. Someone who knows me very well and hates me even more."

Chapter 73

A bbie decided to skip school on Monday and her dad agreed. She was physically ill from the backlash against her mother. Someone started an online petition to make Massachusetts a death penalty state just so her mother could get the needle or the electric chair. She wasn't sure what horrible methods were used to kill people who were sentenced to die. Ty seemed withdrawn lately and she couldn't blame him. Her high school life was in serious jeopardy of being over. Only Mr. Newman checked on her constantly, and checked in with her teachers to make sure she was doing okay. The Rainbow Posse didn't exactly abandon her, but things were a little off.

It was time to reveal her secret. Now that she knew her mother was Mia Lansing, the stalker didn't have that over her head anymore.

She found her father concentrating hard on a cup of coffee at the kitchen table. The morning sunlight seeped through the windows, offering hope of better days ahead, a direct contrast to her dad's dark mood and disheveled appearance. He looked like he hadn't slept, ironed his clothes, taken a shower, shaved, or combed his hair. Her dad, who was always immaculately groomed, now looked like a hobo.

She pulled up a chair and sat next to him. "This is all my fault. I wanted to say something sooner, but I was too scared, and now Mom—"

She broke down before she could even get the rest of the story out.

"None of this is your fault. Some very bad people wanted to hurt your mother."

"You don't understand. The guy who's doing this, setting up Mom, destroying our family, he's been calling and texting me."

Her dad knocked over the cup of coffee, which spilled all over the table and dripped onto the tiled floor. Mahalia lapped it up with her tongue. He didn't notice.

"Who's been sending you text messages?"

"Him. I don't know his name, he wouldn't tell me. He kept saying Mom did bad things and she has to pay, and he said if I told you or anyone else, he would kill you and Miles and then he said he would kill Ty, too, so I didn't know what to do."

Her dad's face turned to stone. "Dad, you're scaring me, say something. Please."

When he spoke, it didn't sound like her dad. The words were coming from some strange creature, one that was caught in a trap of some kind, and was wounded, crying out for relief from unbearable pain. "When did he send you those messages?"

"It started back in November, right before Mom was arrested. He admitted he was the reason for her troubles. I was afraid if I said something, he would come after us for real and after that, things just got worse and worse. I'm so sorry, Dad."

Her father gently wiped her tears with his thumbs. He looked at her worried, like when she fell off her bike as a little girl and scraped her knees. "None of this is your fault, sweetheart, stop feeling responsible. I'm not angry with you. I just wish you had come to me, no matter how scared you were."

"I know, Dad. But he knew stuff about our family, and about me, so I figured the threats were legit."

"Tell me what he said to you during those phone calls, and I'll need to see the text messages on your phone."

Abbie recounted her encounters with the stalker to her dad. If the stalker were in front of them this very minute, she was sure her father would strangle him with his bare hands. She'd never seen him look so angry. He held her close and stroked her hair.

"I'm sorry you were terrorized and so scared you couldn't come to me. I have good news, though. That awful man won't be contacting you ever again."

"He won't? How do you know?"

"He's dead."

"Really? Are you sure?"

"It's been confirmed."

Abbie was a compassionate girl but she couldn't feel sorry that the evil stalker was dead. She was beyond happy. "Does that mean Mom is coming home soon? The DA won't take the case to a grand jury?"

"Not exactly, sweetheart."

"Why not? The bad guy is dead. They have to let Mom go."

"Because we need proof on our side. The dead stalker was working with someone else. That someone is the mastermind behind the plot to frame your mother and we believe she's been sending anonymous tips to the police. She hasn't been caught yet, but she will. I promise."

Abbie sobbed in her father's arms. "It's not fair, Dad," she said in between ragged breaths. "I'm sick of it. So sick of being scared, so sick of Mom being in jail, so sick of the nightmare that just won't end. When do we get to wake up, Dad? When?"

"Don't give up now. Just think of your favorite movies. This is the part where it seems all hope is lost. Then the hero finds an inner strength and slays the bad guy, right?"

Abbie looked up at him. "Right," she said, wiping her nose with the back of her hand. "Right. We need to find our inner strength to defeat the bad guy."

"Exactly."

"How are we going to do that?"

"Well, sweetheart," he said, kissing her on the head, "sometimes we must go to some dark places in order to find the light."

Abbie didn't like the sound of that and didn't want to know what it meant. Her dad was a determined guy who was used to getting his way, so she wasn't about to question him. All she needed to know about his plan was that it would bring her mother home.

She thought her dad could use some cheering up though, after the heavy conversation they just had. She wanted to lighten the mood.

"I have big news."

"What is it?"

"I don't know how you'll feel about it. To me it's the best news."

"Then I think I'll be okay with it."

"It happened. Finally."

Her dad stared at her, his eyes wide with alarm. "What finally happened?"

Abbie chewed her bottom lip and twirled a strand of hair. "Ty and I kissed at the Platinum Ball."

"Oh."

"Are you mad?"

"I knew it would happen one day, your first kiss. I'm glad it was Ty."

"You mean that?"

"Yes. After the incident in the chapel, I was worried about you. Spare me the details, though. I don't want to hear about some guy shoving his tongue down your throat. You're still my baby girl."

"Are you a prude, Dad?" Abbie teased. "Don't worry. I'm saving all the juicy details for Mom. She'll appreciate it."

A sad cloud passed over her dad's face.

"Promise me when Mom comes home, you guys will try to hold it together."

"Hold what together?"

"Your marriage." Abbie held her father's hand. "I know it sucked for you, her betrayal. You can't divorce her, Dad. She forgave you. I know she lied to you about a bunch of stuff but she didn't do it to hurt you. You told me yourself that sometimes you have to go to dark places to get to the light. Well, sometimes you have to lie to survive, right?"

"It's complicated."

"I know, Dad. You think I'm just a kid, but I understand."

"Don't you have some girlie thing you should be doing? Giggling with your girlfriends about Ty or harassing me for money to go shopping? Polishing your toes, picking your nose?"

"Dad, that's gross."

"Sorry, that last one is Miles."

"I can take a hint. I know when my company is no longer appreciated," she said, grinning. "I'll go find someone who wants to hang out with me."

Chapter 74

Breakfast was awkward. Abbie couldn't believe her uncle was sitting right there with them in the kitchen, a real life relative of her mom's. Miles was especially excited. They stayed up late the night before asking all kinds of questions about what their mom was like as a kid, and how they grew up. Her dad just sat off in the corner scowling. She learned where her mom got her love of cars and motorcycles from and that she had been a daddy's girl, much like Abbie was. Her uncle didn't talk much about her grandma, only to say she and Mom didn't get along and her grandpa always tried to keep the peace. This morning, Michael couldn't keep his eyes off Rayne, and kept peeking at her when he thought no one was watching. He was totally crushing on her.

"I want to apologize again for showing up uninvited," her uncle Michael said to her dad. "I hope Mia can see Daddy before he passes. I'm praying real hard on that one."

Abbie was sad to hear her grandpa was dying of Alzheimer's and she would never get to meet him. "Do you have any pictures of him?"

"I sure do. As soon as we get your mama all squared away, y'all can come on down to Kenner and I'll show you all the pictures of the family."

Rayne began to clear away the breakfast dishes and Abbie noticed her uncle trying to help but she would have none of it. "Please, you're Mrs. Cooper's brother. You don't need to help with the dishes."

"I don't mind at all. Let me pitch in."

After breakfast, Jason gathered everyone in the living room for a reality and sanity check. He had to be honest about what they were in for if the grand jury indicted Shelby on murder charges. Michael was looking at the wedding portrait above the fireplace.

"Your sister never sent you a wedding photo?" he asked.

"No, sir. I only have a couple of pictures of Abbie and Miles when they were still babies. I'm glad my sister met you, though."

Michael moved closer to the fireplace, as if something was drawing his attention. "Well, will you look at that," he said, picking up the pair of crystal swans. "These are beautiful," he said turning them over in his hands.

"They were an anniversary gift from me to your sister."

"Swans, huh? Don't they—"

"Mate for life."

"I see," Michael said, flashing a mouthful of teeth. "Well, that's pretty special if you ask me."

He was about to put the swans back when one of them dropped on the hardwood floor directly beneath the fireplace. The eye of the swan fell out.

A mortified Michael reached down to pick it up. The apology died on his lips and a strange look came over his face. "What in the heck is this?"

Jason crossed the space to see what he was talking about. Miles, Abbie, and Rayne gathered around, too. He picked up the eye of the bird and something else. His anger at Michael's carelessness in dropping the object disappeared. A tiny camera was hidden inside the swan. It looked like someone drilled around the eye to make a small hole, inserted the camera, and replaced the eye.

"Oh my God, Dad, is that a spy camera?" Abbie asked.

"That's pretty clever," Rayne said. "Who would think to put a camera in there?"

Jason struggled to conceal his anger and frustration. He had the place swept for bugs before he installed security cameras on the property and hired armed guards. The woman calling herself Mia Lansing had found a way to breach the fortress he had created around the house. He was on to her, a fact he couldn't discuss with anyone. He would have his revenge. The clock was ticking.

"Seems to me whoever did this has been to your house before and knows the importance of those swans," Michael observed. "It's like mocking you and my sister by putting that camera in there. They don't think you have the good sense God gave you to figure out that's how they know all of your business. "

Jason held the tiny camera, no bigger than a quarter in his hand. All thoughts of the meeting he had planned to prep the family for what was coming next flew out of his head and everyone went off to occupy themselves. Jason removed his cell phone from his pocket and placed a call to Tom Bilko.

PART VIII:

KILLER CONFESSIONS

Chapter 75

I come out of the bathroom to find Jason pacing. I'm wrapped in a large white fluffy bathrobe with the Ritz-Carlton logo embroidered over the pocket. My hair is dripping wet. I could have spent hours in the shower, scrubbing away the past ninety days spent in a jail cell. I had to stop eventually, when my skin was so raw, it felt like I was stung by a swarm of angry bees. When Alan Rose showed up with Jason at the prison earlier in the day and told me I was a free woman, my knees almost buckled with relief. I expressed to Alan I was forever in his debt, and wouldn't stop sobbing in Jason's arms.

"Should we order room service?" he asks.

"Yes. I'm starving."

While Jason orders food, I make my way to the window that offers a great view of Boston Common. People are going about their business on the clear, cold afternoon, bundled in hats, gloves, scarves and jackets. I didn't feel him come up behind me. I melt into him when he wraps his arms around me. "You smell good," he says, nuzzling my neck.

"It's nice to feel human again. How long before you think the news breaks?"

He takes my hand and I follow him. He points out an armchair and I sit. He moves behind me and begins to massage my neck and shoulders, which feels like heaven.

"Hard to say. I'm just glad that Alan got the grand jury to rule in our favor, and the DA will be dropping the charges. What happens next, it's up to law enforcement to find her and prosecute her. I don't want you worrying about that."

"I do worry. When she realizes I'm out, she might disappear and we may never catch her, leaving her to strike again in the future."

"We'll find her. I'm sure of it."

"I'm sorry, Jason," I say, turning to him.

"What for?"

"For hurting you. Pretending everything was fine while our lives were burning to the ground. However, I never stopped loving you. Wanting you. Needing you."

"What are you asking me?"

"It's what I need from you. Forgiveness."

I cup his face with my hands. My eyes dare him to be honest.

"Forgiveness is a journey, Shelby. I don't know how long it will take me to get there. I believed becoming CEO of Orphion would be the ultimate achievement of my life. When I made the decision to quit, I realized that not leaving my mark on the business world didn't terrify me as much as the possibility of living the rest of my life without my family in tact."

He resumes pacing. "What is it, Jason?"

He smiles. "Nothing."

"You can talk to me, baby."

"I want to talk. But, not with words."

He picks me up as if I were no heavier than a loaf of bread and tosses me in the middle of the king sized bed.

Three sessions later, I'm satiated but exhausted and securely tucked in Jason's arm. He refuses to let me move an inch. My eyelids are heavy. Sleep beckons. Then I hear the words that will shatter my soul forever.

"Shelby, Vivian knows who 'Mia Lansing' is."

Chapter 76

We arrive at the hospice on Dublin Street in New Orleans and enter the grand foyer with its dual grand staircases, one on each side. The staff is helpful and accommodating, happy to have Mr. Lansing's daughter come to see him. Michael accompanies me down the long, sterile hallway with white doors to the right. He's been through this a thousand times. Now that the fog has lifted, I can only imagine how tough it has been for him being the sole caregiver. I used my money as a substitute for what our father needed most: my presence. My stomach is doing flip-flops as we pull up to the white door with the number 27 emblazoned in gold letters.

Michael knocks gently then opens the door. I stand behind him and follow him into a room with rich hardwood flooring and natural light, with a door that leads to a balcony in warmer weather. His back is turned to us. I see all-white hair, a feeble frame hunched over. My hands begin to tremble. My brother takes mine in his and squeezes. It was always Michael and me against the world until I was kicked out. Looks like it was just going to be the two of us, and Daddy, just the way it always was.

Michael called him. "Daddy, I brought someone here to see you."

No response. It was my cue to speak. My throat feels like someone dumped broken glass in it. I speak slowly. "Daddy, it's Mia."

No response. I turn to Michael, whimpering. "Hush," he says. "Mia?"

Michael looks at me. "That's the most he's said in weeks. His speech is leaving him day by day."

Daddy slowly turns his head and my knees buckle. Michael's strong arms catch me before I hit the floor. Daddy is drooling all over himself, his face worn by age and the ravages of his disease. I barely recognize him as the father I knew and adored. I inch closer to the bed. He struggles to turn all the way around. I ask Michael to help me position him so we can face each other.

He stares at me then tries to raise his hand to my face. I press my face into his hand and for a moment, it's just the two of us in the entire world. My brain floods with memories: His mechanic outfit, blue overalls and a navy blue baseball cap. Me, five years old, sitting on his lap as we skim through the latest issue of *Popular Mechanics* pointing out each other's favorite cars. The moment I dropped Michael as a baby and he tried to protect me from my mother by saying it was his fault. Mama beat me anyway.

The heartbreak on his face when I told him I was pregnant at fifteen, that Anton Devereaux was the father. The money he squeezed into my hands the day I walked out of his life forever. The way he clutched Michael, as if he knew he was losing one child for good and he had to hold on tight to the remaining one. The times I picked up the phone to call him and didn't have the courage to do it in the end. How courageous is it to visit a dying man?

"Mia."

I look into his eyes. I see flashes of recognition. He's present in the moment but I know it's fleeting.

"I'm here, Daddy."

He speaks slowly, as if each word causes him pain. "I got...I got your bread," he breathes heavily, "pudding."

"Thank you, Daddy. I'm not giving Michael any. He told Mama on me."

He tries to smile. It's painful for him. It's time to let him lie down, rest.

"Baby?"

Michael and I exchange pained glances. "He's with Anton."

"Good."

I hug his emaciated frame. "I love you, Daddy."

It won't be long now.

Chapter 77

A nton was wrapping up some paperwork in the church rectory when his secretary Julia appeared at the door. "You have a visitor," she announced.

He glanced at his watch. "It's almost six. I don't have any more appointments for the day. Who is it?"

"Lee Newman. I hear you're looking for me."

Julia disappeared and in her place stood an intense young man. He was polished, sophisticated. Anton couldn't ignore the cloud of hostility that floated around him.

"Please come in," Anton said, gesturing for him to take a seat across from the desk.

His guest walked in, but declined the offer of a seat.

"I don't know anyone named Lee," Anton said, puzzled. "Who told you I was looking for you?"

"James Dillon. An old friend from Baltimore."

The hairs on the back of his neck tingled. Thanks to Martin's resources, Anton tracked his son to Baltimore where James Dillon ran a group home. He was only able to confirm that Rowan once lived at the shelter but had moved on to parts unknown in his early teens. Anton failed to see the connection between Rowan and this

Lee Newman, since James never mentioned him.

Anton observed Lee closely. His eyes wandered around the office and landed on a photo on the desk: Anton's thirteen-year old daughter Sarah. He cleared his throat loudly.

"What can I do for you, Mr. Newman?"

"Nothing," he answered in clipped tones. "Why are you looking for me?"

"Mr. Newman," Anton said with a nervous chuckle, "I think there's been a mistake. I've never heard of you before until a few minutes ago."

"I know. You were looking for Rowan Jackson, correct?"

"You know Rowan?" Anton latched on to whatever hope this stranger seemed to be offering, no matter how small. With his daughter now on an experimental new drug, thanks to Shelby, a favor he could never repay, would it be greedy of him to hope that now, after twenty-five years, he would finally find his son?

His question was met with stony silence.

"Am I missing something?" he asked, trying to break the awkward silence that seemed to stretch on for eons.

"You missed more than 'something.' Twenty-five years to be precise."

The truth crashed into him, knocking him senseless. Anton undid the top button of his shirt and began to sweat.

"Come closer, have a look. I always wondered which parent I looked like. There was no one around to tell me."

"You're Rowan?" Anton asked, his voice low.

"Was Rowan. I attempted to rob a man who was in Baltimore on business when I was thirteen. It was the best thing I ever did. Turns out his brother, Lee, was passionate about helping unwanted children. When Jake Newman took me in and adopted me, I took his brother's name to honor his memory."

Anton was at a loss. He'd thought about what it would be like if he ever came face-to-face with his adult son, but never dreamed said son would just stroll into his life one day. He was unprepared for it.

"Your mother looked for you, a long time ago."

"Obviously not hard enough, because here I am," he said, stretching his arms out.

"I'm sorry."

"Don't be. You both did me a favor. The two of you, from the looks of things didn't want to be parents."

"It's complicated."

"It always is, isn't it?"

Lee sat down and crossed his legs, as if he were now ready to be entertained by whatever story Anton invented. "Go ahead, tell me why my birth mother threw me away and your part in it. I know she was a teenage mother who left me in a New Orleans hospital. You can pick it up from there."

Anton's throat felt parched. There was no escaping this ambush, so he told Lee the sad, pathetic story surrounding his birth. No matter what spin he put on it, there was no way to disguise the ugliness of it. The simple fact was Lee was unwanted by both his biological parents. In his eyes, circumstances probably didn't matter.

Lee didn't react, his face an unreadable mask. "What changed? Why go through the trouble to try and find me now?"

Anton didn't have the guts to tell Lee why he was searching for him in the first place. That would be cruel and unusual punishment, so he told a half-truth.

"I didn't know what happened to your mother after she found out she was pregnant. Then last year, my daughter got very sick and was dying. I took it as a sign that I should try to find you. I wanted my daughter to know her only sibling. I thought it would also be a chance for me to make amends."

He couldn't tell if Lee believed him or not. His unreadable mask was still firmly in place. He was a handsome guy, took his mother's youthful features, but he had Anton's eyes. He could also see Shelby's brother, Michael, in him. No DNA test was needed. This was his and Shelby's son.

"Do you take me a fool, Pastor Devereaux?"

Anton didn't like the way the word *Pastor* sounded coming from Lee's lips.

"How can I take you for a fool since we just met?"

Lee uncrossed his legs and leaned forward, his eyes pinned on Anton, hard as two concrete blocks. "I attended your church last Sunday. Wonderful sermon about forgiveness. A little self-serving if you ask me, but I was glad to hear your daughter Sarah is doing better and may not need a bone marrow after all."

Shame washed over Anton. He fiddled with the frame that held Sarah's photo. All hope of building a relationship with his son just disappeared. They never had a beginning yet the end was here. He had to accept that. Lee owed him nothing. He owed Lee everything.

"There's nothing I can say that would make this okay. Not my guilt over the years. Not going to your mother's house to try and fix things, only to be told she didn't live there anymore and no one knew what happened to her. Not my fear that you would reject me the way I did you."

A momentary flash of sympathy crossed Lee's features and disappeared quickly, as if it had never occurred. "Do you know where my birth mother is now? What's her name?"

Anton was so busy dealing with his own turmoil that he hadn't given a thought to the Shelby part of the equation. How much should he tell Lee? Shelby had the right to tell her side of things but their son was sitting in his office asking questions—questions to which he deserved honest answers.

Lee noticed Anton's hesitation. "What, is she dead?"

"Oh, no, she isn't."

"Then what's the big deal?"

"I don't know how to tell you this. She should be the one to tell you."

"Is she a criminal?"

Anton coughed. Lee eased back into his chair, and pinched his nose.

"So, my mother is a criminal. The gene pool is so fascinating. I guess that means I shouldn't reproduce."

Anton cringed. "Your mother isn't exactly a criminal. She's had some legal troubles as of late. They'll be resolved soon."

"Oh, I see. She's innocent, the mantra of criminals everywhere. What's her name? One day when I'm bored I might research her."

"I'm sure you've heard of the Cooper family. They've been in the news lately."

"Yes. It's a tragedy. Abbie Cooper is one of my students. I'm a Guidance Counselor at Saint. Matthews Academy. I've met the

Coopers on a few occasions. What do they have to do with my birth mother?"

Anton took deep breaths. He was about to disrupt this boy's life again.

"Lee, Shelby Cooper is your mother. Abbie Cooper is your half-sister."

The attitude of cool indifference vanished, replaced by shock and bewilderment. "I don't believe you. You're wrong."

"It's the truth, Lee."

"I just visited her in jail. There was not a flicker of recognition on her part. Aren't mothers supposed to recognize their children, something about the genetic bond? This woman looked straight at me and didn't even flinch. No way she gave birth to me."

Lee stared at Anton, his eyes begging for a different story, a story that would change his maternal origins. A story that would tell him anyone but Shelby Cooper was his mother.

"She's a good person Lee. I'm the one who deserves your anger. I almost ruined her life and then I abandoned her."

Lee shook his head. "Makes sense that you would defend her. What happened after she wasn't 15 anymore? What happened when you became a grown man? What's your excuse?"

Anton had none. He and Shelby had discussed this very point. "We didn't think we deserved to have you in our lives after we screwed up so badly. We were cowards."

"You're right. The two of you didn't deserve me. You're a liar and opportunist. She's a selfish, heartless woman. You wasted your time pastor. I hope I never run into either one of you again, as long as I'm alive."

Chapter 78

Mia Lansing stared at her reflection in the bathroom mirror of the apartment she would soon vacate. She finger combed her blonde hair and ran her index finger over her cherry red lips. "Perfection," she purred. It had been a wild ride and it was time to say goodbye. Everything had worked out just the way she wanted it to, and now, she would claim her prize.

"What do an Academy Award winning makeup artist and I have in common?" she asked her reflection. "We're both fucking geniuses."

She served up a cruel laugh and began peeling off her face, ripping the forehead apart with her fingers, then the cheeks, the chin and the neck, dumping each piece in the trash. When she was satisfied there was no trace left of her alternate identity, she let her own black hair loose from the confines of a hair clip. She brushed it all out, letting it fall past her shoulders. Then she washed her face clean.

"Glad that's over with," she said to her mocha brown reflection. "Now, I just need to make the name change official. Vivian Cooper has a nice ring to it, doesn't it?"

She laughed at her own anecdote. The Coopers were so

331

obsessed with their precious Shelby that they couldn't see what was right in front of them. It was sickening how they were all pretending she was a saint, the best at everything. But Vivian knew better. Thanks to a friend who made up some of the most beautiful faces on film, she was able to straddle two different worlds, grabbing them both by the tail and bending them to her will. It was fun. It had made her unstoppable.

Now, they would never find out the truth. In a couple of days, she would clean out this apartment, turn in the keys to the management, and take up permanent residence at 68 Meadow Lane until she could convince Jason to send that brat Abbie to a real boarding school far away, none of this local student at a boarding school in town shit. Vivian had already picked out a couple of schools in Switzerland and one in the UK. At least she was giving the brat choices. She could tolerate Miles until he became a problem, then she would get rid of him, too.

Soon, she would be Mrs. Jason Cooper. It wouldn't take much to convince him since they were intimate. Shelby's deceptive games had sealed her fate. There was no way he would keep that marriage going. Shelby would pay for taking her father away from her with her lies. Too bad her idiot mother couldn't see that. Shelby was her favorite. Shelby could do no wrong. Shelby would never lie. It was all her father's fault and he had to go. Nothing was ever the same after her dad left. Daniel March was an outstanding man, a nationally recognized civil rights attorney who fought for those who didn't have a voice. He was a loving father. He didn't deserve to die so violently and alone.

He wouldn't have started drinking if that bitch Shelby hadn't lied about him attacking her. That's when her mother Rita kicked him out of their home and it was a downward spiral ever since. Vivian's first order of business would be to wipe out all traces of Shelby from the house. She knew it would be an uphill battle with that opinionated mini adult Abbie, who had something to say about everything. God, she was annoying. Aunt Vivian knew how to play them all and she would continue to do so.

Chapter 79

Two days after I said goodbye to my daddy, he passed away in his sleep. I'm dazed. I have to face *her* for the first time in twenty-five years. I arrive at the funeral home before anyone else does. I must take care of some last-minute business with my daddy—before the mourners and what's left of our family, Michael and Mama arrive.

He looks peaceful now, in a way that says all business on this earth is finished and he's quite content with the outcome. I caress his face, and then hold his cold hands. "It's just us now, Daddy. Your secret is safe with me." I reach into my purse and pull out the letter. I remove his left shoe and place the letter inside.

"I have a special present for you, Daddy. I only wish I could have given it to you while you were alive. I'm sorry. I'm sorry I didn't come sooner. I thought you didn't want me. You didn't fight for me and I thought I had to forget about you to make it on my own. Now I understand. She had you under her thumb, the way she did all of us.

"I know you want me to forgive her and all I can do is promise to try. You were a good father. It took me a long time to realize that. I married a man who's a great father, too. You didn't get to meet your grandbabies, but I know you'll be looking out for them from up there."

I reach for his gift in my purse and place the key in the pocket of his suit jacket. "Your very own 1964 Shelby Roadster Convertible. There are very few left in the entire world. Now, when you go to heaven, you can drive God around the Kingdom in style."

I begin to sing Mahalia Jackson's "Summertime/Sometimes I feel Like a Motherless Child." It was our favorite song.

We're at the cemetery. Daddy's being buried near a big old magnolia tree. I know he's happy with his final resting place. He was a simple man. The sun is out in full force, an almost cloudless sky in February. No coat is needed at a comfortable fifty-five degrees. I'm dressed in a simple black dress with a matching overcoat, heels, triple strand pearl necklace and matching earrings. On my head is a black, wide-brimmed hat with a cluster of black silk roses. I complete my ensemble with dark sunglasses. What goes on behind the shades is nobody's business.

Most of the mourners have gone and it's just Michael, me, Mamma, and a few family friends scattered around. They lower the casket into the ground and I blow a final kiss to Daddy. I hear someone whisper in my ear. "Well done, Princess."

I whip my head around but don't see anybody. What was that? It sounded like Alessandro. My eyes veer off to my right where I can see the parking lot in the distance. Alessandro smiles at me, and waves. My hand waves back of its own accord. Then he disappears into thin air.

"Who are you waving at?" Michael asks.

"An old friend."

He squints. He sees nothing.

Mama decides to speak up. Twenty-five years have mellowed her out a bit. I guess that's what age is supposed to do. She almost looks like a mother, kind, protective, loving. She invites me to the house for the repass. I explain that I prefer to grieve in private for my father. The truth is, I'm afraid to go back there. She has long since retired from nursing and still lives in the house where I grew up. According to Michael, her days are now filled with fewer and fewer friends, a cruise here and there, and knitting. At least, she's healthy enough to live on her own.

"Michael, I need to talk to your sister."

Michael makes himself scarce. The undertakers dump the last of the dirt over the coffin. She motions to me to walk with her, which I do out of respect. "It's good to see you, Mia," she finally says.

"Are you sure?"

She stops walking and tilts her face toward me. I remove my sunglasses.

"You must hate me."

"I don't."

"Couldn't blame you if you did."

"I don't blame you."

"I'm a different person now."

"Aren't we all?"

"I was grieving and didn't know how to handle it. It just kept getting worse."

I force myself to ask the next logical question. I know she's about to justify why she treated me like some disease she was hell-bent on eradicating. She'd waited forty years to unburden herself. I may as well give her an audience.

"What were you grieving about?"

"Not here," she says. "Let's go to the house."

Chapter 80

The house and yard were well kept. Daddy had done some major remodeling after Michael told me the roof was leaking, the paint was peeling off the walls and everything else that could go wrong did. I paid for the work. That's how I dealt with staying away. If I threw money at whatever problems surfaced, I wouldn't have to face what I was feeling and what happened that night. Nobody would ask anything of me. Only Michael had, repeatedly. I'm glad he did.

Mama and I enter through the kitchen. A few older ladies are busy piling food on platters and tending to whatever is bubbling on the stove.

"Mia is home, y'all," I hear my mother say.

All eyes are on me. I'm surprised by the announcement and don't know what to do so I look through them. Mrs. Wilkes, the neighborhood gossip, as I recall, has a big smile for me. "Welcome home, sugar," she says, opening her massive arms.

After multiple hugs, best wishes and questions about my life up north, we end up in Mama and Daddy's bedroom. I was never allowed in there as a kid, so it was a strange feeling. It was immaculately kept, not a thing out of place and smelled like jasmine oil. I guess the Lansing women have a thing for jasmine oil. Even

Abbie likes to scent her room with it.

Mama directs me to sit in the chair in the corner and she decides to stand.

"When you were born, you didn't come alone."

"I don't know what you mean, Ma'am."

"Just listen. I have to get this out. Your daddy is gone now and ain't no use hiding the truth."

She looks up at the ceiling as if praying for strength. Whatever this is has to be huge if Mama is unsure of herself.

"You came out first. And then your sister did. She was the prettiest little thing you ever did see."

In Mama's world, that meant she was light-skinned like her.

"The Lord had blessed me with twin girls. Then, He turned on me. Maybe for something I did. He took Maddie away. I was beside myself with grief. It wasn't fair. You lived and Maddie didn't. Then I blamed you. It had to be your fault because you survived."

It doesn't surprise me to hear Mama speak this way. However, I'm struck by the fact that I had a twin sister and no one talked about her when I was growing up. Knowing Mama, she probably forbade Daddy from speaking about it. It's awful to lose a child, whether to death or other circumstances.

"Every time I looked at you, it was a reminder of losing Maddie. And your daddy, he just thought you were the moon and the stars. It's as if he didn't care that we had lost her. All his attention was focused on you."

"So, you got angry and decided I didn't deserve to live, that I should have died with my twin?"

She didn't need to say anything; her face told me I was right.

"I just didn't know how to deal with my grief. I'm not saying it was right. I just couldn't see past...I just couldn't—"

"Find a way to love me," I finished for her.

"Your mama knows you'll never forgive her, but I thought you deserved to hear my side of the story."

It's still all about her after all these years. I will never tell her what Daddy told me in the letter, how she used a tragic accident to terrorize him in his own home. That's just between Daddy and me. Now and forever.

"I forgave you a long time ago. I will never forget, though. As for the future, we can take things slow. I can get to know you and you me. That's all I can offer for now. If you need anything at all, I don't care if it's a class or a trip or new clothes or doctor visits, consider it taken care of.

Michael tosses my suitcase in the trunk of his Chevy Malibu and we leave for Louis Armstrong International Airport. Whatever fate awaits me when I return to Boston, I'm ready to face it.

"It's just you and me now, Michael," I say and pat his arm affectionately. "But you're the only one left who can carry on the Lansing name. What about you and Analise? She seems like a nice girl. I can tell she's ready."

"Come on, Mia, you sound like Mama. Always asking when I'm getting married and if I'm ever going to give her grandbabies."

"Okay, you have me worried. About sounding like Mama."

"You and Mama need to leave the past in the past."

"I already have, Michael. I already have."

We remain silent for a moment as the car eats up the miles of highway dotted with trees and businesses.

"Shoot, I almost forgot," Michael said, hitting the steering wheel.

"What?"

"Rayne. Something about her, I meant to tell you. She looks like she could be Anton Devereaux's daughter."

"Strange coincidence, that's all."

"It's more than that. She looks like she could be your daughter, too."

"Don't be ridiculous. I had a baby boy, not a girl."

"How can you be sure? You told me yourself you were drugged out of your mind from anesthesia."

"I think I know the difference between a baby boy and a baby girl. They made quite sure that he was wrapped in a blue blanket."

Michael wants to say something more then thinks the better of it as the signs for the airline terminals came into view. He drops me at the curbside where a pleasant porter checks my bags.

"Please come back and visit me. Let me know when you finally decide to marry Analise."

"What's going to happen to you, Mia?"

"All I can say is that it will be heartbreaking for me and my family."

Chapter 81

The place I once called home is now foreign to me. The happiness that was a part of the very fabric of this house is gone, soiled, decimated by an imposter. We were all taken in. There's an eerie silence in the house. I walk up the grand staircase quietly, one step at a time. My heart is threatening to escape its four chambers, so I hold onto the banister for support. I reach the top then turn left to walk down the hallway. I stop at the door down the hall from my daughter's room. The door is slightly ajar. I push it wide open.

"Hello, Vivian."

My voice frightens her, causing her to pop up like a jack-in-the-box. "Shelby. Oh my God! What are you doing here?"

"We need to talk, don't we?" I shut the door behind me and enter the room, landing on an armchair a few feet away.

"You look—"

"Good for someone who's been in jail?"

"Welcome home. It's good to see you. What happened? Did Jason bribe someone to get you out? Oh my goodness, there's so much to discuss, and the children will be so happy."

For all her joy at seeing me, my best friend has yet to make a move to embrace me. She's nailed to the spot in the middle of the bed where I found her thumbing through bridal magazines. "Jason didn't have to bribe anyone because I didn't do anything wrong. See, our justice system works."

I remove my coat and throw it on the bed, barely missing her. Next, I go to work on my knee-high boots.

"How did you get here? You feeling okay, after your ordeal in prison? I can't imagine what it must have been like."

"Pure hell. The worst part was not being able to see my children, but you already knew that."

"Of course. They missed you terribly. It was really tough on them, especially Miles."

"Then why did you almost destroy their lives?"

I leave my boots in a heap at the foot of the chair. I stand up and edge closer to the bed. Vivian tucks her left hand under her thigh. "What have you been up to, Vivian?"

Just like that, she flips the switch and the real Vivian emerges. "I'm sorry, Shelby. Things have changed. I'm with Jason now. We're going to be married this summer."

I pick up the magazine she was leafing through earlier and begin turning the pages. "Did you know polygamy is illegal in Massachusetts?"

"It's difficult to let go, I know. You'll get used to it. You didn't expect him to stay married to you after all your lies and sleeping around with another man, did you?"

She has declared war. I remove my cashmere gloves slowly and throw them at her. Then hold up my left hand. "Jason can't marry you if he's still married to me, now can he?"

"You know how Jason is. He doesn't want to hurt you and he's waiting for the right time to tell you it's over. We're a real couple. In *every* way."

She gives me a pitying glance. "This is hard, Shelby. With everything you've been through, to come home and find out that your husband has moved on is hard. But, that's life."

"Jason isn't going anywhere. Did you think spreading your legs for him makes you special? It doesn't. You're not that good."

Her eyes widen in surprise.

"Yes, I know about the sexcapades. Jason and I discussed it at length. As revolting as it was, you throwing yourself at him, I saw an opportunity. We both know you were prepared to let me go to prison for a crime I didn't commit. It's what you wanted. So, I did what any woman running out of options would do. I told Jason he had to take one for the team. I told him to screw your brains out for as long as it took to get the proof we needed."

She quivers with shame and humiliation, barely able to look at me. Or, maybe it's uncontained rage, the discovery that she had been played. For someone like Vivian who always believed she was the smartest person in the room, and entitled to everything she wanted, it's a devastating blow. She trusted Jason and truly believed he was in love with her.

"You're a liar," she screams at me. "You're desperate and will say anything. I thought we could be adults about this."

"We are. Haven't we engaged in grown up games? Koczak made a mistake by calling you. The catalyst for putting the pieces together was the photograph you showed Jason. Everyone's face was x'd out except yours. That was a damning piece of evidence. Tom Bilko, remember him? The Private Detective Jason hired to help with my case? He's been shadowing you for weeks and reporting to Jason on your every move, even when you assumed your alternate identity."

"You're a lying, murderous psychopath who was willing to destroy his family for your own selfish gain. I knew how you felt about Jason, and I used it to my advantage because I fight for what belongs to me, by any means necessary. You'll never underestimate me again."

Stunned silence. She doesn't move a muscle. But in a flash, the real Vivian is back.

"You can't stand it that I won. I always win, Shelby."

"Tell me, what exactly did you win?" I fold my arms, my eyes never leaving her face.

"The man that should have been mine in the first place, the life you stole from me."

I look at her like the demented human being she is. "Hmm, I don't recall taking anything from you, Vivian. I don't steal."

"Don't pretend to be innocent. You took my father from me when you cried rape. He was never the same after my mother threw him out. You destroyed our family, after everything we did for you. You were a street rat, a nobody when my mother took you in, and this was the way you thanked her, by lying."

"Your father was a raging alcoholic who tried to rape me during one of his drunken episodes. Rita walked in on it. I didn't have to lie. I'm sorry, your father was no saint. That's all I'll say on the matter out of respect for his memory."

She sneers at me, her eyes raging pools of hatred and malice. "You're a liar and a poser. Pretending to be this wholesome girl that Jason fell for, when in fact, you were a two-bit whore who got knocked up as a teenager and then abandoned your own kid. Then had the nerve to wear white on your wedding day. That was my dress," she says, pointing at me. "I was supposed to wear it on my wedding day. Somehow, you convinced my mother you should wear it. You destroyed that beautiful dress. They had to cut it down to fit your inelegant frame."

I didn't know she was so upset about the dress. Her delusions about her father and her parents' marriage, I get that, but not the dress. Rita March had gotten married in a gorgeous Grace Kelly inspired wedding gown. When Jason proposed, Rita made the decision right away that I would wear the dress and she wouldn't hear anything else to the contrary. Vivian was fine with the decision and didn't seem to care. It had all been an act.

"I'm not going to argue with you about a wedding dress. Maybe Rita gave it to me because she understood I would cherish it and I would feel honored to wear it, which I did. You didn't appreciate her much with your rebellious, ungrateful behavior. You can't blame me for that."

"You were so desperate for love and attention. Always sucking up to her, doing whatever she said like a lap dog. You were pathetic."

She comes off the bed and stands in front of me, wagging her index finger in my face.

"You deserved what you got, and too bad they didn't keep your sorry ass locked up. But you're not going to steal my happiness from me this time, bitch."

"You don't know how to be happy, Vivian, that's the real tragedy of your life. You had two loving parents who gave you everything and it wasn't enough. Didn't matter what you had accomplished or what you had acquired. You're just a big black hole that sucks up everything in your path yet never gets filled."

She shoves me and I stumble backwards, landing on the bed. I get up and shove her harder. She almost loses her balance and winds up in the chair I occupied earlier. I take a few steps towards her. It's my turn to wag my finger in her face. "You're going to listen to me because I've suffered enough. I'm going to tell you what really went down, and when I'm done, you're going to pack your shit and get the hell out of my home and my life."

She recoils as if I've just slapped her.

"Let's start with that damn wedding dress and your relationship with your mother. Rita gave me the dress because she wanted her daughter to wear it on her wedding day. In her heart, I was her true daughter. Rita wasn't your biological mother. You, my dear friend, are the product of an adulterous affair between your father and Rita's sister, Delores. She died giving birth to you and Daniel convinced Rita that the two of them should raise you as their daughter. Rita March was your aunt, not your mother."

I let that sink in for a moment. Vivian looks ghostly. "You're pitiful. I hate you."

"Yes, you've proven just how much. It was all for nothing, though. As for Jason, you had zero chance with him. You were never going to be his wife or mother to my children. God, I wouldn't wish you on any child."

I'm afraid for my safety. "Liar! Liar, liar," Vivian screams, her body racked with rage.

"Calm down. The story is just getting good. Someone as clever as you will appreciate it. Trust me."

She vacates the chair and returns to the bed and the bridal magazine she was thumbing through when I walked in. She's not ready to concede defeat, but I can feel the air slowly seeping out of her—the realization that it had all been for nothing, that she, the clever one who had it all figured out was dead wrong.

"You brought this on yourself, Vivian. No point in getting angry. Posing as a green-eyed blonde, using my birth name? Honestly, Vivian, that's sick, even for you. Why kill that poor psychiatrist, Dr. Singer. Why was it necessary to add to the body count?"

"You think you know everything? You don't." A diabolical smile plays at the corners of her mouth. "Do you know how much your Brazilian lover begged me to spare his life? Said his daughters needed him, they were starting their lives over, and that a woman he loved gave them that second chance. He was in tears. So moving. I knew the woman he referred to was you. That's when I pulled the trigger. Your affair with him was a gift I couldn't ignore. It made setting you up so much easier. He had to die."

I shiver. Goosebumps appear on my arm. I won't bow to her brand of evil. She won't know that I'm devastated all over again listening to her.

"Alessandro was a good man, but he should have left a long time ago. Maybe you did him a favor. His wife doesn't have him to beat on anymore."

"That's cold. Is that how you saw the man you cheated on Jason with? Jason deserves better."

"He certainly doesn't deserve you. No man does. Deep down, part of me always knew you were a cruel, vindictive human being with no conscience."

"Aww, is Shelby mad at me? Don't be, sweetheart. I have a present for you. You have to be nice to me if you want to find out what it is, though."

"I don't need any presents from you, other than your leaving and never contacting me or my family again."

She grins. "Are you sure you don't want your present? You've been wondering about it for over twenty-five years."

My son. What could she possibly know about him? I'll bite. "I already know. He walked into his father's office, days ago."

She looks deflated, that I've taken away her element of surprise. It gives me pleasure to deny her that triumph.

"You only know half the story."

"What?"

"You had twins, dumbass, a boy and a girl. I went to a lot of trouble to find out about them. Aren't you going to thank me?"

"You're making that up. One baby was placed in my arms at the hospital. One. A boy."

"How would you know what you had? You left before they could bring your daughter in. Patty Revington, my mentor at the Art Institute of Chicago and her husband Paul adopted a baby girl. Then I met Rayne. Patty mentioned that she was adopted from an orphanage in New Orleans. Coincidence I thought at first. When Patty told me her teenage mother abandoned her at the hospital, I knew it was no coincidence. I volunteered to do Rayne's hair one day. I had to find out if my hunch was right. One DNA test later to establish a genetic link between the two of you and voila, I found your daughter. It wasn't hard to get your DNA. After all, we were best friends. You left both your kids and never looked back. Yet both of them ended up right here in New England."

I have a sudden flash of memory, Michael telling me that Rayne Revington was a dead ringer for Anton Devereaux. My hands reach up to cover the shock on my face. Vivian smiles that contented smile she always had whenever she put me in my place when we were growing up. It is true. I can't breathe for a minute or two.

"And the best part is," she continues, "Rayne has no idea that when I plucked her from a dead-end job in Bloomington, Indiana, it was to reunite her with her mommy. See how nice I am? She hates you, though. She wants to know why her biological mother didn't want her, so now would be a good time to come up with a convincing story. I have a feeling it won't matter."

Vivian continued her rant. "Rayne got lucky. Your son didn't. After you threw him away like trash, no one wanted to adopt the poor thing. Seems you passed on your defective genes to your sons. He had seizures like Miles. Nobody wants to adopt an unhealthy baby, so the poor thing bounced from foster home to foster home. By the time he was in his teens, he was living on the streets in Baltimore for a while. Somehow, he made it up here until some do-gooder like my mother took pity on him, adopted him, and gave him a last name and a family. Would have introduced myself to him, but I kinda got busy you know, setting you up and such. Now, you owe me two thank you gifts," she says, holding up her index and middle fingers.

It's too much. I head to the corner of the room between the dresser and the laundry basket. I'm overcome with emotion.

"Aww, are the mommy hormones kicking in?" Vivian mocks. "Look on the bright side, you didn't have to change any diapers. Other women already did all the work for you. Now, thank you for stopping by. You can leave now so Jason and I can plan our future."

That comment snaps me out of my emotional pit. "The only

future that's awaiting you is a prison cell."

"I got away with three murders, what makes you think I won't walk away with the man that was meant for me?"

"Because you're not as clever as you think."

"Meaning?"

I have gotten her attention. Gone is the smug, condescending attitude of a few moments ago. "The cops are on to you."

"You can't prove anything. There's nothing connecting me to those murders or setting you up. I win again. See, Shelby, I'm a born winner. You will always be in my shadow."

I point at the ceiling. "Look up."

"Why?"

"Just look up. Look at the smoke detector."

She does but confusion is evident on her face.

"It's a camera and audio device," I say. "It recorded our entire conversation. And, the cops have the house surrounded."

Her face turns vicious and she jumps off the bed and grabs a chair. She places it in the middle of the room. Her intention is obvious to me. "No use in dismantling it. The police were listening. They have everything they need."

She lunges at me and misses.

"Just give yourself up, Vivian. It's over."

"I'm never going to serve one day in prison."

"There's that cockiness again."

Diabolical smile again. "I was diagnosed with a mental disorder in my early twenties. I was seeing Dr. Singer while I was up here. I guess he wasn't that good at his job because he couldn't cure me."

"An insanity defense? You're an insult to people who legitimately suffer from mental illness. It's not something to fool around with. You meticulously planned your crimes and you were completely sane when you committed them. You won't get away with an insanity defense."

She pushes past me and opens the bedroom door. I follow. Something inside of me breaks. It can't end like this. She has to pay. I grab her sweater. She's stronger than me and keeps going. She's in the hallway. I instinctively know she'll head for the stairs and make a run for it.

"Listen to me. You have to turn yourself in. The police have the house surrounded."

She turns around and punches me in the face. It hurts like hell but I have to push through the pain. It's a long hallway and soon, she'll reach the stairs. I grab her again, just as she reaches the top of the stairs. It's a tug of war and I'm pulling with all my might, but she's as strong as an ox. She manages to push me off her, but like a pit bull, I refuse to give up. My main objective now is to buy time, slow her down, so I trip her by sticking my leg out. She falls flat on her ass and I grab one of her legs and try to pull her away from the stairs, back toward the bedroom.

She kicks me with her free leg right in the chest. I fall backward and end up on the floor, too. She takes the opportunity to head for the stairs again. I get up. I have to stop her. She takes the first step in descending the long staircase and I'm right next to her. There's barely enough space for both of us walking side by side.

"They'll find you, there's nowhere you can hide. It's better to turn yourself in now. Have some sense for once."

She doesn't speak. Instead, she lets go of the railing, launches off the step and in slow motion begins to free fall down the stairs. My reflexes aren't fast enough to grab onto her. In the split second it takes me to realize her intention, it's too late. She lands at the bottom of the stairs in a crumpled heap, blood pouring from the back of her skull.

Epilogue

The trees in the backyard are green and vibrant, swaying in the warm breeze. The pool is officially open for summer fun. I sit on the patio of our new home, surrounded by all my children. Vivian was right. I gave birth to twins, an anomaly, to say the least. It's widely accepted that twins skip a generation. That's the story of my life: the oddball. Though I was happy to be cleared of murder charges, I lost the woman I considered my sister. I'm grateful that she reunited me with the daughter I never knew I had. In spite of the darkness she struggled with, I choose to remember her with gratitude.

My family dynamic is complicated now and will take some time to sort itself out. I have two adult children with a man who almost lost the only child he ever cared about. I called Anton and gave him the news about Rayne after Vivian died. He accepted it with grace.

The past several months have been a time of big changes. We couldn't continue to live in our home in Castleview, too many bad memories. Moving the next town over was the least disruptive to the children's lives. Rayne and Lee outright rejected me initially. I had to be patient, give them the space and time they needed to come to grips with the emotional turmoil of discovering, first, that I'm the birth mother who had abandoned them, and second, that they were twins. Things are moving rather slowly, trying to get to know each other but we're trying. I suspect the fact that Lee is fond of Abbie is the only thing that gave me a shot at getting to know my adult children.

"Abbie, when is Ty heading home to New York?" Lee asks. "You must miss him already."

"His parents will be here tomorrow for the graduation ceremony and afterwards, he'll be gone."

"Please tell me he kissed you," Rayne says. "It would be a tragedy if he went off to college and you never got to experience your first kiss with him."

"Wait a minute, time out," Lee says. "What is this, Abbie? Any young man who wants to kiss my sister has to go through me first."

"And my dad," Abbie adds. She looks at me, and smiles. "You see what we're up against, Mom? Dad has reinforcements now. This is not good for my love life."

"So, did he kiss you?" I ask.

"I can't listen to this," Lee says, in mock offense. "Miles, let's head to the pool."

Rayne leans in closer so we can all listen after her brothers hit the water.

"A lady never tells," Abbie teases.

"Are you seriously going to do this to us?" I ask. "Come on."

"It. Was. Amazing! I'll never forget it as long as I live."

All three of us scream like giddy teenagers.

"I'm happy for you, Abbie," Rayne says. "Will you keep in touch?"

"He promised he would but college life is busy. He'll visit during breaks."

Jason comes out of the house with a tray, a bottle of wine, and two wine glasses. The girls excuse themselves and join their brothers in the pool.

"What are we celebrating?" I ask Jason.

"Just got a call on that property we bid on. Looks like we have your restaurant."

I kiss him firmly on the lips.

"Hey, none of that in front of the kids," Rayne yells from the pool.

Jason and I grin. He pours the wine and proposes a toast. "To the future, to our union. Swans for life."

"Swans for life," I say, as we clink our glasses.

We just might be after all.

Author's Note

Dear Reader,

Thank you for reading *Swan Deception*. I hope you enjoyed the turbulent rollercoaster ride with the Coopers. I would be grateful if you could give the gift of an honest review.

The Coopers will be back in *Game of Fear* but this time, Abbie Cooper takes center stage as she battles a dangerous threat to her future and embarks on an unexpected romance.

Thank you for your support.

Jade Browne-Kabogo

Acknowledgements

I'm grateful to Detective Arthur Hall Brewster of the Boston Police Department for his generosity in helping me understand the details surrounding the criminal apprehension and investigation process.

Sandi Hughey for her tireless efforts in tracking down research resources on MCI Framingham Correctional Facility.

Beverly Horne for her thorough and thoughtful evaluation of the manuscript.

My boys Amini and Maximillian, who keep me grounded, and laughing constantly.

Esther Pemberton who pushed me to "tell the truth". That piece of writing advice shall stay with me always.

Upcoming Releases

Game of Fear

Seventeen-year old Abbie Cooper is the poster child for good girls—smart, ambitious, stays out of trouble, and obeys her loving albeit strict parents. As senior year at her elite private school kicks off, she's singular in her focus: do whatever it takes to get into the Ivy League University of her choice. But Abbie is on a collision course with disaster.

It begins with a series of anonymous, untraceable communications. Someone knows what she did—the horrible choice she made that she can never take back. To make matters worse, there's video evidence that could destroy her future before it even begins. Soon Abbie's world is on the brink of collapse, as she struggles to stay one step ahead of a diabolical enemy with no conscience. If Abbie refuses to play his cruel games, the consequences will be destructive and irreversible. If she gives in, she's doomed to become the tragic victim of a twisted adversary whose identity may be too shocking to be believed.

More by the Author

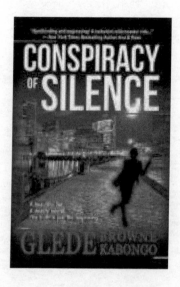

Conspiracy of Silence
#1 Amazon Bestseller
http://www.amazon.com/dp/B00FY5JMZA

A beautiful liar. A deadly secret. The truth is just the beginning...

Boston executive Nina Kasai will do anything to keep her past a secret. But she's about to learn that some secrets are too big to stay buried.

Years ago, Nina fled her affluent suburban home and vowed never to return. The truth now lives within the pages of her hidden diary, and in the mind of a disturbed woman who will never tell. However, when she lands the cover of a prestigious business magazine, everything Nina has worked for—her career, marriage, and sanity hang in the balance. Phillip Copeland, a powerful enemy with secrets of his own wants to be the next Governor of Massachusetts, and warns Nina to keep quiet about what happened all those years ago or else.

As the stakes are raised, Nina realizes the only way to win this game is to tell the truth. But who will believe her when her diary has gone missing and the only other witness isn't talking? To reclaim her life and confront the past she's been running from, Nina must make a gut-wrenching decision that will leave multiple casualties in its wake.

About the Author

Gledé Browne Kabongo is the bestselling author of *Conspiracy of Silence*. Her love affair with books began as a young girl growing up in the Caribbean. The town library overlooked the Atlantic Ocean so becoming a book addict was inevitable.

She holds both an M.S. and B.A. in communications and has worked in marketing communications management for over a decade. When it comes to writing, Gledé describes her female protagonists in terms of brains and beauty, meet wounds and secrets at the corner of courage and vengeance.

Visit her author website (http://www.gledekabongo.com/) for more information and to sign up for the newsletter.

Twitter: https://twitter.com/gkabongo
Facebook: http://www.facebook.com/gledekabongoauthor

Made in the USA
Lexington, KY
28 June 2016